Author Heidi Rice's first love was watc̶h̶i̶... ...̶ ̶̶ ̶S̶u̶r̶-
prisingly, her first proper job was ... ̶... ...̶ ̶̶̶ ̶A̶f̶t̶e̶r̶
spending years sneaking off to read̶ ̶... ̶... ...̶ ̶s̶h̶e̶
was being paid to watch movies she de̶... ...̶ ̶̶ ̶̶ ̶...̶el
of her own.

After several false starts, her first book, *Bedded by a Bad Boy*,
was published by Harlequin Mills & Boon in 2007. Ten years and
twenty-six published novels, novellas and short stories later, she
has nabbed three RITA nominations, become a *USA Today* best-
seller and sold over two million copies of her books worldwide.
Summer at Willow Tree Farm is her second full-length women's
fiction novel.

As you can probably tell, she loves her job, because it involves
sitting down at her computer each day and getting swept up in a
world of high emotions, sensual excitement, funny flawed women,
sexy tortured men and intriguing locations where laundry doesn't
matter. She lives in London with her husband and two sons, and
lots of other gorgeous men who are entirely in her imagination
(unlike the laundry, unfortunately).

Summer at Willow Tree Farm

Heidi Rice

ONE PLACE. MANY STORIES

HQ
An imprint of HarperCollins*Publishers* Ltd
1 London Bridge Street
London SE1 9GF

This edition 2018

3

First published in Great Britain by
HQ, an imprint of HarperCollins*Publishers* Ltd 2017

ISBN: 978-1-84845-690-7

MIX
Paper from
responsible sources
FSC™ C007454

This book is produced from independently certified FSC™ paper
to ensure responsible forest management.

For more information visit: www.harpercollins.co.uk/green

Printed and bound by
CPI Group, Croydon CR0 4YY

To my Mum, who is magnificent

PART ONE: EVERYTHING CHANGES

THEN

Eloise Charlotte Preston's Diary: Do NOT read or you will die.

17 June 1998

My life is actually officially over. And my mum has gone stark raving bonkers. She woke me up while it was still dark yesterday – and it was Sunday, it wasn't even a school day.

She said we were going somewhere really cool and all sorts of other mad stuff about starting a new life. I just listened to my Discman because she was acting weird. But the way she was going on, I thought we were moving somewhere cool, like New York or Disneyworld. And then where did we finally end up... After hours and hours of driving... Wait for it... FLIPPING WILTSHIRE! And not just Wiltshire, but a commune. That's right, a commune. Obviously someone forgot to tell the people here communes went out of fashion a million years ago when hippies went extinct.

Mum said I'm missing school for the rest of the term, which could have been good. But it's not. I miss my friends. It's PE tomorrow and I even miss that! And I won't get to go to Laura Gilchrist's end of year party.

And all this horrible stuff is happening because she's divorcing Dad. But I don't get why we have to leave London and come here? Why can't Dad leave instead? That's what happened when Jess's parents got divorced – she ended up with two cool places to live, her mum's house and her dad's new flat in Chelsea. And I've ended up living in a field.

I keep telling Mum I hate it here, but she just keeps smiling.

Mum's friend Pam is here and she's all smiley too – like me having my whole life ruined is a good thing.

I hate them both. There's not even a TV so I've already missed one episode of Sex and the City *– which I'll probably never see ever again now. Or* Friends. *Or* Beverly Hills 90210 *(although that's not so bad now that Luke Perry's hardly even in it). And, even worse, forget about a computer or the internet, this place doesn't even have a phone. So I can't even ring Jess. She'll probably think I've been kidnapped. I had to write her a letter. How tragic is that?*

The woman that runs this place is called Laura and she's a total psychopath. But her son Art is THE WORST. He's only a year older than me, but he's really scary. He's sort of good-looking, if you fancied Jack in Titanic *you'd probably fancy him too. He's got a tattoo on his arm– which I thought was a little bit cool (it's a big red rose with thorns) until I got a closer look at it today, and realised the petals are actually drops of blood. Yuk! And anyway, no one has a tattoo who isn't a criminal or a biker. All the other kids here, who are miles younger than me and him, follow him around like a pack of wild dogs and treat him like he's God. Which he is so* not.

I bet he's never smiled in his entire life. His jeans are ripped, but not in a good way, and covered in stains like he's never cleaned them ever. And he doesn't seem to go to school, so we were the only kids here today. He totally ignored me when I said hello. Then when I told him the room my mum's given me here is nowhere near as pretty as my room at home (just to make conversation, like a normal person), he made a mean comment about me being like Princess

4

Di. As if that was a bad thing. When EVERYONE loves Princess Di, especially now she's dead.

He called me Princess Drama at supper, so now all the other kids have started calling me it too. They all hate me (AND Princess Di probably) but I don't care because I hate them back.

I told Mum what Art said about me (and Princess Di) and she just smiled AGAIN and told me I shouldn't judge people too harshly before I get to know them properly.

Like I want to get to know Art properly! As if!! Honestly, Mum acts like it's my fault Art's so mean to me. Why is she on his side? When she should be on mine?

I want to go home. I wish I was dead. I might have to kill myself if we stay here. I think I'll start a hunger strike tomorrow and see what Mum does.

If you're reading this, Mum, I'm not kidding!

CHAPTER ONE

'Mom, this pie has Jell-O in it. It tastes weird.'

Eloise Granger eased her foot off the accelerator, to see her son's face screwed up in comical disgust over the remains of his Melton Mowbray pork pie.

The gamey taste and meat jelly was obviously too much of an acquired taste for an American twelve-year-old brought up on meat that had been processed to within an inch of its life. Even for one who had never been a fussy eater she thought, taking in the dimpled skin where Josh's tummy peeped above the waistband of his 'husky boy' shorts.

'Have some popcorn chips instead then.'

'I ate all the popcorn chips already,' Josh whined, his usually sweet nature finally beaten into submission by jet lag and boredom after seven hours in a plane and a total of fifteen hours on the road since they'd left Orchard Habor in Upstate New York yesterday.

'Once we get to Grandma's, I'm sure they'll have supper ready.' Whether it would be edible though was another matter.

If Josh was struggling with the concept of pork pies, what were the chances he would wolf down kale stew or tofu casserole or whatever other vegan weirdness the commune had on the menu tonight?

'Are we almost there?' he said.

'Very nearly.' The rental car hugged a curve, the high-sided banks on either side of the road topped with wild grass and nettles. The stretch of road was familiar, even if it had seemed never-ending too, when she was fourteen and arriving here for the first time with her mum nineteen summers ago. 'Twenty minutes tops.'

At which point I will get to time-travel back to the worst summer of my life.

So I can top it. And possibly myself in the process.

Why did I ever think running away from Dan and our disaster of a marriage to a place I haven't been in nineteen years would be a good idea?

The simple answer was, desperation had set in a week ago when Dan had levelled her with his I've-just-been-caught-with-my-dick-in-someone-else's-cookie-jar-again look and told her his latest mistress was accidentally pregnant. And it had all gone downhill from there – because Ellie hadn't been angry, or upset, or even remotely surprised. She'd just been numb. Numb enough to think that taking her mum up on the invitation she'd been extending to her and Josh for the past four years, ever since Ellie had received that first tentative, white-flag-waving Christmas email from Dee, was a good way of escaping the shit storm that had wrecked her life and her business in Orchard Harbor in less than seven days. Because announcing you were divorcing the town's Golden Boy was the opposite of good publicity for a woman who made her living as a wedding and events planner. Who knew?

Unfortunately, she hadn't stopped feeling numb until she and

Josh had boarded the plane at JFK… And she'd actually had a moment to contemplate the new shit storm she was flying into.

'You said that ten minutes ago.' Josh's whine drilled through Ellie's frontal lobe. But she resisted the urge to snap at her son.

He hadn't complained when she had wrenched him away from everything and everyone he knew, without giving him a proper explanation, and dragged him across an ocean, not to mention two hundred miles of the M3 and the A303 in a tiny Ford Fiesta because that was the only hire car they had left. And he always got cranky when he was hungry. Right now he was probably ravenous, because she'd had to make do with the limited options at the small service station near Stockbridge. Hence the Melton Mowbray debacle.

And, anyway, even a cranky Josh was a welcome distraction from the flood of memories that had kept her awake during the red-eye flight to Heathrow.

What had she been thinking? That swapping one shit storm for another would somehow cancel them out?

'I said that less than a minute ago,' she corrected. 'But you're right, that means it's probably only nineteen minutes now.'

Why was it that when you knew something bad was headed your way, it always took that much longer to arrive? Was it just life's equivalent of slow-motion replays on *America's Funniest Home Videos*? Because she could remember another sunny June day nineteen years ago, when her mum had driven her to Wiltshire, their whole lives packed into the back of the family Range Rover. She had drowned out her mum's fake cheerfulness by listening to Take That's break-up album on a loop, and it had taken for ever to get there then, too.

'I'm bored.' Josh interrupted her maudlin thoughts.

'Why don't you play on your DS?'

'It's out of charge.'

'Why don't you listen to your iPod then?'

'I'm bored with the songs on it. I've listened to them over and over.' She knew how that felt. After that summer, Robbie and his pals had been dead to her for ever.

'Then have a nap. You must be tired.' *Because I'm exhausted.*

Although she doubted she'd sleep any time soon. All the nervous energy careering round her system made her feel as if she were mainlining coke.

'Naps are for babies,' Josh moaned.

'You're my baby, aren't you?'

'Mom!' She could almost hear Josh rolling his eyes. 'Don't say that in front of the new kids, OK. They'll think I'm weird.'

The smile died as she heard the anxious tone, generated by a year of being the 'weird kid' at Charles Hamilton Middle School in Orchard Harbor.

'They won't think you're weird, honey.'

Because I won't let them.

She didn't doubt that if the kids at the commune these days were anything like the ones that had been there when she'd arrived at fourteen for that one fateful summer, she'd have a job keeping Josh's self-esteem intact.

But she was ready for the challenge. This summer she had no job to go to, or marriage to pretend to care about, giving her ample time to concentrate on the two things she did care about: her son, and creating a new grand plan to give him the settled, secure, idyllic family life he deserved.

'Will they think I'm fat?' Josh asked.

Ellie's head hurt. 'No they won't, because you're not. Your

weight is perfectly healthy.' Or healthy enough not to risk giving Josh a complex about it with weight charts and unnecessary diets. That's what the nutritionist had said at any rate, at a cost of two hundred dollars an hour. And, at that price, he must have been right.

'Mom, there's a sign. Is that it?'

Josh's shout jogged Ellie's hands on the steering wheel. She braked in front of the sign, which was no longer a childish drawing of a rainbow on a piece of splintered plywood, but a swirl of hammered bronze. The sign appeared sophisticated, but it announced the entrance to a rutted track that looked like even more of an exhaust-pipe graveyard than it had nineteen years ago.

Sunlight gleamed on the metal swirls which read: 'Willow Tree Organic Farm and Cooperative-Housing Project'.

Underneath was another smaller sign listing – shock of shocks – an email address.

So they'd finally managed to dynamite themselves out of the 1960s then. Was it too much to hope the hippies who ran the place even had Wi-Fi? Perhaps they'd also realised that calling it The Rainbow Commune had conjured up images of stray dogs and filthy children in badly tie-dyed clothing? Unfortunately, the state of the track suggested the name change was nothing more than a cynical rebranding exercise.

A housing co-op is probably just a commune in disguise.

Josh bounced in his seat. 'Let's go, Mom.'

He sounded so keen and enthusiastic. How could she tell him this was likely to be a disaster?

Whatever reception she got, Josh was a sweet, sunny, wonderful boy, and anyone who tried to hurt him would have his big bad mother to answer to. Plus, they didn't have to stay, there was still the Madagascar option, which she had considered a week ago, before settling on Wiltshire.

Ellie crunched the car's gear shift into first, determined to be positive, no matter what. 'I'm sure Granny can't wait to meet you.'

The car bounced down the track, the nerves in Ellie's stomach bouncing with it like a team of obese gymnasts wearing hobnail boots, as she clung to the one bright spot she'd managed to eke out of her dark thoughts during her night flight.

At least Art Dalton, the scourge of her existence that long ago summer, wouldn't still be here. Her mother had never mentioned him or his psychotic cow of a mother Laura, or even her lover Pam, in the emails they'd exchanged in recent years. And Art would be pushing thirty-five. He must have buggered off and got himself a life by now – or at the very least, got himself arrested.

*

'Arthur, they're nearly here.' Dee Preston burst round the side of the farmhouse in a swirl of gypsy skirts and jangling bangles brandishing her mobile phone as if it held the Eighth Wonder of the Universe. 'I got a text from Ellie that she sent from the service station outside Tisbury.'

She grasped Art's arm. His chopping arm. And the axe thunked into the stubborn trunk he'd been trying to shift all day inches from his boot.

'Jesus, Dee, calm down.'

Her round, flushed face beamed at him and his heart shrank in his chest. He knew how much Dee had invested in this visit. If Ellie Preston was the same high-maintenance drama queen now that she'd been at fourteen, though, he didn't hold out much hope of Dee getting the Kodak moment she was hoping for with the daughter who hadn't bothered to come visit her once in nearly twenty years.

'I almost took off my big toe,' he added.

'Stop being such a killjoy.' Dee shoved the phone at him, only stopping short of inserting it into one of his nostrils by a few millimetres. 'Read the text and see for yourself. She sent it twenty minutes ago, she should be here any minute.'

Art plucked the phone from her fingers, before he ended up with a nosebleed, and checked the text. He managed to decipher the words "Josh" and "Love Ellie" from the jumble of letters. Without his thirteen-year-old daughter Toto on hand to read it for him properly or the spare time available to decipher each individual word himself and then compile them into a comprehensible sentence, he had to wing it.

'If she sent it twenty minutes ago, I guess you're right.' He handed back the phone. 'She should be here soon, unless she's got lost.' And, given his present run of shitty luck, that was highly unlikely.

'You have to come,' Dee said, grasping his arm. 'We should welcome them properly, like a community.'

'You've spent the last week redecorating their rooms and the whole weekend baking, isn't that enough?' But even as the grumpy words left his mouth, he was being dragged round the side of the house to the front yard, to join the other families who lived on the farm and had already been assembled.

The twin tides of pride and panic assailed him, as they always did at the endless get-togethers Dee was always organising to build a sense of community.

Toto was corralling Rob and Annie Jackson's twin toddlers.

Ducks and geese from the nearby millpond roamed over the for once not too muddy yard, and everyone stood around in small groups. The sunshine glinted off Maddy Grady's spectacles as she flirted with her boyfriend Jacob Riley. The only two unmarried members of the Project apart from him and Dee, they'd started dating a few weeks after Jacob had come to volunteer for a weekend and then never left. Art shuddered at the memory of the rhythmic thumping coming from Jacob's room the night before and keeping him awake. Even after close to a year, the shine still hadn't worn off their sex life, that was for sure.

'Please smile, Arthur. I don't want you to scare Ellie when she arrives, like you did the first time.'

'What do you mean?' Did Dee know? About the cruel things he'd said to Ellie the night before she'd left that summer? Did she know Ellie wasn't the only one who'd behaved like a selfish little shit? Guilt coalesced in the pit of his stomach.

'You ignored her.' *Was that all?*

'Did I?' Relief coursed through him. Even though that was not the way he remembered Ellie's original arrival at all. Truth was he'd been fascinated by Dee's daughter that day. She'd stepped out of her mother's car, flicked back her Rachel from *Friends* hair, the pastel silk blouse emphasising the buds of her breasts, and the superior scowl on her face making her look like a fairy queen who'd just swallowed a cockroach.

He'd stared, dazzled by how pretty and pristine she was. And she'd pursed her lips into a brittle smile, wrinkled her nose and looked right through him.

Dee glanced his way, before returning her attention to the road. 'To a fourteen-year-old girl, when a good-looking boy doesn't notice you, that's tantamount to a knife through the heart.' Dee craned her neck, eager to see round the corner of the barn, her knotted hands a testament to her nerves as she waited for her prodigal daughter's return. 'Especially one as vulnerable as Ellie was.'

Vulnerable? Was Dee kidding? Beneath the petite figure and the baby-doll face, Ellie Preston had been about as vulnerable as Maggie Thatcher.

'She didn't want me to notice her,' he muttered in his defence. Because she'd done nothing but give him grief when he had.

Dee's gaze flicked away from the road, her pale blue eyes beseeching. 'I know you two never did get along. But please, will you try and be nice, or at least not hostile towards her. It would mean so much to me.'

'Don't worry, I'm not fifteen any more,' he said, trying to keep his voice devoid of tension. 'And neither is Ellie. I'm sure we can act like grown-ups if we put our minds to it.'

And stayed the hell out of each other's way – which was precisely why he hadn't planned on being part of the welcoming committee.

'Ellie runs a very successful event-planning business in America, you know,' Dee said, her voice thick with pride. 'She might have some ideas that could help with our financial troubles.'

'We're not in financial trouble,' he said, determined to take away the worry lines forming on her forehead.

'I know it's nothing you can't fix,' she said, reassuring him instead. 'But maybe Ellie could help you run the place, take some of the burden off your shoulders, while she's here.'

'It's no burden,' he murmured, thinking of the cramped office he'd escaped from for the afternoon, furnished with a dying Hewlett Packard of indeterminate vintage and floor-to-ceiling shelves bulging with folders full of spreadsheets and order forms and invoices, which he had inherited from Dee's dead partner Pam four years ago – and still hadn't got to the bottom of.

While he'd have been more than happy to hand the lot of it over to someone else and run like hell, no way could he hand the mess over to Dee's daughter. As a teenager she'd hated this place with every fibre of her being.

While he might not have the right skills to manage the farm, he wasn't going to let it be bludgeoned to death by a woman who would happily tap dance on its grave.

'Don't worry, I'll figure out something useful for her to do while she's here,' he said wearily, hoping like hell Ellie wasn't planning to stay for the whole summer.

Maybe Princess Drama could shovel the manure into biodegradable bags? Or collect eggs from Martha, their prime layer, who had a homicidal personality disorder that would rival Caligula? Or better yet, help Jacob set the rat traps in the back barn? If he remembered correctly from the summer he'd spent with Ellie, she had a pathological phobia of mice. And the rats in that barn were big enough to give the farm's fifteen-pound ginger tom post-traumatic stress disorder.

The vice around Art's ribs loosened as he imagined the many ways he could persuade Ellie Preston to bugger off back to her very successful event-planning business in America long before the summer was over.

'I know you will.' Dee placed her sun-spotted hand on Art's forearm. 'You always know what to do. You're such a credit to us all.' She gave his arm a reassuring squeeze, the gesture full of maternal affection. The way she'd begun doing nineteen years ago. The day her daughter Ellie had climbed into her father's Mercedes and driven away.

He caught the comforting scent of vanilla essence and lavender while Dee nattered about all the exciting things she was going to do with the grandson she'd never met. And his spirits sank.

Bollocks. He wasn't going to be able to torture Ellie into leaving without upsetting Dee. The headache at his temple hammered at the base of his skull.

Perhaps he'd be able to set Martha the psycho hen on Ellie, but locking her in the barn with the mutant killer rats was probably a non-starter.

'That's them.' Dee's remark cut into his thoughts.

He lifted his head as a red Ford Fiesta bounded into the yard, then stopped. A boy popped out. About Toto's height. His short caramel-brown hair stuck up in a tuft at the crown. He wore high-top sneakers, a grey and blue New York Mets T-shirt, a baseball cap backwards and baggy cargo shorts that slouched on his hips but did nothing to hide his pronounced belly.

'Hey, I'm Josh,' he said in a broad US accent. He shuffled his hand in a half-hearted wave that was both eager and shy.

Dee rushed over to gather him close in a hug. 'Josh, it's so wonderful to meet you. I'm your Granny Dee.'

The boy smiled, his expression both curious and uncomplicated. And Art spotted the railroad-track braces on his teeth.

Ellie's kid couldn't have looked and sounded more like an all-American stereotype if he'd tried. He reminded Art of one of the characters from *Recess*, the cartoon Toto had devoured like kiddie crack a few years ago.

Ellie stepped out of the other side of the car and Art's breathing stopped as he absorbed the short, sharp shock of recognition.

In a pair of faded Levi's rolled up at the hem and a snug lacy vest top that emphasised her small frame, her wild strawberry blonde hair tied up in a haphazard knot to reveal dangly earrings, she looked summery and sexy and casual, and nothing like the pristine, polished, too perfect girl he remembered. But then Dee placed a hand on her daughter's arm, and Ellie's spine stiffened as if someone had shoved a rod up her arse.

Dee began introducing everyone, while the younger kids swarmed round Ellie's son, who seemed astonished by the attention. Toto, like him though, held back.

Then it struck him, as he watched Toto watch the boy, that as the oldest kid here, a card-carrying tomboy and as good as a surrogate grandchild to Dee, his daughter might feel as uncomfortable about the new arrivals as he did. Maybe he should have spoken to Toto about Ellie and her son coming to visit? Was this one of *those* situations that required the sort of 'parent–child' conversation the two of them generally avoided? How was he supposed to know that?

But then Toto stopped watching and marched up to the boy, said something to him and grabbed his hand. The boy's doughy face lit up as he nodded and allowed himself to be dragged off. Toto in the lead as always, like the Pied Piper.

Nope, we're good.

Thank Christ. This situation was enough of a head-wreck already.

Give or take the odd drive-Dad-mad moment, Toto was a brilliant kid. Smart, independent, straightforward and unafraid. And, like him, she wasn't the share-and-discuss type.

So yeah, it was all good. *No feelings talk required.*

Ellie's body remained rigid as she chatted to her mother, while Mike Peveney and Rob Jackson – who had both bought into the Project with their young families a couple of years ago – set about unpacking her car. A few minutes later, they had disgorged enough bags from the two-door compact to spend six months on safari in Kenya rather than a few weeks in Wiltshire.

Digging his fists into the pockets of his work overalls, Art strolled towards the dwindling welcoming party, prepared to follow through on his promise to Dee.

There was no reason why Ellie and he couldn't be civil to each other. She might not even remember him. Much.

But then his gaze snagged on her strappy top and the way the thin cotton stretched tight across her breasts. The firm nubs of her nipples stood out against the fabric.

He heard a cough, and lifted his gaze. A pair of grass-green eyes glared at him. The flush burned the back of his neck, at the thought that he'd just been caught checking her out before he'd even said hello. But then the intriguing tilt at the edges of her eyes went squinty and he noticed the bluish hollows of fatigue underneath.

She looked exhausted.

Her lips pursed and the puddle of pity dried up. The tight smile was as unconvincing as the one nineteen years ago.

'Hello, Arthur,' she said, using the name he hated except when Dee used it. 'You're still here then.'

It wasn't a question, more like a declaration of war.

CHAPTER TWO

*B*ollocks *on toast.*

Art Dalton was still here. And still hot. And most definitely still an arsehole, if the insolent way he'd been inspecting her boobs was anything to go by.

'Yup,' he said, in the gruff tone that had always unnerved her when they were teenagers. As if there were a million things he could say, but wasn't going to.

The nervous tension that had been sitting in her gut during the flight over and the drive here, snaked up Ellie's torso to wrap around her ribs like an anaconda.

Stop freaking out, you ninny. He'll think it's on account of him.

She took two calming breaths, drowning out her mother's information about sleeping arrangements, and took a moment to glance around the yard. Studiously ignoring the man in front of her.

The pungent smell of wet earth and manure hadn't changed, but everything else had. The place didn't look like the site of a recent zombie apocalypse any more. There were no rusting vans and trucks propped up on breeze blocks, no broken furniture lying about. Just a carefully segmented vegetable garden, laid out in rows with a section under glass. There were geese and ducks poking around, but no pack of wild dogs or wild children, just two well-dressed toddlers and a skinny little boy about Josh's age who had taken him off somewhere.

She would check on her son in a minute, after three hours in a car he could do with a run about, but she was reserving judgement on the motives of that skinny boy.

The barn behind the two-storey stone farmhouse had a new roof, the corrugated iron gleaming silver in the sunlight. Even the mud looked industrious. And all three of the men she'd been introduced to had seemed young and ordinary, instead of old and weird. Not a nose ring or multicoloured Mohican in sight.

The anaconda released its stranglehold on her ribs. The place didn't feel as hostile any more.

'Exactly how long are you planning to stay?'

Art's dry enquiry interrupted her mum's running commentary on how pleased she was to meet Josh.

Not hostile – except for Prince Not Charming.

'Because that's a ton of stuff,' he added, the rasp suggesting how much of an effort it was for him to put a whole sentence together.

In worn boots and oil-stained overalls, Art Dalton looked as intimidating as ever – the strong, silent, stroppy type. His tall, whipcord-lean build had a solid strength, accentuated by the workman's biceps that moulded the rolled-up sleeves of his overalls. The old tattoo caught her eye, the once blood-red lines having faded to a dusky pink against sun-browned skin. She dragged her gaze away, before she got fixated. His dark messy hair matched black brows, permanently lowered over his prominent aquiline nose. Sensual lips twisted in a cynical attempt at a smile. At fifteen he'd been the ultimate rebel without a cause, the original Lord of the Flies – both terrifying and exciting.

Not a good combination for a fourteen-year-old girl in the grip of rioting hormones, who missed her friends terribly and had about as much common sense as Daffy Duck. Luckily, she'd kicked Daffy to the kerb nineteen years ago – give or take the odd ill-advised marriage – after Art had rejected her the first time. So it really didn't matter now that he looked like the walking embodiment of 'a bit of rough'. Or exuded the earthy eroticism of *Lady Chatterley's Lover*.

'Stop interrogating her, Arthur.' Dee threaded her arm through Ellie's and led her towards the farmhouse, and away from Art and his surly questions.

'How long *are* you planning to stay?' Dee asked, as they approached the farmhouse.

Lavender bushes, sunflowers and fire-red foxgloves spilled out of the flowerbeds by the door, giving off a heady perfume. A wisteria vine, clinging to the stonework, wound its way around the peaked portico.

'Because you and Josh are welcome to stay for as long as you want,' her mother added.

From the forbidding scowl on his face, she wasn't convinced Art Dalton agreed.

'I don't know. We haven't made any concrete plans yet.' The only concrete plan so far had involved escaping from Orchard Harbor before news of Chelsea Hamilton's pregnancy hit the local gossip grapevine – and turned her and Josh's lives into a soap opera worthy of Argentinian daytime TV.

Ellie would have been able to cope with all the 'well-meant advice' and faux sympathy once the news was out, because she'd been doing that for years, but she wasn't sure Josh could, without eating his own weight in Oreos. The truth was she hadn't even had the guts to tell him yet that Dan and her were separating.

'Then I hope you'll consider staying for a while,' Dee said, the generosity of the gesture making Ellie feel even more uncomfortable.

Her mother had been suggesting she and Josh visit for a while now, not long after that first tentative email with the subject line 'Merry Christmas, Ellie' had appeared in her inbox four years ago. But, prior to that, they'd lost contact for over a decade – separated by the huge chasm that had developed once Ellie had chosen to leave the commune after that one fateful summer and go back to live with her dad. And her mother had opted to stay put with her new girlfriend.

'But there's no need to make a decision yet,' Dee added quickly, obviously picking up on Ellie's reluctance, as she walked ahead past a rack of coats and jackets positioned over a crate full of scuffed sneakers and wellington boots. 'All you and Josh need to do today is settle in, and relax after your long journey.'

The long journey had been a picnic compared to the week that had preceded it, but Ellie allowed herself to be led.

'I'll be serving dinner in a couple of hours,' Dee said. 'But I could get you something to snack on first if you're hungry.'

Her mum's voice drifted over Ellie. 'I'm fine.'

She refrained from suggesting she skip dinner and crash now as her mother opened the door to the communal kitchen. It would be an ordeal attending the communal supper tonight. She didn't find eating with people she didn't know particularly relaxing, but it was the penance she would have to pay for being deranged enough to accept her mum's invitation in the first place. And at least the people who lived here now didn't have inappropriate piercings or judgemental scowls on their faces – every one except Art.

Then again, she hadn't seen Art's mother yet, or her mother's girlfriend Pam. Reunions she was not looking forward to almost as much as the one with Art.

She raised her head to ask about them both, and gasped.

She recognised the sturdy butler sink and the scarred butcher's block table – around which numerous discussions about whether Tony Blair was really a Tory plant had been conducted in her youth – but nothing else looked familiar. The boxes of pamphlets and home-made placards she remembered stacked in every available corner, the wolf-like dog that snarled whenever she ventured into the room and the teetering towers of dirty dishes in the sink were all gone.

The commune's hub had been transformed from revolution central into the set from a country cooking show.

An industrial dishwasher stood in one corner next to the cast-iron splendour of a traditional Aga cooker. The flagstone flooring had been scrubbed clean. The door to the pantry – which had once housed an antique printing press – now stood open to reveal shelves groaning under jars of home-made preserves, while a collection of potted herbs stood in aromatic abundance on the windowsill over the sink.

The delicious smell of garlic and melted cheese drew Ellie's gaze to the home-baked lasagne and tray of roasted vegetables resting on the Aga's hot plate.

Ellie blinked, expecting Hugh Fearnley-Whittingstall to pop out of the pantry at any moment and start demonstrating how to make sloe-gin ice cream.

'What happened?' Had she slipped into an alternative reality?

'What happened to what?' Her mother turned from the cooker, where she'd been taking another tray of vegetables out of the oven.

The light from the window illuminated the streaks of grey in her mother's dark blonde hair. In the shaft of sunlight, Ellie noticed for the first time the speckle of sun blemishes on her mum's skin and the slight thickening around the waistband of her gypsy skirt. But otherwise, Dee Preston, unlike her kitchen, had hardly changed. With her sky-blue eyes, the thick tangle of hair tied up in a topknot, the collection of bangles on her wrist jingling as she basted the vegetables, she looked a good fifteen years younger than her fifty-nine years.

'To the kitchen? To the whole place?' Ellie felt a bit ridiculous when her mother sent her a quizzical look, as if she couldn't imagine what Ellie was getting at. 'It doesn't look anything like I remember it.'

'Oh, well, yes.' Dee glanced around, attempting to locate the differences. 'I suppose it is a bit less cluttered these days.'

'Mum, it was a shit-hole,' Ellie said. 'There was that feral dog that lurked in the corner like the three-headed hellhound from Harry Potter.'

'Fluffy?'

'That dog was called Fluffy?' Clearly someone back then had a sense of humour she'd been unaware of.

Her mum smiled. 'No, the three-headed dog in Harry Potter's called Fluffy. Laura's Irish wolfhound was called Scargill, I think.'

That figured, because Art's mum had been in the forefront of all the revolutionary bollocks Ellie remembered from the bad old days.

'He died years ago,' Dee supplied helpfully. 'He's buried in the back pasture.'

'But it wasn't just the dog,' Ellie continued, silently hoping the Hound of the Baskervilles had died in agony, because it was the least the cantankerous old beast deserved. 'No one ever washed up or cooked anything remotely edible, except you. The whole place stank of unwashed bodies and stale marijuana and it was a hotbed of born-again hippie anarchy.' She swept her hand to encompass the scene before her now, which could have illustrated a feature article in *Country Living*. 'Not home-grown herbs and home-made preserves and home baking. The place looks as if it's been given a makeover by the Shabby Chic Fairy. Seriously, what happened?'

Because she wanted to know.

'Well, Laura left us a few months after you did. And most of the activist element left not long after that, too.'

Laura Dalton had left? Nineteen years ago? So why was her son Art still hanging about? Ellie stopped herself from asking though, because she wasn't interested in what had been going on with Art.

'Where did Laura go?' she asked, deciding that was a safe question.

'She ran off with the local Lib-Dem member of the county council. His name was Rupert something.'

'You are joking?' This was beginning to sound like a *Little Britain* sketch. And not in a good way.

'We were all a bit surprised to be honest, given that Laura had insisted even New Labour were traitors to the cause.' Dee's smile became rueful.

'I thought Laura was a lesbian?' She'd never managed to get to the bottom of how Art had been created, because no one had ever spoken about his father. But given how demonstrative Laura had always been with Delshad, her partner at the commune, Ellie had begun to suspect Art might have originated from a petri dish in a sperm bank.

'So did Laura, I suppose.' Dee tucked a stray tendril behind her ear and picked up a dishcloth to wipe the already pristine table. 'But apparently she wasn't. Or not where Rupert was concerned. She left a note for Art, explaining why she'd left, but he never told me what it said.'

Had his mum just left him behind then? With a note? He'd only been fifteen.

The spurt of sympathy though was blasted into submission by a disturbing memory flash of Art at fifteen. His lean wiry nut-brown body lying in the long grass by the millpond, the bloody ink on his left bicep rippling as he held his…

Heat blossomed in her stomach and crawled over her scalp, the same way it had all those years ago, when she'd watched him unobserved from her vantage point in the derelict mill house and realised what he was doing.

She cut off the memory. But the heat refused to subside as she had another memory flash, closer to home, of the same ink peeking out from the rolled-up sleeve of Art's overalls a few minutes ago.

Note to self: jet lag, a failed marriage and a year with only the occasional duty shag can seriously mess with your mental health. Enough to delude you into fixating on an arsehole like Art Dalton and his tacky tattoo.

She needed to crash, and soon.

'So Laura never came back?' she said. 'Delshad must have been devastated.'

Any sympathy for Art on the other hand would be misguided. She couldn't imagine him being devastated. His mum had probably run off with Rupert the Lib-Dem – and jettisoned her political beliefs and her sexual identity in the process – to get shot of him. After all, he'd been more wild and feral at fifteen than that bloody dog.

'Actually she did come back in a manner of speaking,' Dee said, throwing the dishcloth into the sink.

'Oh?'

'A young man called Jack Harborough turned up five years ago with her ashes in a Tupperware container. He said he'd been living with her in a squat in Tottenham. He had photos of the two of them together. Apparently she died of lung cancer. She did look terribly thin in the photos. Like someone from a concentration camp. Awful,' Dee said mildly. 'That's what roll-ups can do to you.'

Ellie was still trying to get her head around the thought of Laura coming back in a Tupperware container. The thought of the stunningly beautiful radical socialist looking like a Belsen victim simply wouldn't compute.

And she thought her life had become a soap opera.

'Where's Pam?' Ellie heard herself say, deciding she would have to kick the elephant in the room eventually. And getting sidetracked with Laura's story had given her a headache. And some memory flashes she really didn't need to go with the foggy feeling of exhaustion.

Dee's smile didn't falter, but the warmth in her eyes died. 'She's dead, darling. She died four years ago.'

'I didn't know. I'm… I'm sorry, Mum.' The words felt inadequate. And somewhat hypocritical, given the emotion arriving on the heels of the revelation was a massive surge of relief. 'Why didn't you tell me in any of your emails?'

Was Pam's death the reason why Dee had decided to get in touch again out of the blue? Surely it had to be.

Ellie's spine stiffened a bit more. *Get over it.*

It was churlish to feel cheated that her mother's grief had been the only thing prompting her to build bridges that had been broken for so long. Why should her mother's motivations matter? After all, she and her mother weren't close, would never be close – and Ellie's reasons for being here were equally as self-serving as her mother's reasons were for wanting her here.

'I didn't want to bother you with it,' Dee said easily enough. 'After all, you and Pam didn't care for each other.' The words were said without any censure, but Ellie's chest tightened.

Pam had tried to get on with her. It was she who had refused point blank to get on with Pam.

She headed round the table, and laid a palm on her mother's arm. 'Yes, but you cared about Pam.' While Ellie might once have managed to convince herself her mother's affair with another woman was nothing more than a juvenile mid-life crisis, it was hard to escape the fact the two of them had lived together for fifteen years. 'I'm sorry for your loss.'

Her mother's skin felt soft and cool. And the gesture felt awkward, and insincere. Especially when Dee said: 'Thank you, Ellie. You know, it was Pam who begged me to contact you, to re-establish a relationship with you before she died,' she added, confirming Ellie's suspicions. 'And I'm glad I did. It's wonderful to finally have you here.' Dee's hopeful expression did nothing to ease Ellie's guilt or her discomfort. Exactly what was her mother expecting from this visit? 'And I'm so looking forward to getting to know Josh.' Dee patted her fingers. 'He seems like a lovely boy. So open and so very American.'

The mention of Josh gave Ellie a jolt. In the shock of seeing Art and the new improved farm and hearing about Laura's Lib-Dem love shock and Pam's untimely death, she'd completely forgotten about her son.

'I'm sure he will. But who was that boy he went off with?' she asked, her protective-mother instinct charging to the fore.

Actually, it was a bit surprising Josh hadn't returned already. He wasn't usually confident with strangers. Especially strange kids. And the boy who had led him off had reminded Ellie of the wild kids who had roamed the commune before. Skinny with a smudge of something on his chin, his short dark hair sticking up, wearing torn jeans and a grubby T-shirt, his eyes too big for his freckled face, the boy had looked decidedly feral.

'Toto, you mean?' Her mother smiled as if enjoying a private joke.

'Yes, Toto, that was it. He said he was taking Josh to their clubhouse. Is it safe?' She should have asked this before. Josh wasn't the most agile of children. And she didn't want him to feel awkward. Or worse, end up in some hideous initiation ceremony. Like she had. 'Isn't Toto a dog's name?' Why would anyone give their child a name like that?

'Toto's short for Antonia.'

'That boy's a girl?' The obese gymnasts relaxed. Surely a tomboy would be less feral than an actual boy.

'Yes, she's Art's daughter.'

The obese gymnasts began doing backflips in Ellie's stomach. *Less feral, my arse.*

CHAPTER THREE

'Dad, Dad, Dad, you've gotta come quick.'

'Damn it!' Art wheeled back the axe to stop himself from nearly hacking off his foot a second time in one afternoon. 'Toto, what is wrong with you? Don't run up and shout at me when I'm chopping.'

But Toto already had her hand buried in his overalls to drag him who knew where. 'You've got to come. Josh is stuck up a tree and he's going to die if you don't rescue him.'

He placed the axe by the tree stump and gripped his daughter's shoulders to stop them shaking, from either exertion or terror, it was hard to tell.

'Calm down. Who's Josh and what tree is he stuck up?' They'd deal with the dying bit in a minute.

'Josh is the new kid.' Toto gasped between breaths. 'Dee's grandson.'

Crap. Just what he needed, Ellie's kid breaking his neck after they'd been here exactly half an hour. She was just the type to sue them into the ground for child endangerment.

'What tree's he stuck up?'

Toto tried to drag him towards the woods. 'The Clubhouse tree.'

'Can't he just climb down again?' he said. 'There's a ladder. I built the thing myself.'

'No, it's the ladder he's stuck on.'

'How can he be stuck on the ladder?' Had the thing broken? The cost of the lawsuit spiralled up.

'I don't know,' Toto wailed. 'He just did. And now he can't get down and he's afraid and he could fall. And he's way way up, right near the top. If he falls, it's gonna hurt.'

She yanked his overalls. Grasping her wrist, he lifted her fingers off. 'Stop tugging me. I'll go sort it out.'

Toto tried to shoot off ahead of him, but he grabbed her arm.

'Dad! Don't hold me. I need to run back; he'll be scared without me.'

'I'll go. You need to go tell his mum what's going on.' He'd be more than happy never to have Ellie know about this, but just in case her son did end up injuring himself, it was the only responsible thing to do. 'And show her where the tree is.'

Toto nodded. 'Oh, OK.' But, as she tried to dart off towards the farmhouse, he yanked her to a halt again.

'But do me a favour.'

'Yes, Dad?' She waited for his instructions, total and utter trust radiating from her.

And he got light-headed.

He knew Toto's complete faith in him was unlikely to last much longer, but it was still a heady feeling for a man who had spent the first twenty-one years of his life convinced he could never do anything right. He'd strived for the last thirteen years never to abuse Toto's trust, but he was going to have to blur the lines a bit today, to ward off a punitive lawsuit.

'Take your time getting Josh's mum to the Clubhouse,' he said. 'I want to have Josh down before she gets there.'

'OK, Dad.' Toto nodded, her acceptance of the instruction unquestioning as she sped off to find Ellie.

He jogged off towards the forest, hoping like hell the boy hadn't already fallen off the tree and broken his bloody neck.

It took him less than five minutes to get to the Clubhouse. A simple A-frame design he'd built two summers ago in a hundred-year-old horse chestnut near the edge of the coppice woods with Toto's help – or rather hindrance. He hadn't given much thought at the time to the access. Toto could climb like a monkey and would probably have been able to get up the damn tree without the aid of the boards he'd nailed into the trunk. And as the thing had been built precisely so she'd have a refuge from the younger kids when she needed it, the ladder, such as it was, had been an afterthought.

He regretted that decision big time when he spotted Ellie's son stapled to the trunk – a good twenty-five feet off the ground.

How had he got up that high before he froze?

And how was he going to get the kid down? Although the boy wasn't exactly light for his age – he looked about twice as wide as Toto – Art would probably still have been able to sling him over his shoulder. But no way would those boards take the weight of both of them, assuming of course the kid would let him carry him. From the death grip he had on the board, Art figured he was going to have a hell of a time even getting the boy to let go.

Which left only one solution. He would have to talk him down.

Wonderful. Because he was so good at conversation.

'Hey!' he shouted up and then winced, as the boy nodded, butting his forehead into the trunk with a hollow smack. 'It's Josh' isn't it?'

'Yes, sir.'

Sir?

Was that an American thing? He'd never been called 'sir' in his life. Not even by the bank manager.

'I'm sorry, sir,' the boy continued and Art winced again at the plaintive, terrified whimper. 'I got stuck and now I can't get down.' More tremors wracked the kid's body and Art lifted his arm, suddenly worried he might shake himself right off the tree.

'You don't have to be sorry, Josh. Happens to the best of us.'

He climbed the rungs, ignoring the give in each one and hoping he didn't end up breaking his own bloody neck.

'I won't do it again, sir. I promise,' the boy said, sounding more miserable than Toto when she had to do maths homework.

'Let's not worry about next time yet.' He reached the boy. 'I'm right here beneath you, Josh.' He stared at the rungs above the boy's feet, partially hidden by his legs and torso. One of the rungs was a little longer than the others, and if Art eased himself up carefully, he could hold on to it and effectively cradle the kid. Maybe that would help with his fear? Knowing that he'd be caught if he did let go.

'You should get my mom,' the boy said. 'She'll know what to do. And she wouldn't want me bothering you.'

'I'm here now, so I might as well help.' And the last thing he wanted was Josh's mother finding her son in this state. Forget about bothering him, she'd probably murder him. 'I'm going to put my arms around you, Josh. And hold on to the rung under your belly, OK? So I can catch you if you fall.'

The boy nodded, headbutting the trunk again.

Art grasped the rung and hauled himself up, until his chest was resting securely against the boy's back. The child's whole body trembled as if he were in a high wind.

34

The kid was absolutely terrified.

Then Art heard the whimpers. Craning his neck, he could see the side of the boy's face. The silent tears leaked out and dripped down to disappear into the roll of fat where he had pressed his chin into his neck.

'Don't cry, Josh. You're OK, I've got you.' Balancing carefully, he lifted one hand to pat the boy's back, and felt the vibrations, and the heat of the boy's body through the thin cotton.

'Please don't tell Toto,' the boy said.

'Don't tell Toto what?'

'That I cried. I don't want her to think I'm lame as well as fat.'

The boy wasn't exactly thin, but hearing him call himself fat in that sadly accepting voice had a shaft of anger shooting through Art.

'She won't think that,' he said, because he knew his daughter. She didn't judge people by their appearances. 'But if we get down before she gets back, she won't even know.'

'How will I get down?'

Good question. There wasn't a lot of room to manoeuvre. 'Do you think you could move down a step, while I stay in place?'

He heard the sound of swallowing. The shaking was still pretty pronounced. 'I'll try.'

'Good boy,' Art said. He didn't usually bother with positive reinforcement with Toto. But with this kid, he had the feeling it was required.

After what felt like ten hours, but was probably only ten seconds, they'd negotiated one rung down.

He lavished the boy with more praise, the relief loosening his tongue more than usual. The stillness of the summer air seemed eerie as Art waited to hear the boy's mother crashing through the undergrowth ready to issue an injunction. But as they spent an eternity inching their way down the ladder, one tortuous rung at a time, until Art could finally step onto the ground – the sound never came.

Good girl, Toto. She must be escorting Ellie to the Clubhouse via Plymouth.

'You can let go now, Josh.' Relief surged through him as he grabbed the boy round the waist and lifted him the rest of the way down. 'Well done.'

The boy huffed, and then to Art's astonishment wrapped his arms tight around Art's midriff and buried his head against his sternum.

'Thank you, sir. Thank you so much.' The words were muffled against Art's overalls. 'You saved my life.'

Containing his surprise – Toto had never been a big hugger – Art cupped the boy's shoulders to ease him back. 'No thanks necessary. You saved yourself.'

The boy loosened his hold to gaze up at Art. He had a dusty green smear across his cheek and red indentation marks on his forehead. Truth be told, he looked a mess, but then he smiled. His eyes were hazel, with flecks of green in them, and his round face was impossibly young and open, but, in that moment, Art could see the resemblance to his mother — which was weird, because Art was fairly sure he could count on the fingers of one hand the number of times he'd seen Ellie smile her real smile — as opposed to her tight smile, or her sarcastic smile, or her you-are-such-an-arsehole smile.

But that rare real smile had been exactly like her son's. It had made her eyes shine, as if someone had lit a furnace behind them.

'I didn't think I could, but I did, sir.'

'Yes, you did.' Art patted the boy on the shoulder, relieved when Josh let go of him. 'But you don't have to call me "sir". It makes me feel a hundred years old.'

The furnace behind the boy's eyes flared and he giggled. The childish chuckle made Art feel for a moment as if he were lit from within too.

And that's when he heard the sound of someone charging through the forest, from the opposite direction to the farmhouse. That would be Ellie and Toto, back from Plymouth.

'Josh, Josh, are you OK?'

Ellie catapulted from the wooded path that led down to the millpond. Her hair flew out behind her where it had escaped its knot. Even Toto, who was fast as a whippet, was struggling to keep up with mother bear come to rescue her cub.

Josh stepped back out of his arms as Ellie rushed past him to grab her son's shoulders. 'Thank God you're safe.' She stroked his cheek and then touched the abrasions on his forehead. 'What happened to your face?'

'It's OK, Mom. It doesn't hurt.'

A blush had suffused Josh's cheeks.

Ellie was totally overreacting, and she was embarrassing the boy. Her son was twelve, not two. Art figured it was none of his business, though, as she crushed Josh to her bosom, running her hand over his hair. She peered at the treehouse, then fired a glare at Art that could laser stone.

'What was he doing up there? He's afraid of heights.' Her glare travelled back to the treehouse. 'And that thing's a bloody death trap.' Then the glare hit Toto. 'What were you trying to do, kill him? Or just humiliate him?'

Toto shook her head, her eyes popping wide, but remained

mute. Art figured she had to be in shock, because his daughter was usually incredibly hard to shut up.

'Mom, I wanted to go up there,' Josh offered in Toto's defence. 'It's a clubhouse and it's cool.'

Maybe the boy was scared of heights, but he only seemed embarrassed by his mother in full Valkyrie mode. Art gave the boy points for bravery, because the woman looked ready to commit murder.

The killer glare shot back to him. 'Why does it not surprise me that your daughter is as much of a sadist as you used to be?'

Crap, she'd just made it his business.

*

'Chill out, Ellie.'

'Chill out?' Ellie hissed, the obese gymnasts ready to explode out of her ears.

This man and his vicious little minion had nearly killed her son. Not to mention taken her on a trek across most of Wiltshire when she was so exhausted she was ready to faceplant for a week.

She'd chill Art Dalton right into the freezer cabinet if he wasn't careful.

'I will not chill out. And the name's not Ellie, it's Eloise to you.'

His brows wrinkled. Fine, maybe it sounded a bit pompous. She didn't care.

'OK, Eloise.' He rolled the name off his tongue as if it were the punchline to a particularly unfunny joke. 'There's no need to flip out.' He swung a hand towards Josh, who had wriggled out of her arms and was standing beside Art's evil minion. The two children edged closer to Art, as if he were the sane dependable adult in this scenario.

'The boy's safely on terra firma.' Art's patient tone made her want to kick him exceptionally hard, somewhere extremely soft. 'He made the decision to go up there and he got himself down without too much help from me. Toto came to get you as soon as she knew there was a problem. So whatever you're accusing her of, you're wrong.'

'She came to get me and then took me on a guided tour of Wiltshire to bring me to a tree that I know is only five minutes from the farmyard.'

She was getting light-headed again, her lungs aching from the effort to hold back the tortured breaths of her outrage.

They'd done to Josh exactly what Art had done to her all those years ago, Art and the other commune kids. A couple of days after she'd arrived they'd told her she needed to be initiated in their stupid club. And somehow, because she was fascinated by the rough boy, and a bit afraid of him too, she'd agreed to try. And had ended up with the brand new Kookai blouse her dad had bought her for her birthday covered in fresh manure and them all laughing at her.

'I don't want my son near your daughter,' she said. 'I don't want her suggesting he climb up trees, or swim in the millpond or tramp through fields of young bullocks to get a mythical stone that doesn't exist. Do you understand?'

'But, Mom, I want to join Toto's club,' Josh wailed, as if she'd just ruined his life. She ignored him, her gaze focused on Art Dalton's face, and the rigid line of his jaw. Good, at least he didn't look patiently amused any more.

'Toto, why don't you take Josh back to the farmhouse?' Art addressed his daughter. 'Dee can clean him up. It'll be suppertime soon.'

'OK, Dad'; 'Yes, sir,' said Art's daughter and her son in unison.

'Excuse me,' Ellie began, her breath coming in jagged gasps now. 'Who gave you permission to tell my son what to…'

Before she could finish the sentence, the children had dashed off together through the woods, back in the direction of the farmhouse. The direction she should have come from if Art's child hadn't taken her on a five-mile hike while her heart was exploding at the thought of Josh tumbling to his death.

Her temper hit boiling point, the white noise in her ears loud enough to sound like the woods were being dive-bombed by the Red Arrows.

'How dare you tell my son what to do. He's my responsibility not yours. I decide who he–'

'If Dee has her way, he's going to be here the whole summer.' Art's gaze locked on hers, all signs of amusement gone. 'Toto's a good kid and she likes him and they're about the same age. It won't do them any harm to hang out together. He'll be sure to get lots of exercise.'

'I'm not asking you. And don't worry, we're not staying the whole summer. I doubt I'll stay more than one night after this. And if you're talking about his weight with that comment about exercise, you can piss off. It's perfectly healthy.'

'Did I say it wasn't?'

'You implied it.' Other parents always assumed they knew best. That if your child was carrying a little extra weight and theirs wasn't that they knew how to fix it. They knew nothing of Josh's body image issues. His anxieties. The way he could comfort eat his way through a whole quart of rocky road ice cream in two minutes after coming home from school. 'And, believe me, being forced to climb a tree when he's afraid of heights is not going to magically make him lose two stone.'

'No one forced him to climb the tree. And he survived.'

'How do you know that? You don't know anything about him, you only just met him.'

'I know he's a little boy. And little boys need the chance to cut loose now and again. Not get wrapped in cotton wool by their mothers.'

She sputtered. She actually sputtered. The Red Arrows circling her head now. How dare he tell her how to raise her child, when he'd clearly spent no time at all raising his own. 'Oh really, well maybe that explains why your daughter thinks she's a little boy too.'

'At least my daughter doesn't think she's fat.'

'He's not fat.' She wanted to hit him. She squeezed her fingers into a fist, to resist the urge to lash out. 'He has a traumatic relationship with food.'

'Uh-huh? All I've seen so far is his traumatic relationship with you.'

'You son of a bitch.' The Red Arrows hit the sound barrier, the sonic boom going off inside her head as she swung her bunched fist towards his face.

He dodged back, and she hit thin air, flinging herself off balance and tumbling to earth. She body-slammed the ground, her reflexes too dulled by fatigue and incandescent rage to react fast enough to break her fall. Air gushed out, and pain ricocheted through her ribs, tears stinging her eyes.

She heard a curse, as strong hands gripped her waist and hauled her back onto her feet.

'You all right?' His gruff voice reverberated in her head, the low-grade headache now hammering her skull in time with the throbbing pain in what she suspected might be a dislocated shoulder.

'Piss off,' she said, but the expletive lacked heat. She hurt every-where, her pride most of all.

The nausea galloped up her throat as blunt fingers pushed the hair off her brow. 'You look knackered.'

Of course she did, she'd just hit the deck with enough force to puncture a lung.

'I think I'm going to be sick,' she said, her humiliation complete.

'Put your head down.'

His palm cupped the back of her head and suddenly she was staring at the ground between her feet, studying the decaying leaves and a small beetle burrowing into a mound of twigs and wild grass.

'Breath through your nose, it'll go away in a minute.'

She wanted to tell him where he could stick his first aid advice. But she couldn't speak round the lump of anguish, so she watched the beetle.

'When did you last eat?' he asked.

She tried to focus on his voice, which seemed a million miles away. 'Yesterday morning, before we left home.'

'Then you're not likely to be sick,' he said.

The dizziness and nausea began to subside. He released her head, and drew her upright with the hand he had clamped on her upper arm. The feel of his fingers, rough and cool pressing into her biceps, sent sensation zipping through her system.

Which should have been mortifying, but somehow wasn't, because the pain had drifted away, to be replaced by a floating feeling. The warm numbness spread through her body.

'Can you walk?' he asked.

'Of course,' she said, but as she took a step, it was as if she were walking on the moon, about to bounce off into the cosmos.

'Shit, here we go.' She heard the husky words still a million miles away, but now from underwater.

Then she wasn't vertical any more, she was horizontal and focusing on the scar that nicked his chin and made a white sickle shape in the dark stubble.

Her focus faded as she blinked. Once. Twice. The pleasant numbness enveloped her, her limbs going loose and languid, as she sank into a hot bubble bath that smelled of motor oil and laundry detergent and something else – the musty earthy scent of man.

CHAPTER FOUR

Consciousness beckoned through the magical twinkle of stars and the comforting scent of lavender. Ellie's eyelids fluttered open and she found herself cocooned on an iron-framed double bed, the cluster of fairy lights draped over the mantelpiece opposite dotting a hand-sewn coverlet with sparkles of light.

A dark figure appeared from a door to her right, holding a towel, and looking muscular and intimidating in oil-stained overalls. The magical twinkles surrounded him like dancing fairies until he stepped into the light.

Art.

The dull ache in her ribs throbbed as the events before she'd blacked out came back. Her stomach cramped. And she scooted across the bed, ready to heave over the side. 'I need a bucket.'

And after that please leave me alone to die in peace.

The polished wooden boards creaked. And the mattress dipped as Art sat on the bed.

'Here.' He slapped a cold wet cloth on her nape, then lifted her wrist to position her hand over it and hold it in place. 'You don't need a bucket. You're not going to puke.'

She rolled over and propped herself up to glare at him – somewhat miffed the nausea had passed. 'How would you know?'

'Because you haven't eaten anything for twenty-four hours.'

She tried to hold on to her indignation, but she didn't have the strength. Had he carried her all the way up here? And where was here?

The room looked vaguely familiar, but her brain was still too fuzzy to figure out why. 'Where am I?'

'Your old bedroom. Dee redecorated it when she got the email saying you were coming over.'

The room was exquisite. No wonder she hadn't recognised it.

The space was fresh and clean, decorated with bold colours and inspired prints. A couple of huge overstuffed armchairs in one corner sat next to a sturdy wooden dresser, its vibrant yellow paint making a statement against the white walls even in the dappled glow of the fairy lights. New curtains in retro gingham were draped stylishly over long sash windows that looked out into the reddening sky as dusk fell over the woods. The Victorian grandeur of the room looked inviting now instead of forbidding. Under the scent of lavender, Ellie detected the turpentine aroma of new paint.

'It's beautiful,' she murmured.

'She put a lot of hours in fixing it up.'

The pang of guilt hit under her left ventricle, not dull this time, but sharp as a blade. What was she supposed to do with the knowledge that Dee had decided to welcome her back with home-made curtains and newly painted walls and fairy lights, like a treasured, long-lost child?

'I wish she hadn't gone to this much trouble,' she said, knowing the effort her mother had put into redecorating the room would force her to reconsider her plans to leave tomorrow.

Art shrugged. 'She wanted to do it.' Standing up, he thrust his hands into the pockets of his overalls. 'How are the ribs?'

'I'll survive.' She placed a hand on her side. Her embarrassment at the way she'd swung at him and missed more painful right now than the bruises.

She noticed the sunburned column of his throat. Her gaze darted away, the glimpse of chest revealed by the open neck of his overalls making her aware of how much more body hair he had now than he'd had at fifteen. Not something she needed to be noticing.

'Did you carry me all the way up here?' she asked, the thought of those muscular arms holding her aloft not good for her equilibrium.

He nodded.

'Thanks,' she said, grudgingly. 'But you didn't have to do that.'

'You're not heavy. And Dee would have had my hide if I'd left you out there all night.'

The lack of sentiment was strangely comforting. At least she knew exactly where she was with Art.

But, as he put his hand on the doorknob, she felt compelled to add, 'Thanks for getting Josh down from the treehouse. I'll apologise to your daughter next time I see her. I shouldn't have shouted at her.'

She'd been exhausted, and the child had definitely taken them well out of their way to get to the Clubhouse, but still she regretted the outburst – remembering the reputation she'd had at the commune once before.

Princess Drama.

How she'd loathed that nickname and all it implied – that she was a high-maintenance drama queen who was far too prissy and privileged to be included in Art's gang.

'Toto took you that way because I asked her to,' he said at last.

'What?' she said, her shock doing nothing to cauterise the stab of hurt. 'Why would you ask her to do that?'

'What did Toto tell you when she came to get you?' he asked, instead of answering her question.

'That Josh was up a tree and he was about to fall off and break his neck,' she replied.

He swore softly.

'I can't believe you would tell her to take me miles out of our way when you knew my son was in danger and that I would be worried about his safety,' she said, finally finding her voice. 'I know we're not friends.' She was ranting, but at least it disguised the tremor in her voice. 'But I–'

'It wasn't like that,' he interrupted her. 'I only asked her to take her time so I could have Josh down before you got there. I underestimated Toto's flare for the dramatic though, and I'm sorry about that.'

'But…' The simple apology cut her rant off at the knees.

'If it's any consolation, your son was never in danger,' he said. 'He's a brave kid, who handled himself just fine.'

'A brave *fat* kid you mean,' she said, unable to let go of her resentment completely. And unsettled at the realisation that Art's compliment meant something. Why should she care what he thought of her son?

'I never said he was fat. I said he thinks he's fat.' His head dipped to one side, the patient perusal sending heat into her face. 'There's a difference.'

The husky tone wrong-footed her, because it made the frank assessment sound like a compliment, too. Almost.

'No need to apologise to Toto,' he added. 'Your freak out might teach her to dial down on the drama.'

His gaze skimmed back over her, and her misguided belly dissolved into a warm fuzzy puddle of need. Annoyingly.

Clearly being starved of male attention – because she'd had little enough from Dan in recent years – had the potential to make her delusional.

Then her belly added insult to insanity by rumbling loudly enough to be heard in Dorset.

Art's lips kicked up on one side. The tiny suggestion of a smile on his hard, taciturn face made her lungs seize – which only served to remind her she had several bruised ribs.

She hauled in a painful breath as he left the room and captured a lungful of his scent – soap, sweat and motor oil. The warm fuzzy delusion in the pit of her empty stomach returned.

She dragged herself out of the bed and headed to the door Art had come out of, to find a newly painted en suite bathroom, complete with light blue enamelled tiling and a pile of brand-new extra-fluffy towels.

Staring at her smudged face in the mirror above the sink, she splashed cold water on her cheeks.

Step away from the edge, Princess Drama. One almost compliment and an overdue apology does not make Art Dalton less of a dick.

Hearing the click of the bedroom door, she switched off the tap and returned to the bedroom with a towel in her hands.

'Ellie, should you be out of bed?' Her mother placed a dinner tray laden with food, a pitcher of lemonade and a small vase with a bunch of wild flowers on the dresser.

Ellie's stomach growled again, the sight of the wild flowers making her want to weep.

What are you doing, Mum? We missed the chance for our big mother–daughter moment nineteen years ago?

'I'm fine,' she said.

Dee simply smiled. 'OK, but you should eat.' She took the plate of food off the tray. The delicious aroma of roasted garlic had Ellie's stomach protesting even more. 'And then get some rest.'

Ellie dumped the towel on the bed. 'That looks delicious, but I need to go check on Josh first.' And make sure Art's daughter wasn't busy encouraging her son into any other near-death experiences.

'Josh is fine.' Dee placed cutlery beside Ellie's plate and a folded napkin. 'He's downstairs having supper — fielding lots of questions from Toto about his favourite TV shows. I can make sure he gets showered and into bed, if you want? I've done up the room next to mine for him,' she continued, pouring a glass of the lemonade.

The tentative request made Ellie feel like a toad. 'OK. I'm sure he's loving all the attention.' Even if she wasn't.

'That's all settled then.' Her mother smiled at the modest concession as if Ellie had just announced Rod Stewart was coming by to serenade her. 'Now sit down and eat. Have a shower if you want.'

'Thanks, Mum.' Ellie took a gulp of lemonade to ease the new blockage in her throat.

'Josh said he's finished school for the summer, does that mean you can stay?'

Ellie still wasn't convinced that was a great idea, but thinking of all the effort Dee had put into redecorating their bedrooms, she couldn't quite bring herself to say no, outright.

'I haven't booked the return flights yet, so why don't we see how it goes.' She was in no hurry to return to New York, but having an exit strategy made sense.

'That sounds like a plan,' Dee said, seeming happy with the concession. 'Leave the tray outside when you're finished and I'll pick it up later. I have to run our stall at the Artisan Market in Salisbury tomorrow, so if I'm not here when you wake up just help yourself to breakfast. Maddy and Jacob will be about if you need anything. And Art, obviously.'

Obviously.

'But what about everyone else, don't they live on the commune too?' Ellie said.

'They live in their own homes, which are dotted around the seventy acres we have here. Strictly speaking, we stopped being a commune a long time ago. We became a co-housing project about five years back.'

'What's the difference?' Ellie asked. Was this the first rebranding project she'd ever encountered that actually meant something had changed for the better?

'Each family or individual leases a plot of land from us to build their home on. But instead of paying for the leases they help out on the farm – and we all share the surplus. Rob runs the dairy herd, Mike manages the produce side of things and Art contributes his skills, too.'

What skills would those be? How to look hot in overalls?

'Who's "we"?' *Forget about Art and his overalls.*

'Pam left the farm to me in her will,' Dee said. 'But I gave a half-share to Art, when he agreed to manage things. I'm not good with paperwork.'

And Art was? Hadn't Laura always boasted her son was too cool for school?

And now Art owned half the farm. This probably wasn't good. Especially if... 'Does Art have his own place too?' she asked, hopefully.

'No, his room is two doors down.'

Fantastic! The one person she least wanted to be bumping into in the dead of night lived down the hall.

'He works full time on the farm,' Dee continued. 'And so do Mike and Rob, but everyone else has a day job, mostly in Gratesbury, or further afield. Annie and Tess, Rob and Mike's wives, were both in Gratesbury today, which is why you didn't meet them earlier.'

So there was no one staying in the farmhouse to run inter-ference between her and Art except Dee and the children and the canoodling couple she'd met earlier. *Super fantastic.*

'But isn't the whole purpose of the exercise to escape the real world?' Ellie said.

'Not any more.' Dee looked pensive. 'Nowadays we run it like a proper business. The original plan was to have everyone who lived here working here, but it was never viable, so we had to compromise.' Her mother headed to the door. 'By the way, Josh asked if he could come to Salisbury with me and Toto tomorrow to help on the stall if he wakes up in time. Would that be OK?'

'Yes, of course,' she said, then had a thought. 'Could I come and help out on the stall too?' It would be a way of paying her mother back for all her hard work in getting the rooms ready.

'You don't need to do that,' Dee said. 'You're a guest here.'

'I know, but I'd like to.' Having her mother pamper her to within an inch of her life already felt awkward. And keeping busy was also a great way of avoiding the stuff she didn't want to

think about, like Dan and the divorce and her failed business...
Not to mention Art Dalton and his unsettling effect on her.

'Then, I'd love to have you there,' her mother said. 'If you're sure?'

Ellie nodded. 'Absolutely sure.'

After her mother had left the room, Ellie sat at the dresser to tuck into the plate of roasted vegetables and feta and aubergine lasagne. The salty cheese melted on her tongue.

Despite her face-plant in the woods, and the awkwardness with her mother, and Art, the nightmare she'd been fretting about on the journey here hadn't completely materialised. Because Willow Tree Organic Farm and Co-Operative Housing Project was the polar opposite of the Rainbow Commune – give or take the odd death-trap treehouse.

She tore off a chunk of the home-made seedy bread roll beside her plate, and slathered on a layer of what looked like home-churned butter. She took a large bite and chewed, savouring the creamy taste, while trying not to savour the memory of Art's tattooed biceps rounding out the sleeve of his oil-stained overalls and that enticing shadow of chest hair.

So what if Art had unsettled her. And she'd made a bit of a tit of herself by collapsing in the woods.

It was just an inevitable by-product of all the stress she'd been bingeing on for weeks.

Once she'd had a couple of days to get her bearings, and establish a comfortable distance with her mother, she'd be totally immune to Art again, and his half-arsed compliments and his sexy scent.

Whatever happened, Princess Drama would not be popping out to take another bow.

CHAPTER FIVE

The following morning, Dee drifted towards consciousness, her body floating in that tempting half-space between sleep and waking when she couldn't feel all the aches and niggling pains of being a woman approaching sixty. She held on tight to her dream state, feeling Pammy's arms around her midriff, snuggled up against her back, the way they'd woken every morning for years in the big tester bed Art had made for them. She clung on to Pammy's scent, the seductive combination of lemon verbena and tea tree oil. But then consciousness crowded in on her, and the small dresser beside the bed came into focus.

Pammy's keys, her purse and the hairbands she took out just before going to bed each evening were still gone, replaced by the novel Dee had been reading the night before to take her mind off all the thoughts that kept circling in her brain about Ellie's return.

The scent of lemon verbena disappeared, overwhelmed by the scent of the lavender laundry detergent she'd used on the sheets the day before. And the echo of Pammy's off-key whistle – as she showered and got ready to head down to the office and start filing and ordering and doing all those mysterious tasks that Dee had never bothered to know about – faded into silence.

Pammy, I need you here, so much.

Grief hit Dee like a punch to the stomach as she let the miserable memories in: the endless, tedious waits in uncomfortable hospital chairs; Pammy's once vibrant red hair falling out in clumps as she brushed it one morning; and those miserable final days of standing over her partner's bed in Magnolia Ward and willing the woman she no longer recognised to die, so she could be without pain.

Dee rolled over, the clutching pain accompanied by the dull ache in the middle of her back caused by a day spent cooking to welcome Ellie home.

Except this wasn't Ellie's home, and whatever Dee had been hoping for – that Ellie's decision to come visit meant she was eager to try to build a new relationship – seemed even further out of reach now than it had been four years ago when Pam had found an email address for Ellie's event-planning business and suggested contacting her in America.

Ellie and she didn't know each other. And four years of Christmas cards and polite emails and handmade gifts, and a fevered attempt to bribe her way into her daughter's affections with fresh paint and newly made gingham curtains wasn't going to change that. Or absolve Dee of her selfishness that summer, when she'd chosen her lover over her daughter.

She couldn't regret that choice, because she had loved Pam so much. But ever since she'd lost Pam, she'd imagined winning Ellie back. And now she could see exactly how selfish that was too. Especially now she suspected the reasons Ellie had come to visit had nothing to do with her.

Why had her daughter been so exhausted when she'd arrived? She looked as if she hadn't slept properly in weeks. And why hadn't she mentioned her husband, Josh's father? Why hadn't he come with them?

Oh, Pammy, what if we were wrong about this? What if Ellie's never ready to forgive me? What if I'm not even ready to forgive myself?

Dee breathed, waiting for the sting behind her eyelids to subside, before pulling back the bedclothes and padding to the bathroom. After getting dressed, she went to wake Ellie, but her gentle tap received no answer.

Feeling like an intruder, she pushed open the door, and saw her daughter curled in the bed, so sound asleep she reminded Dee of the little girl she'd once known, and had invested so much in.

Dee's heart expanded, with yearning and emptiness, but then she closed the door behind her. She had to make sure she didn't do that again – expect her daughter to fill the gaps in her own life. If Ellie was only here because she was running away from something then Dee could provide a safe haven. No questions asked. After all, Dee knew exactly what it was like to be so desperately unhappy that running away seemed like the only option.

*

Ellie woke up with a start, to discover that she'd overslept. It was nearly noon.

Was her mother still here? Or had she left for Salisbury already? Ellie showered, feeling better rested than she had in weeks. Months even. She'd help herself to breakfast and then head into Salisbury. She had a vague idea where the main square was, hopefully the market would be there.

She could smell the yeasty aroma of freshly baked bread as she headed down the stairs, but jerked to a stop as she entered the farmhouse kitchen.

Heat swept through her system, making her feel like a voyeur, but she could not detach her gaze from the sight in front of her.

Wow, hotness alert.

The young couple she had met the day before were bent over the sink in an embrace that, even though they were both fully clothed, looked pretty close to requiring birth control.

The guy's hands were kneading the girl's backside, while her leg was hooked round his hip and her hands were fisted in his hair as if she were about to launch herself up his torso. Their lips were achieving the sort of suction that would impress a vacuum cleaner convention.

Apparently the country air around here wasn't only good for rest and relaxation. So the activist element may have left the farm, but the free-love element hadn't? What if Josh had walked in on them? Her son would have had a sex-ed lesson almost as graphic as the one she'd had nineteen years ago, when she'd spied on Art by the millpond.

Ellie cleared her throat, loudly.

The girl squealed, and the couple sprung apart as if Ellie had just lobbed a grenade into the room.

'Hi, um, I'm Ellie, Dee's daughter.' She stumbled over the new introductions.

I can't even remember their names and I may well have just prevented them creating their firstborn.

'We met yesterday,' she added.

'This is so embarrassing.' The girl palmed her face. 'I'm Maddy. This is Jacob.' She jogged her thumb towards her boyfriend, who was looking more sheepish than embarrassed.

'And contrary to appearances we're not into exhibitionism. We thought you'd left with your mum.'

'Yeah, sorry about that.' The guy finally spoke, the dimple forming in his cheek suggesting he wasn't that sorry. 'Maddy's insatiable, she can't keep her hands off me.'

Maddy elbowed him in the ribs. 'Shut up, Jay. You're only making it worse.' The girl rolled her eyes. 'I'm really sorry. Jay thinks he's being funny.'

'Hey?' Jacob said, placing his hands on her hips to draw her back against him. 'Who kissed who first?'

'Stop it.' Maddy slapped his hands away. 'You douche canoe.'

'Douche... What? Now?'

Ellie covered her mouth, but the laugh popped out anyway – at the silly insult and Jacob's comical reaction. Maddy chuckled too.

'Why is that funny and I'm not?' Jacob wanted to know.

'Will you do us a favour?' Maddy said, when they had stopped laughing.

'Sure,' Ellie said, liking the couple, who were actually cute, in a pornographic sort of way, and feeling about a million years old.

When had she become such a prude?

If Josh had interrupted them, he would have been absolutely fine after he'd got over the shock.

And the only reason Josh would have found it shocking was because she doubted he'd ever caught Dan and her kissing. The thought made her feel a bit sad. But at least he had never caught them arguing either, that was the main thing. Somewhere in the last ten years, she'd stopped wanting to kiss Dan, or do much of anything else with him, but they had both made sure to protect their son from the fallout of that loss of love. Unfortunately, they'd done such a good job, Ellie was finding it next to impossible to broach the subject of the divorce with her son.

If Josh would be shocked at finding two healthy young adults kissing, he would be even more shocked by that news, and somehow explaining the situation felt like having to rob him of the last of his childhood. He'd weathered so much in recent years, thanks to the bullies at middle school, and she wanted to be able to give him a summer without stress. If things worked out in Wiltshire, why not keep him away from that truth until they returned to New York? Because she knew for sure Dan, the king of avoidance, wasn't going to raise the subject in the weekly Skype chats they'd arranged.

'Don't mention you caught us to Art,' Maddy said, interrupting Ellie's thoughts. 'I'm sure he already thinks I'm a nymphomaniac.'

'Better than being a douche canoe,' Jacob pointed out.

'Don't worry, I won't say a word to Art.' Not a hard promise to keep seeing as she intended to speak to Art as seldom as possible. 'But I wouldn't worry,' she added. 'Art's not the shockable type.' Or he certainly hadn't been at fifteen. Ellie could still remember all the girls who had hung around the farm that summer trying to get his attention – and the long list of ones who had succeeded.

'You know Art?' Maddy's eyes lit with interest.

'We met when we were teenagers. I spent a summer here in the nineties,' Ellie replied.

'How intriguing,' Maddy said. 'Was he as scary then as he is now?'

Ellie coughed out a laugh, enjoying the girl's directness – and her accurate opinion of Art. 'Actually yes.'

'Art's not scary,' Jacob said. 'He's a cool guy.'

'Didn't say he wasn't cool,' Maddy replied. 'But he is

intimidating. He does the whole strong silent moody thing better than Christian Bale's Batman. Even without the aid of a black rubber onesie.'

Ellie laughed again, pleased to discover she wasn't the only one who found Art intimidating – while trying not to imagine him in black rubber.

'Time to haul arse, Miss Nosey Pants.' Jacob took Maddy's hand. 'We're supposed to be helping Rob bring the heifers down from the hill pasture.'

'Nice talking to you, Ellie,' Maddy said as Jacob dragged her towards the door. 'We'll keep our PDAs on the down low from now on. I promise.'

Ellie doubted that when she heard a loud slap followed by Maddy's giggle of protest before the front door slammed.

Locating a jar of granola in the pantry, Ellie ladled out a generous helping of the toasted nuts and seeds then topped it off with some yoghurt and a selection of the freshly picked berries she found in punnets in the fridge.

Five minutes later, she was rinsing her bowl in the sink, when the crash of the door slamming open made her jump.

Batman himself charged into the kitchen holding his hand aloft, blood dripping down his forearm and splattering Dee's sand-blasted stone.

'Move,' he said as he nudged her aside at the sink.

'What happened to your hand?' Ellie asked, as he thrust his hand under the tap.

'I was sharpening one of the rotary blades and I nicked myself.'

Cold water gushed out, and ran red into the sink.

'That's more than a nick.' Ellie leant over his shoulder – the deep ten-centimetre gash bisected his palm and sliced under his thumb. So much for Art's useful skills, the guy couldn't even sharpen a rotary blade without sawing off a hand.

He shot Ellie a caustic look over his shoulder, then shifted to block her view. 'Get me a tea towel. It'll be fine once it's wrapped up.'

'You're going to need more than a tea towel,' she said, as she checked the drawers, finally finding a pile of clean towels and fishing out a fistful. She lifted one from the top of the pile – ominously decorated with pictures of Druid worship at Stonehenge – and handed it to him, the metallic smell of fresh blood making her head swim.

Art wound the towel round his hand, tying the makeshift bandage off with his teeth. The blood started to seep through the fabric.

'You are not serious?' Ellie stepped into his path as he went to leave. 'You need to get that stitched to stop the bleeding.'

'It's fine,' he said through gritted teeth, the mutinous scowl reminding her of Josh when he'd been a fractious toddler. Josh, though, had never been this stubborn, or this stupid.

'Plus it could get infected,' she added. 'And then you'll lose it.'

'Get a grip, Princess Drama.' The old insult might have had more impact if she couldn't see the greasy pallor beneath his scowl.

'No I won't, Captain Dickhead,' she replied.

What was the guy trying to prove? That he could saw off his hand and keep on going? This was beyond ridiculous.

'I'm not kidding,' she continued. 'You need to go to A and E.'

His face paled even more.

Whipping another tea towel off the pile, she took his hand and bound it more tightly in a vain attempt to stem the blood flow. His breath gushed out against her forehead. She tied two more towels together to create a makeshift sling.

'Keep it elevated,' she said, as she knotted the towels at his nape. 'Until we get to Gratesbury.'

If she remembered correctly, there was a minor injuries unit there. Hopefully it was still there or they'd have to carry on to Salisbury, which was at least an hour away.

'I'm not going to a hospital,' he said.

'Yes, you are, because I refuse to let you bleed out all over my mum's kitchen.' Taking his elbow, she led him towards the door. 'Getting the stains out of these flagstones would be a total bitch.'

He shrugged out of her hold. 'If I've got to go, I'll drive myself.'

'With one hand? I don't think so.' She grabbed his elbow again and tugged him towards the door, her temper riding roughshod over the ego slap.

So Art would rather lose a hand then spend twenty minutes in a confined space with her.

'Wait there.' She left him standing in the hallway, as she took the stairs two at a time to get her car keys. 'And stop being a douche canoe.'

'What the hell's a douche canoe?' he shouted after her.

'A guy with way too much testosterone and not nearly enough common sense,' she shouted back, taking a wild guess.

CHAPTER SIX

'For Christ's sake, slow down. I'm not going to bleed to death in the next ten seconds.'

Ellie slanted a look at her passenger. He clung on to the handle above the car door, sweat glistening on his forehead, the blood having soaked through the towels she'd wrapped round his other hand in scarlet blotches.

'I don't care if you bleed to death,' she replied, trying to remain calm – he was a big guy, hopefully he had a few pints to spare. 'What I do care about is you bleeding all over my rental car.' She eased her foot off the accelerator to take the next hairpin bend in the A30. 'I've got to drop it off in Salisbury in a couple of days and I don't want to pay a fine, or have to spend hours cleaning it.'

'If you were worried about your stupid hire car why did you insist on driving me to A and E?'

'Because I stupidly care if you lose your stupid hand.'

'I'm not going to lose my hand.'

'Not on my watch you won't.' She braked at the roundabout on the outskirts of Gratesbury and heard him curse. She wrestled the unfamiliar stick shift into first gear. 'Did you seriously think you were going to carry on playing dodgeball with a rotary blade with half a hand?'

She jammed her foot on the accelerator when she spotted a gap ahead of an articulated lorry.

'Jesus!' He slapped his uninjured hand down on the dash. 'Who taught you to drive?'

'Stop changing the subject.' She took the second exit signposted Gratesbury.

She had checked on her mobile before they set off that the minor injuries unit was still there and open at weekends in the market town. Art's breath caught as she zipped past a tractor with at least an inch to spare on the road that took them past the town's church and secondary school.

'What subject would you rather talk about?' he said drily. 'How much longer we have to live with you at the wheel?'

They headed up the town's main street, which was furnished with a collection of charity shops, pound shops and chintzy tourist-friendly tearooms. The narrow pavements that headed up a steep hill were mostly deserted. Apparently Sunday opening hours still hadn't made it to Gratesbury.

'Now who's being Princess Drama?' she said, taking the side street at the top of the hill past the Somerfield supermarket.

They drove past a collection of old detached stone houses, their high garden walls lovingly decorated with trailing lobelia.

She'd once moaned incessantly about the lack of any fashion options for women under sixty in Gratesbury or the chances of getting a soy vanilla Frappuccino because they didn't even have a Seattle Coffee Company café, which were all the rage in London, when her mother had brought her here during that summer. But in retrospect, weekend trips to the town had been a quaint and pleasant way to spend the afternoon – and the Women's Institute market had done a phenomenal lemon drizzle cake.

The road narrowed ahead and seemed to be coming to a dead end. 'Where is this place?' she asked, wondering why she hadn't spotted the sign.

Art stilled beside her. A brief glance confirmed his face had gone deathly white. Sweat dripped down his temple to furrow through the stubble on his jaw. It was a sunny day, and pleasantly warm, but not that warm.

She wondered how many more pints he could afford to lose, because the metallic smell had begun to permeate the whole car.

'No idea,' he said. 'I've never been to it before.'

He closed his eyes and pressed his head into the headrest, the tight grimace signalling how much pain he must be in.

She almost felt bad about the Princess Drama crack. The man was nothing if not stoic.

She slowed the car, and finally spotted a blue sign emblazoned with the NHS insignia. 'At last, found it.'

He shifted beside her as she drove into an almost empty car park. The one-story utilitarian building had a glass front and an ambulance bay with a paramedics van parked in it.

'I hope it's actually open,' she said.

Still no comment.

'Do you want to wait here while I investigate?' she asked, concerned he might be about to pass out for real.

'Sure.'

The bloody towel covering his injured hand had started to seep onto his T-shirt.

She got out of the car and sprinted across the lot, propelled by panic.

Art Dalton might be a pain in the arse, but she really would prefer it if he didn't die in her rental car. Not only would that be a difficult one to explain to the car hire company, but she had a sneaking feeling her mum would be devastated.

*

'Art, wake up, it's open and the receptionist says the doctor can see you straight away.'

'I wasn't asleep.' Art dragged his eyes open, because some bugger had attached ten-ton weighs to his lids. Ellie's intent green gaze roamed over his face.

He must really look like shit for her to actually be anxious about him, although maybe her anxiety was more to do with the threat to her upholstery than the threat to his health.

He certainly felt like shit. His hand was throbbing as if someone had tried to hack it off with a chainsaw – not completely untrue. But worse was the sick sensation in his belly, and the anxiety that had his chest in a death grip as he stared at the plate glass panel twenty feet away.

He hated hospitals. Really hated them.

He'd been trying to convince himself all the way here, this wasn't strictly speaking a hospital, more like a glorified GP's surgery. And it looked deserted. He wouldn't walk in and be accosted with the sound of hurrying feet slapping against linoleum, the smell of blood and urine and bleach, or the beep of monitors, phones ringing, hushed conversations or shouted demands, or worse, the groans and mumbles of other people's pain – everything that had haunted him in nightmares for years.

Even so, he'd rather risk losing his hand than have to walk through those sliding glass doors in the next few minutes…

Worst of all was the knowledge that if he hadn't been thinking about Ellie, while he was supposed to be concentrating on sharpening the blade to start the cut-out on his latest commission, he wouldn't have got into this fix in the first place.

'Haul arse, Art, let's get this over with.' Ellie sounded exasperated and anxious.

'Give me a moment,' he said.

He needed to hide the fact he was not only terrified of going inside that building, but also terrified of losing it in front of her.

'What for? Do you want to wait until you need a blood transfusion or something?' The high note of panic gave lie to the snark.

And spurred him into action.

'Fine, let's do this thing.' He tried to sound sure.

He gave his head a quick shake, to clear the fog enveloping him, and grabbed a hold of the car door while ignoring the rabbiting heartbeat punching his ribs. And the nausea sitting like a roaring lion under his sternum.

Do not puke.

He placed his feet on the tarmac, levered himself out of the car and staggered, his balance shot.

Ellie caught him round the waist. 'Don't you dare fall on top of me, Dalton.' Banding a supporting arm around his back, she propped his good arm over her shoulder. 'If you go, I'm going to go with you, because you're too much of a big lummox for me to catch. And I'm telling you now, I will be severely pissed off if that happens.' The snippy motormouth monologue was weirdly comforting.

'I'm OK.' He tried to take some of his weight off her, even though his equilibrium was iffy at best, the scent of her – summer flowers and sultry spice – as disturbing as the prospect of flattening her in an NHS car park.

'Shut up, and lean on me,' she said, holding him upright.

He gave up objecting – he didn't have the strength to walk and argue at the same time.

The shaking hit his knees as the glass doors slid open, the electric hiss bringing with it the sucker punch of memory.

'Don't make a fuss, Arty. Everything will be OK. As long as you don't tell, baby.'

His mummy's voice whispered in his ear while the scary man with a white mask over his face kept prodding at his tummy, making the screaming agony a thousand times worse.

'Art, you're not really going to pass out are you? I can go and get a wheelchair?' Ellie's frantic questions beckoned him back to the present.

He breathed, ignoring the lion now roaring in his ears. And realised he'd yet to cross the threshold.

'I'm fine, Princess Drama.' But he didn't feel fine, he felt terrible. She didn't comment, so he knew he must look terrible too.

He forced his feet to carry him through the door and back into purgatory, grateful for the feel of her flush against his side, her fingers digging into his hip. He clung on to her, reminding himself every step of the way that the throbbing pain was coming from his hand now and not his stomach. And wasn't anywhere near as diabolical as it had been when he was a boy.

'Ouch, nasty.' The female doctor snapped on a pair of surgical gloves then unwrapped the layers of blood-soaked tea towels and dropped them in a surgical waste disposal unit. 'How did you do this, Mr Dalton?'

'Rotary blade slipped,' Art supplied, in his usual talkative fashion from his perch on the gurney. The room was sunny and smelled of orange blossoms, not bleach or blood like most hospitals. Ellie was surprised Art hadn't kicked up a fuss when she'd followed him into the treatment room. But then, from the pasty face, she wasn't sure he would notice if she started tap-dancing naked in front of him.

'At least it's a reasonably clean incision.' The physician, who was called Susan Grant according to the nametag pinned to her white coat, wiped away the sluggish seep of blood with a succession of antiseptic wipes. 'And you don't appear to have severed any tendons. But it's deep, so it's going to need quite a few stitches.'

Ellie cringed as the woman, who had a pleasantly upbeat and efficient manner, began to probe at the cut.

If Art could feel it, he wasn't letting on, his eyelids sinking to half-mast, as if he were struggling to remain awake.

He looked dreadful, but not as dreadful as he'd looked when they'd been entering the building. The electrical hum of the doors had triggered and, for a split second, he'd looked completely terrified, the whites of his eyes showing. She'd said something to him, worried he was about to keel over and take her down with him, and she'd had the strangest feeling she'd called him back from somewhere far away.

What was that about?

Because Art definitely wasn't the swooning type, even after managing to hack off half a hand. Something else had been going on, something other than his injury, because he looked as if he'd rather do anything in that moment than take a single step into the medical centre.

'When was your last tetanus shot?' the doctor asked.

Art shook his head, his eyelids drooping.

The doctor turned to Ellie. 'Do you know if he's had any recent boosters? I think he may be a bit shocky.'

'No, I'm afraid not.' This would probably be a good time to say she was just the taxi service. But after the episode as they entered the centre, she wasn't going anywhere.

'All right.' The doctor turned back to Art. 'I think we'll err on the side of caution and give you one just in case. I'm going to call the nurse so she can help me stitch you up.' She applied a dressing to the wound as she spoke, the thick wadding absorbing the worst of the blood, which seemed to have finally stopped flowing so copiously. 'In the meantime, Ms… ?'

'Preston,' Ellie said, then realised she'd given her maiden name.

'Ms Preston. Could you help him get his T-shirt off.' She lifted a gown off a neat stack in the corner of the room. 'And get him into one of these.'

Ellie took the gown, before the doctor disappeared out of the door.

She stared at the neat blue and red geometric pattern on the starched cotton then back at Art. She was going to have to undress him?

Suck it up. You've seen a lot more of him than just his chest.

So what if the memory of seeing his chest hair peeking out of his overalls had made her react like a nun yesterday evening.

'Art?' She nudged his shoulder. His lids snapped open, but his eyes were blank for a moment, as if he wasn't sure where he was.

'We've got to get your T-shirt off.' She held the gown aloft. 'And put this on.'

'I can do it,' he said, or rather croaked, still channelling he who shall never need any help.

He yanked up the hem of his T-shirt with his good hand. Then swore as the wad of cotton got stuck. With his sore hand dangling in space, his face covered by the blood-soaked shirt and some phenomenal abdominal muscles trembling with the effort he was making to try to yank the garment the rest of the way off, he looked stuck fast.

'Ready for some help yet?' Ellie quipped.

The reply was an annoyed grunt.

'I'm going to take that as a yes.' After dumping the gown on the bed, Ellie circled his wrist with gentle fingers, and eased his injured hand through the armhole, ignoring the sight of the dark hair fanning out across the defined slabs of his pectoral muscles.

There was not an ounce of extra belly fat on the man, the black elastic of his boxer briefs peeking over the low-slung waistband of his jeans. The black hair around his nipples tapered into a thin line to bisect the ridges of his six-pack.

The hot flush struck somewhere around her backbone and raced up her spine as she dragged the T-shirt over his head.

He groaned, cradling his hand as he positioned it in his lap. She spotted the ridged white scar that had shocked her all those summers ago. She'd only seen it from a distance then.

She could see it more clearly now, illuminated by the treatment room's harsh fluorescent light. It still looked nasty, but for the first time she noticed the tiny white dots that travelled up either side of the line trailing out of his groin all the way to the bottom of his ribcage.

When had the injury happened? Was this where his fear of hospitals came from? Because it looked like he had once had at least fifty stitches in a wound that must surely have been life-threatening.

She dragged her gaze away not wanting to get caught staring, but Art seemed unconcerned, or uninterested, busy trying to unfold the gown and put it on with one hand.

'Here, let me.' She took the gown and held it for him to thread his arms through. For once he didn't protest, or insist he could do it himself.

She edged it up over his shoulders, standing on tiptoe – because even hunched over, his shoulders were impressive. Clearly spending hours on end rotary-blading things and doing whatever else was needed to keep a seventy-acre farm going was better for the male physique than pumping iron in a gym.

'What?'

Her gaze snapped to his. And she realised she'd been caught staring.

What a shame those impressive shoulders came with his not-nearly-as impressive personality.

'Nothing.' She sat on the moulded plastic chair in the corner of the room, grateful his distracting chest was now covered in the blue and red geometric cotton of the gown. 'How are you feeling?'

'Like shit.' He adjusted his hand on his lap. 'I'm guessing I look pretty terrific in this outfit too?'

'Not at all, the red triangles blend with the bloodstains beautifully.'

He gave a gruff cough, which might almost have been mistaken for a laugh.

A small amount of colour had returned to his face. Whatever had spooked him seemed to be passing. While he could hardly be described as comfortable, he didn't look as if he wanted to bolt for the door.

'You don't have to hang around,' he said. 'I can make my own way back when I'm done.'

'Uh-huh, were you planning to jog back to the farm then?'

He coughed again, coming even closer to a laugh. 'Did anyone ever tell you, your bedside manner is rubbish?'

'Good thing I never considered becoming a nurse then, isn't it?' she said and was rewarded with an actual honest to goodness chuckle this time, albeit rough enough to sound as if someone had been sandpapering his larynx.

'You're not wrong.'

The door opened and Dr Grant walked into the room, followed by an older woman dressed in bright blue nurse's scrubs and wheeling a metal trolley laden with what Ellie assumed must be the supplies needed to stitch Art's hand.

'OK, Mr Dalton, Tina is going to give you a tetanus shot and something to numb your hand and then I'll get to work,' Dr Grant said.

Art straightened on the bed, making the gown slip off one shoulder.

Apparently, the entertainment portion of the afternoon was now officially over. Sympathy whispered through Ellie. However annoying he was, and however many times he'd been stitched up before, this was liable to be unpleasant. And from the tension on his face, he knew exactly how unpleasant.

Watching Art get tortured wouldn't have bothered her nineteen years ago after the way things had ended between them. But as the doctor and her assistant injected him, cleaned and irrigated the nasty gash and finally proceeded to stitch him – while Art remained stoic and silent and uncomplaining throughout the whole ordeal – Ellie had to admit that seeing him in pain now actually did bother her, a little bit.

*

'You are not driving. Are you bonkers?' Ellie marched ahead of Art across the car park and ignored his beyond stupid suggestion.

'Why not? I'm fine now. And I'm a safer driver than you are.'

'You're not fine.' She clicked the locks with the key fob and flung open the door. Settling in the driver's seat, she waited for Art to climb in on the other side. The mulish expression on his face didn't bother her as much as the white bandage on his hand which covered thirty-two stitches. She knew this because she had counted every single one.

As he wrestled with the seat belt with his right hand, she remembered that he was left handed. She turned on the ignition and left him to struggle with the seat belt on his own.

'I can drive one-handed,' he said. 'And even one-handed, I've got a better chance of getting us back alive than you have.'

'Hardly. You've been shot full of enough painkillers to fell an ox, plus driving will only open up the wound.' She crunched the gears, shifted into reverse, and wheeled into a three-point turn. Art gripped the dash like an old woman. She ignored the not-so-subtle hint. 'And even though that would totally serve you right,' she added, 'the good Dr Grant's just wasted twenty minutes stitching you up.' Twenty minutes that had felt like twenty years. 'And I'm not going to let you undo all her hard work just because you're an idiot.'

A dark brow hitched up his forehead. 'Since when did you become my keeper?'

'Don't worry, I'll be resigning the position as soon as is humanly possible.' With that in mind she accelerated down the country lane that led to the town's main street. 'And anyway, this is my car, so you don't get a say.'

He didn't reply, finally having conceded defeat. Feeling magnanimous in victory, she eased her foot off the accelerator as they headed over the speed bumps on the outskirts of town, and took her time getting onto the roundabout, waiting for a space big enough not to require the need to play chicken with any articulated lorries.

They'd been driving along the A30 for a good ten minutes, before he finally spoke again. 'Thanks for helping me out. The cut was worse than I thought.'

The admission sounded weary and grudging.

'Just a tad,' she said, unable to resist a smile at his frown.

They drove on, the road passing the newbuilds on the outskirts of Gratesbury to wind through a landscape of fields banked by high hedges.

His eyelids kept drifting to half-mast and then popping open again. She remembered Josh doing the same thing as a toddler, when he was exhausted but didn't want to go to bed. The thought made her think of Art as a boy, and the terror on his face when they'd walk into the unit.

'Why didn't you tell me you have a phobia of hospitals?'

His eyelids jerked open. He stared at her, the slow blink making her aware of exactly how long his lashes were.

He had the most amazing eyes, the tawny hazelnut brown embedded with flecks of gold. The bloodshot quality added to the glittery sheen of the low-grade temperature the good Dr Grant had told her to keep an eye on – because, at some point during today's drama, she *had* become Art's keeper.

'I haven't got a phobia. I just don't like them much,' he said, but his gaze flicked away as he said it and she knew he was lying.

How about that? She could still tell if Art Dalton was or was not speaking the truth. The way she had all those years ago.

It was a heady feeling, like discovering a superpower she thought she'd lost.

She drove down the track that led to the farm, recalling their exchange in the treatment room before Dr Grant had returned to give Art his thirty-two stitches.

OK, maybe she wasn't totally immune to Art's non-charms. But there would be no more flirting, with or without abs. Handling the fallout from one disastrous relationship was more than enough incentive to keep her libido on lockdown for the next decade, let alone the rest of the summer.

CHAPTER SEVEN

Driving into the farmyard, with Art dozing in the passenger seat, Ellie spotted a woman busy loading a muddy four-by-four while a young girl danced around beside her.

Art jerked awake as Ellie braked. As he hauled himself out of the car, the woman rushed towards them, the little girl bouncing behind her.

'Art, what the hell happened to your hand?' The woman's eyebrows drew together. Tall and slim, with her long mahogany-coloured hair tied back in a ponytail, she looked elegant even in an ensemble of faded jeans, a baggy T-shirt and wellington boots.

'Just had a disagreement with the rotary blade.' Art lifted his bandaged hand as if to prove it was still attached. 'It's sorted.'

'Give or take thirty-two stitches,' Ellie added.

Art shot her his stop-being-a-drama-queen look.

'Thirty-two stitches! In one hand?' The woman crossed her arms over her chest, her concern escalating. 'That sounds like some disagreement.'

'Mummy, has Art lost his fingers?' The girl clung to her mother's leg, her eyes widening with a combination of fear and fascination. A puff of wild red hair surrounded a face covered in freckles, making her look like Little Orphan Annie after she'd been electrocuted.

'No, sweetie, they're still there,' the woman murmured patting the child's head. 'Just about,' she added under her breath.

Art crouched down and wiggled his fingers inside the bandage. 'See, Melody, it's all good.' Straightening, he swept a sharp look over Ellie and Melody's mother. 'Stop scaring the children, ladies.' He lifted the bag of medication out of Ellie's hand. 'I've got work to do.' He rubbed the girl's hair. 'Bye, Melly,' he said, then headed across the yard and disappeared behind the farmhouse.

What work did he think he was going to be doing on a farm with an injured hand? Ellie wondered, but stopped herself from shouting after him. Time to relinquish her responsibilities as Art's keeper.

'There goes the most stubborn guy on the planet,' remarked the woman standing beside her.

'You have no idea,' Ellie murmured, the stomach muscles that had been knotted tight ever since Art had raced into the kitchen dripping blood finally starting to relax. 'I had to practically kidnap him to get him to the doctor's.'

'Why does that not surprise me,' the woman said, before unfolding her arms and offering Ellie her hand. 'Hi, Tess Peveney, I'm Mike's wife. You're Dee's daughter?'

Ellie nodded, returning the firm handshake.

Mike had to be the red-headed guy she'd met the day before. Melody had obviously inherited her father's mercurial hair.

'Ellie Preston,' she introduced herself, her maiden name coming out more naturally this time. 'It's nice to meet you.'

'You too. Sorry I missed the welcoming party yesterday. I was busy suffering the tortures of hell in Gratesbury. Otherwise known as helping out at a birthday party for sixteen four-year-old girls.' She tucked her hands into the back pockets of her jeans and shuddered. 'If I hear "Let It Go" or see another pink balloon, Barbie cupcake or sparkly deely bopper again in this lifetime I may have to be sectioned.'

Ellie laughed. 'That sounds almost as traumatic as having to drag a bleeding man to Gratesbury's minor injury unit.'

Tess grinned. 'Nope, it's much worse. I think I may actually have post-traumatic *Frozen* disorder.'

'I like *Frozen*, Mummy,' Melody piped up, hopping from one leg to the other. 'Anna and Elsa are the best.'

'I know how much you love *Frozen*, baby.' Tess rolled her eyes for Ellie's benefit, before addressing her daughter. 'Run into the farmhouse and have a pee before we head for Salisbury.'

'Do I have to?' Melody begged, wiggling furiously.

Swinging her daughter around, Tess gave her a pat on the bottom. 'Yes, because you need to…' Taking a deep breath she launched into the *Frozen* anthem… '*Let it go…Let it go.*'

Her daughter ran off, struggling to complete the song's chorus around her delighted giggles.

'Are you going anywhere near the market in Salisbury?' Ellie asked, once they had both stopped laughing. 'I was supposed to be helping out my mum today on the stall.'

'Actually, that's exactly where we're headed. Melly and I just finished baking the stall's supply of strawberry shortbread and sourdough loaves. Or rather I baked and Melly ate as many straw-berries as she could cram into her mouth.' She swung round to indicate the trays she'd been loading into the car when Ellie and Art had arrived. 'Why don't you tag along?'

'That would be terrific,' Ellie said, pleased to get the chance to escape her unnecessary concerns about Art. Spending the rest of the afternoon in the company of women seemed like the perfect antidote to the morning's drama.

*

Situated in the historic centre of Salisbury, the city's main square had served the population since medieval times as a thriving community market. Presided over on one side by the majestic Georgian columns of the Guildhall, which now housed the city council, and hemmed by the patchwork of shopfronts ranging in style from half-timbered Tudor to redbrick Victorian, eight hundred years of the city's history was here. As Ellie muscled her way from the car park behind the square through the crowds of shoppers buying everything from home-made soap to burritos, it was clear the Artisan Market was still a thriving place of commerce in the present day.

Indian spices blended with the scent of freshly roasted coffee and patchouli oil. The standard-issue green gazebos vied for space with gleaming metal food trucks and striped awnings, while the jubilant Caribbean riff of a steel band floated over the shouts of the traders and the general hubbub of people enjoying a sunny June afternoon getting lots of retail therapy. A pair of elderly ladies in floral prints inspected a stall laden with hand-sewn cushions next to a gang of teenagers with tattoos and nose rings clustered around another stall peddling multicoloured cupcakes.

'How long has this market been in operation?' Ellie shouted to Tess as they made their way through the labyrinth, laden down with a tray each of the strawberry shortbread Tess had baked. The few times she'd been to Salisbury in her teens all Ellie could remember was a market full of jumble sale knock-offs that she'd looked down her nose at as a London teenager with vast fashion sophistication.

Tess glanced back, Melody clinging to the hem of her T-shirt so as not to get lost in the crowd. 'The Artisan Market? Quite a while. It's a brilliant venue for us. It attracts a great foodie crowd. But, unfortunately, it's only on one Sunday a month. Dee also runs a stall at the farmers' market here every Wednesday and the general markets, on Tuesdays and Saturdays, when she's not manning stalls at other farmers' markets around the county.'

'That must require a huge amount of work, doing all that baking?' Ellie said, readjusting the tray. Her arms were already aching and they had two trays of bread still to transport.

'We don't just sell baked goods,' Tess said. 'Dee does amazing jams and preserves too. And Annie is a whizz with pastry – she's on a mission to single-handedly reintroduce the wonder of quiche to the south-west of England – and Annie's husband Rob makes some very nice elderflower fizz when he has the time,' Tess replied. 'But yeah, time is a problem because most of us are stuck doing day jobs. So Dee is the one who has to bear the brunt of the work.' Tess shouldered her tray and sidestepped a queue of people lining up to buy themselves a dosa wrap from a Bombay street food stall. 'Most of the speciality markets don't run after Christmas,' Tess continued. 'So there is some chance to stock up and catch up on our sleep. But as most of our merchandise is freshly prepared, not much. And, to be honest, the time spent travelling to venues and setting up, and then clearing out, is also pretty prohibitive.'

Ellie spotted her mother's stall ahead of them. The queue was even longer than at the dosa wrap one, with her mother in the centre of it all busy chatting with one of her customers while Josh and Toto packed their order into folding cake boxes.

Seeing them approaching, Dee raised a hand to greet them both.

Tess ducked round the crowd. She stacked her own tray and lifted Ellie's out of tired arms, then began adding the cakes to the dwindling supplies on display.

'Mom, me and Toto have been working all morning.' Josh tugged Ellie's arm to get her attention. 'And Granny Dee says she's going to pay us.' He did a jaw-breaking yawn as Dee looped an arm around his shoulders.

'He's been terrific,' Dee said. 'A natural salesman just like Toto.'

Josh grinned up at his grandmother, basking in her praise, and Ellie felt the burst of warmth in her chest. However many mistakes she'd made in the last few months, however much she'd let Josh down, the hare-brained decision to bring him to Wiltshire might turn out better than expected in some regards.

However stilted her own relationship with Dee, Josh seemed more relaxed than she'd seen him in months.

Not so Toto though. The wave of regret was swift and fairly painful for Ellie as the girl's gaze darted away from her.

Art had told her not to apologise to Toto, but then he was, and had always been, a hard arse. Having watched Josh struggle for over a year to find acceptance with any of the judgemental little body fascists at the expensive private school he attended in Orchard Harbor, Ellie knew she owed Art's daughter an apology.

But that would have to wait, until after she'd given Dee news of the morning's events at A and E. She drew Dee to one side while Josh and Toto helped Tess deal with the queue of customers.

'Mum, I need to tell you something,' she said.

'I hope you don't mind that I didn't wake you,' Dee said. 'But you looked so peaceful, I didn't want to disturb you.'

'I don't mind.' Ellie smiled, strangely touched. When was the last time anyone had put her needs first? 'Actually, as it turns out, it was a fortuitous thing I was at the farm, because Art had an accident and I had to take him to Gratesbury to get his hand stitched up.'

The colour leached out of Dee's face. 'Is he OK?'

'Yes, as long as he doesn't try playing dodgeball with a rotary blade again.'

Ellie gave her mother's hands a reassuring squeeze when her colour failed to return. 'He's woozy from all the medication and not too happy with me. And I'm afraid your kitchen looks like the set of a slasher movie, but otherwise he's fine.'

'He let you take him to the hospital?' Dee asked.

So Dee knew about Art's hospital phobia? Ellie wondered if her mother knew where it came from. And anything about that gruesome scar on his stomach?

'I insisted,' she said.

Dee squeezed Ellie's hands back then let them go. 'I'm sure that's an understatement.' She gave a breathless laugh. 'But thank you. And thank goodness you were there.' She tucked her hair behind her ear in a nervous gesture.

Ellie wanted to question her mother further about Art's phobia, when Toto's panicked voice interrupted them.

'Is my dad OK?' The cake box in her hands had been scrunched into a ball. 'Is he going to die?'

'No, of course he isn't.' Dee captured the girl's slender shoulders and folded her into a hard hug. 'He cut his hand, but Ellie looked after him and it's all fixed now.' Dee sent Ellie a look of gratitude over Toto's head.

Toto nodded mutely while concentrating on the mangled cardboard in her hands: 'Thank you for looking out for my dad,' she mumbled. 'I'm sorry I made you mad yesterday.'

'You don't need to be sorry,' Ellie said. 'I was tired and cranky yesterday. I hope *you* can forgive *me*?'

'OK,' the girl whispered, but the wary expression remained. 'Can I go home and make sure Dad's alive? Please?'

'Yes, of course,' Dee said, but Ellie could see the concern cross her mother's face. There were still two trays of bread to unload from the car, plus there were several hours to go yet before the market closed and the queue was only getting longer.

Ellie touched her mother's arm. 'Mum, you go ahead and take Toto and Josh back to the farmhouse.' From the way Josh was yawning, she suspected the jet lag was about to slam into him. 'I can assist Tess on the stall.'

It took quite a lot of effort to persuade Dee, but Ellie eventually managed to corral her mother and all three of the children to the car park – Melody having decided that hanging out with Josh and Toto would be much more fun than manning a market stall for the rest of the afternoon. After seeing them off, two questions nagged at her as she began the trek back to the stall with a tray of sourdough loaves.

Where had Art's hospital phobia come from?

And where was Toto's mother?

CHAPTER EIGHT

Two days later, Ellie sat in the kitchen and chewed at a ragged thumbnail after a morning spent picking strawberries with Josh for Dee's latest batch of shortbread.

Nicole at Nails R Us on the corner of Main and Fifth in Orchard Harbor would have a fit if she could see the state of Ellie's manicure.

'Why don't I show you how to use the bread maker this afternoon?' her mother said, as she slid a plate of fennel and endive salad in front of her with a bowl of freshly baked bread rolls. 'We've got a batch to make for tomorrow's market in Swindon and it's a lot less hard on the hands.'

Ellie breathed in the yeasty aroma and picked up her fork. 'I'd certainly be quite happy never to see another strawberry again in this lifetime.'

But, as she tucked into her lunch, she recalled the hushed conversations and hidden looks directed at her during her visits to Nicole, as she pretended she didn't know her husband had flirted with most of the women there and probably slept with a few of them too. Chipped polish and fruit stains suddenly seemed a small price to pay not to have to do the walk of shame each week at the local beauty parlour.

And running herself ragged with Tess on Sunday afternoon on the farm's market stall had been an even better distraction than picking strawberries until her manicure died. Chatting to customers, wrapping what felt like a million cakes and loaves in paper until her fingers ached, and ringing the mounting sales up on the stall's antique till had been so much more exhilarating than all the small talk she'd had to endure with her fair-weather friends in Orchard Harbor.

As she and Tess had packed up the empty trays, swept the debris, folded away the farm's tables and gazebo and loaded everything into Tess's car, the sense of achievement and camaraderie had been immense – so much more rewarding than attempting to ingratiate herself with women who she suspected had viewed her with pity or contempt.

'Rob's wife Annie does a mean manicure.' Dee put a plate in front of Josh and took his DS out of his hands to replace it with a fork. 'You, Tess, Maddy and Annie should arrange a girls' night in soon so you can get your nails fixed.'

'I'd love that,' Ellie said as she split open a roll and slathered it with butter. She'd met Annie yesterday, and had warmed to her instantly. A petite woman with the will of a Trojan and a broad Northern accent, Annie Jackson had been busy corralling her twin toddlers, Jamie and Freddie, while she dropped off some of her husband's home-made elderflower fizz for the weekend's stall. Of course, the two of them had been forced to sample some of it with a slice of Dee's banana nut bread. By the time they'd moved on to coffee, they'd discussed everything from the current state of US politics to the pee hazards involved when changing the nappies of baby boys. Ellie had conceded that Josh's aim was nowhere near as hazardous as Annie's two boys.

'I'll suggest it to Annie, then, so you guys can all get together soon,' said her mother.

'Won't you be joining us?' Ellie asked, surprised that the thought didn't feel as uncomfortable as it probably would have three days ago, when she'd arrived.

Her mother picked up her fork. 'I'm afraid manicures are totally wasted on me.' The wistful tone told Ellie that there was more to the refusal, but she didn't push. Maybe her mother was just being diplomatic, and wanted to let Ellie get to know the other co-op women on her own terms.

As Ellie finished her lunch, she watched Josh plough through his salad. While he'd never been a fussy eater, he wasn't a particularly adventurous one either, but the last three days of exercise and fresh air had turned that around. As soon as Toto got home from school, the two of them headed off on another adventure and stayed out until supper.

In an attempt not to freak out when he returned each evening either covered in mud or with some unexplained raw spot on his elbow or chin, Ellie had kept busy, helping her mother with the cooking and KP duties. Dee had given her endless assurances that Toto knew how to stay safe on the farm, but even so Ellie had set some ground rules – such as no climbing on the combine harvester, or playing handsy with Art's rotary blade.

And here was her reward. Not only had Josh spent very little time on his DS in the last few days, she suspected he'd never eaten so many fresh vegetables in his life. He was a little boy. A boisterous little boy, who had been overcautious for too long.

His nutritionist back home would be ecstatic.

'When will Toto be back from school?' Josh asked, around a mouthful of bread roll.

'Not till four,' Ellie replied. She'd learnt the bus schedule off by heart, because Josh asked the same question every lunchtime.

'But that's hours away and I'm bored,' he said. 'Toto says she's got weeks and weeks of school left and I won't have anything to do all day when she's gone.'

'You liked helping with the strawberries, didn't you?' Ellie asked. Why hadn't she considered how bored Josh was likely to be with Toto at school most of the day?

'But we've finished that,' Josh said. 'And it's not as good as building a hideout with Toto.'

'Maybe you could go and hang out with Melody until Toto gets back?' Ellie said. Her mother looked after Tess's daughter each morning while Tess was at work in Gratesbury, and Ellie knew Josh had helped to entertain her the day before.

'Melody's OK, but she's only four,' Josh said, exasperated. 'And she's a girl. All she wants to do is play with her doll. And sing dumb songs, really loud.'

Ellie didn't think it would help to point out Toto was a girl too.

'I tell you what, Josh,' Dee cut in. 'Why don't I ring up the head teacher at Toto's school this afternoon? Maybe you could go for a visit tomorrow? Would you like that?'

Josh chewed his lip – a sure sign of the nervousness and trepidation that had dogged his time in Charles Hamilton Middle School. Ellie was about to intervene, and explain to her mother that school was a problematic environment for Josh, when her son surprised her.

'I could go to Toto's school with her?' He actually sounded curious.

'I can't promise anything,' Dee said. 'But if you'd like to go in with Toto for the day tomorrow, and try it out, I could certainly ask her head teacher. Marjorie's a friend of mine and a lovely lady and I'm sure if I explained everything there might be a way to make it work. They have exchange visits with children from France all the time. I don't see why this should be any different.'

'Yes!' Josh punched the air and bounced out of his seat. 'Just wait till I tell Toto. I'm going to go get my stuff ready.' He shot out of the room and Ellie heard him racing up the stairs.

'Do you really think the head teacher will go for the idea?' she asked her mother. 'I don't want to get his hopes up.' Especially as she'd never seen Josh this enthusiastic about the thought of attending school.

'Toto's school is a new school, so they have places to fill at the moment. And Marjorie is the local organiser for the Women's Institute – if there's a way to make it happen, she'll find it.'

'I'm sure she will but what if...'

'We'll find something else for Josh to do,' her mother interrupted gently. 'There's a million and one chores round here. Maybe he could help Art out in the workshop?'

'And risk getting his hand chopped off? I don't think so.'

Plus, she couldn't see Art going for that idea. Art had taken his trademark sullenness to a whole new level in the last few days, skulking at the opposite end of the table during supper time as he picked at his food with his uninjured hand, his beard growth starting to make him look like a particularly disreputable pirate. Only last night, he'd chastised Toto for giggling too much at one of Jacob's jokes. Toto had taken the harsh comment in her stride, obviously used to her father's moods, but Josh had looked terrified. Her son tended to get anxious around men at the best of times, probably because he'd spent so much of his childhood trying and failing to attract Dan's attention.

And Art, with his no-frills parenting, was a great deal more intimidating than Dan.

'It may surprise you to know that Art is actually great with kids,' Dee said. 'And he's never usually clumsy. I still can't imagine how he cut himself so badly.'

Ellie was reserving judgement on Art's way with children. Toto and Melody might adore him, and Josh was clearly in awe of him, plus she could remember how he'd managed to hypnotise the other children at the commune when they'd been teenagers together, but that did not mean she was going to expose a child as sensitive as Josh to Art's moods.

And she didn't trust Dee's opinion on Art, because it was fairly obvious she was a founder member of the Art Dalton Appreciation Society.

Ellie carried their used dishes to the sink and rinsed them off. 'Here's hoping the school visit pans out, so we never have to consider the nuclear option.'

'I'll go ring Marjorie now and see what she says,' her mother announced as she placed the rest of the dishes in the sink. 'Could you do me a favour while I'm handling that?'

'Sure,' Ellie said, placing a rinsed plate on the draining board.

'Would you take some salad and bread into Art in the study?' Dee opened a drawer and rummaged around. 'And check up on him while you're at it. I'm worried that hand may have got infected, he's been so grumpy the last couple of days.'

Ellie dried her hands. 'Isn't that his natural state?'

What exactly did her mother mean by 'check up on him'? She'd already done her shift as Art's keeper.

'I'm worried about him.' Dee pulled a thin pencil-sized leather case from the drawer then held it towards Ellie.

'What's that?' Ellie stared at the case as if it contained an unexploded nuclear warhead.

Please don't let this be what I think it is.

'A thermometer,' Dee replied, shattering Ellie's hopes. 'All you need to do is take his temperature. It won't take you a minute and it will put my mind at rest.'

Yeah, but it's liable to make my mind explode.

'I'm not sure I'm comfortable taking his temperature.' *Like, at all.*

'Why not?'

'Because I hardly know the guy.' *And what I do know is only going to make this situation more supremely uncomfortable.*

'Don't be silly.' Dee lifted Ellie's hand and slapped the thermometer into her palm. 'Just get him to hold it under his tongue for two minutes. He's more likely to do it for you than me.'

'Why on earth would you think that?' Ellie asked. Was her mother delusional?

'Because he let you drive him to the hospital,' Dee said, as if that made any sense at all. 'And he hates hospitals.'

So saying, Dee rushed off, leaving Ellie holding the nuclear warhead.

Shoving the thermometer into her back pocket, she trooped down the hallway towards the office at the back of the house and rapped on the door.

'Go away. I'm busy.'

Apparently, Mr Grumpy had gone from cranky to super cranky since yesterday evening.

With the nuclear warhead branding her bottom through her jeans, Ellie opened the door, certain that no superpower on earth was liable to stop this situation blowing up in her face.

She braced herself as she stepped into the cramped room. Art sat crouched over some papers, his hair swept back in untidy rows as if he'd spent the day running agitated fingers through it. An ancient desktop computer hummed in the corner like a demented bumble bee. The once white bandage was now an unhealthy shade of grey where his hand rested on the table.

'Hi.'

He swung round, looking surprised for a moment. And then pissed off.

Quelle surprise.

'What do you want?'

She whipped the thermometer out of her back pocket like Harry Potter preparing to do the Expelliarmus Spell.

If only.

'I've got good news and bad news,' she said. Time to go on the offensive. There was no point being a wimp around Art, because he would stomp all over her. So he was having his temperature taken now even if she had to shove her wand right up his bum.

He eyeballed the thermometer. 'What's the bad news?'

'The bad news is I'm here on a mission from my mother to take your temperature.'

'So, what's the good news?'

'You're going to hate this even more than I do.'

*

I do not believe it!

Art stared at the thermometer – and wanted to punch a wall. Unfortunately, he couldn't, because one hand was throbbing like a rotten tooth and damaging the other one would leave him helpless.

Damn Dee for siccing her daughter on him. And damn Ellie for looking like she was enjoying this. 'I don't have a temperature.'

'Tell that to my mum, she's worried about you.'

'Go back and tell her yourself.'

She stepped into the room and closed the door, making the space feel even more claustrophobic than usual. He could smell her, that fresh spicy scent that had enveloped him while he'd dozed off in the car on the way back from the clinic.

'Unfortunately for both of us –' she propped her bottom on the desk '– that's not going to wash when you haven't eaten a full meal in days.'

'I'm not hungry.' Like he was going to tell her the real reason he wasn't eating. She'd probably crack a rib laughing.

She shook her head. 'Nope, that won't work either. Unless you've suddenly become a closet anorexic. And I'm afraid if you have that's only going to make Dee worry more.'

'She's not my keeper and neither are you.'

'Yes, I believe you said that already.'

'So why aren't you listening?'

She opened the leather case and dropped the glass tube into her palm. 'What exactly is so terrifying about having your temperature taken?'

'I don't have a temperature.' He grabbed her other hand and slapped it onto his forehead, to prove the point.

The feel of her palm, cool and soft, pressed to his skin didn't help with the tugging sensation deep in his abdomen. He dropped her hand.

'Satisfied?' He cleared his throat, because the word had come out on a husky rumble.

Ellie pressed her palm into her jeans, and scrubbed it down her thigh.

'I am. Dee won't be.' She wielded the thermometer like a light-saber. 'Unless I hand her conclusive proof, she'll only harass you herself. So stop being a pain in the arse and stick this under your tongue for two minutes.'

He was debating whether to do it, just to get this over with and her and her subtle sexy scent the hell out of his office, when his stomach growled like a marauding mountain lion that hadn't been properly fed for two days – probably because it hadn't.

Ellie glanced pointedly at his belly. 'Not hungry, huh?'

'Bloody hell.' He grabbed the thermometer – with the wrong hand.

Lightning lanced through his palm and shot up his arm. He swore viciously, jerking his hand back and cradling it against his midriff as the burning pain kicked up several thousand degrees.

'Did that hurt?'

'Of course it hurt, I've got about a hundred stitches in it. Now go away.' He rocked, waiting for the lancing pain to subside, not caring that he was being an arsehole. He hadn't asked her to come in here and harass him. His head felt like someone was trying to hook out his eyeballs with a coat hanger, his stomach was so empty it was practically inside out and now his hand was about to drop off altogether. The only thing that could make his misery any more complete was having Ellie Preston leaning over him with a worried look on her face.

Bingo.

'I've got work to do,' he added, the pain finally dulling to just about manageable.

Work that gave him a headache at the best of times. And which had transported him into a whole new level of purgatory since Sunday.

'Dr Grant gave you some heavy duty painkillers, why aren't you using them?'

Because they made him feel woozy and gave him nightmares. He'd woken up the first night sweating and swearing and thrashing about like a madman in the grip of a dream that had felt far too real. He hadn't taken the painkillers since.

'Bugger off.'

'No.' She pushed away from the desk and lifted his wrist.

He flinched. 'Don't.'

'I'm not going to hurt you. I'm just going to take the bandage off.'

'What for?'

'Because look at it.' She cradled his hand, holding it up. 'It's filthy.'

She had a point. He'd done his best but it had been next to impossible to wash and dress himself one-handed, let alone eat and write and attend to all the other chores he had piling up around him. Keeping the bandage dry and clean, as the doctor had recommended, had been the least of his worries.

'You try keeping a bandage clean in a farmyard,' he said, but the truth was, the fight had drained out of him.

He flinched as she peeled off the surgical tape around his wrist.

'It's OK, I'll be gentle,' she murmured, her blonde hair close to his nose as she bent over his hand and unwound the grubby bandage.

She eased off the gauze and he sucked in a breath.

Big mistake. His lungs filled with the scent of her shampoo.

Spice and musk and summer flowers all overlaid with the scent of her.

He shifted in his seat, disturbed by the liquid tug in his groin.

'Yikes,' she whispered and then raised her head.

He winced as he got a look at the raw, reddened skin. The stitches sat like thin black slugs stapled into the swollen flesh.

'No wonder it hurts.' Her eyes met his, the concern in them disturbing and captivating at one and the same time. 'Stay there, I'm going to ring the clinic.'

'I'm not going back there,' he said, trying to sound demonstrative, even though he knew he might have to. He wasn't such an idiot that he'd risk losing his hand. But anything less than that and he was prepared to fight like hell to stay put. He hadn't had one of those nightmares in years. He did not want them becoming a regular occurrence again.

She nodded slowly, the knowledge in her eyes somehow more disturbing than the argument he'd been expecting. 'Duly noted, but don't panic. It might not be necessary.'

She headed for the door. 'As long as you do exactly what I say.' She smiled, the twist of her lips decidedly smug. 'I hope you realise, you're now entirely at my mercy, Dalton.'

*

'I sneaked all this stuff past Dee and called the clinic from my mobile so she wouldn't hear me on the house phone. Which meant trekking all the way to the far corner of the vegetable garden, because that's the only sodding place I can get a signal.' Ellie dabbed at the angry swelling with the antiseptic wipes, keeping a tight grip on Art's wrist in case he flinched. Although, as usual, he was the picture of stoicism.

Frankly a little less stoicism and a lot more common sense would have gone a long way in the last couple of days. Who the heck was so flipping stoic they let their hand rot off? She tore open another of the wipes she'd filched from Dee's first aid supplies.

'Why did you have to sneak them past her?' he asked, as if he honestly didn't know.

She dabbed at the stitches again, making sure they were clean, before ripping open the packet of sterile gauze with her teeth.

'If she'd seen me carting this lot in here, she would have been fussing over you for the next decade.'

Holding the gauze in place, she began wrapping his hand with the bandage.

Once she was satisfied it was suitably covered, she tore the ends and tied it.

She placed his hand back on the desk. 'So you totally owe me one.'

He nodded. And his lips twitched. The almost smile had her heart knocking against her ribs.

She'd genuinely panicked he was going to have to get his hand amputated when she'd seen what he'd managed to do to the wound. Thank God, the clinic nurse had been a lot less worried once Ellie had finally got her on the line.

The instructions had been simple. Check his temperature. Clean and re-dress the hand. Dose him up with painkillers. Get him to his GP's for a course of antibiotics. Tell him to stop being an idiot.

His temperature had been in the normal range. He'd refused the heavy duty painkillers but agreed to take Nurofen and paracetamol, she'd changed the bandage, and made an appointment for him at the GP in Gratesbury for this afternoon, so the first four directives had already been covered. All that remained now was to impress upon him what an idiot he was being. And re-check the wound every day, reapplying new dressings if necessary, the stitches could come out in a week's time and as long as he didn't get it infected again all should be well.

'What did the clinic say?' he asked.

'The nurse basically said if you don't have a temperature, it's probably just a localised infection. But you need to keep an eye on it and get a course of antibiotics.' She began packing the contraband supplies back into the box. 'Which means you can go to the GP's this afternoon and *I'm* keeping an eye on it from now on, because you're obviously incapable of doing that.' She scooped up the empty wipe packets and dumped them into the bin under his desk.

The crisis had been averted. Art wasn't going to lose his hand just yet. And Dee hadn't discovered what a twerp he was.

'So why don't you tell me now exactly why you haven't been eating your food?' Ellie asked, still irritated by his cavalier attitude. 'And don't give me any bullshit, because I can still rat you out to Dee.'

He watched her, his eyes narrowing, but he didn't look away when he said: 'I'm left-handed.'

'So what?'

'So I can't eat with my right hand, it goes all over the place.'

'Let me get this straight, you've been starving yourself because you're worried about making a mess? Are you kidding me?'

He looked at his injured hand, cradled in his lap, the tips of his ears turning an interesting shade of red.

'Why didn't you ask for help, Art?' she asked, not quite ready to give him a break. He might be a man, but that did not mean he got to be a total moron. 'I could have cut up your food for you, or Dee, or even Toto.'

He tapped the fingers of his good hand on the desk. 'No one's cutting up my food.'

'It's better than starving to death.'

He shrugged, the stubborn expression suggesting she hadn't won that argument. 'It's not that bad, I managed to find some finger food from the pantry after Dee had gone to bed to keep me going.'

So he'd been raiding the pantry in the middle of the night, simply to avoid having to ask Dee to give him food he could eat with his fingers?

'Very clever,' she said. 'Except Dee now thinks you're about to die of malnutrition.'

'She doesn't have to worry. I've been looking after myself for years.'

'Of course she has to worry, she loves you.'

He frowned. Apparently this was news to him.

'And whether or not you can look after yourself is debatable, frankly.'

'It feels good now.' He lifted his bandaged hand off the table and cradled it back in his lap.

'That's only because the Nurofen is kicking in.' She took the rest of the packet out of the first aid box and placed it on top of the paperwork he'd been doing when she walked in. Whatever he'd been writing, it looked a mess. The spidery scrawl barely legible. 'Make sure you keep dosed up on them until the antibiotics kick in. You're sure you don't want to take the other stuff the doctor gave you tonight? It should help you sleep.'

He glanced away. 'Yeah, maybe, if it's still sore I'll take some tonight.'

Hmm, no he wouldn't. She wondered if he had a phobia of painkillers as well as hospitals.

Luckily, getting to the bottom of Art Dalton's bizarre behaviour was not her concern.

'And talk to Mum about the food situation. Or I will.'

He considered the request. The pulse in her neck throbbed as she waited for a response.

It suddenly seemed vitally important she make him understand he needed to keep her mum informed. Or she'd worry. Which was fairly ironic.

What right did she have to insist he be a better surrogate son to Dee, when she'd been an absentee daughter for nineteen years?

'I'll talk to her,' he said at last.

'Good.' She wiped her hands on her jeans, nervous and not sure why.

She closed the first aid box, tucked it under her arm. 'I should get these back to the pantry.'

Art caught her wrist in his good hand. 'Listen, thanks, Ellie.'

She looked down, the feel of the rough calluses against delicate skin triggering a memory she didn't want.

He let her go.

Had he remembered it too? Because that would be mortifying.

'I owe you one,' he said.

'Too right you do,' she replied. 'But there's no need to thank me, because I plan to collect, when you're least expecting it.'

A smile touched the corner of his mouth. 'Why am I getting the feeling I'm going to live to regret this?'

'Probably because you are.'

CHAPTER NINE

'I don't need you to do the paperwork,' Art asserted. 'I've got a system.'

Ellie cast a critical eye over the mess on Art's desk, more than ready to call in yesterday's debt.

From the pile of order forms and invoices, the files stacked up in dusty towers on the windowsill, and the Excel spreadsheet open on the computer that hadn't been updated since yesterday, it was obvious the man didn't have the first clue what he was doing. Plus, there was his injured hand to consider. He couldn't even hold a pen properly.

No wonder this job gave him a headache. It was giving her a headache just watching him struggle with it, hunched over his desk with all the enthusiasm of Bob Cratchit on Christmas morning.

She had hinted heavily during last night's supper, but, true to form, Art hadn't asked for her help. So she'd been forced to demand he take it.

And lo and behold, as soon as she had, she'd smacked straight into Art's I-Don't-Ask-For-Help-Because-I-Have-Testicles bol-locks.

She fixed Art with her best Testicles-Be-Damned look. 'What system is that exactly?'

She'd tried to bring it up subtly, because she knew male egos could be delicate things. But Art's ego was clearly too stubborn to appreciate subtlety.

'*My*. System.'

'All right, and I don't suppose the fact you can't even hold a pen is going to interfere with your system?' She whisked the sheet of paper he'd been slaving over when she'd walked in off the desk. 'What exactly is this supposed to say?' But, as she scanned the scrawl, she realised the atrocious handwriting wasn't the only problem. 'You can't even spell.'

The minute the words were out of her mouth, she regretted them. Art had once boasted about how he didn't do school, and his ego had always seemed more than robust enough.

But when he grabbed the sheet back from her, she knew she'd embarrassed him. And she suspected it had nothing to do with his ego or his testicles, and everything to do with the fact he had some sort of learning difficulty. Because no matter how little schooling you'd had, no one forgot how to spell 'the'.

'Thanks for the observation,' he said. 'Now piss off.'

'I'm sorry.'

'I don't need your apology. I need you to piss off.' He sounded mad now rather than embarrassed, which had to be a default position to salvage his pride.

'Why are you in charge of the paperwork if you're dyslexic?'

The look he sent her was one of deep suspicion. She supposed she deserved that. 'I took it on because Dee asked me to do it when Pam died.'

So Dee had asked Art and Art had said yes, even though it was probably the very last job he would want to take on, because he had been here and Ellie hadn't.

'Does Dee know you have a learning difficulty?' she asked, but of course she must know. Perhaps Dee didn't realise how severe it was.

'Stop making it sound like it's a big deal. I'm managing OK. I know how to use spell check. I get Toto to read and double-check anything important. Being dyslexic doesn't make me an imbecile.'

The flat tone made Ellie wonder how many times he'd had to defend his intelligence before. Probably hundreds. No wonder he'd never been a big fan of school.

'But surely you could use *some* help? At least until your hand is healed?'

'Why are you so keen to help me out with this shit?' The suspicion was back.

'Because it's not shit to me. I love doing admin. Balancing budgets, organising schedules, managing overheads are my passion. While other women can have orgasms over a new pair of Jimmy Choos, I can have an orgasm over a balanced IRS return, or a fully itemised Excel spreadsheet.'

'Jimmy who?'

'Only the greatest shoe designer in the world ever,' she said, waving away the ignorant comment. 'I want to be useful while I'm here. And, as much as I've enjoyed doing kitchen chores with my mum and picking a billion strawberries, that's not the best use of my skill set.'

'Maybe you could feed the chickens?'

'I don't think so. One of the hens nearly pecked Josh to death yesterday. And animals tend to like him. They don't tend to like me.'

'Then I've got the perfect job, you could help Jacob set the rat traps in the back barn.'

'No way!' she shrieked, her skin crawling at the thought of being anywhere within a twenty-mile radius of a rat. She was about to tell him that when she noticed the sly tilt of his lips. 'You sadist, you enjoyed that.'

He chuckled. 'Maybe a bit.'

'Now you've had your little joke, I should remind you that you owe me one.'

'I wondered when you were going to bring that up,' he said, but he was still smiling. Not just a sadist. But a smug one to boot. The bastard.

'Don't even make jokes about rats, it's not funny.'

'It is if you could have seen your face.'

'Haha,' she said, with a distinct lack of amusement. 'I'm calling in the debt. You have an admin ninja in your midst and I'm going to force you to use her, unless you want to be a welcher.'

He laughed, the sound doing strange things to the muscles in her abdomen. He really was sinfully handsome. For a smug sadistic bastard. The pirate scruff on his face caused by his inability to shave only added to his rugged, bit-of-rough appeal.

'All right, knock yourself out.' He dumped the sheet of paper onto one of the many piles on his desk. 'But only if you promise not to screw with my system.'

'Absolutely not.'

She so *was* screwing with his screwy system. She could already feel the adrenaline charging through her veins at the thought of getting her hands on the stacks of files and turning the Manhattan skyline effect he had going on into something ordered and efficient and – oh, the joy of it – properly alphabetised. That delving into the farm's accounts would also allow her to satisfy her curiosity about the project's financial situation was just an added benefit.

'And my debt to you is paid in full as of now,' he added.

'Understood.'

And not a problem, seeing how big he was going to owe her, once she'd finished ordering and alphabetising his rubbish system to within an inch of its life.

CHAPTER TEN

The following Monday, Ellie was elbow deep in a pile of order forms dating back to when Madonna was still a virgin when Dee popped her head round the study door.

'Tess and Annie are here to pick up their kids. We're just about to have some tea and...' Dee paused in mid-sentence to step into the room. 'My goodness, you've certainly made a few changes in here.'

Ellie stood and dusted off her jeans, surveying the damage she'd done to Art's so-called system. She'd seen very little of him over the weekend. But whatever he'd been doing, at least his hand seemed to be healing because she noticed this morning at breakfast he'd managed to shave off the hipster beard.

'I know it looks like a hatchet job,' she said, 'but most of this paperwork can be binned. You only need tax records dating back six years and–'

'That's wonderful,' Dee interrupted with an absent smile, obviously not that interested in the tax regulations. 'It looks like you've definitely earned a break. And Tess has already got the kettle on.'

'A tea break sounds like a great idea,' Ellie said.

The nerves dancing in her stomach began to do the polka.

How could she swap small talk over tea and cake and not mention what she had discovered in the last three days about the farm's financial situation?

Almost as soon as she'd begun delving into the accounts, it had become clear the business needed to make some substantial changes if it was going to survive much longer. But exactly how aware was Art of the financial cliff they were teetering on the edge of, and how much had he told Dee?

She did not want to step into the middle of an emotional minefield. She and her mum hadn't discussed the past. Their relationship, such as it was, was still fragile and at times awkward. The last thing Ellie wanted to do was challenge Dee's loyalty to Art or her faith in this place. Especially as she knew she would lose. Just like she had nineteen years ago, when her mother had decided to stay here with Pam and Art, instead of returning to London with her.

Ellie was well over that betrayal now. She'd made her own life and her own spectacular mistakes, and if her marriage to Dan had taught her one thing it had been to be emotionally self-sufficient.

But was she really ready to test that theory? And have her mum reject her again? And, perhaps more importantly, did she really want to challenge Art's authority over the accounts? Because that's what she'd be doing. If her relationship with her mother was fragile, her relationship with Art was even more problematic. That something about him still tugged at her, still made her want to delve behind his stoic, taciturn shield and find out what kind of man lay beneath, was not something she wanted – or needed – to encourage. Because she had a distinct feeling the man behind the shield was as much of a hard arse as the one in front of it.

But how could she keep the farm's financial problems a secret?

And if she told her mother how precarious things were, wasn't it her duty to make constructive suggestions to help her sort it out?

To add to her confusion, she'd found something in Pam's old files that had intrigued her. And got her thinking of a possible solution. But it was a long shot, which might fail, even if Dee and Annie and Tess were interested in hearing about it.

Not surprisingly, the nerves in her stomach were dancing a jig by the time she followed her mother into the kitchen. Tess and Annie were busy setting the table, with her mother's legendary lemon drizzle cake getting pride of place. Annie's twins were corralled in the playpen Dee kept in the kitchen and Melody was hard at work colouring in a picture of her favourite Disney princess, Anna from *Frozen*.

Seeing the children made Ellie think of Josh, which did nothing to calm her jittery stomach.

His taster day at Gratesbury Secondary had been a roaring success on Friday and the head teacher had called that evening to suggest he attend classes for the rest of the term as an exchange student. Josh had been enthusiastic and so Ellie had been forced to bottle her concerns when she'd sent him off on the bus that morning wearing his brand-new Gratesbury Secondary sweatshirt.

Thoughts of Josh reminded her of the conversation they'd had last night when she'd explained in great depth why they mustn't forget they were only visitors here. Maybe she should be taking her own advice?

Quite apart from her rocky relationship with Art, did she really have the right to suggest something that could be risky and would require a great deal of work when her own business hadn't exactly been a roaring success and she was only here for the summer?

'We've come to rescue you from the horror of the farm's

accounts.' Tess pulled out a chair for Ellie and patted the seat. 'Now sit down and take a load off. What do you need? Coffee? Tea? Gin? Whisky? Crystal meth?'

'Coffee would be fab, if it's not too much trouble,' Ellie said. The nerves tap danced along her oesophagus as Annie concentrated on chopping off a slab of lemon drizzle. And Tess began ladling coffee into the cafetière.

Was it her imagination, or was no one making eye contact with her?

'I'll have one too, Tess,' Dee remarked as she sat down beside Ellie.

'Your mum says you've been hard at work on the accounts all weekend.' Annie nudged the loaded plate across the table. 'So either you're a masochist or it's even worse than we thought.'

The bold statement delivered in Annie's no-nonsense accent and the concern on all three of their faces made two things clear.

The coffee and cake invitation hadn't been as spontaneous as it appeared. And the farm's dodgy financial situation was not going to be news to any of them.

This was an intervention pure and simple.

The good news was it was an intervention that was long overdue and that Ellie could wholeheartedly support, except…

She took a generous bite of lemon drizzle and let the rich, tart taste melt in her mouth, the nerves starting to jitterbug in her stomach as if they were in the final round of *Dancing with the Stars*.

Whatever her past issues with Dee, the opinion of all three of these women, their friendship and respect, had come to mean something to her, and she didn't want to muck that up.

She sipped the coffee Tess placed in front of her, and swallowed the cake. Surely there was no harm in at least telling them the whole truth about the farm's finances?

'From what I've seen so far, your financial situation isn't good,' she said. 'Certainly not if you want to keep the business viable for the foreseeable future. Or even the next twelve months, frankly.'

Tess sighed, Annie swore and Dee looked devastated. And it was that crestfallen look that had all Ellie's caution jumping up and darting right out the window into the bright summer day.

Sod it, Dee was her mum. And she'd welcomed her and Josh here when they'd needed a place to stay. This suggestion didn't have to have anything to do with Art. She was over-complicating things.

'But I found something that might provide a solution,' she heard herself saying. Pam's idea was a good one, she'd laid the ground-work for something that could save this place. And however inappropriate it might be for Ellie to be making this suggestion, it was entirely up to them what they did with it. 'Or at the very least is worth considering.'

Dee's head came up. 'What is it?'

'We're all ears,' Tess chipped in.

Here goes nothing.

Ellie watched their faces, and took an unsteady breath, her stomach having jitterbugged right into her throat. 'How do you feel about opening a farm shop and café on the premises?'

PART TWO: RELIGHT MY FIRE

THEN

Eloise Charlotte Preston's Diary: Anyone who reads this will die a horrible death in total agony (worse than Jack's in *Titanic*. MUCH worse).

1 July 1998

Two absolutely shocking things happened today and I don't even know which is the most shocking.

FIRST BIG SHOCK OF THE DAY: I saw my mum and Pam kissing in the kitchen. Not a friendly peck but real snogging. Like Pam was trying to explore my mum's tonsils. I mean, yuk! Who wants to see their mum kissing anyone? I wouldn't even want to see her kissing Dad. What if my mum is in love with Pam? Is she really going to divorce Dad? She wasn't just saying that! We may never go back to London. We've been here three weeks now and I've lost all hope. I'm going to have to write my dad and ask him to come get me.

I'll have to do it tomorrow, though, because seeing Mum kissing Pam wasn't the only shock of the day and after this shock I totally forgot to write to my dad.

SECOND BIG SHOCK OF THE DAY: I saw Art TOTALLY NAKED. I was hiding out in the old mill house after seeing Mum and Pam, when I spied him swimming in the millpond all by himself. I wanted to call out to him – it was hot and I wanted to go swimming too – but I didn't call out in the end because I knew he'd just be nasty to me like he always is when I try to talk to him or join in with stuff. Plus, I'd been crying, so he'd probably call me Princess Drama again.

So I kept quiet and watched him swimming instead, and when he came out of the water, he had no swimming trunks on. He didn't even have his underpants!!! And I could see EVERYTHING. His bum (very white compared to the rest of him) and all the places he's got hair and even his you-know-what.

He has a huge scar on his stomach, which actually made me feel a bit sad for him. How the fudge-sicle did he get that? Did someone try to kill him? I know he's super annoying but he's not THAT annoying! I willed him not to put his clothes on because I wanted to go on looking and – guess what – he didn't. He smoked a cigarette first, like that's perfectly normal to do when you're stark naked (as if!) and then he laid down in the grass and started to stroke his whatsit.

No really, he did!

He got all red in the face and started moaning and groaning and he was going for it so much I thought he might chafe himself. I almost laughed at first, because it did look pretty silly, but the laugh got stuck somewhere. And I got hot all over instead.

If Art had caught me watching, he would DEFINITELY have killed me. But that only made it more exciting.

Tomorrow I'm going back to the millpond and see if I can catch him doing it again. It totally took my mind off Mum and Pam – and the thought of having to be here for ever.

Even though Art's not Leonardo DiCaprio (because Leonardo DiCaprio would never be so mean to me), he's still almost as good-looking as him. And, let's face it, I'm never going to get to see Leo naked or jacking off, especially if I get stuck in Wiltshire for the rest of my life.

But here's the really cool thing: this evening when Art called me

Princess Drama, I just thought about that big scar on his tummy and how he has a white bum and how he moans when he's jacking off, and it totally didn't bother me. In fact, I couldn't help smiling. He looked really surprised, and then he shut up.

And, you know what, I don't even care if he calls me Princess Drama again. Because Art just isn't that scary any more.

CHAPTER ELEVEN

I still can't believe they said yes.

Ellie stacked the pages that had finished spewing out of the co-op's ageing printer, then stapled them into batches. She paused, aware her fingers were trembling, the memory of Tess, Annie and Dee's enthusiastic support four days ago for her farm shop and café suggestion still a bit unnerving.

Of course, it had been a qualified yes. A yes that the four of them at the Lemon Drizzle Summit had decided to keep secret from the rest of the co-op, even Annie and Tess's husbands, until Ellie could work out a coherent business plan.

The business plan that she was supposed to be presenting to everyone in approximately two minutes. No wonder her fingers were trembling.

Over the past week, she'd got stuck into her role as the new admin manager while also spending the last four days creating that business plan, which had meant contacting the Council Planning Department, looking at the financial projections in more detail, checking out investment possibilities and doing about a billion and one spreadsheets.

On top of that she had also taken it upon herself to finish

correlating, alphabetising and reorganising all the paperwork, and worked out a system for filing the VAT and tax returns online.

The work had exhausted her, requiring ten-hour work days which had included some important field trips with Tess, a couple of meetings with their gang of four to hash out tonight's presentation, a trip to the local bank to schmooze the manager and hours spent bent over the new laptop she'd bought to replace the ageing computer Art had inherited from Pam. She'd even taken it to bed with her last night so that she would be fully prepared for tonight's meeting.

But now it was show time, and the storm of anxiety in the pit of her stomach from four days ago, when she had first suggested this idea to Dee, Tess and Annie, had become a Force Ten gale.

It shouldn't be this important to her, that she – or rather they – got the vote of confidence they needed to go ahead with the shop. She stuck the printouts under her arm and headed out of the office.

It wasn't that important. She was blowing this out of proportion. She had nothing to prove to her mother, or anyone else. This was just an idea. And it wasn't even her idea, it had been Pam's idea originally. If everyone else decided it was rubbish, it would be absolutely fine. And if they went for it, she could hardly take the credit.

The smell of freshly made coffee wafted around her as she walked down the corridor and through the kitchen door. Everyone sat round the table, chatting amiably, and she was struck anew by how much the place had changed from nineteen years ago. But then she'd changed too. The thought strengthened her resolve, as her mother and Tess and Annie threw her reassuring smiles from the head of the table.

Everyone gave her warm greetings, even the sleepy Melody sitting in her father's lap with her thumb tucked in her mouth.

Everyone accept Art, who stood apart, propping up the sink, his hands wrapped round a mug of her mother's coffee.

She shook off the trickle of apprehension. This wasn't personal. And she needed to stop making it so. But, even so, her gaze lingered on him.

In a V-neck T-shirt that offered a tantalising glimpse of dark springy curls, and faded jeans that moulded to his long legs, his freshly showered hair slicked back from his forehead, he looked clean and probably smelled delicious. The memory of his scent, infused with hints of man musk and motor oil and the industrial cleaner he used to wash it off, spiced the air even though she was too far away to smell it.

Their eyes connected, and awareness skittered over her skin.

She ran her tongue over dry lips, recalling their meeting in the corridor outside her room the previous evening, while he was padding back from the bathroom, a towel hooked round his hips, his legs and feet and chest bare. Moisture had collected on the dark curls to drip through his six-pack. He had grunted a greeting and carried on walking, giving her the opportunity to follow his retreating arse down the corridor. His flexing glutes barely concealed by the towel.

She hadn't slept very well last night.

He blew over the steaming coffee, never losing eye contact, and she felt the phantom gush of breath whisper over the skin of her cleavage.

Her mother bustled past, cutting off her line of vision. Ellie straightened, jerked out of her trance.

Get a clue, Princess Drama.

She had a meeting to chair. An important meeting. And entering into a fugue state over the memory of Art's V was inappropriate. Not to mention distracting.

'Everyone's here.' Her mother handed her a cup of coffee.

Ellie concentrated on adding a dollop of cream. She took a sip and placed the mug on the table, dispelling thoughts of Art and her inappropriate scent fantasies. She handed the stack of printouts to Annie to pass round.

Art glanced at his copy, before stuffing it into his back pocket. Her heart did a somersault.

He's dyslexic. It's a fairly common learning disability. Get over it.

She cleared her throat. 'Hi, everyone, thanks so much for coming tonight to the meeting me and my mum, and Tess and Annie have called.' She launched into the introduction the four of them had prepared. 'Hopefully this won't take too long, but Tess, Annie, Dee and I have been working on something.' She paused. 'An idea, a fairly radical idea, but we think an exciting one, that we wanted to present to you guys.'

'You can keep us as long as you like, if Dee's walnut dream cake is involved,' Rob Jackson, Annie's husband, announced while cutting himself a slice of cake almost as large as the head of his toddler son Freddie who was squirming on his lap. Freddie reached out to sink his fingers into the frosting.

Ellie coughed out a laugh. But it sounded trite and forced.

What was she actually doing here? Her CSUB certificate said she had five years' event-planning experience and knew how to get good flow round the food and beverages area during a non-profit fund-raiser. It did not mean that she could save this business, especially as her own business had already collapsed into a quagmire – not unlike the chemical potties she'd hired for the Orchard Harbor Jazz-ateers' centenary festival last year.

She gripped the sheet of paper, feeling as if she had a spotlight shining on all her misplaced hubris and imperfections.

She took a steadying breath and talked herself out of the pit in her head. That jazz festival had been an event for three hundred people, and she'd managed to find replacement toilets at the last minute so none of the Jazz-ateers had been forced to crap al fresco in the driving rain.

The failure of her business hadn't been her fault. And she had every intention of trying to resurrect it, in some form or another, when she returned to the US and the scandal of her impending divorce and Chelsea Hamilton's baby bump died down. She could do this. She could present a well-intentioned business initiative to the families living on this fledgling housing co-op. Whether they chose to follow through on it would then be out of her hands.

'Do you want to tell everyone Pammy's idea?' Her mother's suggestion cut through the fog of insecurities. Ellie looked up from the sheet grasped in her hands to find eight pairs of eyes focused on her. Everyone except Freddie Jackson, who was bouncing up and down on his dad's lap as if he'd just swallowed a pound of crack cocaine instead of a fistful of coffee frosting.

Only one pair of eyes held her gaze though, searing right through her composure to the washed-up event planner beneath.

'Yes, of course.' She glanced at the first bullet point on her notes. *Ignore Art, he can't intimidate you any more.*

'Basically, we called this meeting because after having looked closely at the project's accounts, I think the co-op needs to think about investigating new avenues for profit growth to create a sustainable future.'

'The project's purpose is to create a sustainable living for every-one here. We're not trying to make ourselves rich.' Art's terse tone sliced right through Ellie's composure.

Her bouncing stomach went into a tailspin.

She'd expected debate and discussion, and possibly some prob-ing questions about what qualified her to make suggestions about the project's future when she wasn't a resident. What she hadn't expected – or been prepared for – was to have the plan dismissed before she'd even presented it.

Suddenly all she could hear was the fake concern in Caroline Myerson's voice as her final client sacked her, because having an event planner in the midst of an acrimonious divorce hadn't been the sort of vibe Caroline had wanted for her thirtieth wedding anniversary celebration.

'I'm not talking about getting rich,' Ellie managed, clinging to her composure before her confidence crumbled completely. 'I'm talking about establishing more of a financial cushion. At the moment you're skirting the edge of financial ruin every time you need to buy a new piece of farm equipment or...'

'That sounds serious,' Jacob said, bouncing the other Jackson twin on his knee. 'Are we about to go bankrupt?'

Art jerked away from the sink, the indolent pose history. 'That's bullshit. We've been in profit for the last two years.'

By a few hundred pounds.

Ellie swallowed down the retort with a gulp of coffee. Her purpose had never been to scare anyone.

Relax, rewind, re-engage.

She repeated the mantra that had seen her through the early days in Orchard Harbor, when she'd been touting for business and getting knocked back at every turn. If she could schmooze the ladies who lunched, she could schmooze the good people of Willow Tree Farm.

'I didn't say you're about to go bankrupt,' Ellie qualified, Art's glare making her agonisingly self-conscious. Why was he being so combative? Even with his literacy issues, he must know the project was one broken boiler or Inland Revenue audit away from serious problems. 'Your finances aren't on a solid enough footing. You need more revenue to increase your available operating capital, not just to insulate yourselves against emergencies but also to make up for the shortfall in your income during the winter months.'

'And Ellie's discovered that Pam had a brilliant idea five years ago, which never got actioned...' Tess sent Dee a consoling smile '...because of her illness, but which might be able to save all our bacons.'

'Brilliant ideas are always welcome here,' her husband Mike chimed in, his enthusiasm in marked contrast to Art's antipathy.

At least someone was willing to listen without prejudice.

Ellie glanced back at her hit sheet, memorising the bullet points until her fingers had stopped trembling and her stomach didn't feel as if it were about to plummet to the stone floor.

'OK,' Ellie began again. 'Before I outline Pam's idea, I want to give you an overview of why it could work.' She kept her voice steady. Sounding confident was as important as being confident. 'Basically, by far your most profitable venture is the products and produce you sell at the community markets in the region. I worked with Tess on the stall the Sunday before last and it was obvious you have a lot of regular customers in Salisbury alone. In contrast, revenue from orders for the dairy products and organic produce straight from the farm are much harder to come by because of the competition from the big supermarkets.'

'That's been a problem since we started the business,' Rob said, with Mike nodding in agreement. 'There aren't enough independent outlets nearby to sell to, our yield is too small to attract the supermarkets and it's against the farm's ethics to transport our goods long distance. When we get a new contract, the feedback's always really good, but we're struggling to find enough stockists at a wholesale price that can sustain our profit margins – which is why we started selling the surplus at the local farmers' markets.'

'All of which is exactly my point and where Pam's idea comes in,' Ellie said, beginning to warm to her cause. 'Five years ago, Pam submitted a planning application for a change of use for the back barn.' Ellie glanced at her mum. 'She didn't tell anyone, because we think she may have wanted it to be a surprise. And then she was diagnosed and well...' She paused, not sure how to continue.

'The thing is, Ellie found the application approval in Pam's files,' Dee kicked in. 'So we could go ahead with Pam's idea now, without having to wade through too much red tape, because Pam has already done all that for us.' The emotion in Dee's voice had Ellie swallowing the block of emotion in her own throat.

How come she had never realised exactly how much her mother had loved Pam that long ago summer?

'A change of use to what?' Rob asked.

'A shop and café,' Ellie said, then paused, remembering to breathe. No one said anything, so she continued, desperate to fill the silence. 'Pam wanted to turn the back barn into a shop and café for Dee. You're in an even stronger position now to launch such a venture after your success locally. Rather than being at the whim of other local stockists or having to transport your surplus to a whole network of community markets around the region – and be at the mercy of their timetables – you could sell everything you produce on the farm, and all the products you make for the markets right here. You've got a great range of stuff, which local people obviously love, and it would effectively cut out the middleman.'

The silence continued for a moment, but then suddenly everyone started talking at once.

'Damn, that is a brilliant idea, why the hell didn't we think of that ourselves?' Mike said.

'There's sure as hell a gap in the market locally,' Rob spoke over him, while trying to fend off Freddie, who was happily combing his dad's hair with sticky fingers.

'And the real brilliance of it,' Annie cut in, 'is that we have all the labour and talent we need right here to make it happen. The four of us have already worked out a possible timetable.' She flung her arm out to indicate Ellie as well as Dee and Tess. 'To renovate the barn and then open by the beginning of August so we can launch during the summer. It's tight and it's going to be hard work, but we think it's doable.'

'Who's going to run the place once it's open?' Rob asked.

Tess grinned. 'That's the best part. The plan would be for me and Annie to jack in our jobs. We could share the childcare, and we were already baking like insane people in our spare time to supply the community market stalls we attend so it wouldn't be that much more work.'

'I'd be happy to help out with childcare or baking chores when I get home from work in the evenings,' Maddy said, the enthusiastic smile she sent Ellie full of gratitude. 'Maybe me and Jay could give up our jobs too, eventually? Our dream was to work on the farm and it might actually become a reality if this works.'

'Anything I bake would probably poison the customers,' Jacob said, his enthusiasm almost as pronounced as Maddy's. 'But I spent some time in foster care as a teenager, so I know how to ride herd on younger kids.' Little Jamie Jackson chortled on his knee in confirmation. 'And I would ace the customer service given my astonishing charm.'

'Yeah right, Mr Lover Man.' Maddy laughed.

'How would we publicise the place?' Mike asked. 'We certainly don't have the funds to advertise?'

'And how are we going to fund the renovation?' Rob said.

Ellie held up her hands to halt the flow of questions. 'If you want to take a look at the business plan I've printed out, it includes suggestions for marketing and PR, as well as some costings for the original set up and running costs.' She'd done her homework on this in the past four days. 'But in answer to your specific questions,' she smiled at Mike and Rob. 'I agree, paid advertising is too expensive and won't necessarily pay off. To start with we need to keep costs as low as possible. But you've already got a great customer base. While we're setting up the shop, I'd suggest giving out flyers at all those markets, to get the word to your customers that they can get your great products any time of the week if they're willing to travel to the shop. From the enthusiasm of people in Salisbury, I don't think that's going to be too big an ask.' She carried on talking as everyone began reading their printouts. All except Art, who she noticed was the only one who hadn't made a comment yet about the idea. 'The truth is, there's no better advertisement for what you do than the products themselves,' she continued. 'That said, there's also tons of stuff we can do especially with social media and I'd be happy to set up a website while I'm here. I designed one for my own business and it's not hard. When it comes to the regulations, I've checked with the council and the planning approval still stands, plus Dee already has all the necessary health and safety documentation for the stuff she sells at farmers' markets, all the other red tape will be to do with the building conversion for the shop itself.'

'Isn't that going to need a lot of work?' Jacob said, lifting his head from studying the business plan. 'It's almost derelict.'

Ellie cleared her throat. She was on shakier ground here, knowing absolutely nothing about construction. But she'd braved a walking tour of the facility with Dee and Tess even under threat of rat sightings, and read through Pam's original specs for the conversion, so she wasn't going to be deterred. 'The back barn is actually a beautiful old Victorian building. The high ceiling and exposed beams will look magnificent once they've been cleaned up. It also shouldn't be too expensive to get the running water and electricity connected from the dairy barn.'

'What about the rat problem?'

At last, he speaks.

The nerves in Ellie's stomach spiked. Art's caustic comment was accompanied by his trademark scowl. Apparently there was one member of the co-op who had not been won over. Yet.

This time she was ready for him, encouraged by the positive response from everyone else. Pasting a helpful smile on her face, she prepared to schmooze the unschmoozable.

'We'll call in an exterminator,' Ellie said. 'Obviously you haven't felt the need to invest in one up till now, because you're only using that barn as a dumping ground for defective equipment. But I had a quick chat with Bill Greenman in Gratesbury who runs the hardware store and does pest control on the side.'

'We know who Bill is,' Art interrupted. 'Because the rest of us actually live here.' The observation struck right at the heart of Ellie's insecurities, and she was sure Art knew it.

'OK, well…' She forced herself to continue in the same upbeat manner, determined not to be put off by his attitude. 'Bill said once we renovate the building and put in a proper floor, we'll probably find the problem has remedied itself. But either way, he'd be happy to come by and check out the situation and will eradicate any remaining vermin in return for a year's supply of Dee's apple and almond polenta cake.'

'You've done a ton of work on this,' Rob said, as he finished leafing through her business plan. 'And I for one am really impressed,' he added, looking pointedly at Art.

'I got a lot of help with it from Tess, Annie and my mum,' Ellie said, feeling oddly teary at the chorus of approval from everyone else in the face of Art's continued silence.

'Bugger that! We did virtually nothing,' Annie said, getting nods of agreement from Tess and Dee. 'This is Ellie's baby and she's done nearly all the work. And we wanted to ask her if she would consider managing the shop, at least until she goes back home?'

Ellie's stomach went into free fall as all the co-op residents except Art chimed in.

'I don't know…' She hadn't even considered it. After all, she was only here for the summer. But, as Tess and Annie and Dee continued to try to persuade her, she sniffed and smiled, and found herself agreeing to the request.

As everyone started clapping and cheering, the wave of approval almost knocked her off her feet. What was making her so overemotional? This really wasn't that significant. She'd had nothing else to do in the last week and she'd enjoyed working on the business plan – having a project like this to sink her teeth into was exactly what she loved doing. The planning, preparation and troubleshooting before and during a job were the things she'd excelled at as an event coordinator. But still, she couldn't deny the feeling of achievement and acceptance that both humbled and excited her as everyone began to talk at once about the project and Tess and Annie both came up to thank her.

Her mum pushed a plate of walnut coffee cake in front of her. 'I think you've earned this,' she said.

'Why don't we take a vote and make the Willow Tree Farm Shop and Café Project official?' Mike Peveney said, placing an arm round his wife's shoulders as Tess sent her a thumbs-up.

Ellie wanted to kiss the man. To kiss all of them.

'All in favour... ?' Annie shouted.

'Where are we going to get the money from?' Art's surly tone sliced through the optimism filling the room like a machete, hacking down the forest of raised hands in its wake.

Ellie stared back at him, trying not to take his negativity personally.

'Your costing says fifty grand,' he continued, when she remained silent. 'I think that's underestimating it. You want to get it up to code, it's going to cost more than that. And you just finished pointing out we don't have fifty grand to spare.'

She stared at her papers, to give herself a chance to calm down and stop her voice betraying her thoughts. 'The plan was for us to all chip in with our labour to do the grunt work, the painting and decorating et cetera, in any free time we have,' she said.

Dee had also been singing Art's praises as a possible project manager, because he supposedly had major skills in carpentry and construction.

So much for that idea.

'Pam had done costings on the main expenses, which will

be hooking up the water and electricity, laying a proper floor and fitting out the kitchen.'

'And her costings are five years out of date.' Art dragged a hand through his hair. 'It'll cost more now. And you still haven't said where this magic fifty grand is coming from.'

'I factored in a five per cent increase in those costs for inflation,' Ellie replied, her voice rising in counterpoint to his. The rest of the company had gone silent, glancing from her to Art, obviously scenting the tension between them. 'We'll have to get a business loan, but there are grants we can apply for too.'

'If you think all this is going to happen in five weeks, you're nuts,' Art replied. 'Even if we could get the finance in place, how the hell is everyone going to find the time in their schedules? We're all busting our balls already to keep this place afloat and you–'

'Art,' Dee intervened. 'Stop it. We're all adults here and we can decide for ourselves whether this is something we can devote enough time to or not. Between the four of us...' She paused to encompass herself, Ellie, Tess and Annie. 'We've worked out a detailed schedule, which includes an estimate of exactly how much time it's going to take. It's daunting,' she continued. 'We all know that. But we four will be doing the bulk of the work and this would give us all a chance to work towards achieving our dream for this place, which was Pam's dream too, instead of just keeping our heads above water. And that's why, for me, it'll be worth every extra hour I spend busting my backside to make it happen.'

The emotion in Ellie's throat swelled back up again. That her mother had backed the project was one thing, that she'd stood up to Art to do it seemed even more significant. She swallowed, determined not to get sidetracked by feelings that were nineteen years past their sell-by date.

'I agree with Dee,' Rob added. 'Plus you need to chill out, Art. You're getting worked up about nothing. This is just a vote to give Ellie the go-ahead to get confirmed estimates and check out the situation with a loan. If you'd actually bothered to read this like the rest of us–' he held up the business plan then slapped it back down on the table '–before getting your bollocks in a twist, you'd know that.'

Ellie knew full well why Art hadn't read the plan more carefully. But she couldn't muster any sympathy for him.

His enmity felt personal because it was personal, just like it had been nineteen summers ago when he had made her life hell. She hadn't belonged then, she'd been the outsider, and he'd rubbed her nose in it. This time the tables were turned, the members of the co-op had welcomed her, had given her a stake, albeit temporary, in this place. And he resented that. She might not want to get sidetracked by the past, but he appeared to be stuck there.

'So are we all finally ready to take a vote?' Annie said, lifting her eyebrows at Ellie in exasperation.

The vote was carried, with only one abstention – who left the kitchen without another word.

No one commented further on Art's behaviour, everyone keen to congratulate Ellie and talk about all the things they could contribute in the weeks ahead, if they could secure the loan and turn Pam's dream into a reality.

After about an hour, all the enthusiasm and excitement had begun to wane, as tired children whined for attention. Toto and Josh appeared to demand their supper and Maddy and Jacob disappeared upstairs as everyone else began to pack up their kids and head home.

'Don't worry, Art will come around. Especially when he sees

how brilliant this is gonna be,' Annie commented as she left with the now exhausted Freddie snuggled in her arms.

Once everyone had gone and Toto and Josh had been sent to bed, Ellie helped her mother put the used coffee mugs and plates into the industrial dishwasher. But Art's intervention kept running through her head.

He'd managed to cast a shadow over what had been an otherwise energising and exciting evening full of potential for the future.

The man was the anti-karma.

'Don't be angry with him,' Dee said, as she loaded the last of the cutlery and set the machine.

'Angry with who?' Ellie scooped the cake crumbs off the table, refusing to meet her mother's eyes.

She really didn't want to think about Art and his shitty attitude because it was totally destroying her happy buzz. And reminding her of the distance between her and her mother. That absolutely did not bother her. She wasn't a teenager any more and she was not about to get into another pissing contest with Art over her mother's affections. He'd already won that one, but apparently he didn't even have the good grace to be magnanimous about it.

Dee rested cool fingers on the tight muscles of Ellie's forearm. 'Art's not good with change.'

The justification spiked Ellie's temper. 'Art's also not good with people generally. And me in particular.'

And she'd never done anything to deserve it. Not nineteen years ago and certainly not now.

'He can be difficult when he feels threatened,' her mother continued, as if this was still all about Art. 'He had to deal with so much when he was younger. And I suspect it was the only way he could cope.'

'Like what? What exactly did he have to cope with that gives him the right to be an arsey prick for the rest of his natural life?' Because she really wanted to know now. She'd been so pathetically grateful for her mother's support. But why should she be? Didn't she deserve at least a little support from her own mother?

Why had her mother always protected Art? Why was she still excusing his behaviour even now? Her mother didn't know the full extent of what had happened between the two of them back then, and Ellie certainly didn't intend to enlighten her, because neither of them would come out of it looking good. But she was not about to let Art treat her like that again.

'I got some of it out of Laura,' Dee said, not disputing that Art was an arsey prick. *So you're OK with that, are you, Mum?* 'And some of it in confidence from Art. And the rest I can only guess at,' Dee continued, being annoyingly cryptic. 'But you mustn't take his manner to heart. It's just his way.'

She so would take it to heart, because she had been the one tonight taking the direct hit. But she could see there was no mileage in arguing the toss with the president of the Art Dalton Fan Club. Her mother had declared on Art's side when she'd made the decision to stay at the commune and become Art's surrogate mum instead of coming home to London to be Ellie's real mum.

The futile resentment burned the back of her throat, but she forced herself to ignore it.

Ultimately, she'd survived without her mother, she and her father had muddled through on their own.

She heaved out a sigh and tried to take stock.

She'd made progress with Dee in the last two weeks. She didn't want to revisit all those old resentments. It was ancient history now. And anyway, her mum wasn't the one with a case to answer here. Dee wasn't the one who had comprehensively tried to screw her over tonight for no good reason.

'Don't worry, Mum. I've had to deal with more than a few difficult clients in my time.'

Although dealing with a budget-busting change in the entrée from salmon to scallops twenty-four hours before a banquet for five hundred accountants at the end of a team-building weekend didn't seem quite as daunting right now as corralling six foot two of hard-arsed macho diva.

'I can handle Art Dalton,' she finished.

Or she would be able to, once she'd given him a crash course in why not to piss on Ellie Preston's parade.

*

Dee watched her daughter leave the kitchen, the temper in her stride a welcome change from the nervous tremor in her fingers at the start of the meeting. She picked up the cloth Ellie had left on the table, rinsed it at the sink and draped it over the tap.

You can't smooth over everything, Dee. Sometimes you just have to let bad things happen and then deal with it the best you can.

Pammy's words rang in her head, the way they had a million times since that summer. Sentiment mixed with loneliness in the pit of her stomach making her feel tired.

She could go and warn Art that Ellie was on the warpath, but she wasn't sure he deserved the heads-up. He had been out of order during the meeting.

She switched off the kitchen light, and closed the door on the memory. As well as the idea of interfering any more than was strictly necessary in The Ellie and Art Show.

Ellie and she had problems that didn't involve Art. Problems that Dee had been too much of a coward in the last two weeks to discuss with her daughter. But it was good to know Ellie was now a successful independent career woman – the wobble earlier in the evening could only have been performance anxiety. She certainly wasn't the vulnerable, lonely, insecure girl who'd been torn between two parents who had both shoved her needs aside to make themselves happy.

Stop beating yourself up about that, Dee. You did what you had to do, we both did. One day Ellie will understand.

Pammy's words pushed the guilt back, a little.

Her daughter was keeping a lot of secrets, secrets that she didn't trust Dee enough to share. She still hadn't mentioned her husband. And Josh hardly ever mentioned his dad either. And how had Ellie been able to leave her event-planning business for a whole summer, when surely that was the most lucrative time for such a business?

These were all questions Dee wanted to ask, but still didn't feel she had the right to ask. The farm shop wasn't just a terrific initiative to solve the farm's financial problems and a wonderful way to honour the woman she'd loved, it also had the potential to give Dee the thing she'd yearned for – to reforge the relationship with her daughter. To make it strong and true again. The way it had been before that difficult summer. She didn't want to jinx this chance. Which meant Art was on his own if he continued to behave like a dick.

For all his lack of communication skills, Art was not that angry, reckless boy any more. He was a strong, capable and caring man, who, against all the odds, had lived up to the responsibility of parenting a child solo. And Dee had formed a strong bond with him in the last nineteen years.

But he could also be a moody bugger.

Mounting the stairs to her room, Dee could hear Ellie further down the hallway laying down bedtime law to Josh.

'Ten past ten on a school night is ten minutes past lights out, so you need to get in that bathroom now or you're going to be brushing your teeth in the dark.'

Josh's answering plea was way too tired to gain a reprieve.

Dee entered her room, rubbing the tight muscles in her neck.

She heard Ellie's shower go on in the bathroom down the hall as she went in to start her own night-time ritual, the flicker of concern turning into admiration.

Her daughter was certainly no pushover any more. Time to step back and watch The Ellie and Art Show from the sidelines.

Dee removed her make-up and waited to hear Ellie's shower switch off before she stepped into hers. The boiler hadn't been able to cope with two showers at once for over a decade, no matter how often Art overhauled it.

Art would be in his workshop putting his carpentry skills to good use, burying any wayward emotions under a pile of sawdust and lumber. The way he always did when he had stuff to process. The way he'd been doing almost every night until the early hours ever since Ellie had arrived.

Dee shifted her head to one side, letting the heating jets pummel the tight muscles.

Stupid of her not to realise the significance of that until now.

CHAPTER TWELVE

Art snapped on the protective goggles and yanked the cord to kick-start the saw's reconditioned motor. The blade chugged to life, rotating with blurring speed as the cord snapped back.

Taking a piece of walnut wood out of the pile he'd marked up earlier, he took a deep breath into his nose. The scent of sawdust and turpentine snagged on his tonsils, making him cough.

He needed to calm down. Operating power tools when you wanted to punch something could be hazardous. And letting Ellie Preston mess with his head had nearly cost him his left hand a fortnight ago.

He scrubbed a sweaty palm against his jeans, let go of the breath about to explode in his lungs.

Threading the board against the blade, he shaved off the excess two centimetres. He had forty boards to plane, ready for tomorrow morning, when he was due to get stuck into the second phase of the commission he'd started a month ago.

It was hot, tiresome, and dangerous work, if you didn't know what you were doing, or weren't paying attention. And Ellie Preston had distracted him enough already for one night. Make that one fortnight. If she was really planning to stay the whole summer, he needed to find better ways to avoid her – that actually involved avoiding her – because every single second spent in her company was seared on his consciousness.

Letting her handle the project's admin should have been the perfect solution. Not only did it mean he no longer had to do a job that he wasn't qualified for and would happily have sacrificed his left nut to be shot of, it also meant he had the perfect excuse to stay locked in his workshop for the daylight hours and well away from the house and her. But the nights had been another matter. Yesterday evening he'd come out of the bathroom and all but tripped over her in the hallway.

Her lips had issued a shocked gasp, her eyes focusing on his naked chest. The long slow glide over wet flesh had burned off the condensation left from his power shower in two seconds flat. Then she'd edged back against the wall as he sent her a mumbled apology and trotted off down the corridor to his room feeling her eyes on his backside every step of the way.

The sibilant buzz of the saw didn't do much to downgrade his temper.

Ellie's presentation had been coherent and articulate and, if he had been able to read her printout, he had no doubt she would have made a convincing argument on paper for going ahead with Pam's scheme. She certainly seemed to have convinced everyone else it was a great idea. But it wasn't, for the simple reason that Ellie didn't live here, she didn't belong here and she wasn't going to stay.

The door crashed against the frame, making his fingers jerk on the saw. Thrusting up the googles, he squinted through the fog of sawdust at the vision in pyjamas – were those dancing pink elephants? – that stood in the doorway of his workshop. She mouthed something and he flicked the switch on the saw.

The buzzing faded.

What was she doing here? In his place? His sanctuary? He'd made a point of not telling her about the workshop, precisely because she had invaded enough of his territory already.

'I want to have a word with you,' she announced.

Her hair hung in damp strands, the drying ends curling around her face in mad corkscrews. Without the sheen of lipstick and the smudge of eyeliner that she usually wore, she looked not much older than the first time he'd laid eyes on her. The top two buttons of her pyjama top were undone, playing peek-a-boo with the worn vest beneath. She crossed her arms under her breasts, making them sway under her top. Her chin lifted in challenge, and he realised two things at once. Ellie was in a major snit. And she wasn't wearing a bra.

Terrific.

*

'Sorry, have I struck you dumb? Because you seemed to be talkative enough during tonight's meeting?' The righteous indignation that had been pumping through Ellie's veins while she got ready for bed was like the lava from a long dormant volcano finally ready to blow.

She'd been waiting for Art to come home for two hours while she lay on her bed and relived tonight's meeting. And he hadn't shown.

So if the mountain of macho bollocks wouldn't come to Ellie, Ellie would damn well come to the mountain.

He'd ambushed her in the meeting. Had done his utmost to make her feel useless and insignificant and insecure. And she wasn't going to let that pass for another second, let alone another night.

She'd spent the whole of her marriage to Dan avoiding difficult conversations, because she'd been scared of what she would discover, and look how that had turned out?

Even so, she'd planned to be calm and dignified with a hint of steel when she'd ventured out to find Art's 'workshop'.

But calm and dignified had got lost somewhere while she'd been stumbling around the outbuildings in the dark, getting her best bunny slippers covered in mud.

The workshop wasn't what she had expected. She'd assumed 'workshop' was guy code for man cave. Apparently not, because Art looked as if he was actually working in his workshop. His thick muscular arms and that blasted tattoo were sheened with sweat, his T-shirt speckled with dirt, the dust on his face giving him panda eyes as he tore off his safety goggles.

There wasn't a single creature comfort in the cavernous barn, just the overpowering smell of tree resin from the freshly cut lumber and the chemical smell of turpentine.

What looked like the chassis of a trailer stood in the middle of the concrete floor with a wooden frame built on to it. A ladder led to a hayloft, which was piled with wood of all different descriptions and thicknesses. And there was the shell of something laid out on the floor, the wood shaped into curves with a series of clamps. She noticed the sketches pinned to the board above the workbench, along with some photographs of what looked like gypsy caravans. Were they previous projects? She envisioned the finished product from the template on the floor, and realised the caravan had to be one of the 'sundries' mentioned in the accounts – the sundries that had managed to tip the balance of the co-op's accounts into credit. Despite all his downsides – and they were legion – Art clearly had some talents, as Dee had insisted.

The circular saw Art had been using to shave a plank of wood gleamed in the light from the single bulb hanging from the vaulted ceiling twenty feet above their heads. A shudder rippled down Ellie's spine – was that the blade he'd cut himself on? He was lucky he hadn't lost a limb.

'What words do you want to have? I'm busy here.'

The surly statement zapped Ellie's attention back to the man.

Electrical energy and pissed-off vibes zinged in the air around him. She tightened her arms under her breasts, and felt them sway under her pyjama top. Why had she decided to come out here in her nightclothes?

'I'd love to know if that stick up your backside is a permanent fixture,' she said, relocating her temper. 'Or whether you just shove it up there for my benefit?'

He tugged the goggles the rest of the way off his head, making his sweaty hair stick up in indignant tuffs, and dumped them on the worktable. 'You need to go, I'm not in the mood for an argument.'

The words were laced with enough restraint of the gritted-teeth variety to send a prickle of warning through the short hairs of her scalp. But the lava bubbling below her solar plexus was having none of it.

'Maybe you should have thought of that before you decided to behave like such a prick and play "who's got the biggest penis" with me in tonight's meeting.'

'I was not being a prick. I was voicing genuine concerns.'

'You were rude and obnoxious and unnecessarily confrontational. That makes you the definition of a prick in my book.'

Fury flared, turning his hazelnut eyes to a hot vibrant choco-late. His mouth drew into a tight line, the plaintive hoot of an owl the only sound puncturing the silence.

So they were going to play it that way? were they? The way he'd played it nineteen years ago, not speaking, just glowering, expecting her to figure out what the hell was going on in his head using what? A Jedi mind meld? Or some other kind of freaky psychic ability no woman actually possessed.

Fine. She would speak and he could bloody well listen.

'I've spent the last four days working my butt off on that business plan. If you've got genuine concerns and are prepared to be constructive, I'm more than willing to listen to them. But instead you attacked and belittled me in front of everyone. Why?'

'Because you overstepped the mark. You were supposed to be sorting out some paperwork, not coming up with ideas that could run us all into the ground.'

The derogatory comment, ground out through a jaw locked harder than granite, froze the lava in her chest. Emotions careered through her, scouring her insides.

'How many times do I have to tell you,' she said, struggling to regain her composure, her certainty, 'it won't run us into the ground.'

'There is no "us". Not for you.'

And there it was, out in the open. The hostility that had been riding just beneath the surface ever since she'd arrived. It shouldn't feel like a blow, another cut below the knees, she didn't need his approval. But somehow it did.

'I'm as invested in this project as anyone,' she said.

'And yet you'll leave at the end of the summer without a

backward glance.' The scorched earth gaze he levelled at her probably wasn't a good idea with all the dry lumber around.

'This isn't about the shop, is it? It's about me.' At least he was finally admitting it. 'What did I ever do to make you dislike me so much?' she asked, finally through tiptoeing around the twenty-ton pachyderm doing backflips in the centre of the room. 'When I came here nineteen years ago with my mother, I got the same reception. And I never understood why. Why you bullied me and made fun of me and went out of your way to exclude me.' That the memories still hurt only humiliated her more.

He blinked, his face rigid. 'I was a bastard. I admit it. But you took it too hard,' he said, as if that excused the hurt he'd caused.

And it had got so much worse the day before she'd left, the day before her father had arrived. She had no intention of rehashing that scene again, and she certainly didn't expect the apology she wasn't going to get. But she'd be damned if she wasn't going to rail against the injustice of his accusations.

'Maybe I was oversensitive,' she said. 'I was fourteen years old, trying to process stuff I didn't understand. But let's be clear about the real reason I left with my dad that day. It was you Art, you were the reason, because you went out of your way to make me feel like shit that whole summer.'

'You made a choice to break Dee's heart,' he said. 'How the hell is that my fault?'

The low blow knocked her back on her heels, tapping right into the emotions she'd been determined to ignore.

'My relationship with my mother is none of your business.' She pushed back. She'd already let one man trample her self-esteem and her self-confidence into the mud.

But she didn't feel particularly strong when instead of backing down, he stepped forward. 'That would be the relationship you've ignored for the last nineteen years, would it?'

His gaze drifted up to her hair, as she breathed in a lungful of salty sweat and fresh sawdust, and the electrical attraction arced between them like a lightning strike.

'Back off.' She slapped a palm against his chest, feeling cornered.

Solid strength strained against the soft cotton, prickly with wood splinters. But then he swore softly and stepped away, his breathing almost as ragged as hers.

She looked away, the shot of adrenaline, the heady feeling of déjà vu unmistakeable. And all the more disturbing for it.

When was the last time she'd felt that basic, elemental connection? The sharp, insistent tug of desire? So long ago, she almost hadn't recognised it.

She rubbed her stinging palm on her pyjama bottoms, feeling more exposed than she had nineteen years ago.

Fabulous, this was just what she needed, her libido to come out of hiding and start behaving like a lunatic. And not with any man, but with Art. A man she could barely have a civil conversation with. A man with whom she had a history. A man who had made it fairly clear he despised her.

'I have nothing more to say to you,' she murmured, suddenly desperate to escape that searing gaze which seemed able to locate every one of her insecurities and expose them.

'Wait.' He seized her arm. 'We're not finished here.'

His thumb touched the pulse on the inside of her elbow, and that heady shot of adrenaline careered round her system again. Panic soon followed.

'Yes, we are.' She shook off his hold. 'This conversation is over.'

He held up his hands, but the dilated pupils suggested he'd felt that brutal shot of desire too. Which was so not good. 'I've got something to say to you, and I want you to listen.'

She rubbed the inside of her elbow, where his touch had branded the skin. 'Why should I?'

She could see the struggle cross his face.

'Because I was here and you weren't,' he said. 'You weren't here to see what it did to her when you left. I don't want to see her hurt that way again.'

'I don't plan to hurt her.' Despite the denial, guilt coalesced in the pit of her stomach, heavy and indigestible, like a wodge of unleavened dough.

His Adam's apple bobbed. 'Maybe you don't plan to,' he said. 'But you will.'

What could she say to that? She wasn't even sure what he was accusing her of? It had been her mother's choice to abandon her, not the other way around. Hadn't it?

'Losing Pam nearly destroyed her,' he said, the sincerity in his voice cutting through all Ellie's defences. 'She had to watch the woman she loved, the only person who stuck by her no matter what, die a slow and painful death.' He waved his arm to encompass the workshop and the farm beyond. 'This place means everything to Dee, because it's all she's got left of Pam.'

'Which is all the more reason to try everything to save it.' Why couldn't he see that? Was this all simply because he had no faith in her? Why couldn't he at least give her a chance? 'I know the idea has come out of left field, but it really is a good...'

'I knew about the damn planning application, Pam and I worked on it together,' he said, the revelation shocking her into silence.

'But if you knew about it, why didn't you say something sooner?'

'Because Pam told me not to. She was going to surprise Dee, on the anniversary of their civil partnership. But then she got diagnosed with stage four breast cancer and she wanted me to bury the idea. She didn't want to risk Dee losing the farm as well as her.'

'I... I didn't know that. But if you went along with it then, why are you so against the idea now?'

'Because it's too big of a risk. What if the shop doesn't work? It'll be like losing Pam all over again for Dee. It's easy for you, it's just some project to keep you occupied before you go home again, but for Dee it could mean losing every damn thing that matters to her.'

If she'd wanted evidence that Art did feelings, other than stubbornness or temper, she had it now. But she also had evidence that every damn thing that mattered to Dee didn't include her.

'She's not going to lose anything,' she said, suddenly weary. She couldn't fight this battle all over again. 'It's a good idea. And I promise you, even though I'm going back to the US at the end of the summer, I am totally invested in making this work.' And she was even more invested now because it turned out she had something to prove to Art as well as Dee. 'Perhaps you should try trusting me on that?'

The suggestion hung in the air between them, the blank look on his face all the answer she needed.

What had she been thinking? Persuading Art to trust anyone, especially her, was about as likely as persuading him to join a Spice Girls tribute band.

She braced herself for the inevitable slap down. But instead of telling her where she could shove her trust, he simply said, 'It's not like I have much of a choice now, is it?'

She didn't reply, as he walked back to the workbench. Not sure what to say, the grudging acceptance about as far from a vote of confidence as it was possible to get.

The saw roared to life.

She stood and watched him for a moment, her emotions in turmoil, as he snapped the goggles back on and worked the wood.

He handled the plank with easy competence, his large callused hands stroking the grain. The hairs on his forearms misted with sawdust, more flecks standing out against the sweat pooling at his clavicle.

The inappropriate heat flooded in her abdomen to go with the rising feeling of inadequacy. She shot out of the workshop into the night.

She wrapped her arms around herself, trembling despite the warm evening, and spotted the lantern her mother had left burning in the farmhouse window so Art could find his way home in the darkness. The ball of anxiety knotted in her abdomen.

Art knew her mother now better than she ever could. And whose fault was that, really? His, for being such a bastard to her that whole summer, or hers, for letting the way he treated her mean more than it should?

However much she might want to dismiss his criticisms of her and the shop project as envy, resentment, his fear of change or simply his trademark Art bullheadedness, she had to accept that underlying all that were some genuine concerns. And if he ever found out how badly she'd stuffed up her own business, not to mention her marriage, he'd think he was even more justified in believing she had no way of pulling this off.

What Art refused to believe, though, because the man clearly had serious trust issues, was that she was prepared to do everything in her power to make sure the shop was a success. And all she had to do to prove that, to him and her mum and everyone else at the co-op, not to mention herself, was make absolutely sure this was one thing she did not stuff up.

She trudged back to the farmhouse in her ruined bunny slippers.

No pressure at all then.

CHAPTER THIRTEEN

'Right, so which man-killing pedi colour are you?' Annie delved into her tray of nail polishes, lifting the sample bottles as she read the titles. 'Juicy Hibis-Kiss? Guilty Pleasure Dominance? Or Tangerine Tigress? Those are my suggestions, to go with your Hot Raspberry Wine fingernails.'

Ellie squinted at the different colours. 'They all sound very... suggestive.'

It had been a week since her showdown with Art and she had been working her butt off. And this evening's celebration was her reward. After seven days of working on grant applications, construction estimates, work schedules, polishing the business plan, setting up a Twitter and Facebook account and beginning a design on WordPress for the new website, she, Tess, Dee and Annie had spent the afternoon in Mr Hegley's office at the NatWest bank in Gratesbury explaining exactly why the Willow Tree Farm Shop and Café was going to be the best investment he'd ever made. And, unlike Art, Mr Hegley had agreed with them.

So now she, Tess, Maddy and Annie were treating themselves to a mani–pedi girls' night in. The buzz from celebrating their success, not to mention two glasses of Rob's elderflower champagne, and an hour of girl talk, though, had left her feeling far too euphoric to make informed choices about toenail polish.

'Yeah, Annie,' Tess said, as she topped up everyone's glass, 'don't you have any colours that aren't pornographic?'

Maddy snorted out a laugh while wiggling her recently painted toes. 'Don't knock it. I think Jacob is gonna go insane when he gets a load of my Spoilt Diva toes.'

Given the amount of noise that had been coming out of the bathroom last night before the two of them had sheepishly appeared, Ellie wasn't convinced Jacob needed any more encouragement.

'I have two toddlers under three, who never sleep simultaneously,' Annie said. 'I need all the help I can get in that department – so stop knocking my toe polish choices. And for those of us who *are* looking for some action…' She grinned at Ellie as she pulled a bottle of glittery scarlet polish from the tray and wiggled it. 'I can highly recommend Art of Seduction. This polish even managed to get a rise out of a man who has to get up at 4 a.m. every morning to milk a herd of cows.'

Tess and Maddy laughed, while Ellie took a judicious sip of her champagne.

'*Art* of Seduction?' she said. 'Is that supposed to be a hint?'

Annie's grin widened. 'Surely I'm not the only one who noticed the little *frisson* between you two while he was objecting to our project last Friday.' She shook the bottle and lifted her eyebrows. 'What do you say? Shall we knock Mr Dalton dead?'

'Unfortunately, I think it would take more than hot nail polish to knock that man dead,' Ellie said, the mention of Art putting a dent in her euphoria. She'd been avoiding him since last Friday night, but then he'd been avoiding her right back. She'd hoped he would turn up for the meeting they'd called this evening before supper to officially launch the project, but no, he'd been absent.

And OK, maybe there had been a slight frisson between them since she'd arrived, but she did not plan to dwell on it.

'So what's the deal between you two?' Tess asked.

'He thinks the project is going to fail,' Ellie said, offering her glass to Maddy for a top-up, 'but that's absolutely fine because I am going to prove him wrong.' And today had put her one step closer to that goal, whether he had been there to acknowledge their success or not.

'There's more to it than that,' Tess said. 'If it was just about the project, I don't think he would have been so passionate about his objections. I think he said more in that meeting than he's said all year.'

And more later that evening than he'd probably said in an entire decade, but Ellie had decided that wasn't significant, and she refused to let it undermine her confidence any further.

'Art's passions aren't my concern, thank goodness,' she said. 'The deal is we've just never got along.'

'*Never?*' Annie's interest perked up as she dabbed Ellie's big toenail with the glittery polish, having made the choice for her. 'I wonder why? Sounds like you two have got quite a history?'

'Yeah, what exactly *is* your history?' Maddy said from her perch on the arm of the couch.

'I told you all, our history is we spent a summer together, we didn't get on, and then I left. That's it,' Ellie said, downing the rest of her champagne.

'Did you ever bang each other?' Tess asked.

The bubbles hit Ellie's tonsils and exploded into a coughing fit. Maddy thumped her back.

'Jesus, Tess, no we did not,' Ellie said, once she'd managed to draw a full breath. 'I was only fourteen. And anyway, why would I want to bang Art? I don't even fancy him.' And even if that was a lie, she had exceptionally good impulse control.

'Why not?' Annie said. 'He's gorgeous and available and he's a guaranteed orgasm.'

'How exactly do you know that?' It was Tess's turn to choke on her champagne. 'You're a happily married woman.'

'So what? I can appreciate a good-looking guy, can't I?' Annie said, her head bent over Ellie's toes. 'Don't look so outraged,' she added, for Tess's benefit. 'I only know about his orgasm prowess by proxy.'

'Whose proxy?' Maddy asked.

'Daisy Mayhew. She works at the Haymaker at the bottom of Candlewick Hill part-time and dated him briefly last summer. She was very disappointed when he stopped calling her. *Very* disappointed.'

'Why are we talking about Art?' Ellie said. She so did not need to hear about Art's orgasm-on-demand capabilities. She had a damn frisson to control. 'This is supposed to be a girls' night in, which means no man talk. It's boring.'

'What kind of tedious girls' nights in do you go to?' Annie said, pausing mid-brush to stare at Ellie as if she'd lost her mind. 'Man talk is *never* boring – especially if it involves Aidan Turner and a scythe.'

'Fine, we can talk about *Poldark*,' Ellie conceded. 'But let's not talk about Art.'

'I think the lady protesteth too much.' Maddy misquoted Shakespeare.

'I'm just not interested in talking about Art,' Ellie said,

protesting way too much. 'Or his enormous scythe.' But, as she said it, the memory of him lying by the millpond and chafing himself to orgasm blasted into her brain and made her cheeks go almost as scarlet as the glittery polish on her toes.

'How exactly do you know his scythe is enormous? If you've never slept with him?' Annie said, going all Hercule Poirot as she blew on Ellie's toes. 'Because that just happens to be something else Daisy mentioned. A lot.'

Ellie put down her glass. She needed to go easy on the booze, because all three of her friends were now watching her with rapt attention. 'Um, I may possibly have seen it once. In a non-sexual...' she cleared her throat '...an *almost* non-sexual context.'

'Almost?' Tess said. 'We definitely need details.' The other two nodded.

'I'm not sure I know you well enough to tell you,' Ellie hedged.

'We will be very discreet,' Tess said, then glanced at Annie. 'Well, Annie won't be, but me and Maddy can gag her.'

'Hey!' Annie said, pausing in the toe painting to look out-raged.

Ellie laughed, and it occurred to her that she wanted to tell them. Maybe she'd only known the three of them for less than a month, but she really liked them, and it had been so long since she'd had real female friends. So long, in fact, she'd forgotten how good it felt to have women she could confide in. And, what the heck, she'd been holding on to this guilty secret for nineteen years, why not share?

'OK, fine, I know all about Art's scythe because I spied on him once by the millpond, when he was naked and very busy...' she paused, to take a fortifying sip of bubbles '...doing what boys of fifteen tend to do a lot.'

Maddy gasped, Tess snorted and Annie purred.

'Wow, that is even hotter than Aidan Turner doing the bare-chested scythe boogie. I think Mr Annie is going to be whistling when he gets up to milk those cows tomorrow.'

'Does Art know? That you saw him?' Tess probed, still rapt.

'Are you joking?' Ellie said, enjoying their interest maybe more than she should. 'He would have eviscerated me. We had this love–hate relationship going all summer… Well, more hate–hate really.' Not unlike now. 'But I will admit that was probably the most erotic thing I've ever seen in my life.' Because just thinking about it now was making all the saliva dry up in her mouth. She took a sip of her champagne. The others looked riveted. So was she really. 'But we never got it together… I was only fourteen and he was a complete bastard.' Most of the time.

'So now's your chance, why not go for it?' Maddy said, clearly drunk. Or delusional. Or both. 'Art's hot for an older guy.'

Older guy? He wasn't that old.

'And a guaranteed orgasm with an enormous scythe,' Maddy finished, proving she was definitely both drunk *and* delusional.

'Eh, hello, he hates me, and I'm still married.' Ellie danced her ring finger in front of the three of them Beyoncé style. Then she noticed the Hot Raspberry Wine polish, which clashed with the ring on said finger, and had a searing moment of clarity.

After spending twelve years honouring the band of 24-carat white gold Dan had slipped on her finger in the Orchard County courthouse, for the first time ever her ring didn't feel relevant any more. Had they ever really been married? If she was the only one of them to take their vows seriously?

Maybe it was the wine talking, but still the realisation felt profound.

154

'You're getting a divorce,' Annie said as if reading her mind. 'Because Dan Jr was a cheating rat and is about to have a child by another woman. So I don't think you should consider yourself *that* married.'

Ellie frowned. Was Annie right?

'I guess we are separated,' she heard herself say.

'Precisely, so why should you let that stop you jumping Art? It didn't stop your husband from jumping Josh's teacher,' Annie said, with barefaced Northern logic.

The others made sounds of approval.

Ellie didn't comment. Why had she confided in Annie and the others when she hadn't yet told Dee about the divorce? Or Josh? She stared into her champagne flute.

Ah yes, wines.

Never have a mani–pedi girly night with wine, after years without decent sex and five days of intensive girl bonding over too much paperwork.

'All done.' Annie placed Ellie's completed foot back onto the cushion she'd arranged on a footstool. 'You're now armed and dangerous.' She wiggled her eyebrows lasciviously. 'Should you decide to take Dalton down.'

"That's not going to happen,' she said.

Even if her marriage was over, there was still Josh to think about. Jumping Art would only confuse him. Not to mention the somewhat bigger roadblock, they didn't actually like each other.

But, even so, Ellie found herself admiring the glittery sparkle on her toes from the light of Annie's living room fire as Annie cracked her fingers and announced, 'Right, Tess, you're next for the man killer toenail treatment.'

Ellie was still on an elderflower-and-girl-power high as she and Maddy strolled back across the fields together from Annie's house serenaded by the scent of evening jasmine and manure and guided by the glow of a full moon. They headed towards the light in the farmhouse kitchen once they came out of the woods.

A wave of sentiment washed over Ellie. It was past midnight, so everyone would have been in bed hours ago – the first thing she'd discovered about farm life was that it did not allow for late nights – which meant Dee had left the lights on for her tonight. It probably shouldn't matter to her, but somehow it did.

Maddy giggled as they entered the farmhouse, obviously drunker than Ellie. 'I hope Jay's not too fast asleep yet.'

'If he is, he won't be for long,' Ellie teased, enjoying the younger woman's delight. 'I'll get the lights. See you tomorrow for the start of Phase Two.' They were due to start clearing out the back barn tomorrow afternoon. 'But don't exhaust Jacob too much, we need him to move heavy machinery tomorrow.'

Accomplishment and excitement surged through Ellie to add to the general light-headedness from their boozy evening as Maddy stumbled up the stairs.

'No worries, I'll do all the work,' Maddy whispered, still giggling.

OK, that was way too much information.

Ellie opened the kitchen door, planning to hunt up some nibbles and a nightcap to give Maddy time to introduce Jacob to the delights of Spoilt Diva nail polish and then crash out, because she did not need to be hearing the two of them going for it after the discussion they'd had at Annie's about potential hook-ups.

She realised her mistake, though, when she entered the room and spotted Mr Guaranteed Orgasm himself hunched over a plate piled high with her mother's moussaka.

Their eyes met, and he swallowed.

'Hi,' she said, heat flushing through her. *Bugger*.

He nodded a greeting, looking as pleased to see her as she was to see him. i.e.: not at all. His biceps bunched against the short sleeves of his T-shirt as he scooped up another enormous mouthful of moussaka. And then the significance of his presence in the kitchen at this hour dawned on her.

For Pete's sake, had Art been eating every night at midnight then, just to avoid seeing her at supper time?

'We got the loan approved today,' she said.

This was bonkers. He might not like of the shop, but it was going ahead anyway. And it was going to be a huge success – at which point she would take great pleasure in telling him 'I told you so'. But, until then, they needed to find a way to work together. Art had gone out of his way, once upon a time, to make her feel excluded, but she was going to be the bigger and better person here and include him whether he wanted to be included or not.

He swallowed down another mouthful. 'I heard,' he said. No word of congratulations or encouragement.

Great, so he's still being a wanker about the whole thing.

He carried on eating, clearly attempting to finish his meal before they had anything resembling an actual conversation.

Sod that. Maybe she couldn't get Art onside with the project, but she'd had enough of his sulking. And now was the perfect time to call a truce, while she was buoyed up on a wave of success, girl power and Rob's elderflower champagne – and armed with man-killer toenails.

She headed for the pantry in search of some additional Dutch courage. The bottles of sloe gin lined up in myriad shades of red and pink on the top shelf made her heart – and the warm hum in her stomach – jump for joy.

She snagged a bottle and walked back into the kitchen to see Art scraping the last of his moussaka off the earthenware bowl. Lifting two shot glasses from the sideboard, she placed them on the table in front of him with a decisive click and prised open the bottle's stopper with her thumbs. 'Fancy joining me for a drink?'

Dark eyes met hers, the question in them almost as potent as the suspicion rolling off him.

'Unless, of course, you're scared of me,' she added.

His brows lowered and a muscle in his jaw ticked against the day's growth of stubble.

Strike one to Princess Drama.

'Why would I be scared of you?' he said flatly, as if he hadn't just risked indigestion to get out of her way.

She poured a liberal dose of gin into the shot glasses. 'Fabulous. Then drink up.'

He eyed the glass then wrapped his hand around it. The raw, reddened scar from his tango with the rotary blade drew her gaze before he lifted the glass to his lips and bolted the generous shot down in one.

The glass cracked back against the table as he smacked his lips, that dark gaze never straying from her face.

Game on.

She lifted her own glass and floored it.

The perfumed drink roared down her throat like liquid fire, hitting her tonsils with a one-two punch. She gulped down the cough, her eyes watering like a faucet.

Waiting for her hand to steady, she refilled the glasses.

His eyebrow hooked up again. 'Really?'

She picked up her glass. 'Here's to Mr Hegley,' she said. 'A man who recognises a great investment when he sees one.' Then drained the glass.

The gin went down without a problem this time, probably because the lining of her throat had already been cauterised.

Art was still studying her, with that inscrutable expression on his face.

For a moment she thought she might have gone too far. Was he about to walk out, leaving her sitting there, with her foolish desire to end the animosity between them pooling round her deadly toenails in a puddle of despair.

But then he lifted one shoulder in a nonchalant shrug, tipped the glass towards her in a silent toast, and chugged it down.

Triumph – sweet and heady and possibly a tad out of proportion to what she had actually achieved – charged through her system alongside the fiery shot of alcohol.

She reached for the bottle, to refill. Maybe she couldn't get Art onside with the project, but getting pissed with him suddenly seemed like the perfect compromise. But, as her fingers closed over the bottle, his palm wrapped around her hand. The touch was electrifying, zapping endorphins up her arm and down through her torso.

'Slow down,' he said.

She prised her hand out from under his.

'How much did you have at Annie's?' he asked.

Not enough.

'Not much… Only two glasses.' Or had it been three? Because she suddenly felt more drunk than she had a moment ago.

'Right.' He didn't look convinced. 'How about we take a break.' He hooked the stopper back onto the gin bottle, before carrying his bowl to the sink.

Ellie let her gaze drift over him, taking the opportunity to admire all his more basic qualities unobserved. Maddy was right, he was a phenomenally hot guy, dark and rugged, with that edge of raw earthy animal magnetism which made women everywhere – even happily married Aidan Turner fans like Annie – take notice. And tonight, his personality deficiencies didn't seem particularly important. If anything, that air of inscrutability and stoicism made him… well, extra hot.

Everything about Art was so refreshingly straightforward. He didn't try to bamboozle women with empty charm, which was mighty seductive to a woman who had spent the last twelve years living with a compulsive liar.

His back muscles flexed beneath the well-worn T-shirt while he rinsed out his bowl and propped it on the draining board. The alcohol hit ground zero and the hum in her belly built to a slow-burning fire.

Nope, I have not had nearly enough alcohol.

He flicked the water off his hands, wiped them on a tea towel, then headed towards the door.

Need and bravado gathered in her stomach. 'Where are you going?'

He stopped. 'I've got stuff to finish in the workshop.'

'Would that stuff involve operating power tools?'

His lips quirked. 'Perhaps.'

The mellow heat in her belly got jittery. Art was definitely less of a wanker when he smiled.

'Then I'm afraid, I'll have to object,' she said. 'I am in no condition to drive you back to A and E tonight.' Pulling the chair out beside her, she slapped the seat. 'Join me. You've had too much to be sober and not enough to be drunk. I think we should remedy that.'

'Why?'

'Because I'm half pissed already. And it's always a bad idea to do that without company.'

He settled in the seat beside her and she absorbed the stroke to her ego. Then she popped the stopper on the gin bottle.

'Fair warning, you should watch yourself with that stuff,' he said, as she poured. 'The hangovers are brutal.'

'I'll risk it, if you will.' She lifted the bottle, charmed that he might actually care about the state of her head in the morning.

He nodded and she poured them both another shot.

'How about we stop when we're cross-eyed,' she said. 'Or we've told each other all our most embarrassing secrets. Whichever is the quicker?' She blinked. 'Then again, you have a head start, because most of mine involve you.'

He laughed, the sound gruff enough to be rusty.

They drank in silence – the endorphins firing through her body didn't exactly make it companionable silence, but it wasn't awkward. Much.

As Art drank without speaking, it occurred to her he never felt the need to fill the silence, like most people. Was that what made him such an enigma? Or was it just the ten-foot high wall with barbed wire fencing he erected around his emotions?

Ellie slopped some more gin into her glass. Why not take a pop at the Berlin Wall? Now they were actually playing nice.

'Did you ever wonder,' she asked, 'how we both ended up with mums that were lesbians?'

'No.'

The one syllable answer did not deter her. Drawing Art out was going to require perseverance, but he was dealing with an admin ninja who could talk the notoriously cautious Mr Hegley into a fifty grand bank loan. Plus, they had all night. Or at least until 5 a.m., when Dee would come down to start mixing up her first batch of dough for the loaves she sold at the farmers' market in Gillingham every other Saturday morning. Art didn't know it yet, but he didn't stand a chance.

'Is that because your mum turned out to be a faker?' she said.

'She wasn't a faker.' Art's work-roughened hand picked up the bottle and tipped it into his own glass. He squinted at her, and she wondered if he were short-sighted. Or drunker than he looked. And if he knew how that intense, penetrating look had always made butterflies flutter around in her stomach?

'Living with my old man would turn any woman into a lesbian,' he added.

'You had a father?' The words popped out, propelled by the complete lack of inhibition caused by the floaty buzz of the gin.

His lids lowered. 'Of course. Did you think I was an immaculate conception?'

'No, I thought you were a sperm bank conception.'

Art coughed, spraying gin across the table. She slapped him on the back, feeling the tensing muscles under his T-shirt. He drew a steady breath. Took another gulp of his gin. 'I wish. He might have been a medical student then, instead of an arsehole.'

'How was he an arsehole?' she asked. Had she hit the jackpot already? Was Art actually going to talk about himself?

He stared into his glass. 'He drank too much. He hit her. He hit me. Usual arsehole behaviour.'

Her heart did a backflip at the nonchalant tone. 'That's dreadful.' She frowned. 'But since when does being in an abusive relationship change your sexual orientation?'

Art leant back, the intense look making the butterflies in her stomach feel inebriated. 'It doesn't, necessarily. But I have a theory about human sexuality.'

That Art had a theory about anything seemed both incongruous and sort of hot, that he had a theory about human sexuality seemed even hotter. 'What's your theory?'

'We may think we're either gay or straight, but in reality everyone falls somewhere on a spectrum between the two.' He frowned. 'I figure we're all a little...' He took a contemplative sip of gin. 'Shit, there's a word for it.'

'Bi-curious?' she supplied.

He slammed his glass on the table and pointed a finger at her. 'That's it. Bi-curious. I figure some of us our brave enough or, in my mum's case, unhappy enough to see where those urges take us.'

His theory sounded enlightened, especially for a guy as solidly heterosexual as he was. But then he did have a daughter who wanted to be a boy.

'Fair enough,' she said. 'But, be honest, have you ever wanted to shag another guy?'

He considered that for a minute. 'I guess not. But guys have wanted to shag me. And I found it pretty flattering, so that probably puts me on the spectrum.'

'Art! That's astonishing.' So astonishing, she couldn't quite believe it. He was so earthy and straightforward. The smell of him, the look of him, the gruff voice and surly silent charisma.

'What is?'

'You're a secret metrosexual.'

He chuckled. 'No shit.' He placed his glass on the table, then leaned forward, spreading his knees, to draw closer. 'Is that better than being a douche canoe?'

'Absolutely,' she murmured, distracted by the ticking pulse in his neck for the first time. He had a lovely neck, strong and muscular and not too wide, the shadow of his stubble visible from just above his Adam's apple. Reddened skin looped across his collarbone where he'd worn his T-shirt in the sun. The working man's tan. She got fixated on the well of his clavicle, thinking of the warm blood pulsating through the vein under the skin. And the salty taste that would gather on her tongue if she flicked it over the pulse point.

Warmth settled over the butterflies now jitterbugging in drunken glee.

'Have you ever kissed a girl?' The rough, low sound of his voice was even deeper than usual. The spice of awareness danced between them, the lingering aroma of Dee's vegetable moussaka overwhelmed by the phantom scent of sultry summer heat.

Her gaze rose from his throat. His irises were the colour of chocolate. Rich milk chocolate with hints of coffee and caramel. *Yum.*

'Don't tell me you're one of those guys who fantasises about women making out?' she said.

'Are you evading the question?' he said, evading the question. 'I have kissed a girl,' she murmured.

'Really?' His eyes flared as he lifted his hand, his big work-roughened hand. The long blunt finger trailed up her arm, tracing the veins in her wrist. She stared at the short blunt nails, the wide bridge of his knuckles, the nicks and cuts and abrasions from the physical labour he did with his hands every day – the jagged line that ran down the webbing between his thumb and his forefinger which she'd watched being sewn up three weeks ago – as the tip of his finger travelled all the way to her elbow. His finger swept across the inside, triggering a multitude of sensations, both brutally exciting and not exciting enough.

'What was it like?' he said, the husky tone of voice reverberating in her clitoris.

'Hot.' *But not as hot as this. Not even close.*

His thumb pressed into the inside of her elbow, as his fingers wrapped around her arm. He tugged her towards him, until his lips were only a whisper away from hers. 'Do guys kiss different to girls?'

She could smell the juniper sweetness of the gin on his breath, see the dilated pupils.

Who knew? Art was a cheap drunk.

Her insides clenched and released. The butterflies, their wings on fire, fluttered frantically. 'I couldn't tell you, I've never done a thorough comparison.'

He blinked, in slow motion, the thick lashes lowering and then rising again on half speed. 'I'm a little pissed,' he said. 'But I think we should remedy that.'

His other hand lifted to curl around her neck. The long fingers threading into her hair, the rough caress glorious against the sensitive skin of her nape. Until his large palm supported her skull.

Her hands fastened on his waist, dipping under the hem of his shirt to find warm, firm flesh.

'So do I,' she whispered.

His mouth captured hers, the press of his lips firm and wet and hot.

She opened for him as his tongue delved, her mind spinning, comparisons forgotten as he yanked her closer.

Heat shot like a fireball into her nipple as one big hand cupped her breast. Her thumbs pressed into his ribs to hold on to him as he sucked on her tongue. She delved back, getting deeper into the recesses of his mouth, chasing the sweet spice of the gin, the hot spice of arousal.

Her breathing hitched as he drew away then propped his forehead against hers. Strong fingers massaged her nape, anchoring her arm to his side.

'You're good at that.' He groaned.

'Ditto.' She chuckled – which had to be the gin.

Her fingertips slid back down to his waist and he shivered.

'So what's the verdict?' he said, his gruff voice thick with temptation. 'Guys or girls?'

'Hard to tell,' she said, his confidence contagious. 'I may need more evidence.'

He laughed, the sound deep and rough. His thumb circled the tight muscles in her shoulder – which relaxed and wept with joy, for the first time in months.

'If I kiss you again, I won't be able to stop,' he said. 'And we'll both regret it in the morning.'

'I know.' She straightened away from him, trying to clear the gin-soaked fog from her brain as her gaze roamed over that devastating face.

As she took in the tanned skin drawn tight across high cheekbones, the aquiline nose, the tapered brows, those wide lips, tipped up now in a tantalisingly lopsided smile, she knew that starting something with Art would not be a good idea, but that didn't make it any less tempting.

The possibility of having sex with a guy who might actually notice whether or not she had an orgasm was a pretty powerful mojo. And somehow she knew Art would notice.

'I should go to bed,' she said. Time to get her wayward mojo under control.

As she stood up, she swayed.

He stood too, resting a hand on her hip to steady her. 'You OK?'

'Yes, I'm just exceptionally drunk.' She glanced down at the now empty bottle of sloe gin. 'You're right, that stuff is lethal.'

He took her wrist as she turned to go. 'Hold on.'

Walking to the sink, he tugged her with him. He took a glass from the shelf above the sink, and filled it with water. He presented it to her.

'Drink it, or you'll wish you were dead in the morning.'

She chugged down the lot. He poured her another glass and she drank that too. She handed the glass back to him. 'Thanks.'

'Goodnight, Ellie,' he murmured.

She staggered out of the room, feeling dazed, and drunk and desperately disappointed.

CHAPTER FOURTEEN

Dee stood under the shower spray, the needle-sharp streams massaging the knotted muscles of her upper spine, and began to catalogue all the 'stuff' she had to do today as she waited for the hollow ache that was always there after dreaming of Pammy to subside.

She had two dozen loaves to bake for Gillingham market and, once that was done, she had a celebratory meal to plan for everyone to enjoy once the first phase of the barn clear-out was completed.

The forecast was for a balmy evening, so she would get Josh and Toto to help her put the trestle tables out in the yard, adding fairy lights and lanterns for an air of celebration – to symbolise the launching of this exciting new venture to secure the co-op's future. She smiled as she leaned into the mirror to apply moisturiser and suncream – thinking of all the high spirits and high fives yesterday evening at the news of the bank loan being approved – and ignored the new twinge in her back.

An array of salads would be perfect to start the feast – maybe the carrot and ginger, baked aubergine and mint yoghurt, plus some faro and roasted red pepper, she'd have to check her pantry.

She'd pick up fresh salmon to bake with lime and organic lamb for kebabs in Gillingham while she was at the farmers' market, maybe do a trade-off with Donald Allsop and Christy Jenkins who ran the relevant stalls – if not she knew they'd give her a good price. Perhaps she'd pull out the Yotam Ottolenghi cookbook Tess had given her for Christmas to spice up the menu with something new. She rarely stuck to the recipes verbatim, because where was the fun in that, but Yotam never failed to inspire her.

Her back twinged again. The only thing she needed to make sure of was that nothing on her menu required her to spend six hours standing at the stove stirring boiling fruit like she had yesterday while making gooseberry jam to stock the shop when it was ready.

She added a layer of concealer and rimmed her mouth with gloss. Maybe it was a vain indulgence, seeing as no one was going to see her who was likely to notice. She shrugged off the depressing thought as she dropped the lipstick back into her make-up bag. As she picked a shirt from the wardrobe, she spotted the one outfit of Pam's that she'd kept. The outfit Pam had worn to their civil partnership a year before her terminal cancer diagnosis.

Dee stroked the emerald green lace.

They'd been so stupidly happy that day, not knowing what was in store for them. Tucking the body-con dress behind a set of overalls, she closed the closet door on the painful memories, and the aching sense of loss that would never completely go away.

Pammy was gone now. And she wasn't ever coming back. But Ellie was here. And so was Josh. Life was so fickle and unpredictable, you needed to grab every ounce of happiness where you could.

Maybe today would be a good day to finally begin to breach the chasm that still existed between them, and ask Ellie about her life in America. She'd made a point of not pressing, not pushing Ellie for details, but it was becoming glaringly apparent that Ellie still hadn't mentioned Josh's father. Not once. Something was wrong, and Dee had begun to despair of Ellie ever coming to her.

She laced up her Converse pumps, tied her hair up and headed down the stairs. Would it really be so terrible to probe gently? Just to make sure everything was OK? If Ellie wasn't receptive, or it seemed too intrusive, she could always just back off again.

Dee brewed coffee in the quiet kitchen, got flour and yeast out and began measuring out by eye the ingredients in her bread maker for the morning batch. She grabbed some buttermilk from the pantry.

Sourdough today, with sunflower and poppy seeds. And maybe a focaccia with the sun-dried tomatoes she'd left soaking in olive oil yesterday. She'd make an extra couple of loaves to add to tonight's feast.

As she grabbed a couple of packets of yeast to add to the mix, the dull ache in her lower back returned. What she wouldn't give right now to feel Pammy's strong hands digging into the sore muscles, taking the pain away and replacing it with the delicious ache of sexual arousal. Dee blinked, the stinging in her tear duct surprising her.

She tipped the ingredients into a large earthenware bowl, and began dribbling in the water. She definitely needed the distraction of kneading by hand today.

She heard the tread of someone on the stairs.

Ellie wandered into the room, her eyes snapping shut as she covered her face with her forearm. 'Crap.'

'Everything all right?' Dee asked, concerned by the grey pallor of Ellie's skin as she reached over to tug the curtain closed. 'Do you want to go back to bed?' she asked. 'I could bring you up some tea?' It was barely six o'clock. And a Saturday. The back barn clear-out wasn't scheduled to start until midday, so no one else needed to be up at this ungodly hour on a weekend except her and Rob, who'd be busy in the dairy barn organising the milking.

Ellie slumped into one of the chairs.

'No tea,' she groaned. 'Just lots more water. This is all self-inflicted so I don't deserve your sympathy.'

Dee wiped her hands on her apron. Of course, Ellie had gone over to Annie's last night with Maddy and Tess.

'You got into this state getting a manicure?' she said, shocked. Maddy was young and occasionally reckless, but both Annie and Tess had young children and she wouldn't have expected them to drink to excess.

Ellie lifted bloodshot eyes. Dee winced, she could see the headache in them and it did not look pretty.

'No, your sloe gin did actually, once I got back here,' Ellie countered. 'And please keep your voice down or my head may shatter into a billion pieces.'

Dee filled a glass with home-made lemonade from the pitcher she kept in the fridge and hunted out a couple of extra-strength painkillers.

Ellie groaned her appreciation, then chased the painkillers with a long gulp of the lemonade.

Anxiety leapt in Dee's chest. She'd been trying to respect Ellie's boundaries, not to probe into her daughter's personal life until she was willing and eager to talk about it. But if something was wrong, she wanted Ellie to know she was here for her. The truth was, she hadn't been a mother to Ellie for nineteen years. Cooking and cleaning and redecorating wasn't enough. Ever since Ellie had made the choice to leave with her father, Dee had not been present in her daughter's life – the postcards and emails and home-made gifts she'd sent over the last four years could never replace all the things they'd lost that day. And that had always been Dee's fault for making decisions that had ultimately pushed her daughter away. It was way past time to remedy that.

Sitting down beside Ellie, she took her daughter's hand. 'Sweetheart, why were you drinking on your own? Is something the matter?'

'I wasn't drinking on my own precisely,' Ellie said, the pallor replaced by a burning in her cheeks. 'I had Art for company.'

'Art?' Dee said, trying for nonchalant and missing by several miles. 'That's…' *Astonishing? Intriguing?* 'Surprising,' she settled on.

Ellie didn't elaborate.

'I thought you and Art were avoiding each other?' she said.

'Not any more,' Ellie said, not sounding at all pleased about the new development.

Dee knew Art still had issues about the project, he'd been noticeably absent from the back barn roster – the only one of the co-op's members not to commit to devoting some time to the clear-out today. And, as part of her don't-get-in-Ellie's-face initiative, Dee had deliberately avoided making a comment about the obvious tension between the two of them.

But she'd ignored the animosity between Ellie and Art once before. During her first summer at the farm. At that time all she'd seen in Art was a boy whose desperate need for affection had made him do foolish things – and because of her pity for that boy, she had never taken Ellie's complaints about him seri-ously. Especially as they had died down after a while. She'd even become convinced Ellie had a little crush on him. But perhaps if she'd done more then, to support Ellie, her daughter wouldn't have felt so isolated.

The two of them were adults now and she needed to respect that. And intervening would feel a bit like trying to mediate between her two children, because Art had become like a son to her over the years. But that didn't mean she couldn't probe. Gently.

'Did something happen between you two last night?' Dee asked and watched the pink flags light up Ellie's cheeks.

OK, something definitely happened, the question is what?

*

'Nothing significant,' Ellie said, her cheeks burning like flamethrowers. 'We started drinking, and somehow managed to polish off a whole bottle of your sloe gin.'

And if my head didn't feel as if it was being crushed in an enormous vice, I might be able to lie about that with some conviction.

Had she seriously got tipsy with Art and snogged him last night? In the kitchen? And how on earth, when she was currently sporting a hangover that might well kill her, could she still remember every single minute detail of that kiss?

In way too much minute detail.

After nineteen years, she'd finally discovered what it felt like to have Art's mouth on hers and it had been so good. And so not good.

It was perfectly acceptable to entertain a few prurient thoughts about a guy over elderflower champagne and killer nail polish, it was quite another to go the full lip monty with him the first time you caught him alone.

Thank God Art had called a halt, or they may have ended up doing something even more dangerous. But what if he hadn't?

After a week of proving herself with the project, securing her role as an admin superstar and distancing herself from the one person who had the ability to totally screw up her whole summer, she'd plunged right off a cliff in the space of one kiss.

What was wrong with her? She was here to escape from the stupid decisions of her youth, not dig up more of them for a do-over.

She should not have kissed Art, but, even more worrying, why had he kissed her? The tiny part of her brain still capable of operating without pain had been trying to puzzle that one out for an hour and she hadn't come up with an obvious answer. She couldn't remember much of what had been said – metrosexual, bi-curious and arsehole were floating around in there somewhere, but that wasn't a lot of help. The only possible mitigating factor was that she had a vague recollection of Art being drunk too. So maybe that kiss wasn't part of some sneaky scheme to expose her frailties. That small consolation hadn't stopped the euphoria and confidence of the night before from plunging into the toilet this morning.

And now she had her mum, looking all fierce and protective on her behalf.

'A whole bottle?' Dee said, looking suitably shocked. 'Why did you do that?'

I know, right. 'I don't know, but if this hangover is anything to go by, it was a mistake that will not be repeated.' And it wasn't the only one.

'Is he still sulking about the shop?' Dee asked.

Ellie felt stupidly touched. So her mum thought Art was still being a dick about the shop too? Why did it feel so important to know that? She was not in competition with Art. Far from it, unfortunately.

'Yes, I think so,' she said. Although, to be honest it was hard to know how Art still felt about the shop, seeing as that was one thing they had not discussed, as far as she could remember.

'Well, I suppose it's a good thing that you're not avoiding each other any more?'

Not really. Actually, not at all.

Kissing men who disliked you and getting off on it was right up there in the annals of stupid decisions with marrying men that couldn't stay faithful and never getting off at all.

Dee got up and walked back around the kitchen table to punch the dough she'd been working on when Ellie had walked in.

The soft puff of air escaping sounded like a jet engine landing inside Ellie's head.

'Can I ask you a question, Ellie?'

'I suppose.' *Please don't let it be about Art.*

'What's going on with Josh's father?'

Please don't let it be about that either.

'Why do you ask?' Ellie said, in a pathetic attempt to stall for time. She was so not ready to have this conversation while her head was exploding – and damage limitation on her latest catastrophe was still one life-threatening hangover away.

'You never speak with him when he Skypes Josh,' her mother said. 'And I wondered why he didn't come with you?' Dee sprinkled flour over the kitchen table and plopped the dough on top. 'Three months is a long time for Josh and you to be away from him, and for you to be away from your business.' Dee plunged her knuckles into the dough, and began to stretch and tear it. 'I just wanted to make sure everything was all right?'

Emotion Ellie hadn't even realised was there burned her larynx, as she suddenly envisioned herself as Dee's ball of dough being contorted into all sorts of impossible positions.

'It's complicated,' she finally managed to mumble.

'I'm sure it is, marriages always are,' her mother said, the understanding in her voice somehow unbearably poignant.

No wonder she didn't want to tell her mum about Dan and the divorce. Because it would force her to admit how stupid she had been – about her determination to keep her marriage going no matter what. A part of her had always condemned her mum for giving up too easily, for not trying harder to resist Pam, to make things work with her dad, but what if her mum had just been a great deal braver and more honest than she was?

At least her mum had loved Pam, while Ellie wasn't entirely convinced she had ever really loved Dan.

What she'd been was dazzled by his golden boy good looks, and his confidence and charm. When they'd first met, she'd been doing grunt work on a J-1 visa at the Marshall Creek Summer Camp in Sarasota and Dan had been the camp's sailing instructor. Impossibly cute and so effortlessly sexy, he could make every person at the camp with ovaries, and quite a few without, hyperventilate.

At the time, she'd convinced herself she was special. The only one who could make him hyperventilate back, during all those sweaty, furtive encounters in the boathouse after lights out, which had eventually produced Josh.

If only she'd known then what she knew now, that Dan had never been hyperventilating just for her.

'Dan and I are getting a divorce. He got Josh's middle school teacher pregnant. I thought it would be good for Josh and I to be away from Orchard Harbor for the summer when everyone finds out.'

'Oh Ellie, I...'

'Wait, that's not all,' she said, to halt the outpouring of support she wasn't sure she deserved. 'I don't have to worry about taking a break from my business, because...' She hesitated. Why was this the hardest part? She thought of Art's accusations last Friday. That would be why.

'It's a total disaster. In fact, I don't really have a business any more.' She stared down at her hands, feeling sick with humiliation and guilt. 'Once I kicked Dan out of the house, all my clients deserted me, because I no longer had the kudos of being Senator Granger's daughter-in-law. And why would anyone else want to hire Events by Eloise when it was owned by a woman who had been cheated on all over town and had pretended not to notice.'

Surely that was the worse part, that ever since she'd first caught Dan cheating, she'd secretly known he'd never stopped, but she'd kept the façade of her perfect marriage to Senator Granger's son going for the sake of appearances and little else. She'd kidded herself she'd been keeping it going for Josh, but how could that be true, when Dan had given their son almost as little attention as he gave her?

She gulped down the last of her lemonade, the tart sweet taste doing nothing to ease the dryness in her throat.

'Maybe Art's right to be sceptical about my abilities to pull this off,' she said. 'I went to see him after the meeting when we agreed the project and he made it clear he thinks this is just a vanity project for me, that I'm just using it to pass the time until I go home.'

'Art had absolutely no right to say that.' The total and utter faith in her mother's voice made tears well up Ellie's throat.

'I swear that's genuinely not true,' Ellie said, the need to prove herself to her mother suddenly paramount. 'I really want the shop to work. But maybe he's right to be wary. I've failed at my marriage and my business. What if I'm just using this project as a chance to shore up my confidence after all those other screw ups. And what happens if I screw this up, too?'

Her mother swooped down, pressing flour-covered palms to her clammy cheeks. 'You're not going to screw it up.' Dee gripped her head, to get the message across. 'And you're not a failure. Frankly, it sounds like your husband failed in the marriage, not you.'

'The shop might not be a success though.' Did her mother understand that? That she might lose everything Pam had left her? 'It's a risk.'

'And it's a risk we're all willing to take because real failure would be not taking that chance and letting the co-op die by slow degrees through our own inaction.' Dee folded Ellie into a hug.

'Art doesn't think so,' Ellie said against her mother's bosom. The pointless tears started to make her sinuses ache almost as much as her head.

'That's because Art finds it next to impossible to trust anyone, after what happened with Laura and then with Alicia.'

Alicia? Who's Alicia?

Ellie shut the question down. Because thinking about Art just made her head hurt more.

'Does Josh know? About the divorce?' her mother said.

Ellie shook her head. 'I don't know how to tell him.'

How had her mother handled it?

'I don't want to ruin his summer,' she added. 'He's having such a good time. He's even enjoying going to school with Toto.'

The novelty of his accent and his encyclopedic knowledge of Pokémon and the Marvel Universe had transformed him from the weird kid to the cool kid and he was loving it.

'Then don't tell him yet,' her mother said, making it sound so simple.

How would she handle it if Josh responded the same way she had to the news? With tantrums and diva strops and endless complaints? Not that Josh was likely to do that, because it wasn't in his nature to have a diva strop, but even so...

Ellie began to shake, the enormity of everything she'd been avoiding closing in on her. Her mother clasped her harder, the smell of fresh herbs and yeast surrounded her.

'But every time I think about it...' Or every time she avoided thinking about it. 'Every time I hear him talking to Dan.' And every time she avoided talking to Dan too, in case he brought it up and asked why she hadn't told Josh yet. 'I feel so dishonest.'

'It's not dishonest, there's no rush,' Dee said. 'I piled so much onto you when I brought you here,' she murmured against her hair. 'Much more than you were capable of handling and, as a result, I lost you. That you're being cautious is not a sign of failure or dishonesty. It's a sign of your selflessness and your love.'

Ellie clung on to her mother. And hugged her tight, really tight, for the first time since she was a little girl. She could feel the rise and fall of her mother's breathing, that solid strength that had always been there, and that had been gone when she returned to London with her father.

'I did so many things wrong that summer.' Her mother's breast rose and fell as she gave a heavy sigh. 'Pam and I should have waited longer to come here, but she was…' Her mother's voice faltered and Ellie shifted back to look into her mother's face.

Unlined and pale, Dee's face appeared younger than her years, but today Ellie could see the grief, that hollow sadness that would never lift.

'You and Pam were together?' she asked. 'Before that summer?'

'Yes, we'd been seeing each other for two years. Your father and I hadn't had a physical relationship for a long time.'

Ellie sniffed. 'Two years? But you never said anything?' How had her mother kept that a secret for so long?

She thought of Pammy, the woman she'd tried so hard to hate that summer, but who had never shown her anything but consideration.

'Why hadn't you and Dad had a physical relationship for years?' Had her mother always been a lesbian then?

Dee sat down heavily beside her, studied her hands, twisting the ring she always kept on her finger, the ring Pam had given her.

'He cheated on me the first time, less than a year after we married. He couldn't be faithful, and I tried to ignore it at first, but eventually there wasn't really any need to, because we lived separate lives in the same house. He had a mistress and I didn't mind.' Her mother sent her a weak smile that spoke of how much she'd endured.

Ellie felt the twist of humiliation in her own chest, recalling all those times she had gone to an event in Orchard County with Dan, and known her husband wasn't being faithful. And every time she'd made a conscious decision to ignore the evidence.

'When I met Pammy,' Dee said, 'I discovered what it was actually like to be in love. Passionately in love. And I realised

I had never felt that way about your father. So no wonder he wasn't faithful to me.'

Ellie took her mother's hands, and rubbed her thumbs across the knuckles, slightly swollen from all the hours she put in kneading dough or stirring something. The map of tiny cuts, the red mark across the base of the thumb where she must have burned herself.

She met her mum's gaze, the pale blue eyes misty with tears. 'If he couldn't remain faithful, that's his fault not yours. He didn't deserve you.'

Just like Dan hadn't deserved her.

'And anyway it was Pam you loved.'

Her mother's lips curled on one side, the smile weak, but there. 'I know. But I always loved you more than anything. You were my child. And because I chose to stay here, you stopped believing that.'

'You couldn't have stayed with him, and I made the choice to go back to London, so what choice did you have?' Why had it taken her so long to see this?

Her mother touched her cheek. 'Don't let me off so lightly, Ellie. You were a child and I was your mother. I've been over the events of that summer again and again over the years, once we'd grown so far apart, and I tried to figure out what I could have done differently. And I came to the conclusion, it was a mistake to bring you here. A selfish decision I made without taking your feelings into account.' She glanced around the cosy country kitchen, and for the first time Ellie saw it through her mother's eyes. How much she'd done to the place. 'It wasn't ready. You weren't ready.'

Ellie squeezed her mum's hand. 'I'm ready now, and so is this place. You've made it into something really beautiful, Mum. Josh loves it here.'

Her mother turned her hand palm up, and squeezed back. 'I'm glad.'

As she helped her mother with the bread making, the painkillers finally kicked in. She felt lighter, more in control, less fragile, the gut-wrenching feeling of anxiety – that had haunted her ever since the day she'd been eviscerated by Caroline Myerson over a crust-less crab salad sandwich when the woman had sacked her over afternoon tea in the Myerson Memorial Golf Club – was gone for the first time in a month.

She didn't feel so alone any more. Her father's infidelity had given her a connection with her mum she had not expected, and she had her new friends – Tess, Annie and Maddy – to do silly girly things with. And she had a ton of challenging exciting work to keep herself busy…

Which ought to prevent her from doing any more silly girly things with Art.

And thankfully Art was still refusing to get involved with the project, so once they got stuck into the construction, she'd be unlikely to see him much. Plus, she was embarking on a lifetime sloe gin ban.

All good.

And she was totally not interested in finding out about Alicia. Not. At. All.

CHAPTER FIFTEEN

Art crouched on the front steps of the bow-top Romany caravan, scratching the label on the beer he'd pulled out of the van's icebox, and watched the merriment in the farmyard below.

They'd been at it most of the day and evening, clearing the years and years worth of junk out of the back barn. And now they were reaping their reward, tucking into the feast Dee had spent hours preparing. George Michael belted out some golden oldie from the eighties, the lyrics bouncing over the coppice woods in the muggy evening towards Art's perch at the top of the rise. It wasn't full dark yet, but the fairy lights Dee and the kids had strung across the yard twinkled in the half-light adding a festive flavour to the occasion as everyone settled onto the bench seats, filling their plates from the bowls and platters Dee had laid out on a side table.

While he sat up on the hill alone, having somehow morphed into Shrek.

They were planning another whole day of it tomorrow to get the building ready for the concrete mixer arriving on Monday. The heavy construction needed was minimal – replacing the ground slab and sandblasting and then repointing the brickwork was all that was necessary. He knew because he'd assessed the structure five years ago for Pam's planning application. The barn itself was solid and already fit for purpose – give or take twenty years of accumulated crap. The bulk of the work to convert it into commercial premises would be in the fit-out. They'd need to add a customer toilet, sort out the plumbing and electrics, build in the shelving and cabinets and the kitchen units. And then he guessed Dee would supervise the decorating. But if they were going for a rustic look, which made sense, he doubted she'd go overboard on fancy design stuff.

Five weeks in total according to the business plan Ellie had done, which he'd spent the last week deciphering. The schedule would be tight. Very tight. To make it work, they'd need a good project manager. However much of an admin ninja Ellie was, he would bet his left nut she knew sod all about construction.

He did. He'd run the project to convert the dairy barn with Rob. And even though he had found the reading and writing part hard, he was certified as both a plumber and electrician.

He'd been mulling it over for the last week, ever since the original planning meeting and his argument with Ellie in the workshop. Maybe he'd underestimated her. The passion and determination in her eyes surprised him. And did it really matter what her motives were? He still had reservations about the whole thing, but when he'd heard about the bank loan being approved yesterday, his last chance of talking sense into everyone had been shot. Pam's farm shop was happening, whether he wanted it to or not.

As he'd sat in the deserted kitchen last night, eating alone for the sixth night in a row, he'd been considering speaking to Ellie the next morning and offering his services. If for no other reason than to make sure she and the rest of the amateurs didn't screw it up. If they were going to do this thing, they needed to do it right.

But that was before Ellie had stumbled into the kitchen at midnight, half-cut and far too cute in her tight jeans and mad hair, and challenged him to a drinking contest. The sloe gin and his reckless libido had done the rest.

She'd tasted nothing like the way he'd once imagined she would. Not that he'd imagined kissing her back then, if he could help it. She'd been a kid. A pushy, smart-arsed, pampered kid who thought she was better than him, so why the bloody hell would he want to kiss her? But the day before she'd left the commune, there had been one moment when he had not been completely immune.

That insane split second urge had come back to torture him ever since Ellie had returned. But it wasn't until last night that the enormity of the problem had surfaced.

She'd been squinting at him, listening to some rubbish he was spouting off the top of his head about human sexuality – where had *that* come from? Her eyes had been all squiffy and unfocused, but sheened with something that his trashed brain had taken to be admiration, and the only coherent thought running through his head had been the same as the one from that day nineteen years ago.

I want to taste you.

But this time, he'd been unable to resist acting on it. And instead of being sweet and proper and stuck up, Ellie's taste had been raw, needy and real enough to make him moan.

Even at fourteen, Ellie Preston had not been good for his mental health. Now she was a disaster zone.

He lifted the lid on the icebox at his feet and dumped the unopened bottle of beer back inside. Booze had got him into this pickle.

Kissing Ellie would have been bad back in the nineties, when she'd been young and annoying and he'd been monumentally screwed up, but kissing her now felt worse. Not only was Ellie married, she was also heading up a project that could mess up all their lives if it failed, and she was the prodigal daughter Dee had been desperate to welcome back ever since Pam's death.

What if Ellie told Dee what she'd told him a week ago, about why she'd left that summer? Would Dee think he was nothing more than a big fat cuckoo who had kicked her own child out of the nest, to move in himself? It hadn't been like that, he hadn't meant it to be like that, but that's what it would look like.

And then Dee would have to choose between him and Ellie, and she wasn't going to choose him. Because no one ever had, not even his own mother.

How could he offer to be the project manager now? It would only make him look more guilty. More desperate for an affection he wasn't even sure he deserved any more.

Maybe he could give Rob some pointers and persuade him to take on the job. It would save the expense of getting an outside contractor. And keep him well out of Ellie's orbit for the rest of the summer, which was clearly where he needed to be before he gave in to any more suicidal urges.

Of course, he'd have to offer to take over Rob's early morning milking schedule. But having to get up at 4 a.m. each day for a month to commune with a load of cows ought to teach him to keep his stupid mouth away from Ellie's.

He listened to the indistinguishable murmur of conversation drifting up from the farmyard now that Dee had turned down George. Josh and Toto shouted and laughed, getting chased round the yard by one of the Jackson twins, while the adults sat jammed together finishing their meal in the twilight.

His gaze tracked instinctively to Ellie, who was tucked in between Jacob and Rob, her blonde hair shining in the glimmer of the fairy lights. He ran his tongue over his lips, tasting the perfumed echo of the gin. His pulse spiked at the memory of her soft sob of breath. The darting licks of her tongue as she explored his mouth.

He adjusted his jeans, feeling the pressure as the blood flowed into his lap.

He definitely needed to stay away from her.

'I thought I'd find you up here.'

He jolted at the sound of Dee's voice as her figure separated from the shadow of the trees.

'I brought you some supper.' She lifted the plate of food she held. 'No need for you to go hungry while you sulk.' She breathed deeply as she made her way to the top of the small hill.

'I'm not sulking.' *If only it were that simple.*

Dee sent him a sceptical side eye as she handed him the plate then produced a knife and fork wrapped in a napkin from the back pocket of her jeans.

'Then why didn't you come down to have supper with the rest of us?'

He perched the plate on his knees, and picked up a kebab. Tearing a cube of lamb off with his teeth, he took his time chewing the spicy, succulent meat.

She waited for him to swallow.

As they sat together in the gathering darkness, the fairy lights from the farmyard illuminating the scene below, the guilt felt as if it might choke him.

Who was he kidding? Maybe he hadn't deliberately tried to make Ellie leave that summer, but he had been a total shit to her most of the time. And the reason for that, it seemed so obvious now, was jealousy. She'd had Dee and he hadn't. What would he do if he lost Dee's friendship? If she stopped caring about him sitting up here on his own? If she stopped worrying about whether he'd eaten or not? He'd always hated being fussed over, but what if Dee never fussed over him again? He was so used to it now he would miss it.

'I had some stuff to finish up in the workshop,' he said, in answer to her question – an answer that was almost true.

'Then why are you sitting all the way up here on your own instead of finishing up that stuff in the workshop?'

She had him there.

'Because I finished and I wanted some quiet.' That was better, more convincing. 'I wasn't in the mood for company.' Which was actually true. He certainly wasn't in the mood for a particular person's company.

'So is this a problem with the project still, or is it Ellie?'

The fork he'd been using to shovel up a mouthful of Dee's salad selection clattered onto the plate. 'What?'

Dee sighed. 'Are you still sulking about the project going ahead, or is this an issue with Ellie? Because she spoke to me this morning, in the grips of a terrible hangover, and told me you two had come to an accord.'

An accord? Is that what they were calling it?

'We had a few drinks, that was all.' Panic skittered up his spine. What else had Ellie told her mother? 'And I told you I'm not sulking.' *Much*.

'She also told me what you accused her of after our initial project meeting.'

Oh hell. The guilt hissed and twisted inside him like a snake. 'I've got legitimate concerns about the project.'

'Which have been duly noted,' Dee said, patiently. She didn't sound angry, just resigned. He wasn't sure what was worse. 'And, as I told you then, you don't have to protect me, to protect any of us. Ellie didn't come up with this idea all on her own. We came up with it together. So you need to stop being so hostile towards her.'

She knew. He could hear it in her voice. The disappointment. The distance. Ellie had told her everything. All the stupid, nasty things he'd done as a teenager to push her away, to make her feel like dirt, and now Dee was here to cut him loose. And, the worst of it was, he knew on some level he deserved it.

He ducked his head, staring at the plate half full of the colourful salads she'd brought up to him, not hungry any more. 'I'm sorry, I never meant to make her go,' he said, resigned too now.

His relationship with Dee would never be the same again. But whose fault was that? Ever since Ellie had returned, it had been bound to come out. What an arse wipe he'd been as a kid. He'd been hostile towards Ellie as soon as she had reappeared, because he'd been scared. Maybe if he'd managed to stay away from Ellie, managed not to let all those self-destructive urges come out of hiding last night, he wouldn't have exposed himself to this. But he hadn't and now Dee knew. That she'd spent nineteen years without a daughter, because of him.

'Could you be more specific about what you're apologising for?' Dee said.

'I didn't mean to make her leave that summer. I actually liked her,' he said in his defence, trying to explain the unexplainable. 'But I didn't really figure that out until she'd gone and by then it was too late.' He was talking nonsense, like a politician trying to cover his tracks.

Dee pressed a hand to his thigh. 'Art, look at me.'

He turned, steeling himself for the contempt he expected, but all she did was smile. The kind, caring smile he had come to rely on without even realising it.

'What on earth are you talking about?' she said.

She didn't know. For a moment, relief surged. Ellie hadn't said anything. Why hadn't Ellie said anything? Had it been the kiss? Maybe she hadn't been as freaked out about it as he had? Was that a good thing? But, as Dee continued to smile at him, her brows furrowed, waiting for a coherent answer, the relief fizzled out. Maybe she didn't know yet, but he was going to have to tell her. And take the risk, because he could not live with this hanging over him.

'I thought Ellie told you,' he said.

'Told me what?'

'That the reason she left that day with her dad was because of me. She came to see me the afternoon before, and I made her cry.'

She sighed, but the smile didn't falter. 'Oh, Art, don't be an idiot.'

OK, that wasn't the reaction he'd expected. He guessed it had to be better than what he had been expecting, but the smile seemed almost pitying now, which couldn't be good. 'Why does that make me an idiot?'

'Ellie didn't leave because of you.'

'Yes, she did, she told me she did, a week ago.' He wasn't sure why he was arguing the point, but it seemed important to come clean about it all.

'She left for a whole host of reasons,' Dee said. 'I'm sure your behaviour towards her didn't help, and she may even have persuaded herself it was the cause, but the truth was she was vulnerable then, and so were you. And I was the one who didn't recognise that. It was my job to make her feel secure and loved, not yours.'

'But you don't know all the things I–'

'And I don't want to know.' Dee pressed a finger to his lips, halting the confession he was about to make. 'You were a child back then, unloved and broken, nothing you did then would change my opinion of you now.'

'Thanks.' He ducked his head, embarrassed by how much that meant to him.

She touched his cheek, forcing his gaze back to hers. 'Didn't it ever occur to you that once Ellie left, I needed you, too?'

'I guess not.'

'I'll admit my affection for you at first was probably transference. When Laura ran off with Rupert, I knew I could be useful to you and being useful helped me deal with losing Ellie.' Moisture collected at the corners of her eyes.

Panic gripped him again. 'Jesus, Dee, please don't cry. I didn't mean to remind you of all that.'

She sniffed and wiped a thumb under her eyelid to collect the drop. 'Don't be silly. I'm not sad. Ellie's back now and we're going to rebuild our relationship. We've already made a good start.'

'Then why are you crying?'

'I'm sad that you still don't realise how important you are, to me and Toto and everyone else here.'

'Not that important,' he said. 'I managed to totally screw up the farm's management.'

However badly he'd treated Ellie way back when, and however stupid the decision to kiss her last night while she was pissed, he could have done without her pointing out to the whole co-op what a loser he was as a manager.

'Stop it,' Dee said, impatiently. 'You took on a job you hated, because I asked you to, and you never once complained. And the farm's financial situation is not your fault. You need to stop blaming yourself all the time. You did the same with Alicia and it drove me mad.'

His stomach plummeted. Please God, they were not going to talk about Alicia now. How had a simple apology turned into his worst nightmare?

'Alicia was fragile,' he said. 'I screwed her, got her pregnant and then kicked her out. Toto doesn't have a mother because I made a mess of things.'

'Alicia was a twenty-six-year-old woman and you were seventeen when you first started screwing each other on a regular basis, so I think you're kidding yourself if you think you seduced her.'

Dee's crude assessment of his affair with Alicia was a slap to his pride, but the revelation that Dee had known about them from the start added a nice thick layer of humiliation.

'You didn't mess up Alicia,' Dee stressed. 'She had serious addiction issues, which she made no effort to solve. You did the right thing kicking her out and Toto is better off because of it.'

Was she? There was something Ellie had shouted at him her first day on the farm that had been torturing him ever since. And he couldn't hold on to his guilt about that a moment longer.

'Toto wants to be a boy,' he said. 'How is that better off?' His daughter had gender identity issues for Chrissake.

'Toto doesn't want to be a boy,' Dee said, dismissing his fears with an impatient flick of her wrist. 'She wants to be like you. But, even if she did want to be a boy, why would that be a bad thing?'

'Because she's not one?' Wasn't it obvious? What exactly were they talking about now? This was precisely why he didn't get involved in these sorts of conversations. They never made any sense.

'Does Toto strike you as a child who is unhappy in her own skin?' Dee asked him sternly.

'No... I... I guess not.'

'Then stop talking nonsense.' She glanced at his plate. 'Are you going to finish that?'

He scooped another forkful of salad, grateful that they weren't talking about his failings as a father any more. Or about Ellie. Because even if Dee was OK with what had happened nineteen years ago, he didn't think she would be OK with what had happened last night.

He ate in silence. His appetite returned as he shovelled the cacophony of salad flavours into his mouth, chewed off another bite of the lamb.

Everyone was packing the tables and chairs away in the farmyard. He scanned the shadows for Ellie, but couldn't find her. His stomach dipped as a light turned on in the farmhouse kitchen. He scraped the plate.

Dee stood and took it from him. 'Can I ask you a favour?'

'Sure,' he said, hoping it wasn't going to involve any more in-depth discussions about his past screw ups.

'We need you to be project manager.'

'Rob can do it. I can offer to handle the milking. I don't have time to...'

'Can't you make time?' Dee cut through the excuse with a smile of encouragement. 'Ellie's under a huge amount of pressure with this project. She's handling all the permits and licences, trying to sort out a grant with the Rural Enterprise Advisor, liaising with the FARMA rep, speaking to the council about getting all the certificates we need to confirm the planning situation, working out produce rotas and me, her and Tess are going to be spending two days in Somerset next week at an intensive farm-shop management course. On top of all that, she's emotionally fragile, she's come here while in the middle of divorcing her husband.'

She's what? A shot of adrenaline had his just-eaten meal dancing in time with his pulse.

'Now that you're speaking to each other again–' Dee was still talking while his mind reeled from the news '–there's nothing stopping you from working together. Rob hasn't got anywhere near as much experience as you. So you're the best one to take on the project manager's role.'

What could he say? He'd just got through acknowledging how much Dee meant to him. He'd never be able to repay her for all the support she'd shown him over the years. And she was right, on paper he looked like the perfect fit for the job.

But the next five weeks would be hell. Not only would he have to pull eighteen-hour days to keep the project on schedule and make sure he didn't slip up with this, the way he'd slipped up with the farm's financials, but Ellie would be there with him, every step of the way. Ellie and her lips promising that tart, sexy taste that he had not been able to resist last night. How would he stand it?

But then Dee said: 'Please, Art, do this for me.' And he knew he couldn't refuse.

'OK.'

'Thank you.' Dee leant down and kissed his forehead. 'Do you want to come down and tell Ellie now? She'll be so pleased.'

He shook his head. He doubted that. And, if by some miracle

she was, she might get out the sloe gin again to celebrate and then where would they be?

'You tell her. I can go over the logistics tomorrow while we finish clearing out the barn.' And when he'd be guaranteed to have an audience of at least twelve people.

'We? So you're joining us for the rest of the clear-out?' Dee sounded so pleased, he felt like even more of a fraud.

'If I'm going to be project manager, I need to get acquainted with my crew.' And keep busy enough to forget about one of them. 'I think I'll stay in the van tonight,' he added.

Dee nodded. She was used to him sleeping up here on his own when he needed a people break and he certainly needed one now. He'd originally built the thing for Toto's sixth birthday, so they could have some father–daughter bonding time away from everyone. They'd roast marshmallows, get tucked up in their sleeping bags, and he'd usually nod off while he listened to Toto's motormouth commentary on her latest favourite book or TV show, because with Toto there was rarely a gap in the conversation. But they hadn't used it much in the last few years, and they hadn't been up here at all this summer, not since Josh had arrived.

'I'll see you tomorrow.' Dee brushed a hand over his hair. The familiar touch which he'd taken for granted so often – made his chest hurt.

She lit the lantern to lead herself back through the darkness, but turned as she reached the treeline. 'By the way, don't mention the divorce to Josh, or Toto. Josh doesn't know about it yet. Ellie's waiting to find the right time to discuss it with him. So she doesn't ruin his summer with the news.'

Lucky Josh.

He wished someone could have kept the news from him too.

Dee disappeared into the trees, and then reappeared down below, the lantern bobbing as she came out of the woods and headed into the farmhouse.

He reached back into the icebox.

Even without Jacob and Maddy within earshot breaking the sound barrier, he had a feeling he wasn't going to be getting a lot of sleep tonight. The damage to his peace of mind had already been done.

He was having a bloody beer.

CHAPTER SIXTEEN

'Jacob, wait up, where are you headed?' Ellie raced out of the farmhouse to waylay Jacob as he crossed the farmyard.

'The lumber yard, near Gratesbury. Art needs me to pick up some extra wood for the shelving in the condiments section.' Jacob tugged open the truck door, the smile on his face weary and forced.

Ellie's sympathy spiked. According to Maddy, Jacob's passionate defender while she and Dee had been busy every evening making jams and preserves to stock the shop, Art had been a monster in the last week. They were now three weeks into the fit-out and it was on schedule. But Ellie knew Art and his crew, which included Jacob and Mike, had been putting in a lot of extra hours to keep it that way. And Art wasn't the most tactful person at the best of times. She also knew that Jacob wasn't getting a lot of sleep at night, because neither was she.

She'd tried pointing out to Maddy that maybe less sex and more sleep would make everyone less grumpy, but Maddy hadn't taken the hint.

'Perfect. I need a lift into Gratesbury,' she said. 'I've got some paperwork to go through with Rick Chastain at the Rural Enterprise Office about the grant.'

'Climb aboard.' Jacob gripped her elbow to help her into the cab, then got in on the driver's side. 'How's the grant looking?'

'Very positive. Rick thinks we'll get it no problem. It's going to cover the cost of all the second-hand equipment we've ordered for the kitchen and café, which is great.' She'd spent hours last week with Dee and Annie scouring a second-hand catering equipment barn in Andover and had managed to buy everything they needed for a lot less than they'd budgeted for, leaving enough to buy some extras, including a state-of-the-art espresso machine. 'And the cost of the signage for the A30 *and* the A303.'

'That's cool.' Jacob pulled off the sweat-soaked bandana covering his forehead and wiped the back of his neck. He really did look shattered. She had to have another word with Maddy. Young love was all well and good, but she didn't want one of their crew having a heart attack from too much sex, especially not before the shop was ready. That the rhythmic thuds and occasional moans from Jacob's room every night were also keeping her on edge when she really did not need to be was another consideration.

'Who's doing the signs?' Jacob asked.

He reversed out of the car park and drove along the farm track, the truck coasting down the newly laid asphalt without a single bump.

'We're going to use Helena Jacobs again.' The gorgeous hammered bronze sign she'd done for the co-op five years ago would be replicated in neon for the hoardings which Ellie was having put up two weeks from now.

Ellie's insides twitched and quivered at the thought of everything that still needed to be done before the grand opening on Saturday the fifth of August. Even without the noise coming from Jacob's room every night, sleep would probably still have eluded her – the many to-do lists she had on the go bouncing in her mind's eye like malevolent hyperactive sheep.

Maybe she should consider pushing the launch back? To give them all a chance to relax and take stock before they started welcoming their customers. When she and Tess and Dee had attended the Setting Up a Farm Shop course a week ago run by FARMA at Wellhaven Farm, the instructor had pointed out that great customer service was key to making any farm shop a success. Customers would be looking for personal, friendly, upbeat service. It was difficult for anyone to do friendly and upbeat when they were exhausted. If they didn't take a breather, they could all end up breathing fire like Art over their new clientele.

They needed to be on their best game when the shop opened, especially her, Dee and Tess, who would be doing the bulk of the shopkeeping.

Why not put back the launch for a week? They could organise a little social event for everyone to celebrate finishing the shop, and then take a leisurely week to get ready? She'd have to reorganise some of the social media campaigns she'd been working on, talk to the team and check nothing else would be affected, but otherwise she couldn't see a problem.

Ellie added the thought to the to-do list in her head marked: 'Brilliant ideas you don't have time to think about until it's too late to do anything about them'. Her stress kicked up another notch.

Jacob grunted a reply as they sped down the A30 towards Gratesbury. Ellie noticed his fingers white-knuckling on the wheel. Had Art been more of a dragon than usual today? Even when tired, Jacob usually had a joke or a cheeky smile on hand to cheer up the biggest grump.

'Is everything going OK on the build?' she asked.

'Yeah, sure, give or take the odd screw up,' Jacob said, but she noticed his fingers bunch at the fairly innocuous question. He was wound tighter than a ball of high-tension wire. 'Most of which are mine,' he murmured under his breath. But she heard the comment as he switched on the radio.

The cab filled with the sound of Rihanna Finding Love in a Hopeless Place. For some reason Ellie had a flashback to Art and that kiss three weeks ago now.

She'd seen very little of him since. Except the day he'd turned up to help with the second day of the barn clear-out, and told her he would take over the project management. She'd been so surprised, and so grateful, she hadn't questioned him about his sudden change of heart. And avoiding each other had been easy after that day, because she was mostly locked in her office – or rather his office – or in the kitchen helping Dee with the food prep and rotas, or on her course. While Art had been supervising the construction crew and then organising the fit-out. And doing a spectacular job despite all the gripes from Maddy about his arsey behaviour.

Art's arsey tendencies were beginning to look totally under-appreciated when it came to getting this project in on time. She'd wandered past the barn a few times in the last fortnight, usually to track down Toto and Josh and drag them home for supper, and every time she had, she'd spied him up a ladder, or contorted under a counter busy hammering, or screwing or sanding in the lamplight.

Art was the last to leave most nights and the first to arrive every morning and also living proof that men in toolbelts had a hunk factor off the charts.

So if Jacob was having a tough time with him, while Ellie

sympathised, she would feel like a hypocrite if she sympathised too much. But maybe finding out what exactly was putting that tension into Jacob's voice, and making this project so miserable for him, was something she could do. As much as she didn't want to intervene between Art and his crew, he wasn't always the most empathetic of people. Perhaps he could do with some help from her, behind the scenes, to smooth things over.

She switched off the radio. 'Are you sure everything's OK, Jacob?'

He gave her a quizzical look that didn't quite convince. 'Sure.'

'Maddy said you and Art have been having a few run-ins...' She gave him a lead in.

He shrugged. 'It's nothing major. Maddy was exaggerating.'

From the totally defeated look on Jacob's face, Ellie didn't think Maddy was exaggerating.

'I know everyone's tired,' she persevered, determined to get to the bottom of the problem, 'and this has been a tough schedule, but if Art's being unreasonable, I can have a word with him.' Even though she'd rather saw off an arm than have to talk to him face to face, especially in that toolbelt.

Jacob shook his head. 'He's not being unreasonable. I've been screwing up. He's entitled to jump on me when that happens.'

'How bad are the screw ups?' Ellie asked.

Jacob tapped his thumb on the steering wheel, looking more miserable by the second. 'Pretty bad. I misread the plans and cut the wood to the wrong length yesterday for the shelves, which is why we're having to get in a new batch now. And I left the drill charging overnight, and blew out the battery.'

That didn't sound great, especially the bit about buying new lumber, as the budget was tight. She could see why Art would be unhappy, but making Jacob more stressed wasn't going to help.

'I don't know what's wrong with me. I've worked on tons of construction projects before I came here,' Jacob said. 'None of which mean as much to me as this one. But I just can't seem to get my head in the game. Art's right to be mad with me. I've been behaving like a twat.'

Ellie patted his knee. 'First of all, you have to stop beating yourself up, or you're just going to get more stressed and make more mistakes.'

'I suppose.'

'Perhaps you should also consider suggesting to Maddy that she stay in her own room for the next couple of nights.'

Jacob turned to her, his face colouring – which meant he had to be exhausted, because she'd never seen him embarrassed before. 'You can hear us?'

'I'm not deaf. And those walls are not sound-proofed either.' She remembered what it had been like between her and Dan when they'd first got together at the summer camp, and even after their wedding. The sex had been constant. A terrific way to avoid all the stuff that they didn't have in common, like constancy and trust and maturity. Then the sex had become like a chore, Dan had been distracted, uninterested and she had quickly become uninterested too. There had really been no way back from that, once she'd discovered why Dan wasn't that interested in making her feel desired any more, because he was too busy servicing loads of other women.

'I'm sorry,' Jacob said. 'That's pretty mortifying.'

'It's not that bad,' she said, cutting Jacob some slack. 'But really it might be in your best interests too to give yourselves a bit of a rest. Particularly you. You're doing hard physical labour during the day so you need your sleep at night.' They all did.

Jacob nodded. 'I just… I don't know how to tell Maddy no. I don't want her to feel rejected on top of everything else.'

'On top of what else?'

Unlike her and Dan, it was obvious Jacob and Maddy had a great deal more going on in their relationship. You just had to see them together to know that, chatting and grinning at each other like idiots. Surely a little sleep break wouldn't kill their relationship.

'I've messed up with our place, too.'

'What place?'

'We're building our own place, in the back pasture near the stream. We got the main frame up in May. I was supposed to be finishing it. But what with one thing and another I haven't made any progress on it for months.' He thumped his palm against the steering wheel. 'We've been together now over a year…' He hesitated, then sent Ellie a look so full of yearning, her pulse thickened. She'd never seen this side to Jacob before. Not jokey and teasing, but serious and intense. She felt honoured that he would confide in her. 'I want to ask Maddy to marry me, but I can't ask her until I finish the cabin. I don't want to risk her saying no.'

No way would Maddy say no. But the thought of having to survive a wedding night with the two of them in the room next door focused Ellie's mind.

'How much is there still to do on your place?' Maybe there was a better way to solve this problem. And give them all a decent night's sleep.

'Not a lot. The floor needs tiling. The walls need painting. And the bathroom needs to be plumbed in. It's all there. It's like a month's worth tops of evening and weekend work, but I haven't got it done. We've been trying to do it in the spare hours we have. I'm not a trained plumber so it means reading the manual, but

Maddy usually comes over to help and...' He cleared his throat. 'We don't always get a lot done.'

Yes, Ellie could well imagine.

'Isn't Art a certified plumber? Couldn't he show you how? It would probably be quicker?' And if he was there to act as a gooseberry, maybe Maddy would keep her hands off Jacob long enough for him to actually read the manual.

'I don't feel right asking him.'

'Why not?'

He huffed out a laugh. 'I'm not Art's favourite person at the moment. And he's already super busy.'

Art obviously slept like a rock. Or he would be a lot more incentivised to help Jacob and Maddy out. And get them the hell out of the room between his and Ellie's. 'I tell you what, Jacob, why don't you leave it with me? I'll see if I can persuade him.'

'Really? You'll talk to Art?'

'Why not?' She could think of one reason why not – that insane kiss. But that had been over three weeks ago now. Heck, Art might even have forgotten it. And getting a decent night's sleep would surely be worth it. 'Pick me up on Candlestick Hill once you've finished at the lumber yard. I'll have a chat to him when we get back.'

All she had to do was beard the dragon in his den and not get fixated on his lips. Or his toolbelt. Easy-peasy.

*

They arrived back at the farmyard an hour later, Ellie buoyed by her chat with Rick who said the grant application was just a rubber-stamping exercise now. She'd also managed to nip into

Helena's workshop on Candlestick Hill to see the signs in progress. Two more things to tick off two of her to-do lists. Jacob too seemed a little less downtrodden as he began unloading the lumber. Probably hoping she was going to work a miracle with Art.

'Do you want some help taking this in?' Ellie asked, psyching herself up for a quiet chat with their project manager. It wasn't as if they hadn't spoken to each other since the kiss. And confronting him in a work environment would make it easy to keep things on a professional level.

Jacob threw her a pair of work gloves. 'That would be great, but don't take anything too heavy. I can get one of the lads to help bring in the rest.'

With a load of lumber under her arm, Ellie followed Jacob past the farmhouse and across the yard. The sounds of hammering and drilling greeted them, floating on a breeze perfumed by the apples in the orchard. Ellie's spirits soared as she rounded the blasted stone of the barn's back wall.

It had been over a week since she'd had a chance to look in on the build in the daylight and the changes were amazing. Huge bricked arches led into the cavernous interior of the barn, its high ceilings suspended by oak beams. The darkly stained wood looked elegant and yet earthy against the recently plastered walls. Light flooded in from the domed glass Art had suggested adding at the construction stage in the cavity that had once been the old barn doors.

With the cabinets and shelving being built at one end, while the kitchen equipment was being installed at the other, the space was a hive of men – and one woman – busy doing everything from sanding wood to laying ceramic tiles. She spotted Mike in one corner painting the plasterwork in the fresh lime green Dee had suggested. She knew from the financials that Art had hired a bunch of workers from Gratesbury to steamroll through the final week of construction, so Dee and Tess could get in next weekend to start putting in the finishing design touches and arrange the produce for the opening.

Once that happened, it was going to look incredible. It looked incredible already. How had Art managed to get all this done in only three weeks? Her admiration for him increased.

She scanned the interior, and then she spotted him, standing at the main kitchen counter. The faded tattoo flexed on his biceps as he shuffled and rearranged the plans and then began to explain something on them to Rob. His thick wavy hair was sheened with sweat and a fine layer of dust. The toolbelt lay low on his hips like a western gunslinger's bullet belt.

His head came up as she and Jacob picked their way through the melee to pile the lumber on a workbench. Her gaze connected with Art's and the lick of sensation crossed her lips.

Pushing a pencil behind his ear, he walked towards them. He gave her a cursory nod of greeting then addressed Jacob. 'The carpenter's arriving tomorrow at eight and I need this stuff re-cut by then so he can get started. Don't fuck it up.'

Colour slashed across Jacob's cheeks, the hopeful smile from moments ago gone. 'No problem,' he said.

The banging and hammering had stopped as everyone observed the exchange. Who knew construction workers were nosier than the housewives of Orchard Habor? Poor Jacob.

'Have you rechecked the plans? Made sure you've got the right sizing this time?' Art said, the tone harsh.

'I'll do it now,' Jacob murmured and ducked his head, making the long walk towards Rob as all the workers watched him.

Art went to walk off and Ellie touched his arm. The skin burned under her fingertips as his gaze slanted down to where she grazed the tattoo.

Her hand dropped. 'Do you have to be so arsey with him?' she said, beneath her breath, so as not to clue in their audience. 'He hero-worships you, and he's exhausted.'

'Yeah, but his exhaustion is of his own making,' Art fired back. 'I didn't get a wink of sleep last night either, but, unlike Jacob, my sleepless night was a lot less fun.'

So Art didn't sleep like a rock. No wonder he was so arsey. He was getting as little sleep as she was. Why the thought of them both lying in their separate beds on either side of Jacob's room listening to the young couple having sex should seem arousing she had no idea.

'I know what you mean,' she said. Art's eyes narrowed and what was supposed to be a simple confidence suddenly felt far too intimate. 'But there is a solution,' she said, trying to keep her mind on business and off the strange current that arced between her and Art like a blowtorch.

'What solution?'

'You could help Jacob finish off the house he's building,' she said, a little breathless as another solution tried to butt into her brain.

Jumping Art is not and will never be a solution.

Art dragged a hand through his hair, the frown on his face an odd combination of relief and frustration. 'I haven't got time for that. I'm up to my tits doing this.'

Fair point.

'I was thinking of putting the launch back a week. So we could take more time to plan it. But that would give us an extra weekend once the build's completed. We could all chip in. Get their place finished together, turn it into a social event. Like in *Witness*.'

'Like in what?'

'*Witness*, the old Harrison Ford movie,' she explained. 'He joins the Amish, dances to Sam Cooke with the female lead, who's Amish and has never danced before,' she added. 'In just about the most romantic movie scene ever.' *So not the point.* 'Then they all build a barn, in an afternoon.' She was babbling and Art's expression had merely shifted from clueless to completely unimpressed. So Art wasn't a classic eighties movie fan. Figured. 'Jacob says they only have a bit to do.' Forget about Harrison dancing in a barn, it wasn't helping. 'If we got it done, they could have their own place. And we'd all get a decent night's sleep again.'

Art tucked his thumbs into the toolbelt. 'You want me to pay the crew to work an extra weekend after the build's finished, just so Jacob and Maddy can carrying on banging like rabbits?'

'And we don't have to hear it,' she said. Why was he being deliberately obtuse, and putting more X-rated pictures in her head that she so did not need to be there? 'We won't need to pay the crew, the co-op residents can do it. Even Toto and Josh know how to slap on a bit of paint. We can put everyone to work. Dee will do food. It can be another great community event.'

'Because I love those so much,' he said, but the rigid tic in his jaw had softened.

'You'll love this one,' she said, ignoring the sarcasm. 'Just think, there'll be no more midnight moaning and groaning and shouts of "I'm coming, Jay," for us all to enjoy.' OK, maybe that was a bit too much information, because Art's eyes had darkened again, and heat was spreading up her neck like a wildfire.

'Have you got time to organise this?' he asked.

'I'll fit it in.' She'd just start a new to-do list titled: 'Operation Porn No More'.

'I'll think about it,' he said.

She let the air slip out of her lungs – was that relief, or regret?

'But just to be clear,' he added. 'I'm no Harrison Ford.'

As he strolled back across the work area, her gaze slipped over the muscles of his back under the sweat-stained T-shirt and landed on his butt, displayed in battered jeans, the low-slung toolbelt bumping against his hip.

Ellie would have to agree with him. Art Dalton was a whole lot more dangerous than Harrison Ford.

CHAPTER SEVENTEEN

'Put the halloumi over there and I'll give the chickens another turn,' Dee directed, while Ellie finished setting out napkins and cutlery.

Ellie placed the plate of grilled cheese on the trestle tables they'd set up in a copse of trees next to the stream running in front of Jacob and Maddy's cabin. Standing back, she brushed sweat-soaked hair off her brow, and took a moment to admire the magnificent spread her mother had brought from the farmhouse. August sunshine beamed through the canopy of trees, illuminating the feast of salads and baked goods.

The sound of birds and insects filled the air around the small-holding. The manic activity of this morning, as everyone chipped in to finish the dwelling, had finally tapered off. She knew Art was inside busy laying the last of the bathroom tiling with Jacob, while Annie and Tess were helping Maddy finish off the painting chores in the sitting room. Josh and Toto had been commissioned to entertain Melody after covering themselves with paint. The two of them scrambled around on the banks of the stream, building a mud palace with Melody for her extensive collection of *Frozen* figurines. Mike was hauling the last of the debris into the truck to take back to the farmhouse skip, having already made up the bed frame in the newly painted bedroom, while Rob was riding herd on his toddler sons, who had an unenviable knack of always running off in different directions.

After starting at eight the previous morning, they were almost finished, ready to chow down on Dee's early evening meal in the fading sunshine.

The timber-framed bungalow was perfect for a young couple just starting out, the simple wooden three-room structure topped with a sloping roof of reclaimed slate. Jacob and Maddy had spent their last night in the farmhouse yesterday and there had not been a peep out of them all night. But Ellie still hadn't slept well – she hoped the quiet wasn't going to get to her when they were gone. With Josh in his box room between Toto's room and her mother's master bedroom on the opposite side of the house, it would just be Art and herself in the east wing of the farmhouse from now on. Thank goodness she had her own en suite bathroom and wouldn't have to share one with him, because hearing the distant hum of his shower yesterday evening when she'd been lying in bed had been enough of a distraction.

Art emerged from the cabin and unhooked his toolbelt to drape it over the porch rail. She felt the odd bump in her chest that always accompanied sights of Art these days, as he strolled towards the tables across the meadow grass.

'Food, thank God. I'm starving.' He rolled up the sleeves of his work shirt. His dark hair gleamed, the stubble on his jaw and the crisp curls of chest hair against sun-browned skin shiny in the sunlight. Her heart bumped again.

No one wore sweat and sawdust better than Art Dalton.

He leant over the table to pluck one of Dee's feta tartlets off the centrepiece. And got a swift slap on the back of his hand from her mother.

'Go and wash up in the stream before you touch that,' Dee said.

As Dee turned back to the barbecue drum, and the chickens slow-roasting over cedar wood charcoal, Art sneaked a tartlet and popped it in his mouth.

He pressed a finger to his lips while he chewed and winked at her. Silly to get dazzled by Art's mostly non-existent charm, but she couldn't resist the quick grin in response to his playfulness.

He headed over to the stream to do as he was told and she watched him go.

The plaster-streaked cotton of his work shirt stretched across his back as he crouched down to examine the *Frozen* palace on the stream bank. Melody pressed next to his knee, resting her hand on his nape as she pointed out all the palace's design features. His large hand came round to rest on her waist and give it a squeeze as he spoke to her – probably about the construction properties of the palace. Toto joined them, her jeans caked in mud up to her thighs and her hands even filthier.

Ellie couldn't hear the conversation, the girls' voices drowned out by the rush of the stream, the whistle and coo of a nearby bird and the noise of the Jackson boys running rings around their father. But she didn't need to hear the conversation to notice the tilt of Art's head and then the slow nods as he listened intently.

He rinsed his hands, then stood up, flicking the excess water over Melody who giggled. Then he rested a hand on the back of Toto's neck – she dived out of the way, giggling too. Josh stood back through it all, shielding his eyes against the sun, then bobbed his head when Art addressed him. The shy smile on his face as Art directed all three of the children to wash up had Ellie's heart tumbling over in her chest.

Art's communication skills might be lacking, but his listening skills were exemplary.

The thought of that focused, intent look brought back memories of their kiss in the kitchen. The kiss she still hadn't managed to completely forget.

'He's wonderful with them, isn't he?'

Her mother's voice hauled Ellie out of her Art appreciation moment.

'Yes,' she mumbled, as she fidgeted with the table layout.

'I have to admit I had my reservations when Alicia got pregnant. I didn't think Art would be able to cope with the responsibility. But seeing him and Toto together...' Her mother gave a quiet sigh of contentment. Dee's gaze shifted to Ellie, the true blue of her eyes misty with memory. 'You should never underestimate how much people can do when tested.'

Ellie nodded, realising how much she had once underestimated Art too. 'So Alicia was Toto's mother?' she asked, unable to contain her curiosity any longer.

'Yes, she lived here for four years. Her and a couple of her friends...' Her mother paused. 'They came from London. Said they wanted to try alternative living.'

'Where is she now?' If she'd only lived at the farm for a few years had she left when Toto was still a baby? Ellie observed Art down by the stream, busy washing off Melody's hands while Toto and Josh splashed about nearby getting wet but not a lot less muddy.

Toto was thirteen, which meant by her calculation Art would only have been twenty-one when she was born. Had he been a single dad right from the start? How had he coped? Even with

Dee's help? She could remember how much hard work young children were and she'd had a housekeeper and a maid while Josh was little, hired by her father-in-law, who had insisted that Granger women didn't waste time on housework when they could pay someone else to do it for them.

'We don't know,' Dee said, the edge in her voice unlike her. Dee rarely had a bad word to say about anyone. But it was clear Toto's mother had managed to fit herself into that exclusive group. 'She left before Toto's first birthday and hasn't been back in touch since. I can't say I'm upset about that. She had a lot of problems, but it's hard to feel sympathetic when she abandoned her own child without a backwards glance.'

So many questions twirled around in Ellie's brain. How long had Alicia and Art been an item? Did he miss her? And what were the 'problems' her mum was alluding to so cryptically? Other than being a monumentally crap mother?

She forced them back though, as Tess and Maddy and Annie joined them to help carve the chickens. And Rob attempted to wrestle his boys into the two high chairs set out at one end of the table.

As Ellie laid a serving platter of barbecued chicken in front of Rob, she observed Art heading back from the stream. He clasped Melody's hand as she chattered away like a magpie. The older kids trailed behind, now wet as well as muddy.

Questions about Art's past were probably best left unsaid. And unanswered. He had always been an enigma, and the only other time she'd tried to satisfy her curiosity about him, when she was fourteen, it had not ended well.

*

'Folks, I need your attention for a minute.' Jacob looked ready to burst as he tinked his glass with a knife. But, as he pushed back his chair to stand and swept the hair out of his eyes, Ellie could see the nerves.

'First, I wanted to say thanks, from Maddy and me.'

Maddy whooped and cheered.

'I'm sure Ellie and Art are going to particularly appreciate us being gone,' he added, his trademark cheeky grin back.

Ellie's gaze connected with Art's across the table as everyone else laughed. The sun was dipping towards the horizon on the other side of Jacob and Maddy's cabin, throwing Art's face into shadow, but she could feel his gaze on her before he turned to toast Jacob with his glass of home-made apple cider.

'Why do you think I got up at six this morning to finish that bloody bathroom.' Art's growl rippled across Ellie's skin, and she shivered despite the warmth of the evening.

She detached her gaze from Art, only to find Annie watching her with a 'just jump him already' look on her face.

She took a sip of her own cider and ignored it. She'd already decided that jumping Art was not a solution. Maybe they didn't hate each other any more, and maybe they'd managed to forge a good if distant working relationship during the shop build, but they were hardly best buddies.

One insane kiss and a couple of hot looks did not a friendship make.

Jacob cleared his throat loudly as the table fell silent again.

'I wanted to let you all know how much this means to us both. But especially to me, because I've been carrying something around in my pocket for over a month now.' He pulled a small velvet box out of the front pocket of his jeans.

A hush descended over the whole company. Even Jamie Jackson stopped rapping a chicken bone on his high chair as if aware of the gravity of the occasion.

'I had planned to do this in private.' Jacob cleared his throat again, staring intently at Maddy. 'So that if the answer was no, I wouldn't look like a complete twat.' He thrust his fingers through his hair, his nerves palpable now.

Maddy had been struck dumb. Obviously she hadn't been expecting this as much as Jacob thought.

'But I figured, what the hell? Why not do it in public, in front of all the people I admire and trust most in the world? If I'm going to makc a twat of myself, why not go the full twat while I'm at it?'

He turned to Maddy and opened the box, the tremble in his fingers visible. A silver ring embedded with tiny diamonds shone gold in the dying sunlight.

He pulled out his chair and knelt in the grass in front of Maddy, his usually smooth movements clumsy. 'Maddy... I... Oh shit. For God's sake put me out of my misery here.'

The beaming smile that spread across Maddy's face was an answer in itself. 'If that's your idea of a proposal, it's a piss poor one.'

Jacob chuckled, still looking a little unsure. 'If that's your idea of an acceptance, it's an even piss poorer one.'

'I guess we must be made for each other then.' Maddy threw her arms around Jacob's neck, her corkscrew curls bobbing round her shoulders. 'Yes, yes, yes.'

Jacob roared with pleasure then rose to swing his new fiancée round in his arms. Everyone surged to their feet, shouting congratulations and applauding. Toto and Josh whooped and whistled, dancing around behind Jacob and Maddy, who were now kissing as if their lives depended on it, while Jamie Jackson screwed up his face and screamed his lungs out as if he were being murdered.

Ellie's heart jitterbugged. These two had their whole lives ahead of them and, unlike her and Dan, she didn't think they were going to bugger it up. Because they didn't just love each other, they liked each other too.

But, as her gaze travelled round the table at all these people she had come to like so much too, it snagged on Art again. Unlike the others, he wasn't watching the kissing couple, he was watching her.

She looked away, the heat spreading up her scalp, and everything inside going tight and achy and fluttery. *Blast*.

*

'Ellie, could I speak to you a minute?' Maddy still beamed like a solar-powered flashlight, her cheeks rosy with the apple cider they'd used to toast the couple.

'Of course, what do you want to speak about?' Ellie said, handing her mother the box of bowls they'd just finished washing out in Maddy's new kitchen

Dee headed out towards the tractor they were loading.

Maddy's smile spread as she whispered, 'Wedding plans.'

Ellie laughed. 'Don't want to waste any time?'

'Are you kidding? It took him so long to propose, I want this done before he changes his mind.'

Lifting the box with the last of the leftovers they'd saved, Ellie nodded to the bag of cutlery and plastic plates they had to load before they could head back to the farmhouse. 'Give me a hand with that and we can walk and talk.'

Hauling the equipment together, past Art and Jacob who were busy dismantling the barbecue, Maddy nudged her arm. 'I want to do it this summer, while you and Josh are still here. When are you planning to head back to the US?'

The sweet thrill that Maddy would be so keen to include them in her special day was accompanied by a pang of longing.

It was already the sixth of August, the shop was due to open next weekend and they'd already made huge inroads into getting the newly refurbished building stocked. All her thoughts and planning had been focused on the launch. But once they were up and running, she only had three weeks of summer left before the school term started in the US. She'd emailed a lawyer a week ago about the divorce proceedings, but had basically avoided thinking about that too – wilfully putting off any negotiations with Dan and his legal representatives about the splitting of their assets and his visitation rights. For goodness' sake, she still hadn't even spoken to Josh yet about the divorce – the thought of having that conversation still giving her panic attacks. That Dan hadn't raised it in any of his Skype calls with Josh suggested he was more than happy to avoid it too.

'I suppose we'll have to head back at the beginning of September.'

'That soon?' Maddy sounded shocked. Ellie knew how she felt.

Why hadn't she given this any thought? She was an event planner for goodness' sake. Planning for the future was her forte. She needed to stop avoiding thinking about what would happen once their summer was over.

'I'm afraid so. I need to get Josh settled in a new school.' In truth, she should go back now to get everything done she needed to get done. But no way was she abandoning the project when they would need her the most.

'I thought he was going to school with Toto in Gratesbury?'

'That was only supposed to be a temporary arrangement for the last few weeks of the summer term.'

The children had broken up two weeks ago, and had been disappearing each day on different adventures in the woods, or hanging out with Tess and Melody, to avoid getting roped into helping out with the shop.

'You can't go back so soon after the shop has opened,' Maddy said. 'You have to bask in the fruits of your labour. Why don't you ask the school if Josh can enrol there for the autumn term?'

The simple suggestion had the weight in Ellie's stomach jumping. Maddy was right. If the head teacher still had some spare spaces to fill, why not let Josh start back at school here with Toto? It would save her having to put an arbitrary end date on their stay before she was ready.

Maybe it was a cop-out. Another excuse not to face reality. But she'd started the shop project, she was responsible for its success and she couldn't possibly leave her mother in the lurch after all Dee had done for them both.

They would still have to go back. But Dan hadn't contacted her directly since they'd left Orchard Harbor, so he was obviously tied up with Chelsea and preparations for the baby. And she still had no desire to walk back into that minefield before she absolutely had to. Plus, Josh had enjoyed going to school with Toto for the last few weeks before the summer break. He'd made new friends, loved his teacher Miss Morely. Would it be so terrible to extend their stay until the end of September?

'I could definitely think about it,' Ellie said, as they stacked the boxes and bags into the truck bed.

'That's terrific,' Maddy said. 'Because I wanted to ask you a huge favour.'

Ellie smiled, feeling lighter already. 'Which is?'

'Would you plan our wedding?'

'Oh…' she murmured, torn. She wanted to say yes. Weddings had always been her favourite events to plan in Orchard Harbor. All that positive energy. Plus, she'd adored taking the stress off the bride and groom so they could feel relaxed as their big day approached. And with Maddy and Jacob, the joy of doing that would be all the greater, because they had become friends. Giving them a great start to their marriage would be the perfect gift. But if she committed to this, wouldn't she be committing to so much more? She wasn't a permanent part of this community, and she needed to remember that.

'Before you say no,' Maddy jumped in, her face a picture of determination, 'it's only going to be a small affair. My mum and dad will come and a few of my friends from Richmond where I grew up. Jay's got no family to speak of, so he'll just be inviting some of his old mates from Bristol. Even factoring in everyone from the co-op we're talking fifty people tops. And I've already got a dress.'

'Really?' Ellie said, impressed.

'I found it a month ago in the Oxfam shop in Salisbury. Antique lace and satin, bias cut, and it fits so perfectly. I thought it might be a sign so I bought it. I thought I'd sew in some sequins along the neckline to give it a bit of bling.' Maddy hummed with pleasure. 'Seriously, I love it so much, if Jay hadn't asked me soon I would have had to do the asking.'

Ellie laughed. 'And there I was thinking you were as surprised as the rest of us when he proposed.'

'I was astonished. But only because it's taken him so bloody long.'

They both laughed at that one.

Dee came round the back of the tractor to join them, having just corralled Josh and Toto into the trailer they'd hitched up to carry the tables and chairs the short ride across the meadow and through the fields back to the farmhouse. 'What are you two laughing about?'

'The stupidity of wedding proposal etiquette,' Maddy piped up. 'Whose daft idea was it to leave that job to men? Seriously, it's so much easier to be a lesbian.'

Dee's smile was wobbly round the edges. 'It is now. But we had to wait a long time to even get that option.'

Maddy sobered. 'God, sorry, I didn't even think of that. I didn't mean to be crass.'

'You're a woman in love, on one of the most exciting days of her life.' Dee patted Maddy's cheek. 'Crass is allowed.'

'Maddy and I are talking about wedding plans,' Ellie cut in, to give Maddy time to extricate her foot from her mouth.

'That's marvellous,' Dee said. 'I love weddings. Are you planning to have it here?'

'Absolutely.' Maddy nodded, her embarrassment forgotten in the rush of excitement lighting her eyes. 'Do you think we could do it in four weeks?'

It was Dee and Ellie's turn to looked shocked.

'Are you joking?' 'Four weeks!' they blurted out in unison.

'I know it's a bit mad,' Maddy said, 'but I can't wait to get hitched. And we're only talking about a glorified party. I don't want too much fuss. As long as I can wear my dress I'm good.'

'But why the rush?' Ellie said, confused now.

'I want it to be in the summertime, so we can all be outside,' Maddy said, her eyes still bright with enthusiasm. 'We could have it one Saturday evening after closing the shop. String fairy lights across the farmyard like we did after the barn clear-out. Maybe add lanterns and flowers to make it magical.'

Ellie could already envision it, but, even so, four weeks wasn't long. Maddy might think a wedding was nothing more than a glorified party, but even with a small guest list, it would be an important event in the young couple's life. And if she was planning it, she wanted to do it right. 'We could still make it magical at the end of September?' she offered.

'We?' Dee said. 'Will you still be here then?' The hope in her voice made Ellie's mind up for her.

'Yes, I thought I could stay till the end of September. As long as Miss Durden is happy to have Josh enrolled for the start of term. I want to make sure the shop is properly secure before I hand over the reins and head back to the US.'

'Sweetheart, that's marvellous.' Her mother gripped her hands, the pleasure in her voice swelling the ache in Ellie's chest. She'd have to talk to Josh about the divorce, and their long-term plans for the future before he started school again with Toto, so he didn't get confused. But, for now, why not extend their summer an extra month?

'I'll ring Marjorie tomorrow and have a chat about the logistics,' Dee added.

Ellie smiled. This was the right thing to do, she couldn't possibly run out on everyone right after the opening. And now they had a wedding to plan.

'So there's no need for you to rush the wedding,' Ellie said, addressing Maddy again. 'We could schedule for the end of

September, and give ourselves another three weeks of planning time. Two months is much more doable than one.'

Maddy's face went spotlight red. She slanted a furtive look across the meadow to where Art and Jacob were now sharing a beer with Rob and Annie Jackson. The Peveneys had already headed home with a sleepy Melody.

'Actually, there kind of is a need to rush the wedding.' She swallowed audibly, her excitement and joy palpable in the evening light as she placed a hand over her abdomen. 'I want to be sure I'm not too pregnant to fit into that dress.'

CHAPTER EIGHTEEN

Ellie picked her way through the woods, the moon and the floating buzz of the dragonflies edging her path. Crickets rustled in the muggy midsummer air. It had been a hot day, and the night was close and uncomfortable.

She'd tried to get an early night once they'd returned from Maddy and Jacob's house-building party, but she'd been lying in bed, listening to the sounds of the house settle around her as Dee put Toto and Josh to bed, and Art tramped up the stairs then back down again, probably to put a few extra hours in at the workshop.

And sleep had eluded her.

The woods had beckoned. The thought of a midnight walk to the millpond was too tantalising to resist. Having made the decision to stay in Wiltshire another month, she had hoped that her anxiety about returning to the US would have begun to calm, but if anything it had got worse.

She felt edgy and tense, her insides hollow and achy and somehow heavy after the news of Maddy's pregnancy. She was overjoyed for the couple, of course she was. Maddy had confided in her and Dee that she intended to tell Jacob tonight, their first night in their new home. And Ellie had no doubt at all that he would be ecstatic. She also had no doubt at all that Jacob would make a brilliant dad, because he was more than ready to take on that responsibility.

But the news had made her think about the night she and Dan had discovered together they were expecting Josh. The panic, the anxiety, and the trauma of what had followed, when they'd gone to the family planning clinic to discuss their options and she'd run out again in tears, deciding to keep the baby no matter what.

She adored Josh now, of course she did. He meant everything to her. He was the only good thing to have come out of their marriage. And, because of him, she could never regret the decision she'd made that day. But the memory of Dan's face, confused and scared and yet supportive, as she'd told him her decision and he'd struggled to do the right thing, still haunted her. Dan hadn't been ready for that commitment. And neither had she.

Was that the real reason he'd always found it so hard to be faithful? And why she'd allowed herself to go through the motions for so long, while knowing she no longer loved him? The failure of their marriage was an indictment of both of them really and all the immature decisions they'd made along the way without ever thinking through the consequences. Until it was too late.

And Josh had paid the price.

She had to speak to her son. Soon. She'd spent the last few hours lying in bed running through all the ways to have that conversation with him, and she still didn't know what to say. How to explain it all. He'd been so happy in the last few months, away from Orchard Harbor, away from the pressures of real life. And so had she. But was avoiding making decisions really an improvement on making the wrong ones?

She heard the splash of water ahead of her and saw the derelict brick structure of the old millhouse looming over the lake ahead, now overgrown with weeds and bracken. A rambling rose bush climbed up one side, its flowers a dark glossy red in the moonlight, making the millhouse look like something out of a fairy tale. A gloomy and derelict fairy tale worthy of a Tim Burton movie. Walking under the weeping willow that shrouded the water's edge, she stopped dead as the splashing became louder, closer, and she realised it wasn't just the lap of water on the bank.

Across the pond, she saw someone powering through the water with swift, fluid strokes. The swimmer's dark hair bobbed as the person stopped and gripped a tree root, to lever themselves out of the water.

Her heartbeat ticked into her throat. The ache in her abdomen sank lower as wide shoulders, followed by a broad back, rose from the dark pond. Rivulets of water slicked the planes of muscle, which tapered to the lighter strip of flesh defining his buttocks, as he climbed onto the bank in one fluid, athletic movement.

Art.

All thoughts of Dan, her marriage and the conversation she still needed to have with Josh evaporated in a firestorm of lust so hot it made her thighs tremble.

Why did the man have to look so gorgeous? And what the heck was he doing swimming naked in the millpond in the middle of the night?

So much for cooling off. She'd be unlikely to sleep for the rest of the week with this vision burned into her brain.

Bending, Art picked up a piece of clothing from the bank. He rubbed the work shirt across ridged abs and then gave his groin a few absent strokes, before dropping the shirt to scoop up his boxer shorts. He stood upright to put them on, and the breath

Ellie had sucked into burning lungs burst out. The shocked gasp sounded like a gunshot in the eerie quiet.

Art's head lifted, and he caught her standing on the opposite bank staring.

Heat suffused her entire body. A hot aching heat that tightened her skin over her bones, tenderised her breasts and made the weight in her abdomen pound in time with her elevated pulse. She forced herself to breathe past the immoveable lump forming in her throat.

He held his boxers in one hand, but made no move to cover himself as if challenging her to look her fill. She took the dare, because she couldn't make herself look away.

Gilded by silvery light, his body was hard and angular, big and yet graceful in its own rough-hewn way. Unlike Dan, who spent hours in the gym perfecting his toned physique, Art's body had the sinewy strength of muscles acquired through physical labour. There was nothing buffed or overly toned, nothing waxed or pretty about him. Even at a distance of twenty yards, she could see the white ridged line of the scar across his belly, the faded petals of his tattoo, the curls of hair on his chest that tapered through his abdomen, the pale outline of his penis where the hair bloomed into a thicket at his groin.

She couldn't make out his expression, but wondered if he could see her cheeks glowing like beacons.

She stood paralysed, the surge of longing burning away all her embarrassment until the only sensation left was the blood pumping through her veins into all those long neglected parts of her anatomy.

He broke eye contact first, to climb into his boxers. Not rushing, but not lingering either.

Ellie fled the riverbank, and retraced her steps back through the woods towards the farmhouse, not running, but not dawdling either.

Each step of the way, she added items to her newest and now most essential to-do list.

Item one: Go into Gratesbury tomorrow and get some sleeping pills.

Item two: Check out the online buying options for vibrators.

Item three: No more midnight trips to the millpond.

Ever.

PART THREE: NEVER FORGET

THEN

Eloise Charlotte Preston's Diary: Bits of you will fall off if you read this… IMPORTANT bits.

12 August 1998

Art finally came back this evening.

He's been gone for three whole days and even though he ignores me and I sort of still hate him, some of the time, I missed him. Which is beyond weird, I know. But when he came in after supper, I got that fluttery sensation in my belly, the same one I get whenever I see him now. Until I saw the state of him then the fluttery sensation felt as if the Spice Girls were doing 'Wannabe' in my tummy.

*His face was all beat up and he had a scrape on his elbow and his shirt was ripped and filthy. Even more than usual. His mum Laura, who I've decided is the biggest bitch on the planet, just laughed and said, 'Who did you piss off this time? Mike Tyson?' I couldn't even believe it. It was like she didn't care at all. I know my mum has been asking after Art. Asking where he is. Even I asked Laura once and all she said was 'How the f*** should I know, I'm not his keeper.' But she is his keeper, she's his mum, isn't she?*

Art may be a meanie a lot of the time, but now I think maybe he's that way because his mother is so horrible to him.

Thank God my mum was there, she made him go with her to the bathroom. Even though he said the F-word at her and told her to leave him alone, she wouldn't. I'm glad, because he looked like he needed a mum. Even I wanted to hug him. I'm beginning to think he's a bit like Laura's dog, snarling and snapping, but he doesn't actually bite anyone. (That said, I would NEVER hug Laura's dog!)

I listened outside the bathroom door while my mum cleaned Art up. She asked him what had happened to him and he didn't say anything for the longest time then he just said: 'Why does it matter?' But he didn't sound angry any more. He just sounded tired. I heard my mum sigh. That deep, sad sigh she sometimes makes when I have a go at her and then she said: 'It matters to me, Arthur.'

I know he doesn't like to be called that, because I've called him it before to annoy him. I thought he would probably say the F-word at my mum again. But all I could hear was this strange choking sound. So I peeked round the bathroom door and I couldn't believe what I saw… My mum was holding his head and hugging him, and he was letting her. His back was shaking and I could see all the cuts and bruises on it, because my mum had made him take off his T-shirt. It looked awful, his ribs were all black and purple on one side like someone had punched him again and again really hard. He wasn't making much sound at all, so it took me a minute to realise he was shaking like that because he was crying.

My mum saw me, and lifted a finger to her lips to tell me not to let Art know I was there. I think maybe she thought I was going to make fun of him. But for the first time ever, I didn't feel like making fun of him. I still don't. AT ALL. And neither do the Spice Girls who are still prancing around in my tummy like lunatics.

I sneaked away. And I've been crying a little bit myself. Even though Art will probably be mean to me again, once he's feeling better, I'll never tell anyone what I saw. I won't even tell Art.

Thank God I've got a mum that knows how to be a mum.

No wonder Art never smiles.

CHAPTER NINETEEN

The day of the shop opening dawned with spitting rain and one of those opaque grey clouds that looked as if it would never lift. Ellie got everyone together and carried on the preparations they could do out of the weather, while praying like a revivalist minister that the sun would come out before they started greeting visitors at 2 p.m.

She was ready to be born again when a few watery rays of sunshine finally pierced the oppressive mist at noon.

Everyone threw off their raincoats and had to race like Olympic athletes to get the bouncy castle they'd hired blown up and erect the marquees and stalls for all the food samples. Dee headed the team putting the finishing touches on the store and the small grouping of café tables. The council's food safety team had been by to inspect the premises the day before, and given everything the green light.

Ellie's heart got trapped in her throat as she glanced at her watch. Twenty minutes to zero hour. She, Tess, Dee, Annie and Maddy had all done a food hygiene course in the last two weeks and spent the day yesterday practising on the espresso machine and the new tills. But, even so, she'd had to take one of her sleeping pills last night to calm the stage fright that kept threatening to explode out of her ears.

She scanned the yard, checking off the last of the to-do lists in her head.

Rob and Art were hooking up the passenger trailer they'd hired for one of the tractors to take visitors on a pick-your-own tour of the farm's strawberry fields. Check. Annie sent her a wave as she arranged the home-made decorations for her cupcake-making stand. Check.

Ellie waved back then, hearing a cheer, she headed round the side of the back barn to the shop entrance.

Josh and Toto and Melody were shrieking and clapping as Mike climbed down from a ladder, having finished hauling up the huge banner the three kids had been painting on a roll of lining paper all week. The colourful and chaotic drawing of cows and ducks and geese, the farmhouse building and the shop, with each of the farm's inhabitants standing in front of it, made Ellie's chest ache, as it flapped in the breeze. She sniffed and then laughed when she spotted two lumpen versions of the *Frozen* princesses standing beside Melody's drawing of herself.

She whipped her phone out and took a photo, planning to add it to the farm's new Instagram account as soon as she had a spare moment.

'Mom, doesn't it look cool?' Josh ran towards her, his face a picture of excitement and pride. She looped an arm round his shoulders as he threw a hand around her waist.

'It looks fabulous, you've all done an amazing job.' She had gifts for all three of them she'd bought in Salisbury on Tuesday while on her food hygiene course, which she planned to give them once today was over – no matter what the outcome. But, as the sun finally broke free of the clouds and glinted off the glitter Melody had insisted on adding to the banner, her heart bounced.

Today was going to be a success, she just knew it.

Tess and Maddy had spent the last two days leafleting in Gillingham and Gratesbury. She'd been blogging and tweeting and Facebooking and Instagramming about the launch until her eyes crossed, and Dee had even managed to secure a small spot on the local radio station through one of her ubiquitous Women's Institute contacts. The signs had gone up yesterday afternoon on the A30 and the A303 and looked amazing. Classy and rustic and inviting, Helena's work reflected everything the shop itself was meant to be.

'Granny said we could help with the ice-cream stand if we wash our hands,' Josh announced.

Toto stood a few feet away holding Melody's hand as the younger girl jumped up and down on one foot.

'I want to do the cupcakes, too,' Melody said.

'Why don't you all go wash up then; people will be arriving very shortly.'

The kids ran around the side of the barn towards the house, whooping and shouting as they went.

Ellie heard a car horn blow, and headed after them. A procession of three cars appeared, coming down the track to park in the new car park. As they stopped and the bank manager, Mr Hegley, and his family got out of the first one, she saw two more cars coming.

She grinned at Jacob, who stood by the bouncy castle, and then sent a thumbs-up to Maddy who had trays of elderflower champagne flutes and free canapés arranged on a table ready to serve all the invited guests who would be arriving first.

'It's show time, people,' she shouted, giving the cue to the six-piece steel band they'd hired from the Salisbury Youth Co-Operative who had set up next to Annie's cupcake stall.

The opening bars of a calypso version of 'Somewhere Over the Rainbow' floated over the farmyard. Every moment of stress and anxiety and panic seemed to lift off Ellie's shoulders in the tinkle of music as her mum's arm came around her and gave her a hard hug.

'We're going to knock this one out of the park,' she said to her mother, whose eyes were already misty.

'Thank you so much, Ellie. For making Pam's dream come true.'

'Don't thank me, Mum, we all made this happen. Every single one of us.' Even Art, who she suspected still had reservations about the shop's success but had worked like a dog for five weeks.

She spotted him standing beside the tractor and their gazes met.

The reservoir of heat, which was always there when she encountered Art, smouldered in her belly. Luckily, in the last week, ever since they'd had their moment by the millpond, she'd been running around like a headless chicken on acid trying to get everything done. And Art had been locked in his workshop finishing off the commission that he'd got behind on during the shop's construction.

She'd crashed into bed each night unable to string a coherent thought together, so there had been no time to fixate on the picture of Art's naked body in the moonlight that had been branded into her brain a week ago. She'd been way too exhausted to even contemplate sex, let alone worry about what that moment had meant and whether it might complicate their relationship. There hadn't even been the need for sleeping pills or exploring vibrator options on Amazon.

He looked away first, bending to recheck the trailer coupling. And the smoulder was joined by a hum at the sight of tight male buttocks in worn denim.

Ellie ignored the leap of panic under her breastbone.

Everything was OK. They were OK. They hadn't spoken to each other since that night. Why should she be scared of what was just a recreational crush? She liked looking at Art. He was an exceptionally good-looking guy. Rugged and raw and appealingly masculine. He excited her. Why wouldn't he? She was a grown woman, who hadn't had sex in nearly a year, and good sex in a whole lot longer.

That didn't mean she'd be nutty enough to act on the attraction, so what harm could it do? He simply provided a chance to fantasise about something other than produce lists or health and safety regulations in her few moments of downtime. Just like he'd once distracted her from her loneliness and confusion nineteen summers ago.

She forced her gaze away from him. As long as she didn't indulge, she would be fine.

Her mum squeezed her shoulders. 'Pam would have been so pleased about all this.'

Ellie's eyes stung, moved by her mother's obvious pride. 'I wish Pam could have been here too,' she said, 'so I could apologise for the mean way I treated her that summer.'

'You were unhappy, Pam understood that,' her mother replied, her smile kind and reassuring. 'No apology was ever necessary... But if there had been...' Her mother released a quiet sigh, her gaze drifting over the activities getting underway as Rob and Mike greeted the bank manager and the two other VIPs and their families who had arrived early. 'What you've done here is more than apology enough.'

The children raced past them, heading for the bouncy castle and the free rides Jacob had promised them. As Ellie tracked their progress, she saw Art disappear in the direction of his workshop.

She ignored the pulse of regret. Art wasn't a people person. She hadn't expected him to get involved with their opening day once the customers arrived. She'd planned to thank him for all his help to date, but that could wait for another day – when she wasn't feeling quite so emotional and she'd got that hum of awareness under complete control.

Plus, looking at Art could be very distracting. And she simply did not have time for any leisure activities today.

Her mother gave Ellie a final hug.

'Now, I think we should go greet our first customers,' Dee said. 'And get this party started in true Willow Tree Farm fashion.'

CHAPTER TWENTY

'Are you sure you don't want me to pay for the jams?'

Ellie plastered an easy smile on her face as she glanced over her shoulder at Malva Hardwicke, whose devil child had just laid waste to two pots of Dee's apple chutney. 'Don't worry about it, Malva.' She bit off the cranky suggestion that Malva keep a tighter rein on the aptly named Damian next time she was in the shop. 'We love having you in the shop and our insurance covers any breakages.'

Not entirely true, but Malva had been in twice already since the shop had opened a week ago and parted with over a hundred pounds. She'd also brought in a couple of her friends. She was the sort of valued local customer they needed to attract. And Damian was three, built like a mini pickup truck, and a complete terror. No one short of Supernanny would be able to keep him from causing death and destruction wherever he went.

Sweeping up the last of the glass and chutney, Ellie made a mental note to give the area a proper clean as soon as they closed in twenty minutes.

'That's so understanding of you,' Malva said, over Damian's shrieks of protest. 'Laureston's Café in Gillingham wasn't nearly so understanding when Damian had a mishap with their cake stand.'

'Really, it's not a problem.' Ellie kept her easy smile in place while making another mental note to put an armed guard around their cake stand next time Damian was in. 'Tess will ring up the rest of your purchases and we hope to see you soon.'

The harassed mother dragged the screaming Damian away with more effusive praise for the shop's customer-friendly attitude. Ellie rubbed her back, aware of the low ache caused by standing at the counter all day making lattes and espressos. A couple of young mums were having a quick coffee and some of Dee's lemon drizzle while their kids played on the train set table Art had built in the corner of the barn. The line to Tess's till was at least five deep. The easy smile dropped from her face though when she saw Maddy coming in from the stockroom hefting a crate of Rob's elderflower champagne.

Ellie dashed round the fresh produce display. 'You shouldn't be carrying that in your condition.'

Maddy grinned as she let Ellie lift the crate out of her hands. 'Oh please, you're almost as bad as Jacob – he won't even let me cook a meal any more.'

'Don't knock it, being pampered is what makes pregnancy worthwhile,' Ellie said, as she began stacking the bottles in the display rack. 'That and the end result.'

Maddy cradled her still mostly non-existent bump. 'We had the second scan yesterday. They found a penis.'

'Congratulations.' Ellie laughed, trying not to remember the last penis she had seen.

'We finished the guest list last night,' Maddy said, as she helped Ellie load Rob's champagne onto the rack. 'Sixty-two people including my great-aunt Maisie, who my mum is insisting on me inviting. I'm sure they won't all come though.'

'If they do, we'll make room for them.' Ellie smiled absently while rethinking the seating plans she'd already roughed out. 'Why don't you two come over on Sunday night?' she offered. 'Dee's done a couple of designs for the official invites for you to take a look at. I think she plans to do a canapé tasting too?'

Maddy clapped. 'Yes please, the ones she suggested sound awesome. Our only problem is going to be narrowing the menu down to five.'

'Great, that's settled then. I'll let Dee know.' Ellie finished putting the last of the bottles on the rack and stacked the empty crate under the produce display. 'By the way, did you find Josh? Was he over at Annie's?' she asked, trying not to sound too anxious.

She'd been anchored to the shop all day and, as rewarding as it was watching the customers come and go, not to mention selling out of their morning batch of loaves in less than two hours, she'd been unable to track down Josh – or Toto – since breakfast that morning.

Maddy shook her head. 'No, he hasn't been over there today.'

'Damn,' she murmured under her breath.

She knew she was tired and out of sorts. The last week had been exhausting – word of mouth had spread since the launch and they'd been rammed with customers every day so far.

But where on earth was Josh? Dee had said earlier he hadn't been by since breakfast and now it was nearly six o'clock. He knew he was supposed to check in with her twice a day when she was in the shop. He'd managed it all this week so far, which only worried her more.

'Why don't you go and have a look for him?' Maddy offered. 'They're probably at one of their hideouts in the woods and completely forgot the time.'

'I can't leave Tess, and there's only twenty minutes before clos-ing,' Ellie said, undecided.

She was probably overreacting. Toto and Josh roamed the farm every day without mishap, bar the odd cut, bruise or nettle rash, it was one of the things that had made this summer so wonderful for her son – the freedom, the exercise, the adventure. But she didn't like that he had forgotten to come home for lunch. He knew that was a deal-breaker for her. And it was especially important this week, so she didn't have to go hunting for him while she was busy in the shop. She'd made that very clear to him every morning.

Maddy placed a hand on her shoulder. 'I'll hold the fort. I'm on tomorrow anyway, so I can get a jump-start checking the stock levels.'

'Are you sure?'

'Absolutely.'

Ellie yanked her Willow Tree Farm apron over her head as she dashed to the storeroom. After hanging it up, she sent Tess and Maddy and the remaining customers a wave as she rushed out the door.

When she found Josh, her son was going to get a long and overwrought lecture on the dangers of giving his mum a panic attack.

*

'I dripped some, sir. I'm sorry.'

Art switched off the portable radio and the blaring rock of Kings of Leon's 'Sex on Fire' died as he yanked down his face mask. Ellie's son stood outside the entrance to the caravan, looking worried.

'Where did you drip it?' he asked, although he doubted it could be that bad. He'd hired the kids this morning to slap the all-weather treatment on the canvas he'd stretched over the main frame last night. It was going to need a couple more coats before he actually got round to painting it, so unless the kid had knocked over a whole pot it was unlikely to be a problem.

Josh gripped the hem of his T-shirt, to show Art a couple of splatters on the logo of Wolverine. 'On myself. And on the floor.'

'Let's take a look.' He needed a break anyway. The interior fit-out was the one part of the process he generally hated. It was intricate, back-breaking work, with his six foot two frame not adapting well to the cramped conditions. And with the temperatures climbing steadily all day, the caravan interior had begun to resemble a Turkish bath about two hours ago. He must have lost at least two pints of his bodily fluids in sweat. Standing up, his knees popped, the cramping in his thighs shooting up to protest in his lower back. He swore softly as he shoved the sandpaper he'd been using into his toolbelt. He pressed his knuckles into the base of his spine as he walked out of the caravan and jumped onto the floor of the workshop.

Josh stood to the side, his face downcast as he gripped the paintbrush. The boy was still pretty shy around him, but he thought they'd made progress today. From the rigid stance it seemed he'd overestimated how much.

Peering round the side of the van, Art spotted Toto, still happily slapping up the treatment, her face covered by one of the masks he'd given them both, her clothes liberally doused with almost as much treatment as the van. He could see the spot where Josh had been working. The treatment had been applied in careful strokes with a lot less collateral damage. The boy hadn't covered as much ground as Toto since they'd finished eating the pizzas he'd brought back from Gratesbury for them both for lunch, but he'd been much more conscientious. Art addressed the boy, whose chin was now buried in his chest.

'I don't see a problem. You've done a good job.'

'I have?'

Art swiped his forearm across his brow to stop the sweat stinging his eyes. 'Sure, you guys have earned your pay. But maybe you should knock off for the day now?'

They'd been at it for hours, taking only a couple of short breaks for cold drinks and then lunch, which had astonished him. Toto generally wasn't great at applying herself. She had the concentration span of a hyperactive gnat, and usually needed to run off steam at least five times a day. But today she'd been hard at it, and he knew that was down to Josh. It had never really occurred to him till now, but the other kids at the co-op were all a lot younger than Toto, and her school friends lived too far away to visit during the holidays, limiting her options when it came to friendships.

Josh had been a godsend this summer. Something that had been brought home to Art as he'd listened to their chatter through the caravan wall, which had included in-depth discussions about everything from American baseball to the great Harry vs. Hermione debate. He had no doubt at all that Toto's diligence had been down to Josh's influence.

He hadn't had a heck of a lot of contact with Ellie's son so far this summer, but he seemed like a good kid. Generally during the summer holidays, ever since Toto had been big enough to negotiate the dangers of farm life, Art had left her to her own devices. She wasn't a whiner or a fusser and she knew that he didn't have time to entertain her. But, even so, most summers he would rope her into a project or two when she got bored. He would have been hard-pressed to do that this summer with the construction work on the shop, but Josh's presence had made it unnecessary.

That said, the boy clearly had issues with him, or maybe just issues with men generally. He must have asked Josh a million times in the last two months to stop calling him 'sir'. And the boy still forgot half the time.

'You don't want me to do it any more?' Josh said, jumping to the wrong conclusion.

Art's irritation level rose. 'That's not what I said.' In fact, he had said exactly the opposite. 'Totes,' he called to his daughter, who had been so engrossed in slapping on the last of the treatment, she hadn't been paying any attention to the conversation. He needed help though, before he freaked the kid out completely. 'How about you guys quit for the night?'

She whipped up her face mask and grinned. 'How much did we earn, we've been at it for hours and hours.'

He pulled his phone out of his pocket and checked the time. Shit, it was nearly six o'clock. For once Toto wasn't exaggerating.

He did not want Ellie storming out here and giving him the third degree about child labour laws, because he'd been avoiding her since the night at the millpond. Having her eyes on him, seeing the way she had watched him before disappearing back into the woods, had stirred up all sorts of visions in his head he hadn't been able to shake. He'd begun to fantasise about taking things between them a whole lot further. Which would not be a wise move on far too many levels.

She was Dee's daughter, she would be going home at the end of the summer, and they didn't really get on – give or take the odd gin-soaked kiss. And, ever since Alicia, he'd always made a point of keeping his sex life separate from his life on the farm.

He'd been the only parent Toto had for the last twelve years, and he didn't plan to confuse his daughter by bringing another woman into his life. Alicia had left when Toto was still too young to remember her – she'd never asked about her mum, and he had absolutely no desire to encourage that conversation. If he and Ellie started something, it could lead to all sorts of complications he didn't need.

But those salient facts held no sway at all with his sex drive. He'd wanted her when she was fourteen, even though she'd been a thorn in his side the whole time, and wanting her now was proving even harder to deny. So the only way to stop things getting out of hand was to avoid her.

'Thirty quid a piece,' he said, pulling his wallet out of his back pocket. The two of them had put in a solid six hours today since Toto had wandered in that morning with Josh in tow and asked it they could earn some money to go to Gratesbury the next day.

Toto whooped. 'You hear that, Josh, we're rich.'

'For real?' The boy's smile spread across his face, brightening his eyes, and reminding Art of Ellie again. Like he needed any reminding.

He counted out three twenties and handed the cash to Josh. 'I told you, you've earned it.'

The boy ran his thumb over the bills, and then lifted his head. His eyes sparkled in the blaze of fluorescent light, looking disturbingly moist.

Art tucked his wallet back into his pocket, something sharp and surreal kicking his ribs. Was the boy about to cry?

'Thank you, sir,' Josh said, his voice thick with what Art hoped to hell weren't tears. Or worse, awe.

'You're welcome.' Art's hand swept out without him thinking it through, and he ruffled the boy's hair. The secret smile that flashed across the child's face was disturbing. What had he done to deserve such adoration? Not a lot, was the answer.

Either the boy was starved for male attention, or he had a very low threshold for his male role models. He had a feeling it might be both. While he didn't know a lot about Ellie's husband, he did know – even though he'd tried not to know, because it shouldn't have been any of his business   that the boy's father only got in touch via Skype once a week. Which made Art sure the guy was a dick.

If Josh were his son, no way would he want to be away from the boy for this long.

Toto broke up the moment, singing and bouncing like Tigger on speed as she grabbed Josh's hands and the two of them danced about.

'The job's not finished till you get the brushes in turpentine and roll up the tarp,' Art interrupted the celebration. Ellie would be in the shop handling the cash out and the clear up until at least six thirty, so he had time to get her son back to the farmhouse before mamma bear showed up to read him the Riot Act.

The children set about rolling up the tarp without too much fuss, still riding high on their good fortune.

'Can you take us into Gratesbury tomorrow to spend it?' Toto asked, as she hefted the heavy bottle of turps off the shelf and began filling the jam jars he kept handy to soak the brushes – splashing liberal amounts of the noxious liquid on the floor.

'Can't, I've got this to finish,' he said.

'Could we take the bus in?'

'Sure.' He nodded, then remembered Ellie's less liberal approach to childcare. 'But Josh will have to get his mum's permission.'

The kids shared a disappointed look and Josh's smile dimmed. So Ellie was unlikely to give the go-ahead to that one? Maybe he shouldn't have given his permission so easily either?

Not for the first time, Ellie's hands-on approach to child-rearing made him question his attitude to Toto. But, as he watched his daughter and Josh finish up, he shrugged off the thought. Toto was a responsible kid, and she went to Gratesbury on the bus every day for school, and Josh had been doing the same in the weeks before the summer break – if Ellie had an issue with her son being more independent that was her problem, not his.

He climbed back into the van, his knees hurting as he crouched back down to finish sanding the bed frame. Another hour finishing up and he could call it a night himself. He'd pulled a couple of all-nighters in the last week to get back on track since the shop had opened. He certainly did not have the energy or inclination to worry about Ellie and her parenting preferences.

He was listening to the kids busy chatting away about how they were going to spend their earnings if Ellie let them go to Gratesbury a few minutes later, when the door banged open and Ellie's voice rang out.

'Josh, what are you doing here? I've been searching for you for fifteen minutes. You were supposed to check in with me at the shop. I've been worried sick.' The monologue was delivered in a pitch that got higher as it went on, not giving the boy a chance to respond.

Art climbed out of the van, his back muscles protesting as he regretted his decision not to kick the kids out a lot sooner.

Wearing a short summer tunic with big red roses stamped all over it and her blonde hair escaping from the topknot she wore while tending the shop, Ellie had her hands on her son's shoulders.

'You didn't go home for lunch and you forgot to check in with me or Dee. You know that's not the deal. You were supposed to—'

'The two of them were working for me.' He interrupted Ellie's tirade.

Ellie's head swung round and, for a moment, she looked surprised to see him. But then the flush of temper on her face was replaced by the flash of awareness. The blood rushed to his groin on cue – doing not one thing to stem his irritation.

Why oh why, even when she was tired and anxious, did Ellie always have to be so bloody irresistible?

*

'Art? I… I didn't know he was in here working with you today.' Ellie was holding it together. But only just.

She hadn't planned to come charging in here. Hadn't planned to make a scene. But she'd heard the children chattering and assumed that Art was elsewhere. Except he wasn't elsewhere. He was here, with that inscrutable look on his face and wearing that bloody toolbelt again, which had the ability to melt all her brain cells – especially when she'd just spent fifteen minutes racing about the farm trying to find her missing son.

'We made sixty pounds, Mom.' Josh broke into her reverie, waving a bunch of twenty pound notes under her nose. 'Thirty pounds each. Can we go to Gratesbury tomorrow to spend it? Art said it was OK.'

Flustered and feeling Art's eyes on her, that penetrating gaze making her feel as if she were under a very large, very powerful microscope, she turned to her son. 'I can't take you to Gratesbury tomorrow. I'll be working in the shop.'

'But you don't have to take us, we can go on our own on the bus.'

'You're not going to Gratesbury on your own.'

'Why not? Toto does it all the time.' The piercing whine in Josh's voice drilled into her temples. She could feel Toto's eyes on her too.

'I said no, Josh.' She knew she could be overprotective. She'd been working on it really hard. Trying to give Josh space and responsibility this summer. But Josh had always been one hundred per cent loyal to her, and having him challenge her in front of Art and Toto felt like a betrayal.

'But I want to go. That's not fair. I've worked really, really hard today.'

'You also forgot to tell me where you were. You know that's important to me, or I'll worry about you.'

'You always worry,' Josh shouted, his face bright with temper. 'And you never let me do anything I want to—'

'Don't talk to your mum like that.' Art's deep voice cut through Josh's outburst.

Josh stilled, his eyes darting down as his whole body went soft, the temper seeping out of him as his face went the colour of Dee's raspberry jam. 'I'm sorry, sir,' he muttered.

Ellie risked a look at Art. Not nearly as shocked by her son's impromptu temper tantrum as she was by the way Art had cut it dead so effortlessly.

The look was a mistake, because it gave her another unhealthy eyeful of the worn sweaty T-shirt, sprinkled with sawdust, which stuck to his musculature in some interesting places.

'And don't call me "sir",' Art said, wearily, as if he'd had to say it a thousand times before. Then he lifted the limp T-shirt and wiped it across his brow, giving her a glimpse of spectacular abs, bisected by the happy trail of dark hair that led beneath his belt. She got a little giddy, as her gaze locked on the jagged scar that trailed across his hip bone. And she recalled the sight of him illuminated in moonlight across the millpond.

Forget a hum or a buzz, liquid fire settled in her abdomen. She tensed her stomach muscles, desperate to ignore it as she dragged her far-too-easily-distracted gaze back to his face.

Unfortunately, that face, the patient gaze rich with knowledge and something a great deal more potent, was no less compelling.

'He did a full day's work. He earned the thirty quid.' Art swept his hand towards the caravan, which was now fully formed in the centre of the cavernous room. 'Toto's been to Gratesbury before on the bus, they'll be fine.'

'What Toto does is your business, what my son does is mine,' she snapped, and immediately felt like a shrew when he sent her an infuriatingly patient nod.

'Your call.' He lifted his hands in surrender.

'But, Mom, I want–'

'Why don't you guys head into the farmhouse.' Art interrupted Josh's cry of protest. 'Go wash up and we'll be there in a bit.'

She wanted to tell the kids to stay. She did not want to be alone with Art. But she didn't move, as they ran off together, obviously keen to have Art fight their battles for them.

She took a calming breath, trying to get her rising temper, and the rising temperature, under control. Why did he still have the ability to turn her on to the point of madness? She wasn't a teenager any more, she ought to be able to control her ridiculous obsession with this man.

'I'd appreciate it if you didn't butt into my relationship with my son,' she said, trying to focus on her anger, instead of the scent of sawdust and man that invaded her personal space as Art strolled past her to unhook the toolbelt and dump it on the workbench. 'I know you think I'm hysterical and irrational and overprotective, but I'm not comfortable with him and Toto going to Gratesbury on their own.'

He faced her. Leaning his butt against the bench, he crossed his arms over his chest. 'Then they won't. I'll tell Toto she can't go either.'

'You... Really? You'd do that?' Surely it could not be that simple. 'But won't Toto be upset?'

'She'll probably moan a bit, but she's thirteen, so she does what I tell her.' Releasing his arms, he turned back to the bench, and began removing the tools from his belt and placing them in a large box.

She should leave now. He'd agreed to do what she asked. But alienating his daughter as well as her son did not seem like a good idea. What if she *was* being irrational? The children went to Gratesbury on their own for school, perhaps giving them this independence wasn't a bad thing?

'But how will you explain your change of heart?' she asked.

He glanced over his shoulder, looking surprised she hadn't left. 'I'll tell her I changed my mind.'

'But she'll know it came from me. I don't want to alienate her.'

He swung around, staring at her now as if she'd just suggested he join the Women's Institute. 'Ellie, what the hell are you on about?'

She struggled to explain herself. 'I like your daughter,' she ventured, attempting to bring the conversation back where it belonged. On neutral, non-confrontational ground. 'She's been wonderful to my son this summer. And I want her to like me. If she figures out that you're forbidding her to go because I've suggested it, she'll hate me. I don't want that to happen.'

'She won't hate you. She'll know you're worried about Josh, and that I worry about her.' He sighed, the sound deep as he ducked his head. 'That's never a bad thing.' The statement was so thoughtful, and so surprising, Ellie was struck dumb for a moment.

'And, for the record,' he added, 'I don't think you're hysterical, or overprotective, or irrational. I think you're a good mother who cares about her son.' The compliment astonished her and humbled her at the same time. Dan had told her so often that she worried too much about Josh – his weight, his situation at school, his insecurities – that she'd allowed it to undermine her confidence. And when Art had accused her of the same thing on her first day on the farm, on some subliminal level, she'd believed him.

But, as she looked at Art, all she could see was the boy she'd once spied getting a hug from her mother, because his own mother had never bothered to give him one.

'Thank you,' she said, moved. 'Although maybe I overdid the mother bear act when I came in.'

His lips quirked and the persistent hum in her abdomen reignited. 'Overdoing it is better than under-doing it.'

Her gaze dropped to his mouth, that potent, persuasive mouth. Her pulse accelerated as he stepped away from the bench. Suddenly she could feel the heat emanating from him, and the ragged remnants of her self-control slipping through her fingers.

'You're knackered,' he said. 'We both are. It's been an exhausting couple of months.'

The blood thundered in her ears when he stopped in front of

her. His height, the breadth of his shoulders, that tempting smile as he towered over her, should have been a warning to step back and get the hell out. But she got fixated on the slow beat of his pulse against the strong column of his neck.

Droplets of sweat sat on his collarbone and dripped into his clavicle. She ran her tongue over her lips, tasting the salt, the desire to lick those drops off almost unbearable.

'You should leave.' The low murmur reverberated through every one of her pulse points. His eyes had darkened to black, the lust-blown pupils edging out the chocolate brown, the rigid line of his jaw darkened by a day's growth of beard.

'I can't,' she said.

Rough callused palms cradled her cheeks, forcing her gaze back to his face.

She sucked in a breath, but didn't draw away, the hard possessive look like a torch paper to her libido, as his fingers threaded into her hair.

'If you don't leave, I'm going to kiss you.' The gruff agony in his voice released something inside her. Something reckless and elemental.

Need blazed through her. Clutching his T-shirt, she dragged him closer. 'I know.'

Then all coherent thought fled as his mouth descended on hers.

His kiss this time was nothing like the one in the kitchen over a month ago. Not gentle or seeking or coaxing. This time his lips, his tongue, were avid and demanding, exploring and exploiting every inch of her mouth. His fingers sank into her hair, sending the pins she'd used to keep it up pinging off the concrete floor like missiles.

The sting of having her hair pulled only made her feel more

alive, more needy, as everything concentrated in her core, the ache building like wildfire. One large hand covered her breast.

He rolled the rigid tip between his thumb and forefinger through cotton and lace. Sensations shot through her, painful darts of longing, terrifying in their intensity.

She tore her mouth away from his. 'Stop, Art. We have to stop.' She flattened her hands on his chest, her cheeks stinging from the abrasion of his stubble.

'I'm sorry,' she said. 'I can't do this. I'm married.' She dropped her hands, hoping the excuse didn't sound as lame to him as it did to her.

Because the truth was, she'd never felt less married in her life. It wasn't loyalty to Dan that was stopping her from doing the wild thing with Art. It was something much more basic than that. Something she would have to examine later – when she wasn't about to spontaneously combust.

He stood silently, the outline of his erection against his cargo shorts evidence that he was as affected as her by the madness which had consumed them.

'It's a monumentally bad idea,' she said, but even she could hear the uncertainty in her voice, the desire to be persuaded otherwise. 'I should go.' She swallowed past the ache in her throat, feeling like the worst kind of fraud.

She didn't look back, didn't dare, but he made no move to stop her, the silence deafening as she shot out of the door.

CHAPTER TWENTY-ONE

'Josh, sweetheart, can I come in?' Ellie pushed the door to her son's bedroom open when the invite wasn't forthcoming.

He lay in bed, his hair damp from his shower, his expression tense and wary as he looked up from the Harry Potter book he was reading.

'Hey,' he said, but the smile he usually gave her when she came in to wish him goodnight was noticeably absent.

She perched on the side of the bed. 'I'm sorry I snapped at you in Art's workshop.'

'OK.' Josh's eyebrows wrinkled, but then he smiled, the bright boyish smile she had become addicted to over the years. 'So can me and Toto go to Gratesbury now?'

Ellie sighed. They'd had another stand-off about the trip over supper, with Toto looking on and Ellie suspected probably judging her the worst mother in the world.

Art hadn't appeared, but for once she was grateful for his avoidance tactics. With her cheeks burning from what she was sure had to be the visible evidence of his kisses in the workshop and her own emotions still all over the place, having him there would probably have sent her right over the edge. But because he hadn't been there, and hadn't appeared after supper either, Ellie had been the one who had to tell the children that neither of them were going to Gratesbury tomorrow.

'I'm sorry, Josh, no, it doesn't. Art and I agreed it wasn't a good idea for you two to go in on your own. As I said, I'll take you on Sunday.'

The hopeful smile flatlined. 'But the good shops aren't open on Sunday.'

'Then we can go on Monday,' she offered.

'That's three whole days away.' It wasn't like Josh to whine, but he was pushing puberty. She needed to prepare herself for the fact that he wasn't going to be her sweet, uncomplicated child for ever.

'I don't believe Art said that,' he continued. 'He's cool. He lets Toto do stuff when she wants to.'

'Josh, please, can we not have another argument about this?'

'I like Art,' he said, the accusatory stare challenging her to disagree with him.

'So do I,' she countered.

Unfortunately, I like him a bit too much.

'No, you don't,' Josh replied. 'You shouted at him.'

'What? No, I didn't.' What was Josh talking about? She hadn't shouted at Art since that first day.

'You don't like him, I know you don't.' Josh manoeuvred himself up in bed.

'That is simply not true. I do like him, he's a good man and a good father and I admire all the work he's done on the shop.'

Josh looked down, gripping the book he'd been reading too tightly.

She tucked a finger under his chin, to tip his face up to hers. The mix of wariness and confusion on his face disturbed her.

'Why do you think I don't like Art?'

Had Josh seen more than she'd wanted him to see? Had he sensed the physical attraction between them, the razor-sharp sexual tension that just kept building and building despite all their best efforts to stop it, and confused it for something else? The thought troubled her. As if this situation wasn't already problematic enough.

'I know you don't like him, because you don't like Daddy either,' he said, and the guilt punched her in the gut.

'What do you mean?' She forced the question out, sick with dread.

She'd never argued with Dan, not in front of Josh. Had always assumed that he had no knowledge of the stresses and strains in their marriage. In fact, she'd prided herself on being able to keep all the anguish and agony of Dan's betrayals, the fallout from their failing relationship away from their son. Josh was the innocent in all this, she didn't want him to have to deal with any of the emotions she'd had to deal with as a teenager, confused and alone and secretly scared that something she had done had led to her parents' break-up.

'Sometimes…' Josh paused, his guileless expression a damning reminder that however close to puberty he might be, he was still a child. 'Sometimes when you speak to Daddy, it's like you're shouting at him in your head. It's like you hate him.'

Ellie felt all her anxiety, all her worries about the divorce coalesce into a great big bundle of regret in the pit of her stomach.

Apparently the conversation she'd been busy avoiding for two months – for years really – was going to happen now. And she didn't exactly feel prepared for it.

Winging it was not her forte. She preferred to plot and plan, consider all the possible pitfalls and work out a strategy before she did anything. But somehow her cowardice had got her into a situation where this conversation had snuck up on her without her preparing for it properly.

Honesty was the only possible policy now. Honesty and courage. What a shame she'd abandoned both years ago.

'First of all, I don't hate your father.'

'Then why do you never talk to him on Skype?'

'Because we're not as good friends any more as we used to be.' She cleared her throat, aware of the white lie in the statement. Had they ever really been friends? No wonder their marriage had been such an abject failure. 'And we've decided to get a divorce.'

Josh stared, his eyes widening, as he processed the information. 'You mean like Jesse Yates's parents?'

'Yes,' she said, having a vague memory of the boy whom Josh had known in elementary school.

Josh's eyes widened as he processed the information. 'Does that mean I'm never going to see Daddy again, like Jesse never saw his daddy?'

'No. Of course not.' She gathered him close in her arms, his wet head snug under her chin as she hugged him tight.

Pulling back, she held Josh by the shoulders. 'Once we get everything sorted in Orchard Harbor, we'll have to live in separate houses, but you'll be able to go and visit him, probably on weekends. And during the holidays.' Why hadn't she considered Josh's feelings? 'We've only been here the whole summer because I thought it would be nice to take a break from everything.'

Just because Josh had never said anything about seeing Dan, just because he'd seemed to be having such a good time on the farm this summer, she still should have consulted him. Of course he missed his dad. Dan might not be the best father, but she knew how much her son craved his attention.

'Do you want to go home? To see your dad? Is that it?' Maybe a good place to start would be to ask Josh how he felt, instead of making the decisions for him.

Josh blinked, his brows wrinkling in concentration before he spoke. 'Not right away,' he said.

The huge surge of relief made her feel light-headed. And she wasn't even sure where it came from. They would have to go back to the US. Maybe not to Orchard Harbor, but somewhere close by – she couldn't separate Josh from his father indefinitely. That had always been understood.

'I like it here,' Josh continued. 'Better than Orchard Harbor. Toto's my best friend ever and even her school isn't too bad. And Granny's so nice to me all the time. But…' He hesitated and stared back at Harry Potter.

'But what, Josh?'

He lifted his shoulder then dropped it. 'When Toto and me were with her dad today…' He looked up at her, worrying his bottom lip in a way she hadn't seen him do in months. 'I wished my dad would do stuff like that with me.'

'Stuff like what?' she asked, but she thought she knew what Josh was trying to say.

Dan didn't do everyday stuff with Josh. He would take him to baseball games and buy VIP seats in the dugout. He would drive him to the beach, if his father's campaign was organising a clambake. He would do impromptu trips to the mall to buy Josh a pair of three hundred dollar high tops. But Dan would never have spent a whole day with his son letting him help paint a caravan, because he had never been able to give his son time and responsibility and the sort of day-to-day attention that didn't come with shiny distractions.

They'd stopped doing family holidays together, because it had become too stressful. Dan would always be organising lavish day trips deep-sea fishing or reef snorkelling which Ellie was sure Josh didn't want to do, but her son would never say he didn't want to do, because he didn't want to disappoint his dad. And she could never tell Dan that Josh didn't want to do it, because she didn't want to be the one to discourage them from spending time together.

Dan swooped in and gave Josh gifts or snippets of 'quality time' to make up for the fact he got bored if he ever had to spend actual time in his son's company.

And that's what Josh had missed when he saw Toto with her father.

'Just stuff,' Josh said, the dejection in his voice making Ellie's insides twist.

However wonderful this summer had been for Josh, however much fun he'd had with his new best friend, roaming the woods, gaining in confidence, becoming part of this community, when he returned home all the old problems would still be there. All they'd really done was run away.

'When we go back to the US, you'll be able to do stuff with your dad, Josh, I promise.'

Because Dan would probably be even busier avoiding spending actual time with his new baby. The rush of anger was fierce and unprecedented, at the thought of how Dan had managed to stuff up all their lives. Not just her and Josh's but quite possibly Chelsea's and her baby's too. She'd always made excuses for Dan. Because she knew deep down, he didn't mean to be careless and selfish and immature. He just was.

But for a second she couldn't help comparing him to Art, who had been in exactly the same situation thanks to another unplanned pregnancy, and had taken all of the responsibility instead of none of it. When they got back to Orchard Harbor, she was going to stop letting Dan off the bloody hook, parenthood wise. She'd told Josh about the divorce and that was a relief, but Dan could tell him about his new sibling.

Because it was way past time Dan got over the shock of becoming an accidental father at twenty-one and grew up.

'I know, but I don't want to go back yet.' Josh's mouth opened in another jaw-breaking yawn. 'Me and Toto have got our holly tree den to finish. And Art said we could help paint the caravan. And I want to see Miss Morely and the other kids at school again like you said.'

Ellie smiled, pleased that neither one of them had to go back and face reality just yet. 'That sounds like a plan, kiddo.' She gathered *The Goblet of Fire* and laid it on his bedside table. 'But now it's time to go to bed.'

He snuggled down in the bed as she lifted the duvet. She kissed his forehead, and smoothed his damp hair, her heart swelling as his eyelids drifted downward, before he mumbled, 'If Daddy came here to visit, we wouldn't have to go back to Orchard Harbor at all.'

If only it could be that simple, she thought, as she wished her son goodnight. As she turned off the light and shut the door to his room, the shadows from the corridor played over the mural Dee had painted for Josh before they'd arrived.

Maybe they'd been running away, but Josh had needed this breather and so had she. This summer had been a positive experience all in all, and they had a whole six weeks left before they had to return to Orchard Harbor and deal with Dan and the divorce and the new baby.

But, as she padded down the corridor, she passed Art's bedroom on the way, and caught herself sweeping her gaze down to the bottom of the door for any signs of light.

The bubble of disappointment formed when there was none.

She pushed the silly reaction to one side as she got ready for bed.

She and Josh had a clear plan of action now, one they were both happy with. She had a wedding to organise and a shop to run for the next six weeks before they flew home. She was going to be super busy tying everything up here and making preparations for their return to New York. She didn't have the time or the energy to get hung up on Art and a couple of inappropriate kisses. And anyway, they'd both agreed that slaking the lust between them was a monumentally bad idea – because it absolutely was.

Her life was enough of a mess already.

But, as she climbed under the newly washed sheet, the phantom scent of sweat and turpentine overwhelmed the lavender and her lips tingled with the memory of that bone-melting kiss.

She shuffled around in her bed trying and failing to get comfortable. The burning question she didn't have an answer for running over and over through her head.

How the hell was she going to survive her new-found hunger for a month and a half, with Mr Guaranteed Orgasm sleeping right down the hall?

CHAPTER TWENTY-TWO

After so many years not even thinking about sex – let alone wanting to actually indulge in any – Ellie had been sure that once she'd made the decision not to have any with Art, her libido would eventually get the message. And start behaving itself.

Wrong.

Two days after his melt-your-brain-cells kiss in the workshop, she lay in bed, watching the fairy lights her mother had draped over the mantel sparkle on the ceiling like stars, and contemplated another sleepless night spent trying not to fixate on all the things she should not want to do with Art Dalton.

Correction: *Did* not want to do.

Of course, it would have been a whole lot easier to convince herself of that, if Art hadn't started popping up all over the place since that moment of insanity in the workshop.

After weeks and weeks of hardly crossing paths with him, now he seemed to be constantly in her face.

Had he always looked at her like that? The way he'd stared at her that night at the millpond? Why hadn't she noticed it before now? Or was she just imagining it? Maybe it was all in her sex-starved, sleep-deprived head? She flopped onto her stomach, and shoved her head under the pillow. But the maddening memory of those dark chocolate eyes on her, refused to piss off.

He'd shown up to dinner on both Saturday and Sunday, his conversation as monosyllabic as usual, but she'd caught him staring at her. His arm had brushed hers as he reached past her for the salt yesterday and it felt as if she'd touched a power line. Was he getting in her face deliberately? Why would he? To what purpose? Was he trying to drive her insane?

They'd agreed, hadn't they? That they weren't going to take this thing further? Or rather she'd said it and he hadn't disagreed. There were so many reasons why them having a sexual relationship had the potential for catastrophe. It would be madness to jeopardise everything she'd found at Willow Tree this summer, for the sake of an endorphin fix…

She'd always been so good at ignoring her desires, subjugating them to the common good, the higher purpose, so how come all Art had to do was look at her a certain way and she had the insane urge to leap across the dinner table and take him down?

The front door shut downstairs, and then the loose floorboard squeaked as footsteps came up the stairs, lighter than usual. She slipped out of bed, grabbed her robe and yanked it on, then tied her hair in a soft knot.

Art had disappeared after dinner – leaving her achy and tense and unable to sleep – to head to the workshop as he did every night. It was now five minutes past midnight. Everyone else had been asleep for hours, and she wanted to sleep, too.

With Maddy and Jacob now happily nesting on the other side of the farm acreage she ought to be getting ten solid hours a night. She *needed* ten solid hours a night, what with the shop chores and all the wedding planning, she had a lot of responsibilities on her shoulder. And she couldn't do any of it efficiently with Art and his 'jump me I dare you' looks turning her into an insomniac.

She'd had enough. This situation required action.

Taking two deep breaths, she whipped open the door as the footsteps approached in the corridor outside.

'Art,' she whispered furiously.

He stopped, his broad body illuminated by the light from her room. She noticed the sheen on his slicked-back hair and the damp patch on his T-shirt. Her gaze travelled down to take in his bare feet. He carried his boots, which would explain the lighter tread on the stairs. Liquid fire tugged at her abdominal muscles. Had he just been for another midnight swim?

Visions of the swim she'd observed two weeks ago swam into her head.

Down, girl.

He didn't move, didn't say anything. No surprise there then. He was going to leave it up to her to handle the awkwardness.

'We need to talk,' she finally managed.

'About what?' His gaze didn't even flicker.

'The WI's new jam-making regulations, what do you think?' she snapped. Was he actually serious?

'Huh?'

'Don't be dense. We need to talk about what happened on Friday evening.' She oscillated her hand between them. 'The... That bloody kiss.'

'What about it?'

'I don't want it to happen again. So you need to stop looking at me like that.'

'Looking at you like what?' he said, as if he didn't know. But his gaze flicked away and she knew either he was lying to himself, or he was lying to her or quite possibly both.

So she hadn't been imagining those hot looks.

'Like you want it to happen again,' she said.

He didn't deny it.

'Look, Art, I'll admit I'm struggling not to…' She paused. Did she really want to give him this much ammunition?

If he'd looked smug, she might have stopped there, but he was giving her that intense look again, the one that made every one of her pulse points throb with unrequited need.

'Not to want to do something about it, too.' There, she'd said it. He didn't respond, not in words, but the muscle in his jaw twitched. 'But we both know it wouldn't stop with a kiss next time,' she carried on. 'And we both agreed that would not be a good idea.'

He stepped into her personal space. The smell of fresh water and the underlying hint of man had her catching her breath, audibly.

'When did I agree to that?'

She tried to get her objections in order, but the sight of him, the smell of him, so close was having a predictable effect.

'We can't have an affair, it would be too awkward, for Dee… And Toto. And it would be beyond confusing for Josh. I only told him three nights ago that I'm divorcing his father. He's still processing that and…'

'Who says they have to find out?'

'But… What?' Her voice trailed off into breathlessness as he bent to put his work boots on. The narrowed expression when he straightened was even more exciting than his damp T-shirt. *Blast the man.*

'How could they not find out?' Was that hope she could hear in her voice? Or madness? 'We all live in the same house? And we both know from Jacob and Maddy that sound carries in this house.' He remained mute as her common sense explanation gathered pace. 'I'm not having sex with you with my son and your daughter and my mother right down the hall.' Of that much she was certain… Or certain-ish. The feral glint in his eyes doing weird things to her resolve. 'They might hear us.'

There were loads of other reasons why this would be a very bad idea, why couldn't she verbalise a single one of them?

'Get some shoes on,' he said.

'What? Why?'

'I've got a place I want you to see.'

'Where?' she said, fairly sure she should not go anywhere with this man. Because she could not trust the endorphins rampaging round her body like teenagers at their first all-night Acid House rave.

His lips tipped up, the elicit smile a devastating combination of smug and sexy. 'It's a surprise.'

She waited two pregnant seconds. Should she go? Could she stay? And spend another night fighting the memory of having that hot avid mouth on hers?

She cursed and shot into her room to slip on walking boots over her bare feet. She must look ridiculous, but when she returned to the doorway, he took her hand and led her down the stairs without a word.

He dragged her out into the starry night, the air warm and still. He found his way in the darkness as if he had twenty-twenty night vision, leading her through the farm outbuildings, past his workshop, and round the back of the shop, and into the woods. The night smelled of wild honeysuckle and wet earth.

They followed the track that circumnavigated the millpond. It reminded her of another night two weeks ago, when she'd foolishly embarked on a midnight stroll.

Where is he taking me? And why am I going? What am I? A lemming?

But the denial eluded her, as his hand flexed on hers. She stumbled over something and his grip tightened.

'You OK?' he asked as he steadied her.

'Yes,' she managed, past burning lungs.

He guided her over a stile and then led her up the hill through the trees. A cloud passed over the moon, but, as her vision adjusted to the darkness, a shape appeared through the treeline at the top of the meadow.

'What's that?' she mumbled, as the shape morphed into a bow-top gypsy caravan similar to the one in his workshop.

'Somewhere private.'

He let go of her hand to climb the steps and swing open the door.

She stopped in the doorway, both unbearably aroused and completely horrified. With herself and him. What was she doing here? What were they doing here? This was still a really bad idea.

But, even as she lectured herself on the sense of letting Art drag her away from the safety of the farmhouse, she couldn't find the will to move.

He dug around in the darkness. A scratching sound was followed by the scent of kerosene. The soft glow of a lamp illuminated the caravan's interior. It was beautiful, compact and cosy but also luxuriously finished. Her pulse skipped and skidded at the sight of the double bed built into the end of the space, covered by a colourful patchwork quilt which had to be her mother's work.

She dragged her gaze away from it, to encounter a series of

expertly finished dark wood cabinets which had to be Art's work, with a gas stove and an icebox on top. Gingham curtains, like the ones in her room, fluttered over the narrow windows propped open on one side. The fresh scent of lemon polish and the fragrant smell of summer flowers infused the air.

'It's exquisite,' she whispered.

'It's useful,' he corrected. He leaned his butt against the cabinet and folded his arms over his chest. The lamplight shifted over the harsh planes of his face. 'We're at least half a mile from the farmhouse, and even further from the other homesteads,' he said, his voice matter of fact. 'No one's gonna disturb us or get traumatised by us being here and doing whatever we want to each other...'

She had to force herself to breathe. The enormity of what he was suggesting so huge she couldn't quite process it in her head. Even though her body was already way ahead of itself, her nipples hard enough to drill nails.

You muppet. Why did you let him bring you here? And why can't you just turn around and run back out into the night? Before you get pressured into doing something you don't want to do.

But annoyingly, despite the provocative things he'd said, and the hot way he was staring at her, she didn't feel pressured. She felt aroused. Hopelessly, stupidly, unbearably aroused.

'We can't,' she said, her voice a great deal less demonstrative than she needed it to be.

He released his arms, and braced his hands on the cabinets behind him, making his shoulders bunch under the damp T-shirt.

He ducked his head, and crossed his legs at the ankle, his fingers tightening on the cabinet edge as he stared down at his work boots. Was he nervous, too?

But then his head came up and he said in that same matter-of-fact voice: 'Why not?'

There was no anger or irritation, it sounded like a genuine question. That deserved a genuine answer. Unfortunately, she couldn't think of a single, solitary one that would make any sense.

After a pregnant pause, she managed, 'Because it would be dishonest?'

Unfortunately, the lift in her voice made it sound more like another question than an answer.

He huffed out a strained laughed, then dropped his head back down to examine his boots some more. When he spoke, his voice rumbled out from his chest, making the hairs on her nape prickle.

'You know what's dishonest?' He trapped her in that tractor beam gaze. 'Pretending we don't want to do this, when we do.'

Pushing himself upright, he walked towards her, each step slow, and careful, as if he were approaching a wild animal that might bolt at any moment.

Her heart beat so fast it felt as if it were going to gallop right out of her mouth. He raised his arm, and slid his hand across her cheek, barely touching.

The calluses on his palm rasped over sensitive skin and her breath gushed out in a rush. His eyes remained locked on hers, as if he were waiting for her to tell him no.

That would be the no that had deserted her seconds ago, no minutes ago, no hours, and weeks and months ago. The first time he'd kissed her. Maybe even before that. The no that had now floated out into the close night never to be heard of again.

His fingers threaded into her hair, and he lowered his lips to hers, but, just as he paused a whisper away, she flattened her hands against his waist.

'I should warn you,' she whispered against his lips, 'I'm not very good at this.'

He lifted his head, and cupped her face in both his palms. 'What?' he said, searching her face.

Why the hell had she said that?

'Forget I said that, let's just do it and see how it goes. It'll probably be OK, I have it on good authority you're a guaranteed orgasm.'

His lips curved, his eyes lighting with amusement. Was he laughing at her?

She pulled back. 'Why are you smiling?'

'Shhh.' He propped his forehead against hers, grinning now.

'Did you just shush me?'

'Stop talking, Ellie.' His fingers curled around her nape then slid into her hair. The top knot released, spilling her hair onto her shoulders. His abdominal muscles jumped under her touch.

'It's going to be good.' He chuckled again, the rusty sound sending a renewed rush of blood to her cheeks. 'I guarantee it.'

The yank in her abdomen became a hot slow glide of pressure, and instead of pushing him away, instead of being outraged, or scared, or indignant, she laughed, too.

He found her ear lobe and bit into the tender flesh. She choked out a sob, all her performance anxiety issues dissolving in the rush of blood to regions that had been neglected for far too long. He nuzzled, sucking the rampaging pulse, as rough hands sank beneath the waistband of her flannel pyjamas to cup her bare bottom.

She jolted, hot breath skating over her skin, as the ache became heavy and insistent.

'It's just sex, Ellie,' he rasped.

Just sex.

She spread her fingers determined to believe it, absorbing the hard planes of muscle and sinew.

Art was a mercurial and enigmatic man. And she had always wanted him, even as a girl. Why not take this for herself? It would be their secret and no one would ever need to know.

The tension that had been punishing her for days, for weeks, sang a hallelujah chorus in her blood. She tipped her head back, and lifted her hands to rub the day-old stubble on his cheeks, loving the rugged feel of him, absorbing the sublime strength in his jaw. Arousal darkened his irises to rich chocolate. Her pulse leapt at the evidence he was as wild for her as she was for him.

She could have this. They could have this. It would be their secret.

'How about it?' he asked.

She nodded, the power of speech having deserted her.

The quick grin made her heart stutter, before he turned his head to bite into her thumb, the playful nip sending sensation shuddering down.

He bent and scooped her into his arms.

She choked out a laugh, exhilarated and overwhelmed, as he carried her to the bed and placed her on the coverlet.

'Time to get naked, Princess Drama,' he said.

She laughed, joy and excitement battling in her chest with the swooping beat of affection.

*

Art felt the rush of blood southwards, as the adrenaline mainlined into his bloodstream.

This was mad. Certifiable. He'd been telling himself that for days, for weeks, ever since she'd watched him from the edge of the millpond. But with his hands on her at last, her subtle sexy scent driving him nuts, mad seemed like the only way to go.

He hadn't been able to stop thinking about her. Hadn't even been able to keep out of her way any more. When she'd told him she wanted it too, had made it clear that whatever she'd said three days ago, her desire for him wasn't in question, he'd had all the permission he needed to demand more.

Everything else was just practicalities. Sex was simple, and satisfying, and would take this ache away.

He perched her on the edge of the bunk, then gripped his T-shirt and hauled it over his head. He flung it aside, gratified when her gaze fixed on his chest. 'Lose the pyjamas.'

'Stop acting like a caveman.' Her chin took on that stubborn tilt he'd become addicted to.

'Then stop wasting time,' he countered. 'We haven't got all night.'

She huffed, but did as she was told, undoing the buttons on the soft cotton top. Underneath was a wispy lacy thing that moulded to her breasts and did nothing to disguise the shadow of her nipples.

Arousal gripped the base of his spine. He kicked off his boots and ripped open his flies, releasing the aching erection confined in his shorts.

'Do you have protection?' she asked, as she wiggled out of her pyjama shorts.

'Yup.' He reached over to prise open the draw on the bedside table, digging out the box of condoms he had stuffed there yesterday, while convincing himself he wasn't going to use them.

Now that she was here, delightfully naked as she perched on

the bed, her arm drawn tight over those lush breasts, he knew that was a big fat lie.

After dropping the box on the bed, he finished tearing off his clothes.

'I see you keep yourself well stocked here.' He noted the sarcasm. Was she jealous? Why should that please him? 'So I'm not the first to be invited to Art's gypsy love nest?'

He smiled at the indignant tone. Unlike other women, an arsey Ellie turned him on – probably because everything about her turned him on.

He'd never had sex with anyone at the farm, not since Alicia. But he wasn't going to tell her that, and give this moment too much significance.

'Do you want to talk about my past conquests?' He picked up the box and tore off the packaging. He tossed out a couple of foil packages, and handed her one. 'Or do you want to do the honours?'

She took the offering, unfolding her arm from across her breasts. The soft mounds jiggled, the puckered nipples making his straining erection pound harder.

'Pretty full of yourself aren't you, Dalton?' she said, as she ripped the package open, and pulled out the rubber.

Taking her shoulders, he pressed her back onto the bed and climbed up to join her. 'If you shut up for two seconds, you're going to be pretty full of me, too.'

She chuckled. But the sound turned to a gasp when he cupped her breasts, the hard nubs of her nipples pressing into his palms.

He watched intently as he played with the tips, and her snarky smile softened. Her breath released on a sob as he kissed her collarbone, then trailed his tongue down to circle the dark rigid areolas. First one, then the other.

At last he nipped with his teeth, loving the feeling of her quivering beneath him, and the sight of her flushed with need as she bucked off the bed. He held her steady, until her palm wrapped around his erection.

He tried to draw away. He didn't want this to be over too soon.

But Ellie had other ideas, her fingers closing around him, running down to the base then gliding to the tip. Her thumb circled, touching and stroking.

He swore against her neck, pumping into her touch. She let him go and pushed against his shoulders.

His eyes flew open, to find her face close to his, the blush blossoming on her cheeks, her hair wild and untamed, her eyes reflecting the fierce desire knotting his gut. She pressed a hand to his shoulder. He rolled away and lay on his back, then, to his amazement, she bent over and licked his erection.

The groan guttered out, rising up through his torso, sawing out of his lungs.

He gathered her hair, to watch her, the sweet glide of her tongue both tentative and somehow determined.

He'd been given head before. But this felt like more. Too much more. The quick exploratory licks gathering his taste, making his whole body jerk with a joy that reached into his soul.

'Bloody hell, Ellie, you have to stop.' He cradled her cheeks and lifted her head. Her gaze connected with his then darted away.

Suddenly she was climbing off the bed, rushing round to scoop up her clothes. 'I knew this would be a disaster.'

He lay for a moment in a state of stunned disbelief. Where had this come from? What had he done wrong? He jackknifed off the bed and went after her. Grabbing her shoulders, he pulled her upright.

'What's up?'

She stood with her back against his chest, shaking, her arms clasping her clothes to cover her breasts. 'I told you, I'm rubbish at this.'

He looped her hair round her ear, pressed a kiss to her neck, where her pulse fluttered furiously. 'Who told you that?'

Why would she even think that? Was this something to do with the husband she was divorcing?

'You did.' The unsteady voice cut through his rising irritation. 'You just asked me to stop.'

He shifted her round in his arms, keeping a tight grip on her in case she tried to bolt again. 'Only because I guaranteed you an orgasm,' he explained, reaching for practicality again. 'That means you get yours first.'

She had her head down, clutching her clothes.

'You can see what you do to me,' he said, the straining erection trapped against her belly. 'Does that look like I'm not enjoying it?'

Her head came up at last. The fierce flush of embarrassment on her face somehow brave and yet stoic with determination. 'I was joking about the orgasm,' she said. 'I probably won't have one. I don't usually. Please don't make a big deal of it.'

He so would make a big deal of it. What was the point of illicit sex if she didn't get off on it too? But he checked his thoughts, feeling the rigid tension in her shoulders, seeing it on her face. The first order of business was to take the pressure off, or neither one of them was going to be getting an orgasm tonight.

'Relax,' he said.

Taking hold of the clothes she was using as a shield, he tugged them gently. She held fast for a moment then let them fall from her grasp. He glided his hands up her arms. And clasped her head.

A shiver raced through her as her lips softened against his, the sigh deep and heartfelt. He massaged her scalp, drawing out the moment, licking and coaxing.

Dragging his mouth from hers with an effort, he led her back to the bed. She lay back, still wary as he climbed over her. He kissed her breasts, those perky nipples, then trailed down, absorbing the rapid rise and fall of her breathing, the sultry spice of her scent.

Hunger consumed him, hunger and an urge he hadn't felt in far too long. To nurture and protect.

*

Ellie raised up on her elbows, shocked when Art parted her knees, his dark head ducking between her legs. She shuddered. 'You don't have to do that.'

Dan had always hated oral sex, unless she was the one doing the honours.

But all thoughts of Dan and her mediocre sex life flowed right out of her head when Art glanced up, the grin fierce and feral. 'Are you kidding? I've been fantasising about this for weeks.'

She lost the ability to breathe let alone protest, as he separated her with his thumbs and blew on the swollen flesh.

'Oh God.'

He explored gently, cautiously at first, as if learning her taste. The leisurely licks tantalising then maddening. Her own caution drifted away on the warm wave of pleasure. She relaxed back onto the bed. Slowly, gradually, letting the liquid warmth replace the tension. But then he lapped at the heart of her, and the rasp of sensation made her jerk.

'Easy,' he whispered against her flesh. Stroking her thighs, her hips, settling her back. Building the pleasure again, tightening the coil in long, incremental licks, moving back towards that beating pulse. She hovered, the vice becoming painful in its intensity as it tightened.

Was that her sobbing, begging, needing him to touch her there again? Then he lapped right over the heart of her, concentrating there, not retreating this time. She bucked off the bed, cried out as the coil released in a rush, detonating in a blissful surge of release.

He continued to lick and suck, squeezing the last drops of the climax out of her. Before rising above her. He licked her juices from bearded lips.

Goodness, was she going to have beard burn on her clit tomorrow?

'No big deal,' he said.

She laughed at the absurdity of how good she felt as she watched him sheath himself with the condom. No big deal, not any more.

He held her hips, and the laugh guttered out as he pressed into her.

She panted, stretched wide, the exquisite feeling so intense it was a little disorientating. He held her bottom to angle her hips, and slid the rest of the way in one slow, glorious thrust.

Her breathing sawed out of her lungs, as he held still for a moment, seated deep, allowing her to adjust to his size. Then he drew out, and rocked back, going deeper still.

'Good?' he asked.

Tenderness engulfed her at the note of uncertainty.

'Yes, very.'

Touching his forehead to hers, he continued that slow, relentless rocking, drawing out, digging in, stroking a place deep inside.

Her whole body began to shake, the pleasure sublime and

intense, the smell of turpentine and lake water that clung to him a potent aphrodisiac.

She dug her heels into his backside, clung to his shoulders, as the rocking lost that slow relentless rhythm, becoming fiercer, more frantic. He shuddered, muffling his hoarse shout of release against her neck.

They lay entwined for several moments, her fingers tangled in his damp hair, the shelf of his shoulder digging into her chest where he'd collapsed on top of her, the pulsing in her sex brutally tender.

Lifting up, he rolled off her and flopped back on the bed.

She let her mind drift, still fogged by the delirium of afterglow – and the glorious sense of achievement.

The tiny part of her that had always blamed herself for Dan's infidelities – because she'd stopped being able to achieve orgasm with him the first time he'd cheated – finally gone for good.

Gradually a parade of fire-breathing dragons, whimsical elves, dancing unicorns, and all manner of mythical creatures painted in bold splashes of colour emerged from the shadows on the caravan ceiling.

She tilted her head, the lantern light flickering across the exquisite illustration. Her chest tightened, the tenderness in her limbs and between her legs butting into her heart.

Art stirred beside her. 'You all right?'

She turned to find him watching her. 'Yes,' she murmured. Should she thank him for the orgasm? No, that was silly, they were even. He'd had one too, hadn't he?

'Who did that?' she asked, studying the ceiling, the subject of unicorns and elves easier to negotiate.

He slung his arm above his head, the awkwardness lifting as they lay together staring at the illustration. 'I did.'

She caught the reticence in his voice. 'Seriously?'

'Yeah.' Was that a blush she could see slashing across his cheekbones? Since when did Art blush?

'It's beautiful.' She examined the detailed painting which wouldn't have looked out of place in a children's picture book. 'And rather… well, romantic.'

Sitting up, he swung his legs off the bunk, presenting his back to her. 'I didn't pick the subject matter.' He climbed off the bunk and dealt with the condom. 'Toto did. She likes magical creatures. She's a Harry Potter nut.'

It wasn't the subject she'd found so touching, but his obvious embarrassment only made the effort he'd taken to fulfil a little girl's wishes all the more sweet. She wondered if he had any clue how devoted he was to his daughter.

All the questions she had about his past, and how he'd come to be a single dad, crowded into her mind.

He bent to fish his boxers off the pile of clothing they'd left on the floor. She stifled the flicker of disappointment when he tugged them on. Had she left those score marks on his back?

The hum of renewed arousal became more pronounced.

She should probably get dressed now too, so they could sneak back to the farmhouse. But, instead, she slipped under the quilt to enjoy the show as he pulled two bottles of beer out of the icebox.

The thought that he might have planned this seduction, had certainly prepared for it, was almost as touching as the fairy-tale creatures he'd painted on the ceiling.

He offered her a bottle. 'You want one?'

'I'd love one,' she said. Her mouth dried as she watched his pecs flex while he popped off the caps against the cabinet edge and slung them in the bin.

She sat, plumping the pillows and drawing the quilt up to cover her breasts. He handed her the cool bottle and perched on the edge of the bed. She rolled it over her forehead, feeling flushed as he took a long gulp.

She sipped her own beer. Swallowed. 'What happened with Toto's mother?'

'Why do you want to know?'

The slight edge in the tone, and the lift of one eyebrow told her loud and clear she was overstepping the bounds of a casual sex-for-sex's-sakes fling.

'I just wondered. Dee mentioned her.' Surely having sex with Art entitled her to satisfy at least some of her curiosity? 'She said she had problems and that she left before Toto's first birthday. Do you miss her?'

'Hardly. I kicked her out.'

'I see,' she said, the abrupt tone making her pulse bobble.

Instead of filling the gaping hole in the conversation, he concentrated on finishing the beer, then shot the bottle into the bin at the end of the caravan. It hit the rim and dropped into the metal container. The perfect slam dunk.

'Why did you kick her out?' she asked, finally forced to fill the gap for him.

He glanced her way, his expression suspiciously blank. 'I woke up one night and found her shooting up next to Toto's crib.'

Standing, he slipped off his boxers, then climbed back onto the bunk. The sight of his erection bobbing up to his belly button shocked her almost as much as the information about Toto's mother.

Seriously? Again already?

She choked on her beer. He grabbed another condom from the pile on the bedside cabinet.

She pressed into the pillows, the liquid pull in her abdomen swift and unstoppable as his hands flattened on the headboard on either side of her head. He swung one knee over her, caging her in. Her gaze glided down his chest as she watched him roll on the condom.

She finished her beer in one long gulp.

He took the empty bottle from her fingers and slung it towards the bin without looking. It landed with a resounding crash. Another direct hit.

She stared into those piercing eyes. Dark, intent and glazed with hunger. For her.

'What if I want to talk some more?' she said, the husky tone of her voice fooling no one – but it was the principle of the thing.

'Then I'll take you back to the farmhouse,' he said, the wry tilt of his lips even more of a turn-on than the challenging tone. 'We're not here to talk.'

The air backed up in her lungs as he took hold of the quilt and gave it a sharp tug. It dropped away, leaving her breasts bare.

He circled one pouting nipple with his tongue. The liquid pull became a definite yank as the peak engorged in a rush.

He lifted his head. 'You want to go back?'

She thrust her fingers into his hair and dragged his mouth towards hers. 'I don't think that will be necessary,' she murmured against his lips. 'Just yet.'

CHAPTER TWENTY-THREE

Ellie skipped up the farmhouse stairs. She had exactly half an hour before she needed to be at the shop to relieve Dee. Just enough time to freshen up after her trip with Mike to another local organic farm who had contacted them about supplying the shop with fresh vine tomatoes, something they didn't grow at Willow Tree.

The visit had been hugely positive; they'd already drawn up a contract. And Guy Hansard, the farm manager, had given them a list of six other farms, one as far away as the outskirts of Winchester, that had heard about Willow Tree Farm Shop and Café and were interested in filling other gaps they had in their inventory.

After only being in business for three weeks they were already getting a reputation for excellent service and high-end organic produce. It would be a while before they could determine how well they were doing financially, but the excellent customer numbers since the launch showed no signs of slacking and their operating profit in the first three weeks had been beyond all expectations. The shop was still a gamble. A big gamble. But Annie and Tess had made the decision to give up their day jobs last week. Something they were both extremely happy about. And Dee had decided to stop attending farmers' markets – because so many of her regulars were already coming to the shop.

It was still early days, but so far the signs looked overwhelmingly positive. Securing several grants to ease the cost of the original set-up also meant they had a financial cushion to carry them over any potential shortfalls in January and February when the custom would naturally drop off.

They.

The word slowed Ellie's step, weighing on her as she entered her bedroom. She was part of this team. Part of this operation. But after a couple of rather tense conversations with Dan on Skype, she'd finally booked her return flights to the US for the end of September. Jacob and Maddy's wedding was on the ninth, giving her three clear weeks after the wedding to put everything in order to hand over the management of the store to Dee, Tess and Annie. And put all the plans in place for the run-up to the Christmas season.

The Christmas season she was going to miss.

She sat at her dressing table, plucking the last of the pins out of her hair.

Buying the return flights this morning had left her in a bit of a funk. And while the visit to McPherson's Organic Farm had helped lift her out of it, a little bit, the thought of everything that awaited her in Orchard Harbor in four weeks' time kept crowding in on her.

She touched her throat, noticing the raw skin from the night before.

And then there was Art.

They'd been sneaking off to the caravan almost every night for the last two weeks. And it had been glorious. Exhilarating and exciting and surprisingly companionable.

The sex had been nothing short of a revelation.

Even in the early throes of her relationship with Dan, when the sex had been plentiful and mostly satisfying, she could see now Dan had been a selfish lover. Making all the decisions about when and where and how much they had. And of course she'd let him, because she was so besotted with him.

With Art it was different. The clandestine dash through the woods at midnight, when she sneaked out to rendezvous with him, was ludicrously exciting because she knew he would be as eager to please her as she was to please him. Together they'd experimented and explored. She felt like a teenager again, but better. As if anything was possible. Young and in lust, but not ashamed to demand her own pleasure.

Perhaps surprisingly though, the quiet moments afterwards, as they basked in afterglow together, before sneaking back to the farmhouse ten minutes apart, had become almost as precious as the orgasms.

Art wasn't comfortable talking about his past, and she didn't have any great desire to talk about hers – not that he'd asked – so she'd curtailed her curiosity, but they'd still found so much to talk about. All that basic day-to-day stuff, which Dan had got bored with as soon as she brought it up, Art listened to with genuine interest. Getting his take on her social media plans for the shop, hearing how work on his latest commission was going, chuckling over something daft that Toto or Josh had said or done had been rewarding in ways she never would have expected.

And discovering that Art was a bit of a snuggler on the sly

had been almost as much of a surprise as discovering how much she still liked sex.

She sighed as she dumped the last pin on the dresser. If only she could talk about him to Tess and Annie.

Keeping their liaison a secret from everyone made sense, and for the last few weeks the secrecy had been as exciting as those midnight dashes through the woods, but she was starting to feel uncomfortable about pretending nothing was going on. And keeping how much she was enjoying herself from them was next to impossible.

Obviously this affair had no future. She was going back to New York soon, and Art had made it very clear he wasn't interested in anything more. And neither was she, of course. Long-distance relationships never worked, and she would need all her energy in the months ahead to finalise her divorce, sort out the custody arrangements with Dan, navigate Josh's situation when his new sibling arrived and find a new place to live – because she had no desire to return to their soulless six-bedroom show home in Orchard Harbor. But even so, what seemed like a simple affair at the outset was starting to become more complicated, and she would love to have had some advice about how to handle it.

She cleansed her face, and re-applied her make-up, ready for the customers.

She was being juvenile. She didn't need her friends' input or advice. It was obvious what was going on here.

She had a crush on Art Dalton. They were having awesome sex. And becoming friends. But, ultimately, that's all this was, a throwback to her youth. She'd been stressed beyond belief when she'd arrived at Willow Tree for the summer, and she'd taken advantage of everything it had to offer. And when she returned to Orchard Harbor her real life would begin again. At least when that happened, she'd have a much better understanding of what she wanted and what she was capable of. And she had Art to thank for that as much as anyone. And four more weeks to enjoy him.

She was staring into the mirror, trying to align her lips in her I-can-do-anything smile before applying a new coat of lipstick when a loud thumping sound made her jump.

What was that? Had it come from her bathroom?

'Is someone there?'

Could it be Josh? Weren't he and Toto busy building a new hideout near Maddy and Jacob's place? Exactly how many hideouts did two kids need?

She heard another muffled thump, definitely coming from the bathroom.

She grabbed her hairbrush off the dresser ready to investigate. Perhaps a squirrel or a bird had got into the room through the window she'd left open in the heat. She whipped the door open, hairbrush raised, ready to do battle with whatever wildlife had invaded her space.

Toto yelped and leapt up from her crouch on the floor, her face ablaze, Ellie's box of panty liners strewn across the floor.

Ellie lowered the hairbrush. 'Toto, what are you doing?' The poor kid looked as if she were about to pass out.

'Nothing,' Toto said, not at all convincingly. She had whipped her hands behind her back when Ellie had opened the door, but Ellie had seen the panty liners in her fists.

'Did you need to borrow some panty liners?' she asked. Toto was thirteen. It was more than possible she was having her periods already.

Toto shook her head vigorously.

Unfortunately for Toto, she wasn't a very convincing liar.

But before Ellie could question her further, Toto dropped the panty liners and went to dart past her. Without thinking about it, Ellie grabbed the girl's arm as she barrelled past. Toto slammed to a stop.

'You can have them back. I'm sorry. I'm sorry,' Toto said, as she struggled to get loose, tears leaking from her eyes. She pulled a wad of liners from her pockets with her free hand and tried to shove them at Ellie. 'Please don't tell my dad.'

She held on as the girl wriggled and squirmed. 'Toto, calm down. It's OK. I won't tell your dad.'

Why was Toto so scared of Art finding out? If his daughter was having to steal essential sanitary items this was partially his fault. She shoved the thought to one side. Not her concern. And there were more pressing concerns for now. The child was in considerable distress and she could only think of one possible reason for that.

'Did you start your periods today?' Ellie asked.

Toto stopped struggling, and tucked her chin into her chest, her breath heaving in and out as if powered by a bellows. Her face was so red now the sprinkle of freckles across her nose stood out like stoplights.

The child's biceps tensed, as she continued to examine the floor. The nod so tiny, Ellie almost didn't catch it.

'How exciting,' Ellie said, trying to put as much of a positive spin as she could on the news in the face of the girl's distress. 'You're welcome to take all the panty liners you need. But you might need something more substantial. Is there a lot of blood?' Hopefully dealing with the practicalities would also put the girl at ease.

'No,' Toto said into her chest, as if the onset of puberty meant the end of life as she knew it. It might well feel that way to a tomboy like Toto, but it really didn't have to.

Had anyone spoken to her about menstruation? Wouldn't Dee have talked to her? Or Art? Surely she would have learned about it at school at least?

Didn't matter. What she needed was reassurance now. And Ellie was the only one here. She could have waited, to pass the buck to Dee – who was the closest thing Toto had to a mother – but she didn't want to. She had come to like this child very much, but she'd never quite managed to bridge the gap she'd created that first day between her and Toto. Here was a chance to change that. And she did not want to mess it up.

'If it's just a few spots, the panty liners will be fine for now.'

Toto nodded. 'OK,' she said, in a small child's voice.

Ellie's throat hurt as she drew the girl into her arms. Maybe it wasn't her place, but the child needed a hug. And she needed to give her one.

Toto's whippet-thin body stiffened, but then yielded.

'It's really not so terrible,' Ellie said, stroking the sweaty hair back from Toto's forehead, letting the huge wave of affection wash through her. What must it have been like to grow up with Art as your only parent? While he was a good man and obviously a caring father, she couldn't imagine he was very in touch with his feminine side.

'Are you in any pain?' she whispered against the girl's head.

Toto shook her head against Ellie's chest as she nudged closer. Warm hands settled on Ellie's lower back.

The gush of love slammed into Ellie, bringing back memories of how much she'd missed her own mum when she'd returned to London with her dad, Nicholas.

Her mother had called frequently at first and come down to visit, but Ellie had made things as hard as she could for Dee, still hurt and angry that her mother had refused to come home – convincing herself that she was glad when her mother had finally got the message and stopped visiting.

But her father Nicholas had been no substitute for all the things she'd lost when she'd pushed Dee out of her life. He'd never been the caregiver in the family and he hadn't really known what to do with Ellie once she'd chosen to return with him to London that summer. So he'd left her to her own devices in the care of a succession of housekeepers, while he carried on as usual, working long hours and dating a succession of glamorous women, some of whom had tried to befriend Ellie, but most of whom hadn't, thank goodness.

Currently dating one of the junior partners in his architectural firm, who wasn't much older than Ellie herself, and with no intention of retiring any time soon, Nicholas Preston still lived in the lofty, immaculately maintained semi-detached Georgian house near Hammersmith Bridge where Ellie had grown up. He'd visited her twice during the twelve years she'd lived in Orchard Harbor, both flying visits that he'd squeezed in around business trips. During both visits, he'd spent more time playing golf with Dan than he had hanging out with her and Josh. Which had been fine by Ellie. They had nothing in common, all their conversations polite and superficial. And while Ellie had never become estranged from her father, the way she had from her mother all those years ago, she could see now her relationship with him had simply never been as important to her. She'd contacted him once since arriving in the UK this summer, and their conversation had been as polite and superficial as always – with them both knowing that he'd be unlikely to find time in his schedule to fit in the vague offer of a day out in London with her and Josh. And that neither of them cared enough about seeing each other to press the point.

Thinking about her dad, made her think of Dan. And how alike her husband and her father were, because – whether by accident or design – they had both ended up being hands-off parents.

Unlike Art.

Maybe Art wasn't the type of guy to talk about menstruation or make sure he was well stocked on teenage sanitary products, but he was entirely present in his daughter's life. And always had been.

Stop thinking about Art.

Planting her hands on Toto's shoulders, she eased the child back. The reddened skin on Toto's cheeks tugged at Ellie's heart.

Toto was a confused little girl who was having to deal with something she was ill prepared for. Time to start acting like the parent here, even if she wasn't Toto's parent.

'Why don't I pop into Gratesbury this afternoon and pick up some other supplies for you. Just in case the flow gets heavier.'

'OK.' Toto frowned. 'But don't get those ginormous things you stick up you. Miss Morely put one in a glass of water in sex-ed and it blew up to the size of a tin can. I don't think they'll fit.'

Ellie bit back a laugh at the pragmatic response. Toto might not be a boy, but she was still a lot like her dad. 'You're probably right. I was thinking more of some sanitary towels. They're easy to use and more appropriate for now. And you'll want one for the night-time.'

'All right,' Toto said. Her head swung round and back. 'But can I keep them in your bathroom?'

'You can if you want to,' Ellie said. 'But it might be more con-venient to have them in the bathroom down the hall.'

The anxiety flashed again. 'I can't, my dad might see them and freak out.'

'You know, your dad probably won't even be surprised. Most girls start their periods around your age, or even sooner. I started mine when I was thirteen, too.' And thank goodness her mum had still been there.

'But...' Toto's brows drew down. 'But Miss Morely said when you start your periods you become a woman. I don't want my dad to know I'm a woman, because it will totally freak him out.'

'Ummm.' Ellie was struck dumb for a moment. Art was certainly gruff and moody at times, but she'd seen a softer more playful side to him in the last couple of weeks. And he certainly wasn't a misogynist. Where would Toto get the idea from that he didn't want her to be a woman?

'What Miss Morely probably meant was it's the first step to becoming a woman, but you've got a long way to go yet before you're an adult,' she said, keeping her voice as neutral as possible. 'But anyway, why do you think your dad would freak out? He likes women.' Ellie felt herself colouring. OK, not cool to be thinking about Art's lovemaking skills while talking to his daughter. 'And he loves you,' she said, trying to pull the conversation back to appropriate. 'You do know that.' Is this why Toto was such a tomboy, because she thought her dad wouldn't accept her if she was a girl?

'Yeah, of course,' Toto said, her puzzled look making Ellie feel foolish. 'He doesn't say it much, but then he doesn't say much of anything anyway.'

Ellie almost smiled. This child knew her father better than anyone.

'But my dad will need to get used to the idea of me being a woman, because, you know, he's a bit weird about that stuff.'

'Weird how?' Ellie asked, confused herself now and hopelessly captivated by this new insight into Art's personality.

'Well, he's never even had a girlfriend,' Toto said. 'I wondered if he might be gay, like Dee, but he doesn't have any boyfriends either, and anyway Dee said he's not when I asked her.'

An embarrassed laugh got trapped under Ellie's breastbone. Just the thought of Toto and Dee having that conversation, and what Art would have made of it, had her forcing out a fake cough. 'Right.'

'I thought for a bit he might like you,' Toto said, the serious tone ridiculously endearing, despite Ellie's discomfort.

'Why would you think that?' she asked, trying not to sound guilty.

Yikes, could this conversation actually get any more awkward?

'Because he looks at you funny sometimes, but Josh says that's probably just indigestion. And he hardly ever talks to you at all. He talks to Tess and Annie more and I know he doesn't like them that way, so I guess not.'

Of course he hardly ever talked to her, because they were keeping their liaison a secret. A secret that was beginning to look a lot less than secret. Was Toto the only one who had picked up on those hot looks?

'I see,' Ellie said.

She actually wasn't Art's girlfriend, not in any real sense, Toto was right about that. But suddenly the relationship they did have – no strings sex as often as their schedules would allow – seemed dishonest and immature. How exactly would they explain themselves to the kids if their secret got out? It wasn't exactly setting a good example – about how to embark on committed adult relationships.

'Would you like him to have a girlfriend?' Ellie prompted.

'I don't know. I guess I never thought about it,' Toto said with unfailing honesty. 'But I think if he did have a girlfriend, he wouldn't be weirded out by periods and stuff. And me becoming a woman.' She paused. 'You know, eventually.'

'That makes sense, I suppose.' A blush blossomed across Ellie's collarbone.

'Why don't you tell him?' Toto said.

'Tell him what?' *Because I have now officially completely drowned the thread of this conversation in my own guilt.*

'About periods and stuff. He might not know much about them because he never had a girlfriend and he never reads.'

'I suppose I could, but he might wonder why I'm telling him,' Ellie said, thoughts of tangled webs and the problem with trying to deceive swimming through her brain.

Toto considered this for a moment. 'I know, you can tell him I've started my periods. Then I won't have to tell him.'

'*Me?*' Ellie said, feeling as if she'd just won a Nobel Prize and jumped off a cliff at one and the same time. She was honoured that Toto trusted her enough to tell her father about such an intimate event in her life, but she was also deeply wary of having that conversation with Art.

Yes, they talked about their kids together, but only in the most superficial way. Wouldn't telling Art about this be stepping over a line? A line they had both agreed they did not want to cross?

And when would she be able to tell him? It was hardly the sort of thing she could mention before or after mind-blowing sex. And they generally avoided each other the rest of the time, so as not to clue anyone into their relationship.

'You could totally tell him,' Toto said, warming to her idea.

'You're a woman and I think he likes you a bit. You could tell him all that stuff about it not being a big deal and he'd have to believe you.'

'Well, Dee's a woman too,' Ellie said, suddenly keen to find a way out. Stepping over this line would not be good for either one of them. 'And Art knows her better than me.' And he certainly trusted Dee more.

'But Dee's old, and I know she doesn't have periods any more. Because I raided her bathroom before I raided yours.' Toto looked concerned. 'Don't you want to tell him? Is he going to be really freaked out?'

'No, not at all.' *Way to go, Ellie, stop scaring her. Time to get your big girl panties on.* 'I'll tell him, it's not a problem.'

'Wicked.' Toto's sudden grin pierced Ellie's heart.

Whatever mistakes Art had made as a parent, he'd done a terrific job raising Toto. She was pragmatic, open and generous of spirit, but most of all she had more empathy and understanding than people twice her age. She'd been a loyal and enthusiastic friend to Josh, hadn't judged him by his appearance as so many of the children in Orchard Harbor had. And now when she was facing puberty without a mum, she was more concerned about how her father was going to handle it than how she was going to handle it herself.

'But don't tell him until Sunday,' Toto added.

'Why Sunday?'

'Because Dee's taking me and Josh to see the teen club double bill at Salisbury Odeon. It's *Harry Potter and the Deathly Hallows Parts One* and *Two* which is like five hours long. If you tell him while we're gone, he'll have lots of time to get used to the news before we get back.'

Well, at least that solved the problem of when to tell Art.

'This is true.' Ellie slung her arm round Toto's shoulder, and gave her a quick squeeze. 'Good thinking, Batman.'

Toto chuckled, the sound sweet and childish and uncomplicated. Ellie's heart swelled, the pang hitting her square in the chest.

She could do this thing. She must not be a wimp.

All she had to do now was figure out how to get Art alone on Sunday afternoon without anyone seeing them together. And how exactly she was going to broach the subject so that she didn't freak him out, or freak them both out when his casual sex fling gave him the news that his daughter was becoming a woman.

No problem.

CHAPTER TWENTY-FOUR

'Give me a couple of the tartlets too and some of Dee's fried chicken,' Ellie said.

Maddy finished packing the picnic basket then rang up the sales. 'Shall I stick this on the shop's expense account?'

'Don't be daft, I'm a paying customer.' Ellie counted out the bills.

'Who's the picnic for?' Annie leaned over from her spot at the espresso machine while she frothed the milk for a family of four who had ordered baby-chinos for their toddlers. 'I thought Josh and Toto were in Salisbury today with Dee?'

'I thought I'd take a book down to the millpond and stuff myself during my day off.'

Annie's eyebrows lifted. 'You're kidding – you're planning to eat all that on your own?'

'Maybe I'll rope in Art,' she said, pretending she'd only just thought of that idea. 'I think he's almost finished the caravan, he might be in the mood to celebrate,' she added, using the strategy she'd worked out over the last few days: hide in plain sight.

Annie and Maddy shared a look. 'You and Art, eh?' Annie said, her look speaking volumes, most of them pornographic. 'I hope your toenail polish is still intact.'

'Hardly,' Ellie said jauntily, taking the teasing in stride. If Annie knew what she and Art had been getting up to in the last fortnight, she'd know hot toenail polish was entirely unnecessary. But this picnic wasn't about seducing Art, it was about fulfilling her promise to Toto, on Toto's timetable. 'But it doesn't matter,' she added. 'Because Art's not going to be seeing my toes.' *Or any other part of my anatomy currently covered.*

One thing she definitely could not do was let this picnic get out of hand. Because that would only confuse the issue further. As if it wasn't confused enough already.

'Pity that,' Annie said with a cheeky grin.

Ellie picked up the basket, and sent Maddy and Annie a wave as she left the shop. 'See you tomorrow, ladies. I've got an important date with *Tess of the D'Urbervilles* and my mum's amuse-bouche.'

Not to mention my friend with benefits. Even though there will be no benefits.

She left the shop, before either of them could question her further. She headed to the farmhouse and grabbed some beer from her mother's pantry. She had a feeling she was going to need some liquid courage for what she had to say to Art – she had no idea how he was going to take the news that Toto was growing up, but she planned to deliver it as painlessly as possible.

Walking through the back orchard, she arrived at Art's workshop.

He stood on a footstool, his T-shirt sprinkled with paint as he dabbed at the intricate ivy motif he was painting on the caravan's front arch. Bruce Springsteen blared out from the radio perched on the front step.

He'd told her last night, after they'd exhausted each other, he only had a few more days to finish off the paintwork before the buyers arrived to get the caravan on Friday. The vehicle looked magnificent, the intricate artwork on the side shining from the fresh coat of varnish – the designs as detailed and exquisite as the rest of it. He wasn't just a master craftsman. He was a talented artist.

She thought back to the first time she'd come into the workshop, ready to confront him about his objections to the shop, and seen the bare bones of the caravan's shell laid out on the floor. It was hard to believe how long ago that felt now. And how much had changed between them.

Her ribs felt as if they were crushing her heart, the rhythmic pounding becoming deep and uneven.

Don't get carried away.

The summer had been a success, that was all, positive and productive. And Art was a part of that. She had repaired her relationship with her mother, rediscovered the joys of project planning with the shop and now the wedding – which was going to be an amazing event to reflect Maddy and Jacob's devotion to one another – and she had reawakened her long-dead libido. She'd recharged her batteries and there was still four weeks to go before she had to say goodbye to everyone.

By which time she would be more than ready to reboot her life and her business in the US.

Art and she had just been enjoying each other, and would continue to enjoy each other for the time they had left together.

No need to overreact.

She tapped on the workshop door. Art swung round. A slow smile spread across his face, softening his features and making the deep pounding in her chest almost painful.

He dropped the brush in a jar of turpentine and switched off The Boss.

'Hi,' she said, choking a little on the simple word of greeting.

'Hey, what are you doing here in the daylight?' he said, but the smile didn't falter. He strode towards her, the graceful, predatory stride making awareness prickle over her skin.

God, she was going to miss him. Miss sex with him, she corrected herself swiftly. Because that's all this was – a physical addiction to a man who had always fascinated her.

'I figured you might want to take a break.' She held up the picnic basket. 'I thought we could have lunch down by the millpond.'

She noticed the flecks of paint on the bronzed hair of his forearms, the spots in his hair as he brushed it off his brow.

He tipped the lid of the basket up, peered inside. 'Dee's fried chicken and Badger beer.' His gaze met hers. 'Yum.'

The rough tone and that searing look made her fairly sure he wasn't talking about the picnic menu.

'You sure we should risk it?' he added.

'Risk what? People seeing us eating a picnic together? I think we can risk that, yes,' she said, just in case he thought 'picnic' was a euphemism for something else.

After scooping the basket out of her hands, he tucked it under his arm and cupped her elbow, to direct her through the workshop door into the sunlight 'Come on then, I'm ravenous.'

He pressed a palm to her lower back, to guide her through the gate then took her hand as they walked through the woods. She should have objected – it would make them look like a couple, if anyone saw them. But somehow she couldn't bring herself to tug her hand out of that possessive grasp.

The scent of flowers and tree resin and the buzz of insects filled the late summer air.

She spotted the millpond ahead through the trees. The clear

water sparkled like a green jewel, the cool depths beckoning. Rambling roses, wild poppies, dandelions and a patchwork of other flowers and plants she couldn't name edged the path in bursts of colour and pockets of perfume. A Cabbage White butterfly flitted ahead of them as if leading the way through the ancient oaks shading their journey. The pond finally appeared like an oasis, the man ahead of her like a dark knight leading her back into temptation.

He led her towards the water's edge – a man on a mission – without saying a single word. Funny to think how much she had come to appreciate Art's silences in the last few weeks as well as his conversation. What she had once considered a weakness had become one of his biggest turn-ons.

Dan had always been a man who could spin virtually anything and was never short of conversation. There was a lot to be said for a man who believed doing was more important than talking about it.

Art stopped beside the weeping willow where she had once sheltered to spy on him in the moonlight. Placing the basket on the bank where the grass gave way to gnarled tree roots, he let go of her hand. She immediately felt the loss of the firm pressure. But then he reached back to take a fistful of his T-shirt and drag it over his head.

Her mouth dried to parchment at the sight of the smooth planes of muscle gilded by sweat.

He crouched to untie his work boots and kick them off, then unbutton the fly on his jeans, knocking her out of her trance.

'What are you doing?' she said, her voice tight and raspy round the ball of lust forming in her throat.

'Swimming.' He peeled off his jeans and his boxers with them.

'After four hours of slapping on paint, in two hundred degree heat, I stink.'

'Are you mad?' She swung her head round, frantically scanning the woods while trying to ignore the rush of adrenaline. 'Anyone could see you?'

Good grief, why did the man have to look so mouth-watering naked.

He placed his hands on her cheeks, forcing her to face him, unashamed about his nakedness. He brushed his thumbs across her cheekbones, the hunger in his eyes accompanied by that wicked smile making her pulse batter her collarbone.

'No one's gonna see us. Rob and Mike are working on the other side of the farm harvesting carrots and marrows. Maddy and Annie are tied up in the shop. Tess is taking Melly to a Princess Party in Gillingham and Dee and the kids are watching five plus hours of Harry and co. finally beating the crap out of Voldemort in Salisbury.'

She captured a lungful of his scent with her indrawn breath. He didn't stink, he smelled delicious, the salty, seductive aroma making the pheromones fire through her bloodstream.

'We've got a three-hour window of opportunity.' His thumbs slid down her throat to toy with the thin straps of her summer dress. He eased a strap off one shoulder blade. 'Let's use it.'

Her stomach started fluttering like the wings of their butterfly guide. 'I didn't come here to have sex.'

His lips quirked in a challenging smile, before he kissed the tip of her nose. 'Your loss.'

Then he turned and ran towards the lake, yelling as if he were trying to wake the dead. He cannonballed into the water, his naked buttocks bunching as he tucked his legs to his chest, before he shattered the glass-like surface with a resounding splash.

Ellie gasped, as chilly beads flickered across the burning skin of her collarbone. The surge of heat powered through her body.

Oh sod it. She toed off her pumps, then shucked off her dress and dumped it by the picnic basket.

This was madness, but it was divine madness. And it was only for one afternoon. She would have lots of time to be a grown-up later.

Her bra and knickers followed, before she raced towards the water's edge, the butterfly flutters sinking deep into her abdomen when he splashed her.

'Come on in, Princess Drama,' he yelled. 'The water's perfect.'

Pinching her nose, she jumped. She hit the frigid water and sucked in a startled gasp. As she plummeted beneath the freezing surface, her stomach plummeted with her.

*

'Don't get ideas, Dalton.' Ellie batted away the lazy touch of Art's fingertip as he teased the edge of her belly button. 'I'm stuffed and shattered, you're not getting an encore.'

She heard him laugh, that deep lazy chuckle, before his shoulder nudged her as he lay down beside her.

'Killjoy,' he said.

She opened her eyes to stare at the waterfall branches of the willow tree shading them from the afternoon sun.

She *was* stuffed – stuffed full of the array of salads and mini quiches and filo pastries and chicken she'd bought from the shop. And completely shattered.

They'd made love in the open air, the lake water drying on chilled skin, after mucking about in the water like a couple of kids for what felt like hours.

So shattered, she was finding it a little hard to breathe. Her chest felt tight at the thought they were unlikely to get another day like today before she left.

She eased over onto her side, and propped her head on her elbow, to study the man who had always been such an enigma. He lay with his eyes closed, relaxed and approachable. His thick lashes fanned across his cheeks. As her gaze drifted down to the strong column of his throat, and the pulse punching his clavicle, she noticed his workman's tan wasn't as visible as it had been earlier in the summer. He must have been working outdoors with his shirt off. Dark curls of chest hair defined the flat discs of his nipples.

Her heart battered her ribs in a haphazard tattoo. Why not admit it, it wasn't only the sex she was going to miss.

He let his hand drop to rest on his belly, drawing her gaze to the jagged scar.

She touched the raised flesh with a fingertip. He tensed, his belly muscles quivering. But his eyes remained closed, and his hand remained still on his stomach, making no move to push her away as she traced the wound over his hipbone – her belly clutching at the thought of how badly he'd once been hurt.

'How did you get this scar?' she asked

His eyes opened, and his mouth curved in a wry smile. 'Why does it matter?'

The words echoed in her consciousness, reminding her of something he had once said to her mother, and she realised the disturbing truth that she'd never had the guts to acknowledge.

'Because you matter to me,' she said.

Apparently she had the guts to acknowledge it now.

*

Art lifted his arms and put his hands behind his head, buying time, trying to look nonchalant, the quietly spoken words making his chest hurt.

He struggled to remember the lies he'd told for years whenever anyone asked about the scar. But, as Ellie refused to relinquish eye contact, those expressive green eyes so full of empathy, he couldn't find the energy to lie about it to her.

If she was expecting some romantic tale of woe, though, she wasn't going to get it. Because there was no way of romanticising the squalor of his childhood.

'I can't tell you exactly, because I blanked most of the details.' And the ones he couldn't blank still gave him nightmares, and turned him into a bowl of jelly whenever he got within a mile of a hospital.

'Was it your arsehole of a father?' she asked.

He stared at her. How did she know about his old man? Oh yeah, the sloe gin chronicles.

'Sort of.' He sat up, and gazed out at the pond, not wanting her eyes on him. Sunlight sparkled on the water. His skin had been clean and fresh from the swim, his muscles loose and languid after their lovemaking. And his belly pleasantly full from the tasty treats she'd piled into the picnic basket, and the bottle of Badger beer they'd shared. But now he felt unclean, the pastry he'd wolfed down with the ale threatening to reappear.

'I caught him slapping Laura and I had some stupid kid's notion that I could stop him. I couldn't. He was strung out on something and he went berserk, kicked me so hard they had to slice me open to stop the bleeding.'

He heard the sharp intake of breath. Then felt her hand on his back. 'How old were you?'

'Six, maybe seven.' He found it hard to remember, because he'd never had much in the way of birthday celebrations in the succession of squats and communes they'd lived in before ending up at the Rainbow. The revolving door of faces and broken furniture, the smell of stale weed and dirty feet, the sound of boozy arguments and the pounding base beat of music played at top volume all blurred into one now, with no specific time or location attached to the memories.

But he could still remember Laura's frantic whispers as they wheeled him into surgery that day, making the gut-wrenching agony that much worse.

You mustn't tell, Arty. They'll take you away from me if you tell.

'Please tell me they had him arrested?'

He glanced over his shoulder, to find Ellie's face so full of fury on his behalf, it made his chest hurt more.

'They didn't know. Laura told me not to say anything. So I didn't.'

Funny to think there had once been a time when he had been terrified of being taken him away from his mother. But then, young children always trusted their parents, until they grew up enough to know not to. Just like Toto had always trusted him.

He picked up a broken branch, flicked it into the water, watched it splash and sink.

'That heartless bitch.' Ellie's voice was tight with anger. 'How could she make you keep it a secret? She should have been protecting you, not him.'

'He'd run off by the time I got let out of the hospital and we never saw him again, so it didn't matter anyway.'

'Of course it did and it still does. You have a phobia of hospitals now. And I bet that's where it comes from.'

'I don't have a phobia. I just don't like them much. But who does?' Maybe they freaked him out more than they should, but who in their right mind enjoyed going to a hospital? 'And Laura wasn't that bad. We kind of deserved each other.'

'How can you say that, Art? No one deserves to be treated the way she treated you.'

He twisted round, enjoying her outrage maybe a bit too much. 'Have you forgotten what a shit I was back then, to you and everyone else?'

'You weren't that bad,' she said. 'I was pretty high maintenance and chronically self-absorbed.'

'Maybe.' He smiled, not sure how to process the fact that they seemed to have become friends as well as bonk buddies in the last few weeks. 'But I'm still sorry for the way I treated you that summer.'

Warm fingers touched his arm. 'Apology accepted. And I'm sorry, too.'

'What for?'

'For making you talk about your father... And your mother.' She looked sincere, her face grave. 'It's obviously a difficult subject.'

'It's not difficult,' he corrected her, because it didn't feel difficult talking about them to her. 'Just boring.'

She nodded, but she was looking at him in a way that made him feel more naked than when they'd been skinny-dipping in the pond.

He started packing their debris back into the basket. He needed something to do with his hands, because the urge to kiss her felt like more than just the urge to start something they didn't have time to finish.

'I didn't mean to ruin the afternoon, this has been…' She hesitated, then smiled, that sweet, straightforward smile that her son had inherited. His heart started beating in a jungle rhythm – deep and erratic and difficult to ignore. 'It's been really nice to talk to you properly.'

'Nice wasn't what I was aiming for,' he said, letting his gaze drift over the bodice of her dress dampened by her bra. 'How about I make up for it tonight?' he suggested. They were just bonk buddies, that was the deal, he needed to remember that.

'I'd like that,' she said, but her smile had disappeared. 'But, before we go, I have something I need to tell you. It's…' She tugged on her bottom lip, unsure. And his heartbeat became even more erratic.

What was this now? And how did he feel about it? When she'd shown up at the workshop a couple of hours ago in the middle of the day, he'd been so stupidly pleased to see her. Not just because she'd looked so hot and happy in the short summer dress, but because it felt important that she'd come to him in the daylight. And he had to wonder why. Because he'd been trying to convince himself for days now that he was perfectly happy keeping their affair on the down-low, the way she'd originally insisted. Trying to persuade himself that he wasn't dissatisfied every time she slipped out of his arms after they'd made love, and got dressed in a rush so she could sneak back to the farmhouse ahead of him.

They couldn't afford to complicate things. Neither one of them wanted to get caught, because it would confuse everyone. Toto and Josh most of all.

But each night, when he'd lie on the caravan bed, his body still humming from afterglow, and wait for her to finish getting dressed in the lamplight, his chest had begun to feel as if a heavy weight was lying on it. And each night he'd found it harder and harder not to give in to the urge to ask her not to go. To ask her to stay with him for the rest of the night. Not because he wanted to jump her again. But because he wanted her with him when he woke up in the morning.

And now, after everything he'd just told her, stuff he'd never told anyone, not even Dee, and the patient way she'd listened, and the compassion and fury shining in her eyes when she had, he was finding it even harder to ignore the boulder on his chest. He didn't want to hope, because that made him feel pathetic. But surely she wouldn't have asked him about all that shit from his past unless she felt the same way – that there might be more going on here than just recreational sex and small talk.

'It's about Toto,' she said.

'Toto?' he said, as his heartbeat downgraded. It wasn't what he'd been expecting her to say, but why was he so disappointed? What exactly had he been hoping to hear? 'What's up with Toto?'

*

'Your daughter started her periods on Friday.'

Ellie watched Art's face, for any adverse reaction, and saw the crease form between his brows.

'She wanted me to tell you,' she added.

One quizzical eyebrow lifted. 'Why did she tell you about it?'

He didn't sound upset, so much as surprised, but there was a wariness there that made the nerves jump and jive in her stomach.

Why did his reaction feel like a slap? Maybe it was just that shocking revelation about his injury, making her feel overemotional? That Art had opened up about his past had felt significant, even though he hadn't seemed to need her outrage or her support – giving the horrific details in a monotone, as if he'd come to terms with those events years ago.

He was a remarkably self-sufficient man, which was what she wanted, wasn't it?

'Not exactly,' she said. 'She was busy raiding my bathroom for sanitary products.'

He swore, the frown remaining in place. 'I'll take her into Gratesbury tomorrow and get her what she needs.'

'I already did that,' she said, trying not to take the curt tone personally.

The frown deepened. 'You didn't need to. I could have handled it.'

OK, that was definitely a slap. She'd worried about overstepping the mark, that Art might resent her involvement, but she hadn't expected his response to be this negative. Especially after the conversation they'd just shared.

He began to pack the rest of the leftovers into the picnic basket, his movements tense.

'Art, I'm sensing a certain amount of animosity here and I'm not sure where it's coming from,' she said, determined to calm the situation for Toto's sake as much as her own. The little girl had been worried her father would freak out about this. Apparently she'd been right. It was her job now to make sure he didn't freak out with his daughter.

He didn't respond, turning his back to tug his T-shirt over his head.

'If you've got a problem with me buying your daughter sanitary products that she needed, when she needed them, I'd like to know why?'

'Let's just drop it,' he said, standing up to stamp on his boots.

I don't think so.

She grabbed her pumps, slipped them on.

He tucked the basket under his arm. 'I'll head back,' he said. 'And drop the basket off for you.'

'Art, wait,' she said, still frantically tying her laces as he stalked off.

She caught up with him on the path, breathless now and battling to keep her own emotions in check. 'What the hell is wrong with you?'

He shrugged off her hand. 'Nothing, I'll talk to Toto when she gets back from Salisbury, tell her not to involve you again.'

'Don't you dare do that,' she said, starting to lose the grip on her temper.

'I'll dare what I goddamn like, she's my daughter.' And there it was again, the slap, but she couldn't let herself care about that. This wasn't about her, or him, it was about Toto and her feelings. 'She should have come to me.'

'She was scared, Art, scared that you'd freak out about her becoming a woman.'

'Why the hell would I freak out about that?'

'Maybe because that's exactly what you're doing.'

'No, I'm not.'

'Yes, you are. You're even freaking out about me talking to her about it.'

'Because she should have come to me,' he said again, as if this were a parental pissing contest.

'Why would she come to you? She needed sanitary products, you weren't likely to have any, now were you? I bet you've never even spoken to her about menstruation either, have you?'

She could tell she had him there from the stubborn look on his face.

'I didn't need to, they handled it at school,' he said, finally. 'She told me all about it. The tampon in the water glass totally freaked her out.'

Ellie had to bite back a smile, the disgruntled tone making her temper fade. 'Yes, she mentioned that to me too. We decided she didn't need any tampons yet.'

'I can get her what she needs,' he said, his face not softening one iota. 'That's my job.'

'She's a practical kid,' Ellie said, grasping for reason and practicality in the face of his intransigence. 'She figured you wouldn't have any. That's all.'

'I suppose...' He hesitated. 'She still seems like a little kid.'

She saw it then, the flicker of dismay and vulnerability, that he was trying so hard not to show her.

Why had she never figured it out before? Even if Art had been a single parent for a lot longer than she had, he had insecurities too. This wasn't about her, about them, it was just about Art's relationship with his daughter.

She placed a hand on his arm, touched by his concern, and felt the muscles tense beneath her fingers. 'And she's still a little kid in every way that counts.'

He dragged his hand through his hair, sending the still damp strands into furrows. He drew in a deep breath, and let it out slowly. 'Thanks for handling it. I'm not great with this stuff.'

'You're better than you think.'

He shook his head. 'No, I'm not. I try my best, but I can't be her mother.'

She heard the regret in his voice. 'From what you told me about Alicia, Toto's better off without her.'

'Maybe. But I sometimes wonder whether...'

'Don't. You're doing a good job. Toto's a wonderful child, confident and secure and well adjusted. She's been wonderful to Josh this summer. Her friendship has meant so much to him, and to me.'

He nodded, his gaze thoughtful, but he looked away before he said, 'Kind of ironic, when you think how we used to fight when we were kids.'

'I know,' she said. But, as he shouldered the basket, and walked beside her through the woods, it occurred to her that in some ways they had become kindred spirits too.

She pushed the feeling back, of companionship, of friendship. She didn't take his hand, wasn't surprised when he didn't offer her his. Something had changed between them today, something profound, that neither one of them could afford to examine too closely – was that why he'd jumped off the handle when she'd mentioned Toto starting her periods?

As they approached the edge of the orchard, she touched his arm again. 'I'll take the basket. I should clear it out and put it away again before Mum and the kids get back.'

He kept it on his shoulder. 'It's OK. We've got time before we have to cover our tracks.' She thought she heard a slight edge to his voice, but convinced herself she must have been imagining it.

She'd gone into this wanting it to be just about sex, and so had he. If it didn't feel like just sex any more that was only because they'd become friends while bonking each other's brains out. The desire to ask for more was a mistake. The desire to reach out to that little boy who had been broken so badly by a mother and eventually a lover who had never been good enough for him was a fool's errand. A fool's errand that she'd been on once before, nineteen years ago. Art had always found it impossible to trust people and just because she now knew why he couldn't, didn't mean she could somehow magically fix that about him.

But, as they walked through the back orchard together, she found herself finding it harder and harder to ignore the stupid, romantic voice inside her that wanted to at least try.

As they approached the door of the farmhouse, she opened her mouth to say something, anything to bridge the gap that seemed to have opened up between them, when she heard a car coming down the track.

'Who's that?' Art said, dumping the basket on the farmhouse's front step.

That wasn't Dee's car. 'It must be a customer,' she said, grateful for the interruption that had stopped her saying something she would no doubt regret.

Instead of taking the fork in the track that led to the shop car park, the gleaming convertible travelled towards them, stopping a few feet away.

Art stepped in front of her, as a man got out of the car.

Her heart shuddered to a stop, the wave of shock swiftly followed by a wave of panic.

Was that...? No, surely not, it couldn't be. What the bloody hell was Dan doing here?

With his chestnut brown hair carefully styled and a pair of Ray-Bans perched on his nose, her soon-to-be-ex-husband looked debonair and dashing – and nothing like an optical illusion.

Even so, the moment felt surreal, suspended in time as Dan strolled towards them, lifting off his sunglasses. But then his gaze landed on Art, taking in their damp hair, the discarded picnic basket. And the welcoming smile turned into a suspicious frown.

'What's going on?' Dan said.

Art touched her waist to push her behind him. 'Who the hell are you?' he said, annoyance snapping in his voice.

'I'm Ellie's husband,' Dan shot back. 'Who the fuck are you?'

PART FOUR: BACK FOR GOOD

Eloise Charlotte Preston <u>DALTON</u>'s Diary

3 September 1998

Ever since I saw Art silent crying on my mum's shoulder, I've realised he is my soul mate. I haven't been able to stop thinking about him. I even dream about him. And I get sad now when he doesn't come to supper – and I used to love it when he didn't come!!

I think I love him. And I'm pretty sure he is in love with me too because:

Reasons:

1) I keep catching him watching me when he thinks I'm not looking.
2) He hasn't had a girlfriend in ages. Girls still come to the commune to see him, but he hardly even talks to them now. And I haven't seen him snogging any of them, not like I saw him snogging Donna Whatshername in the woods a month ago.
3) He hasn't called me Princess Drama in weeks and weeks.
4) When that horrid little Haley called me a posh cow, he told her to shut up. I heard him.
5) Yesterday, when I said hello to him, he said hello back, and not in a mean way, but in a cool way. He even smiled. Almost.

The only problem is, he hasn't said anything. And boys are supposed to say first.

I wrote to Jess about what to do last week, her letter arrived today.

She thinks I should go ahead and tell Art. But just writing that down here makes me feel a little sick. Excited sick, though, like when I went on the roller coaster at Alton Towers and it did a loop the loop. Not sick sick, like I'm actually going to puke. So there is that.

And Jess is an expert about this stuff, because she's been out with about every boy in our class (all except Kev Smith, because he's gross) and she says she had to ask a few of them first because boys can be really slow.

But Art doesn't seem like he'd be slow about this stuff. Not from the way he was kissing Donna Whatsit.

And what if I tell him and then he wants to kiss me? Like he kissed Donna? And he finds out I'm a rubbish kisser? He's had loads of practice and I've had virtually zero. The only boy I ever kissed was Willy Reid in year six and he slobbered so much he nearly drowned me, so I don't even think that counts as practice.

Tomorrow is Friday and all the little kids here go back to school. I'm supposed to be starting the new school Mum has enrolled me in on Monday. So me and Art will be the only ones here all day tomorrow. And my dad is supposedly coming to visit on Saturday (although I'll be amazed if that happens as he keeps saying he's going to come and then he never does – but if he does, I'll probably have to spend some time with him).

So if I'm going to tell Art, I have to tell him tomorrow. Before school starts, and before I chicken out.

If he wants to kiss me, it'll be fine. As long as he doesn't want to have actual sex with me. Like I think he did with Donna, because he had his hand on her boob while he was kissing her. It looked pretty *hot, and Donna was moaning like she loved it, but Jess said it hurts like hell the first time, because her older sister told her. Also what if I'm rubbish at that too??*

But I'm sure he won't want to do sex straight away. We'll have to run away first, so we can be together. Like Jack and Rose would have done in Titanic *if he hadn't frozen to death (I still don't get why she didn't move over and find a spot for him on that door, it was easily big enough for both of them!).*

My mum will be sad I know if me and Art run away, but Mum will understand, because she had to run away too, with Pam.

At least we won't have to worry about Art's mum. She probably won't even notice we're gone.

CHAPTER TWENTY-FIVE

'Dan, I can't believe you would just turn up here without letting me know,' Ellie's voice sounded hoarse, her head pounding from the confrontation she'd ended up having to referee in the farmyard between her not-quite-ex-husband and her current lover.

At least she'd managed to avert a punch-up between them. Although, to be fair, Art had backed off as soon as Dan had made his announcement.

In fact, his face had gone completely blank and he'd walked off without another word. For a moment though, he'd looked… stunned? Angry? Wounded? It was hard to say, because he'd masked it so quickly. But, whatever it was, it had shocked her. And made her feel sick. She would need to speak to Art later. And explain.

She and Dan were separated, they had been for three months, he had no right to turn up and start mouthing off about his marital rights.

But before she could deal with Art, she had to deal with Dan.

She'd corralled him into the farmhouse kitchen, to contain the situation.

'Yeah, well, I can't believe you'd sleep with some goddamn farmer as soon as you arrived in the UK,' Dan said. 'When you haven't slept with me since before goddamn Christmas.'

'Art's not a farmer, he's a talented carpenter and an expert in construction,' she said, reeling from the fury in his tone. Was he actually seriously upset about this? How could he be?

They'd agreed months ago they were getting a divorce. He'd been sleeping with another woman, who was having his baby in approximately six months' time. How did that make her the bad guy?

'Awesome, so I can get him to drill my drywall as well as drill my wife, that makes me feel so much better.'

'Stop being crude.'

'Crude, I'm being crude! You're the one who just banged some other guy while you're married to me.'

'We are getting a divorce. You're having a child with another woman. What about that did you not understand?'

'Chelsea's not pregnant, it was a false alarm,' Dan said. 'We found out a month ago. She hasn't spoken to me since, so I think we can say that relationship is definitely over.'

'But…' Ellie's mind stalled on the news. How did she feel? Relief? Surprise? Shouldn't she feel something? But all she felt was tired and… indifferent. 'So what?'

'So *what*?' It was Dan's turn to look shocked. 'So I came to get you. You and Josh. I've missed you. I want another chance.'

'Dan, you're not serious? Even if Chelsea's not pregnant, our marriage has been over for years.' And it had taken him over a month to make a move once he'd broken up with Chelsea. If he expected her to believe he'd been celibate for four whole weeks, he must think she was more gullible than Mary Poppins.

'Why? Because you've found some farmer to replace me?' he demanded.

'No, because you found a thousand women to replace me.'

'There weren't that many.'

'That many? Is that supposed to make me feel better?'

'OK, I fucked up.'

'"Fucked" being the operative word,' she said, deciding that sometimes crude worked.

Dan gave a long-suffering sigh, as if he were actually the injured party here. 'I screwed up and I'm not proud of it.'

'You screwed up more than once, Dan. A lot more than once. Someone who keeps repeating the same offence is clearly not capable of change. I believed you the first time you said it wasn't going to happen again. I even believed you the second time. But I finally stopped believing and we simply ended up locked in a loveless, sexless relationship in which we were both kidding ourselves that we actually cared enough about each other to stay together when the truth was we were just too lazy and self-absorbed to do anything about it. I'm sorry you came here today. And I'm sorry you saw Art and I together, because you and I are still nominally married.' Was that the real reason she'd been so determined to keep her and Art's liaison a secret, not to protect Josh or Toto, but simply to protect her own reputation? The new stab of guilt sliced under her ribs, making her anxiety increase. 'But what we've been doing together is still none of your business. You left me, Dan, years ago, every time you decided to sleep with another woman, so you don't get to turn up now out of the blue and lay down the law about marital ethics.'

Unfortunately, that fact didn't make her feel any better about the look that had flashed across Art's face when Dan had arrived.

They had shared something this afternoon, something profound. And now she might never know what that something was, because she hadn't had the guts to ask before her ex had turned up.

'Is he better than I am in the sack? Is that it?' Dan sounded frantic. 'I can do better. I know I was selfish sometimes, I got wound up in myself and our sex life suffered. I get that, but I can change that.'

'It's not about the sex.' Exactly how immature was this man?

'Then what the hell is it about?'

'I respect him,' she said.

Art had opened up to her this afternoon for the first time, and she'd had an insight into why he felt the need to close himself off. 'And I know he respects me.' Although he might not respect her much now. 'And that's a basis for something more than we ever had.'

How much more she wasn't going to contemplate right now, not until she'd had a chance to talk to Art. That she was having this conversation with her estranged husband was probably a bit… well… peculiar. But peculiar she could live with. Dan not so much.

The plan had always been to go back to Orchard Harbor. To remake her life there, or nearby, so that Dan could have access to his son. She'd been so careful not to think outside that box. But why should she let Dan call all the shots? Why was she so terrified of acknowledging that there might be other options? Or that she had feelings for Art that went way past those for a casual hook up?

'Don't say that. We could do more counselling to fix that?' Dan said, the tremor in his voice making Ellie stare at him. 'I've found someone more appropriate than Dr Macklin,' he said, naming the couples therapist they'd attended for six months in one last-ditch attempt to save their marriage, while Dan was busy sleeping with Josh's middle school teacher on the sly and getting her not-pregnant. 'I've been to a few sessions already.'

'You've… What?' Ellie's voice rose several octaves. Surely she could not have heard that right. Dan taking responsibility, creating a plan of action, and then actually following through on it? To save their marriage? She'd always been the one doing all the emotional heavy lifting in their relationship. The one who had continually tried to paper over the cracks of what had eventually become a derelict crumbling mess. That Dan had finally decided to shoulder at least some of that burden felt like way too little, way too late. She wasn't convinced there was anything left to build on any more. But after so many years of struggling alone, it felt necessary to at least listen to what he had to say.

'This doctor's a sex therapist, world renowned, based in New York.'

'I don't need sex therapy,' Ellie said. Not any more anyway.

'I know you don't.' Dan looked sheepish, the honey brown hair falling over his brow in artful disarray.

Ellie wasn't buying the embarrassed look, until colour lanced across his cheekbones.

'But I do,' he murmured into his chest.

She didn't speak, wasn't sure she was capable of speech. His eyes finally met hers, the look surprisingly direct for a man whose father was a politician with two terms in the Senate under his belt.

'You're having sex therapy?' she said, just to be sure she hadn't had a breakdown and stress-projected that piece of information.

He nodded, the sheepish look turning to sober introspection, which actually looked genuine. 'I've had a month to think about everything, about where we went wrong.' He cleared his throat. 'Where *I* went wrong. And it all got down to my inability to be faithful. And eventually, after lots of soul-searching and denial, I figured out I needed help. So I found this doctor. She's terrific.'

She. 'The good doctor's a woman?'

Dan let out a half-laugh. 'She's a looker, but not really my type, she has pictures of her grandkids on her desk.'

'Oh.' Now she was back to being confused. And wary. Was Dan actually here because he thought they had a serious chance of repairing their marriage?

If he had done something like this five years ago, she would have been skipping around the room with unconcealed joy. She had never felt less like skipping in her whole entire life.

'I didn't want to come here until I could prove I wasn't just blowing sunshine up your ass again, that I meant it this time, that I can change,' Dan added.

He was actually serious. Not fake, politician sincere, but tentative I'm-trying-here-but-I'm-terrified-it-won't-be-enough sincere.

She hadn't had a glimpse of insecure Dan since the day they discovered she was pregnant and he'd told his father. It was one of the things that had drawn her to him so comprehensively all those years ago. The way he'd stood up for her, stood up for them and their child, against a man who she knew had always terrified him on some visceral level.

She'd clung on to that in the years afterwards, long after that man had disappeared to be replaced by a careless womaniser who hadn't stood up for anything. But, because of her affection for that man, she couldn't bring herself to slap him down. She suddenly felt exhausted, and she noted so did Dan. He'd probably caught the red-eye and she knew he never slept on planes, even in first class, and it was a three-hour drive here from Heathrow.

Plus, there were all her confused feelings for Art to consider too. This was all too sudden. And too much of a tangled mess to discuss while they were both exhausted.

'I don't know what to say. This is… surprising.' How's that for an understatement – the shock reverberating through her reminded her of the moment when the pee stick had turned pink.

'I know, and I'm sure you don't really believe me. Because why would you? But I want to prove to you I can change. That's why I'm here. I wanted to get you both and bring you home.'

Except Orchard Harbor didn't feel like home any more. And hadn't for a while. And wasn't it just perfect timing that she should finally admit that to herself now?

'I have commitments here that I can't break.' And she had absolutely no intention of breaking.

'What? To him?' Dan said, clearly shocked. 'How serious are you about this guy?'

'This isn't about Art,' she said, even though it was, partially. But she hadn't even had a chance to examine her own feelings properly, let alone talk to Art about them. And she certainly had no intention of discussing their relationship with Dan. Because it would feel like a betrayal, which was probably rather ironic, given that she was still officially Dan's wife. 'I'm planning a wedding for two of the co-op's residents…'

'Can't you get someone else to step in?'

'No, I can't. And I don't want to. They're friends of mine and I want to be here for the event.'

'OK, fine.' Dan scrubbed his hands down his face, looking harassed. 'Look, it's not a problem. I can stay here with you and Joshie for a few weeks.'

'You're not staying with us,' she said, horrified. She didn't want

Dan here – that would just complicate the situation even more. 'We're not a couple any more. We're separated.'

Dan threw his hands up in the air. 'Then I'll get a hotel room nearby. I'm not going home without you guys.'

Trust Dan to choose this precise moment to get assertive.

The rumble of an engine drawing up outside the house was followed by the sound of children chattering, and car doors slamming.

'Is that Joshie?' Dan said, and the genuine pleasure on his face had Ellie's heart kicking her ribs.

She had Josh to consider in all this, too. She wasn't even sure what she wanted to do any more. But, whatever happened, she had to put him first. Not herself, not Art and certainly not Dan.

'Yes, he's back from a Harry Potter movie marathon with my mum Dee and Art's daughter, Toto.'

Dan scowled, the pleasure gone. 'Why did the guy name his daughter after a dog?'

'It's short for Antonia,' she heard herself say as the front door opened and footsteps stampeded down the hall.

'Mom, there's a cool car in the yard.' Josh sounded curious, until he entered the kitchen.

'Dad!' He ran full pelt into his father's arms. Dan grunted, laughing, as Josh smacked into his chest.

Dan scooped him up and swung him round. 'Hey, kid, how did you get to be so skinny?' Putting Josh down, he looped his fingers round the boy's upper arm, testing his biceps. 'And where did you get all the muscle?'

Josh beamed at the compliment, and it occurred to Ellie how much her son *had* changed physically in the last three months. She hadn't really noticed it, as the change had been so gradual, but Dan was right. Their son no longer had that pallid, waxy skin from too much time spent indoors on his Xbox. And his sturdy body was solid now rather than flabby. He'd even begun to wear a belt that Dee had found him to hold up his jeans.

As Josh wrapped his arms around his father's waist, she had a vision of the day their son had taken his first steps solo. Dan had squatted down two feet away and beckoned him forward while she held his straining body upright. Josh had staggered towards Dan on unsteady legs, falling forward into his father's arms, and Dan had wrapped him in a bear hug and lavished him with praise. She'd loved Dan without reservation in that moment, even though they'd had an argument that morning about the text entitled 'lonely nights' she'd found from a co-worker on his iPhone.

Josh burrowed his head into his father's chest, his hands grasping the back of his shirt, his cheeks bulging in an ear-splitting grin.

Dee stood back with Toto; they both looked almost as shellshocked as Ellie felt.

'Mum, Toto, this is Dan, Josh's dad.' Ellie did the introductions, because Josh was far too busy absorbing his father to talk.

She couldn't bring herself to ruin the touching reunion between father and son. The argument Josh's arrival had interrupted would have to wait.

Slinging an arm over Josh's shoulder and fixing him to his side, Dan reached out a hand to Dee.

'Hi, Dan Granger, pleased to meet you, ma'am.'

Dan's golden brown hair shone in the light from the window, the day-old scruff on his chiselled, patrician jaw making him look handsome and rugged – a bit like a movie star who had been professionally rumpled for a photo shoot.

He looked like a campaign poster for the perfect son-in-law, wearing that mantle of self-confident charm that she knew he could turn on and off like a light – a golden all-consuming light that dazzled everyone.

If Dan noticed she'd introduced him as Josh's dad instead of her husband, he didn't let on.

'Hello, Dan. Call me Dee,' her mum said, not looking very dazzled as she shook his hand. Maybe Dee was immune to Dan's charm.

Dan nodded at Toto. 'Hey there, Toto. I hear you're Joshie's new friend. He talks a lot about you.'

Toto didn't speak, leaving Dan's hand hanging in mid-air, her freckles standing out more than usual against her flushed skin. Dan pulled his hand back and rubbed it on his chinos before tucking it into his pocket.

So Toto was immune too.

'Don't call me Joshie, Dad. I'm too big for that now,' Josh said, sounding more excited than grumpy.

Dan ruffled his son's hair. 'Sure thing, buddy.' Dan stood back as if assessing Josh's height. 'I reckon you've grown about two inches since I last saw you too.'

It was Josh's turn to blush, clearly overjoyed at his father's praise.

'How long is Dad staying?' Josh asked, his eager smile joined by Dan's querying look. 'Can he stay for the wedding?' Josh pleaded. 'It's gonna be so cool, Dad.' He sent an adoring look at his father. 'Maddy and Jay are getting married and me and Toto are going to be the attendants. We get to scatter rose petals and everything.'

'I'd love to stay,' Dan said, casting a meaningful glance her way.

'Jay's room is free, isn't it, Mum, now that he lives with Maddy?'

Ellie felt some relief that Josh wasn't expecting his parents to share a bedroom. But the thought of moving Dan into the room next to hers, and between her and Art… Her head started to pound in double time. Thick heavy thuds that hit the base of her skull.

How had everything got so screwed up so quickly?

But how could she kill that spark of joy in Josh's eyes? 'That would work for tonight,' she said. She turned to her mother. 'Is that OK with you, Mum?'

'Whatever you want to do is good with me,' Dee said.

Josh punched the air and Dan grinned, having won this round.

It didn't matter. She didn't plan to be in the room next door to his tonight. She needed to go and speak to Art. They'd agreed to meet at the caravan tonight. She just hoped he was still willing to keep that liaison. The thought of having that conversation was filling her with an odd mix of dread and anticipation, which she would have to examine later too.

Dee set about making them coffee and cake. And Josh settled into a never-ending conversation apprising his father of every single thing he'd done in the last three months, while Toto looked on bemused.

Ellie's heart raced into her throat, and threatened to gag her.

Dan's surprise appearance might be one problem even Mum's sticky toffee ginger cake can't solve.

CHAPTER TWENTY-SIX

It took five hours before Ellie could get away. Five hours of panic and irritation. Art hadn't turned up to supper, and she had to be grateful for that. She didn't think the two men would start anything with their children looking on, but why risk it? Even so, having Dan there had felt like an intrusion. He'd tried to make small talk all through dinner, turned on the charm big time with her mum and Toto, and for the first time ever Ellie had realised exactly how self-serving and shallow Dan's charm was.

Even when she'd known he was cheating on her, even during that last conversation in Orchard Harbor, when he'd told her about Chelsea's baby and she'd told him she wanted a divorce, he'd still had a strange sort of hold on her. She'd made excuses for him – convinced herself that in some ways his infidelity was as much her fault as his. Let him talk her into being the one to tell Josh.

But now, she could see what a phoney he was.

All those practised moves, the easy flattery, the way he pretended to listen and laughed in all the right places. Josh had hung on his every word, but neither Toto nor her mum had been taken in by it. And this time, neither had she. She'd take Art's strong steady silences, even his surly moody moments, over Dan's fake razzamatazz any day.

The privileged, indulged youngest child and only son in a family of over-achievers, Dan had been born not to take responsibility for anything. But she'd once loved that the most about him. As a compulsive fixer, she had found it wildly attractive that Dan could look at any problem and say 'screw that, let's go party instead'. So it made perfect sense for her to handle all the details Dan couldn't be bothered with during their marriage: like calling the plumber, or doing the IRS returns, or hiring a nutritionist for Josh when he couldn't stop comfort eating, or a couples therapist for them both when Dan couldn't stop cheating.

But it had eventually left her as the only one who had invested any energy in making their marriage a success.

She'd discovered this afternoon the full extent of all the challenges, all the emotional curveballs Art had been thrown in life and how much he'd had to endure and overcome to survive. It was hard not to compare the two of them now – Dan's pampered patrician beauty and hollow charm to Art's sturdy, solid, blue collar strength and subtle humour – and find Art the much hotter of the two.

But was it really wise to make choices based on her libido again?

After waiting for Dan to take Josh up to bed, she dashed to her room to shower and change. It was a warm night so she slipped on a dress emblazoned with sunflowers that she'd bought in Gratesbury a few weeks ago but hadn't had a chance to wear. The bias cut flattered her figure. She took a bit of extra time with her make-up, adding eyeliner and a quick layer of lip gloss. She'd caught the sun today, her cheeks given a healthy glow.

She left her room as soon as she heard Dee's tread disappear down the corridor.

Maybe it was reckless to go and see Art before everyone had gone to bed. But she couldn't wait any longer to talk to him. And she did not want to have the conversation here.

She left the house, the sun setting behind the back barn. She went to Art's workshop first, just in case he was still finishing the commission, but felt relieved when she found it empty.

She wanted to talk to him in the caravan, because it felt like their safe place. Maybe they'd never had any proper conversations there, because they'd always been way too busy making love, but it felt like the right place to take this next step. To actually discuss their relationship. Such as it was.

Maybe it was foolish and romantic to want to tell Art about her relationship with Dan. He'd never asked her about her husband and she'd never divulged anything, partly because it embarrassed her to know what a spineless coward she'd been all those years in Orchard Harbor. But still she wanted Art to know that Dan had come here uninvited and that she wasn't convinced they could ever be a couple again, no matter how much sex therapy he had.

Dan would still be Josh's father, and for that reason he would always have a place in her life. It wasn't as if she would ever try to change that relationship. But Dan had never been a hands-on dad. And Josh had settled so well here during the summer. As had she. There were all sorts of possibilities that she hadn't even considered before tonight that she wanted Art's take on.

She walked through the woods, the dusk giving the flowers and trees a reddish glow. And her heart leapt and stuttered as she made her way through the gathering darkness and spotted the light shining at the top of the rise.

Art was waiting for her.

She hesitated for a moment as she came out of the trees. Remembering another time, another place not far from here, when she'd once made a similar clandestine dash to see Art in the sunlight of a September weekend afternoon. The memory of what had happened when she'd thrown herself at Art that day still had the power to make her cringe. But she'd been hyped up on teenage hormones then, and her own confused feelings. She'd totally misread that situation. She wasn't that naïve girl any more. She wasn't here to put pressure on Art, to make emotional demands that he had no hope of fulfilling. She just wanted to let him know that Dan's being here hadn't been her idea… And then go from there.

She tapped on the door and pulled it open.

Art sat on the bed, whittling a piece of wood with a wicked-looking knife she'd seen him use before. Her heart leapt at the sight of those large competent hands on the wood, the long scar she'd seen sewn up three months ago. A yearning ache pulsed deep in her abdomen.

He dumped the knife and the piece he was carving on the bedside table. But didn't move towards her.

'Ellie? What are you doing here?' he said.

He sounded surprised to see her. Her heartbeat leapt, but she ignored it.

She was here now, and he didn't look unhappy to see her, that was the main thing. 'I thought we had a date?' she said.

He got off the bed, but instead of approaching her, or smiling, he sent her the same blank look he'd sent her that afternoon before he'd stalked off after Dan's arrival.

'I didn't think you'd keep it,' he said.

Why did he look so tense? Of course, Dan. The fact of Dan, she had some explaining to do about that, which was precisely why she was here.

Get on with it then.

'We're separated, Art. We've been officially separated for over three months. I didn't invite him here and I don't want him here. He has no claim on me. And we both know that.'

'You've put him up in Jacob's old room.'

How did Art know that? 'I know, it's awkward, I realise that. And don't worry, he's going to a hotel tomorrow.' She was also going to start the divorce proceedings. She'd held off on that until her return to Orchard Harbor – stupidly giving Dan false expectations in the process. But how could she have known Chelsea's baby would end up being a phantom pregnancy? There was no point in waiting any longer, especially now there might be other possibilities. Alternatives to returning to Orchard Harbor once the summer was over. 'But I didn't come here just to talk about him, I came to talk about—'

'I'm not worried,' he interrupted her.

'What?' she said, surprised by the flat tone.

'I'm not worried. What you do with your husband is your business.'

'He's not my husband.' Why were they still talking about Dan, when she wanted to talk about them? About the possibilities she hadn't even allowed herself to consider until this afternoon? 'Not really.'

He shrugged, propping his backside on the bunk and crossing his arms over his chest. 'This has got a lot more complicated than it was meant to be.'

'Yes, I know. That's why I wanted to see you. To talk to you.'

She crossed the small space, suddenly desperate to touch him. To see that lazy smile she'd become a little bit addicted to. Why did he seem so distant all of a sudden? This wasn't the man who had leapt on her every night as soon as she arrived. Who hadn't been able to tear her clothes off fast enough. Obviously Dan being here made her continued relationship with Art more problematic. But surely not that problematic. Dan had been her husband in little more than name for a very long time. She didn't owe him any loyalty and she wanted Art to know that.

But how could he, when she'd never told him anything about Dan? She sucked in a careful breath. She had to tell him all of it. Not just her situation with Dan now, but what a pathetic doormat she'd been during most of her marriage.

'Dan started cheating on me about two years after we were married.' She swallowed down the wave of humiliation. This needed to be said, so Art would know her relationship with Dan had been over long before she'd come to Willow Tree Farm. 'And he never stopped. I put up with it, because I think I had some warped idea that I could be better than my mum, that by not running from a bad marriage I could somehow make it better. I was wrong.'

Art raised a hand, palm up. 'Ellie, that's sad and the guy seems like a dick. But I don't see how it's any of my business.'

You don't?

The flat tone, the dispassionate look on his face choked the rest of the agonising confession off in her throat. She tried to make sense of his attitude.

Why should she be hurt by his reaction? It shouldn't feel like a blow. She was being paranoid. All he was saying was that her relationship with Dan had no bearing on his relationship with her.

'You're right. Of course, you're right. And really I'm not here to talk about him. What I want to talk about is us.'

There, she'd finally said it, but instead of looking pleased, or even interested, his face remained blank. 'What us? You mean the sex?'

'No, not the sex, well, not just the sex, I mean...' She was babbling and she knew it, but she couldn't seem to get her thoughts to join up properly, the blank look on his face making the fear suddenly huge. And all-consuming. What was happening here? Because this is not how she had imagined this going, during the five hours she'd been waiting to talk to Art.

Then he reached down, gripped the hem of his T-shirt and yanked it over his head. The sight of his chest, deeply tanned, the muscles bunching in his pecs as he flung away the shirt, had an inevitable effect. Her sex warmed, the throb of arousal thick and potent. But much more potent was the throb of hurt when he unhooked the button fly on his jeans. 'Come on then, let's get on with it. We haven't got all night.'

'What are you doing?' she said, even though it was obvious.

He glanced up, his fingers pausing on his flies, the penetrating stare one she recognised, from nineteen summers ago. 'Getting naked, that's what you're here for, right? A guaranteed orgasm?'

The phrase that they had laughed about once sounded flat and accusatory now.

'No, I didn't. I came to talk to you,' she said.

'But we don't talk, do we? All we do is shag.' Art didn't sound dispassionate any more, he sounded annoyed.

The humiliation became so huge it started to choke off her air supply.

'But I thought... this afternoon.'

'What about this afternoon?' he said, as if she were talking in Mandarin.

The crippling sense of confusion and shame was nothing to the agony eating away at her chest.

All those things she'd come to admire about him so much – his strength, his stoicism, his protectiveness – none of it mattered, because as far as he was concerned, the only thing they'd ever actually shared was sex.

How could she have lost sight of that so easily? Was it the trauma of Dan's surprise appearance? The confidences they'd shared at the pond that afternoon? Confidences that had clearly meant much more to her than they had meant to him.

'I'm sorry,' she said, her voice coming from so far away it felt as if she were on Mars.

He stared. 'What are you sorry for?'

She opened her mouth, but she had no idea where to even start – the bankrupt apology sitting like a lump of coal on her tongue.

She felt as if she'd been slammed back in time nineteen years, because Art had looked as indifferent then as he appeared now.

He'd made her feel so small and insignificant and stupid that day. And she felt the same now. What she'd thought had been a friendship had never been more than a convenient hook-up – two weeks of convenient hook-ups – for him.

'What are you sorry for, Ellie?' he asked again. Patient, persuasive and utterly disinterested.

She pushed the memory back into the recesses of her brain marked 'never going there again'.

'I should go.' She wanted to rail against him, to call him out for being such a bastard again. But what would be the point? She'd only make herself look even more pathetic.

It had been a mistake to come here, a mistake to think that this was anything more than what it was. A mistake that she would have to learn to live with. Again. But one thing she wasn't going to do was give him the satisfaction of knowing a second time how much he'd hurt her.

'Ellie, wait,' he grasped her arm, but she shrugged off his hold, the touch of his fingers almost more than she could bear.

She had to get out of here now. Before she did something really idiotic like burst into tears – or punch him.

'Don't go off in a huff,' he said.

She blinked furiously before turning towards him, locking her jaw to keep her face as calm and dispassionate as his.

'I'm not in a huff.' *Because I'd have to care about you to do that. And I refuse to do that. Any more than you obviously care about me.* 'I just don't think it's a good idea for us to be shagging each other while my husband's here.'

She rushed down the stairs of the caravan and out into the night, all her beautiful, inspiring, empowering thoughts about maybe considering making a life here for herself and her son scattered at her feet like mud-soaked confetti.

It started to rain as she made her way back through the woods, refusing to look back, refusing to care. Art Dalton had only gone and shattered her a second time. But, worst of all, she'd let him.

*

Art watched Ellie dash down the side of the hill towards the tree line, the boulder on his chest growing to the size of an asteroid. He welcomed the pain, because at least it took the edge off the anger that had been driving him ever since her picture-perfect husband had stepped out of his Audi A6 convertible and the sunshine had glinted off the bastard's designer sunglasses.

What had she expected him to say, for fuck's sake? She said she was getting a divorce? That the guy had cheated on her all through their marriage. Which probably explained why Art had been itching to punch the bastard the minute he'd stepped out of the car. But how could he punch her husband? When he was nothing more than the rebound guy. Ellie's casual sex fling. The guaranteed orgasm who got her rocks off each night, but who she didn't even want anyone to know was her lover?

Every sigh and moan, every single sweet sob she'd uttered in his arms had come back to torture him as he'd trudged through the farmyard towards his workshop and spent the day and most of the evening slapping on another two coats of varnish the caravan didn't even need, just so he could have something to do with his hands that didn't involve putting his fingers round her husband's neck and squeezing the life out of him.

She was sorry. For what, exactly? Sorry for looking at him like he meant something this afternoon? Sorry for getting involved in his daughter's life without asking? Sorry for making him believe that just for a second he'd met someone who might actually care enough about him not to treat him like a piece of disposal rubbish, the way his mother had treated him? The way Alicia had treated him by always putting her next fix above him and their child?

He thumped the door of the caravan closed and finished undoing the buttons on his fly. After kicking off his boots and his jeans, he stretched out on the bunk.

His gaze roamed over the illustration of dragons and dwarves, ogres and elves.

It was his own stupid fault. Letting himself get spellbound by the sex and the hint of companionship into believing in a dopey romantic fairy tale every bit as fanciful as the one he'd painted years ago. He'd stopped believing in that shit as a seven-year-old kid, when he'd tried to protect Laura from a man who treated her like crap but whom she had loved more than she had ever loved him.

In the last couple of weeks, hell, months, while he'd watched Ellie work her butt off to make the shop a success, while he'd seen her connect not just with him, but with his daughter and her mother and with all the other co-op residents he'd started buying into the idea that he could make that fairy tale a reality without even being aware of it. That somehow she might stay, if not for him, then at least for her mum and the shop – and he'd finally admitted it to himself the moment her husband had stepped out of his Audi.

Because all he'd been able to think for a split second was that he wanted Ellie to stay. That he wanted her to choose him.

But why would she – when he had never been more than rebound guy? And why would he even want her to?

He leant over to blow out the lantern and let the darkness engulf him.

He was much better off without her. Him and Toto both. Why complicate their lives just for the sake of a great shag?

Especially as Ellie didn't even want to do that any more.

Fine by him.

But, as he lay in the bunk, the asteroid crushing his chest turned into a supernova, sucking all his anger and frustration into a hollow aching void in the pit of his stomach.

*

344

'Ellie, is everything OK?'

Dee stood in the doorway to the kitchen, holding one of her teapots.

Ellie toed off her wellington boots in the hallway. What was her mother doing in the kitchen? Why hadn't she gone to bed? 'Yes, I'm fine, I just…' What? The raft of lame explanations spun through her head.

She just wanted to get back to her room. And wallow in her misery. She felt like she was fourteen years old again. Fragile and pathetic. And she really wasn't.

She'd made a mistake. A stupid, romantic mistake. That was all. Art wasn't her friend, her soul mate. They'd just been having insanely great sex for two solid weeks. Plus, she'd been working herself to the bone for three months, dealing with a divorce, and then Dan had arrived out of the blue and tipped her over into insanity.

It all made perfect sense. Or it would in the morning, once she'd taken a sleeping pill, or possibly four, and got a decent night's sleep for a change.

'I didn't expect you back so soon,' her mother said, her voice gentle.

'What?' Ellie said, the idiotic tears that she refused to shed clogging her throat.

'You don't usually get back from Art's caravan before 2 a.m.'

She just stared at her mother, the wellington boot she'd taken off fell over and hit the hall floor with a loud thump. 'I…' What did she say? Her mother knew. About her and Art. And had obviously known for quite a while.

She wasn't sure what was worse – that she'd lied about it, that she'd been found out, or that it didn't matter any more. Because she would never be making that 2 a.m. dash back through the woods again. Everything had turned upside down and inside out in the space of one evening. She wanted that sense of excitement and exhilaration back – to cover up the huge gaping hole in her chest, that choking sense of confusion, which felt as if it was never going to go away again.

Her mother lifted the teapot. 'Why don't you come into the kitchen and have a cup of chamomile tea.'

She didn't want to talk to her mother about Art. Because it would just make her feel like more of a failure. And a nincompoop. For investing too much in a summer sex fling.

However close she and Dee had become in the last three months, however much of their relationship they'd managed to repair, talking to her mum about her sex life felt like a step too far.

Was that another reason why she'd been so determined to keep her relationship with Art a secret? Because she did not want to invite this sort of conversation? But, as her mother stood waiting for her response, Ellie stalled, too tired and dispirited to come up with another lame excuse. So instead of escaping upstairs, she nodded and trailed after her mum to sit down at the kitchen table.

'Why don't you have a slice of cake?' Dee placed the remnants of the cake they'd eaten that afternoon when Dan had arrived onto the table and lifted the perspex cover.

Ellie shook her head, utterly unable to speak.

Dee sliced off a chunk of the sticky toffee and plopped it on the plate. Then placed it in front of her. 'There's nothing much a sugar rush won't cure,' she said.

Ellie nodded mutely, unconvinced, as she fidgeted with a few of the crumbs that had fallen onto the table.

She could hear her mother moving around the kitchen, filling the kettle, placing it on the Aga hob, going to the pantry to get the tin of dried chamomile flowers that grew wild in the hedgerows, the gush of water as she filled the kettle, the whistle of steam as the kettle boiled. But the sounds felt muffled by the pain in her sinuses, and the pounding in her ears.

'I take it Art decided to stay in the caravan tonight?' her mother said.

Ellie's gaze fixed on the caramelised almonds and fruit peel on the top of Dee's cake. She blinked, trying to dispel the mist forming in front of her eyes.

Then Dee's arms were around her, holding her head to the soft cotton of her lavender-scented T-shirt.

'Just cry, Ellie, don't hold it in.'

They came slowly at first, burning down her cheeks, and then it felt like a tsunami of choking sobs – a wild and turbulent storm wrenched from deep down inside her.

At last she stopped shaking, and Dee gripped her shoulders and drew her gently away. She pulled a tissue out of the pocket of the faded jeans she wore and dabbed at Ellie's cheeks.

'Better?' she said.

'Not much.'

Dee gave a weary chuckle. 'I agree. I've always thought crying is overrated. I've done enough of it since Pam died, and it usually just makes me feel more crap.'

Ellie had to agree, finding the observation stupidly comforting.

Dee levered herself up. She took a strainer from the kitchen drawer, then poured Ellie a mug of the fragrant brew and passed it to her. 'Let's try this next then.'

Feeling weak and still shaky, and not even sure where the storm of tears had come from, or what they were for, Ellie picked

347

the mug up and blew on the tea. She took a cautious sip of the chamomile, glad of her mother's presence even though she still had no idea what to say to her.

'How long have you known?' she asked at last, because it seemed like the obvious question.

Dee smiled. 'About you and Art? Did it start about a fortnight ago?'

Ellie put the mug down. 'You've known all along? Terrific.' She scowled into her mug. 'Now I feel ridiculous as well as mortified.'

'Don't. There isn't much that gets past me. I don't sleep well since…' She paused, letting Ellie fill in the gap.

'Since Pam died.' Ellie reached across the table to squeeze her mother's hand. 'You don't need to feel uncomfortable about saying that, Mum.'

'I don't,' Dee said. 'I just don't want to burden you with all that.' Her smile was sad and somehow pensive. 'A bit like you didn't want to burden me with your love affair with Art.'

'It's not a love affair.' The pang of regret sharpened under her heart. 'It's a sex-for-the-sake-of-it affair.' She sniffed back another pointless tear. 'And anyway, it's over. We decided it wasn't going to work with my husband sleeping in the room between us. A bit too awkward.' Or at least she had decided that.

'Those were an awful lot of tears to mark the end of a sex-for-the-sake-of-it affair.'

'That's not what the tears were about.' Ellie toyed with the slice of sticky toffee, peeled off one of the caramelised almonds and put it in her mouth. The rich burnt sugar tasted like chalk.

'Are you sure?' her mother asked.

The question made Ellie's hand tremble. She took it off the table and tucked it into her lap.

'Yes, of course,' she said, a bit too adamantly to be convincing. 'I'm just tired and uber stressed what with the wedding and now Dan.'

She frowned at the scarred wood of the tabletop, knowing that those weren't the reasons she suddenly felt so crushed and fragile. How ridiculous. What exactly had she been expecting Art to say this evening?

*

Arthur, why are you such a dope?

'So your sex-for-the-sake-of-it affair is definitely over then?' Dee said, trying to quell the urge to march up to the caravan on the rise and give the man himself a good talking-to.

Ellie nodded, the movement so dejected Dee's stomach hurt. She had always hated to see her daughter unhappy. But seeing her broken like this felt so desperately unfair, because it undermined everything Ellie had achieved this summer.

Her daughter had worked so hard to turn herself around. It had been a pleasure, no, an honour, to see how much she'd changed over the last weeks and months from that fragile, insecure, weary woman who had walked into this kitchen in June. But, in the last fortnight, she had seen Ellie truly blossom. And she'd known Art was responsible for that. He was a good man, a steady, responsible, hard-working man, but more than that he was the sort of man her daughter deserved. Handsome on the inside as well as the outside, unlike the shallow entitled young fool who had arrived this afternoon, who clearly believed that all he had to do was flash a pretty smile and he would get anything he desired.

But, unfortunately, Arthur was and always had been his own

worst enemy. His fear of rejection so huge he would turn away the best thing ever to happen to him rather than admit his feelings. But as much as Dee might want to, she couldn't alter that. All she could do was make sure that Ellie didn't let Art's foolishness undermine the woman she'd become over this summer.

Her daughter had some important decisions to make now that her husband had appeared so unexpectedly – and Dee wanted to give her every chance of making the right one. Not just for her, but for Josh too.

'You know what's really ironic?' Ellie sniffed, and took another sip of her chamomile tea. 'I thought I loved Art that summer nineteen years ago.' Her lips tipped up in a watery smile. 'At least this time I didn't humiliate myself beyond belief and fall down that rabbit hole all over again.' Her gaze rose from the cake platter to meet Dee's.

'I always suspected that you had a crush on Arthur that summer,' Dee said. 'But you do know, he had one on you too?'

And if Art had become an expert at disguising his feelings before he'd ever met Ellie, Ellie had learned to do the same in the years since that summer. Which might explain why now they both had no idea how deep those feelings went for each other.

Ellie sent her mother a weary smile that almost broke Dee's heart. 'Um, no, he didn't, Mum. He made that pretty clear at the time.'

So this was the incident Art had referred to the night of the back barn clear-out. The incident that both he and Ellie believed had sent her running away from the commune and back to her father.

Dee tried to smile back. 'He may well have said that at the time. He may well even have believed it, but that's because Arthur is exceptionally good at hiding how he really feels, from himself most of all.'

'Mum.' Ellie sighed, still looking sceptical and unimpressed. 'I know you're Art's biggest fan. And after getting to know him a lot better this summer, I know why. I always wanted to believe he was an arsehole. Because I was still stupidly embarrassed about that rejection. But I know now he's not. He's hard-working, dependable and he's survived a lot in his life. His bitch of a mother just for starters.'

So Art had spoken to Ellie about Laura's neglect; Dee took heart at the news. Maybe he wasn't a completely hopeless case after all.

'He's also a great father to Toto. A much better father than Dan has ever been to Josh that's for sure,' she added. And Dee wondered if Ellie could hear the admiration in her own voice. Did her daughter know she was falling for Art all over again? 'But if you think he's been holding a candle for me all this time, believe me he hasn't. What we had this summer… Briefly.' Colour washed into Ellie's cheeks, making Dee realise how far they'd come in the last three months, but still how far they had to go. 'Was basically just an explosion of pheromones, for both of us. I'm not going back to Orchard Harbor with any regrets about that though. If that's what you're worried about.'

'Why were you so upset then, a minute ago?' Dee asked, deciding that they'd beaten about this particular bush long enough.

Ellie shrugged, but the gesture looked about as nonchalant as the red streaks on her face left by the crying jag. 'Honestly, I think that's just the stress of having Dan here. And feeling like a bit of an idiot, for thinking that…' But then Ellie paused.

'For thinking what?' Dee prompted.

'God, I feel stupid even thinking it, let alone saying it. Could we just let this drop now.' She picked up her tea and took a long sip. 'I need to get to bed, if I'm going to sort out getting Dan into a hotel tomorrow.'

Dee knew she should probably let it drop. And, up to twenty minutes ago, she would have done, believing that no matter how close they'd become in the last few months, she would never earn the right back to give her daughter unsolicited advice. But this moment felt like a crossroads, a chance to finally take that last step towards becoming a mother again. And to take it, she would have to wade through all the please-back-off vibes Ellie was sending her.

'OK, but can I just say something first?'

Ellie's lips pursed and for a moment Dee thought she was going to regret the request, but then she sighed and sat back. 'All right, Mum.'

It was a qualified yes, at best. But Dee planned to run with it.

'Don't underestimate Arthur's feelings for you. Not then and certainly not now. He's spent a great deal of his life protecting himself from hurt. Which makes him a very hard man to get to know. But, from what you've just told me, you do know him.'

'OK,' Ellie said, her face wearing the expression Dee had come to adore in the last few months whenever Ellie had a problem that she was determined to solve.

'And don't underestimate yourself either. You're a strong, intelligent, extremely capable woman. Trust your own judgement, it's much better than you think.'

Ellie smiled, but the sadness still lurked in her eyes. 'I'm not so sure about that. I've made a lot more than one disastrous decision in my life. Just for starters, I spent twelve years married to a man that I'm not sure I ever really loved.'

'Which you're about to correct,' Dee said. 'We all make

disastrous decisions in life, Ellie, for all sorts of reasons, some of them outside our control. Ultimately though, if we learn from them, they don't become disastrous any more, they become the stuff that makes us stronger, better people. I made a mistake bringing you here and then not supporting you as much as I should, not seeing how confused you were, because I was too busy falling in love.'

'Mum, don't blame yourself about that any longer, I...'

'Shhh, what I'm trying to say isn't about blame, or regrets, sweetheart. It's about owning that mistake and knowing that the good thing to come out of that summer was that although I lost you, I had Pam. And eventually I had Arthur too. And I finally escaped from a disastrous marriage.' She picked up Ellie's hands and held on to them, tears filling her eyes. 'Don't you see, Ellie, the reason you left that summer wasn't just because Art was an idiot, or even because of all the mistakes I made, but because you were much stronger and more self-sufficient than you thought. You didn't make a mistake, you made a choice. A reckless choice maybe, you were only fourteen after all, but also a brave choice. I have complete faith that when you decide what to do with your life and Josh's life at the end of this summer, your choice will be equally brave and whatever it is, it'll be the right one for you.'

Dee could see the blank shock on her daughter's face as she finished her speech. And also the confusion and doubt that had been there before. But underneath all that was also the spark of intelligence.

Ellie had been knocked sideways by Dan's arrival and the abrupt end of her affair with Art. But now she was thinking again, making plans.

Now all Dee could do was hope that Arthur took his head out

from up his backside, and Dan Granger didn't turn out to be a complete bastard.

But, even if Art didn't, and Dan did, she knew Ellie would navigate her way through the fallout. After all, she'd managed to do that nineteen years ago, without her mother's help. And this time she would have her mother standing right beside her whatever she decided to do. And she knew it.

My work here is done.

CHAPTER TWENTY-SEVEN

'Hey, Ellie?'

Ellie looked up from her laptop, pausing in her data entry for the week's takings at the shop, to find Toto standing in the office doorway.

After four days of intensive wedding planning, she was exhausted and behind on every task. She didn't need the interruption. But Toto looked unhappy, and she knew why. Her father had been using her as a go-between ever since Dan's arrival.

'What's up, Toto?'

'Dad says he's towed the caravan to the wild meadow behind Jacob and Maddy's place, so it's ready for you and Tess and Annie when you want to decorate it.'

The mention of the caravan made the gaping hole in Ellie's stomach, which had resolutely refused to close up since Sunday, feel even bigger, but she ignored it. Art and she had been avoiding each other since that night, they'd spoken exactly twice. But she didn't have time to feel sad or stressed about that, she had a wedding to stress over instead.

'Thanks, Toto. Tell him that's terrific and we all really appreciate it,' she said, forcing magnanimity into her voice.

It had been Annie's idea to use the caravan for Jacob and Maddy's wedding night, because Maddy's parents would be staying in their cabin.

It would have been a great idea, if Art wasn't using the thing to sleep in at the moment. Art hadn't returned to the farmhouse, even though Dan had moved into a hotel after that first night, at Ellie's insistence. She wasn't sure if Art's absence from the farmhouse had anything to do with their bust-up, or simply because he was running scared from all the wedding prep. But, either way, she hadn't wanted to have a conversation with Art about lending the caravan to Jacob and Maddy, just the thought of that conversation making her feel raw. So she'd made up some excuse as to why Annie should ask him.

That he had agreed to loan it out meant he was without an extra bedroom until after the wedding now, but she wasn't going to worry about where he planned to sleep tonight. Or for the next three nights. It was none of her business. If he decided to sleep back in the house, great. She'd take a sleeping pill and pretend he wasn't there. How hard could it be?

'How did the first day of school go?' she asked Toto, because the child was still hovering.

The poor kid looked harassed. Had Art been as surly with his daughter in the last four days as he'd been with her? She hoped not. But there wasn't a lot she could do about it. Trying to decipher Art and his moods had always given her a headache.

He couldn't be angry about Dan's turning up, because he didn't care enough about her to be jealous. And anyway there was nothing to be jealous of. She'd finally contacted a lawyer, who would be serving Dan with papers as soon as he returned to Orchard Harbor. Which she hoped would be sooner rather than later. She didn't want her whole final three weeks here soured by Dan's presence. She'd have enough time to deal with him when she and Josh got back to the US.

'All right, we did algebra though, which was pants,' Toto said. 'Miss Morely asked after Josh and so did Frankie Bradford. I think they missed him.'

The quietly spoken observation had guilt pressing in on Ellie.

Miss Morely and Frankie Bradford weren't the only ones who had been missing Josh in the last four days. The plan for Josh to go to school with Toto had been nixed by Dan who had wanted to spend some time with the son he'd been 'missing like crazy' for the last three months. Josh had seemed eager to spend time with his dad and Ellie had been pleased that at least Dan seemed focused on his son and not the impossibility of resurrecting their marriage, so she'd been happy to sanction the daily trips Dan had arranged, to go to the movies in Salisbury, or go to a soccer match in Swindon, or today's excursion to Stonehenge. But she knew Toto had missed her best friend terribly.

Ellie had tried not to worry about that too much. Toto and Josh would be separated soon anyway, so they would both have to get used to it. And Ellie couldn't do any more about Toto's unhappiness than she could do about her own. But if Toto had ended up on the sharp end of her father's temper as well as losing Josh's companionship through no fault of her own, that seemed grossly unfair.

Toto ducked her head. 'Do you know when Josh is coming back from Stonehenge?'

'I think he's staying at his dad's hotel tonight in Gratesbury,' she said. 'But he'll have to be back all day on Saturday for the wedding.'

Maddy had asked Josh and Toto to be wedding attendants. Josh had been overjoyed at the prospect, before Dan had arrived. She hoped he hadn't gone off the idea. But, even if he had, he needed to follow through on that commitment.

'But Saturday's two days away.' Toto looked even more dejected as she turned to go. 'I wish his dad hadn't come to visit now.'

You and me both.

'Don't worry, he won't be staying much longer.' Surely Dan would leave after the wedding? She'd told him they were coming back to Orchard Harbor at the end of September, she refused to change her plans just for him. Or for Art, who probably wanted her to leave sooner rather than later now too.

Well, they could both bog off. She'd done enough to keep them both happy. She was making the choice to go back on her terms, which meant staying till the end of September as she'd originally planned.

And she was not going to let either one of them ruin the three weeks she had left. With her mum and her friends, and the shop.

'Toto, wait.' Ellie halted her progress, an idea forming. 'I'm going over to Maddy and Jacob's after we close the shop in about an hour to do some more wedding prep.' The wedding prep that would never end. 'Annie and Tess are meeting me there, we were going to have some supper over there, too. Why don't you come with me?'

It wouldn't hurt the child to spend more time in female company. And they had about a million things to do, most of it grunt work, so an extra pair of hands would not go amiss. Also it would take Toto out of Art's orbit. Maybe take her mind off Josh's absence. And save Ellie from any probing questions from Annie and Tess and Maddy about Dan. Annie had already asked some pointed questions about what Dan was doing here if they were getting a divorce? Having Art's impressionable teenage daughter in their midst ought to halt any more awkward questions, at least until Ellie had the energy to answer them.

'What's wedding prep?' Toto asked, but she looked a little less dejected. Wow, she must be seriously bored.

'We've got to finish tinting the jam jars for the tea lights. And we're decorating the bases of the flower centrepieces Mum's doing for the tables. It should be fun.' Once the wine started flowing. 'Melody will be there.' Although she doubted Melody would be much help to anyone.

Toto's face screwed up, as she considered the invitation. 'Josh is definitely going to his dad's?'

Toto's request for confirmation tore at Ellie's heart. 'Yes, I'm sure he is.'

'I guess I'll come then,' Toto said, not sounding overexcited at the prospect of spending an evening doing arts and crafts with a bunch of grown women. Ellie understood. She'd much rather be doing anything other than wedding prep right about now, too.

Stop being a killjoy.

Ellie forced a smile. 'It's a deal then. I'll see you in an hour by the shop and we can walk over together.'

Toto nodded and left.

The false brightness died on Ellie's face as she turned back to the data entry.

Bloody men, how did they always manage to screw up the best laid plans of women everywhere without even trying.

*

'OK, spill it…' Annie leant across the jam jar she was tinting red and fixed Ellie with her do-not-mess-with-me stare.

So much for Toto being an effective deterrent. Ellie's shield had spent less than twenty minutes painting jam jars, then got bored and headed off into the woods with Melody and Jacob to forage for more ivy for the centrepieces.

'What the hell is going on with you and Art now?' Annie finished.

Now?

Ellie's hands cramped on the reed grass she was weaving through the bases her mother had designed for the flower arrangements.

'Is it the arrival of the smarmy ex that has put a crimp in things?' Annie continued, confirming Ellie's worst fears when Tess and Maddy sent her equally knowing looks – part concern and part curiosity. 'Because, if it is, I'm going to run him off myself.'

The base dropped out of Ellie's numbed fingers. 'Bloody hell, was Art and I's secret liaison actually a secret from anybody at all?'

'Did you really think it would be?' Tess said, still threading dried ivy through the wicker structures Dee had made to hold the rest of the flower centrepieces. 'Once you started looking as if you'd discovered the secret of life. And Art began to smile on a regular basis?'

'Not the secret of life. More like the secret of the female orgasm.' Maddy grinned like someone who had discovered it too, and wasn't ashamed to let everyone know it as often as was humanly possible.

Ellie swore softly under her breath. Not sure whether to be relieved or depressed that her friends had known about the worst kept secret in Wiltshire all along. A week ago, she would have been amused, delighted even, and probably jumped at the chance to tell them everything. Well, almost everything. Now, not so much.

'Wait a minute,' Annie said. '*Were* doing? I thought so, you've stopped having spectacular nooky with Art just because Dan the Skank has turned up.' Apparently Annie hadn't fallen for Dan's charm either. 'I thought we already discussed this. You don't owe him fidelity. And anyway, you're divorcing him. Unless...' Annie's eyes went wide with horror. 'Please don't tell me you've changed your mind about that.'

'No, I spoke to a lawyer two days ago and I've told Dan. I'm not sure he believes me.' In fact, she was fairly positive he didn't believe her, because he had simply told her they could talk it through when they got back to Orchard Harbor, as if there was actually anything left to discuss that didn't involve their lawyers. 'But he'll find out soon enough when he gets home and the papers are waiting for him.'

'Well, thank goodness for that,' Annie said. 'So what's going on with Art then? Why have you stopped looking born again and why has he stopped smiling?'

'We're guessing there's no more secret orgasms going on, but why?' Maddy poured Ellie a glass of wine from the bottle Tess had brought with her.

'Honestly, it's complicated,' Ellie said, feeling like a fraud. Why couldn't she just tell them what she'd told her mum, that she and Art had never been more than a fling?

'We can handle complicated,' Annie said. 'That's what friends are for.'

Ellie's eyes began to sting. The simple statement making her realise that she hadn't cried herself dry during Dee's pep talk the way she thought.

Her mother had been wonderful, so supportive and so insightful. And it had made her even more aware of how much she had gained from this summer – with or without Art's help. And seeing how worried and willing to help Tess and Annie and Maddy were too only confirmed that.

So why did she still feel so shit about the fact that she and Art were over now?

She knew for all his moodiness, and his general unwillingness to talk about his feelings, Art was not an insensitive man. Not by a long shot. If he were, he wouldn't have been so freaked out about Toto's periods, or got so worked up and overprotective of Dee when Ellie had first suggested the shop project, or been so deeply scarred by his father's brutality and his mother's neglect that he'd ended up with a phobia of hospitals. But it seemed somehow that even though she had thought they were friends, had come to care for him, he'd never cared that deeply for her. Not even as a friend. And that hurt. It made her feel less than the way she now realised she had always felt every time Dan had cheated on her. And that was something she never wanted to feel like again.

'If you put an end to it because of your divorce not being final,' Annie continued, 'we're here to make you see the error of your ways.'

Tess and Maddy nodded enthusiastically, having abandoned their art and crafts too.

Ellie sipped her wine, to give herself strength, deeply touched by their support. 'It wasn't Dan's arrival so much as…' She paused. 'As the fact that it was going nowhere. We both knew it would have to end eventually.' Hadn't they? 'It just seemed less awkward to end it before things got messy.'

'So you didn't end it because the ex arrived, you ended it because you didn't want things to get messy?' Annie asked.

'Exactly,' Ellie said, glad that someone could make sense of it all.

'But why would things get messy, if it was just a fling?' she countered.

'I...' Ellie hesitated. Why didn't she have an answer to that?

'And who ended things exactly?' Annie added. 'You or him?'

'I did, I suppose,' Ellie said, although she wasn't even sure about that any more. 'Although he didn't exactly put up much of an objection.' And why did that still hurt?

Ellie felt the tears begin to mist her eyes again.

Oh, for goodness' sake, pull yourself together.

Annie touched her hand. 'What is it, Ellie? Whatever it is we are totally here for you.'

She looked at the ceiling, struggling to keep her eyes dry. God, why was it so hard to say now, even to her friends? 'I've got a really bad feeling I might have been falling in love with him. How idiotic is that?'

'Not idiotic at all,' Tess said, as if she hadn't just said something completely ridiculous. 'Because it's obvious he was falling for you too.'

Ellie wiped away a tear with her fist. Well, at least now she knew she hadn't completely lost her mind. Unfortunately, though, it didn't make her predicament any less tragic. 'No, he wasn't.'

'How can you be sure?' Maddy said. 'Did you ask him?'

'No, thank God. The only saving grace in all this is that I didn't do that.' And that was still the major bright spot on the horizon. 'Believe me, I've been there, done that and I already have the hideous memory of what happened to prove it.'

'You fell in love with Art before? When?' asked Tess, aka Miss Super Intuitive.

'Nineteen years ago, the day before I left, I threw myself at Art. I'd had a crush on him for weeks and I thought he had a crush on me.' Her mum had thought so too, so she hadn't been completely nuts. 'For a moment, I thought…' She pushed her hair back, starting to feel ridiculous all over again. 'I actually thought he was going to kiss me. But, instead of kissing me, he went all stiff and looked horrified. Then he told me to get lost. He told me he didn't kiss little girls. Especially not stuck-up little girls like me.' Good to know she could still cringe about that. 'I was devastated, of course, as only a fourteen-year-old drama queen can be. I didn't think I could survive at the commune after that. So the next day, when my dad arrived to visit me – I told him I wanted to go back to London with him. That I hated the commune and couldn't live there. So we left together. I know now that devastated my mum. And the reason she signed over all her custody rights to him was because after that grand departure, she thought that's what I wanted. She convinced herself I'd been desperately unhappy at the commune, and it was all her fault, when of course I hadn't been and it wasn't. And I suppose I convinced myself of the same thing, because I didn't want to admit the truth, that I'd made a complete tit of myself and thrown myself at Art when he was not remotely interested in me.'

To think she might have done that again was even more humiliating now she thought about it. Her mother had tried to make her feel good about that stupid knee-jerk decision nineteen years ago, wanted her to believe that she'd learned from it, that what she'd done had been brave instead of just monumentally melodramatic, but how could she have learned from that mistake if she hadn't actually owned it until this summer?

'So let me get this straight, you didn't tell him you think you might be falling in love with him this time?' Maddy asked.

'No I did not, thank God.' She could still be relieved about that if nothing else.

'Ellie, is it at all possible that you let that incident...' Annie paused. 'Which I think all of us who have ever been teenage girls in love will admit sounds pretty horrific,' she added. 'But is it possible that it was so awful you let it colour how you read his reaction this time around?'

Ellie thought about it, for a few seconds. Then shuddered. No, she wasn't going to get delusional again, not even for Annie. 'Yes, but that doesn't mean I'm wrong. He looked right through me, Annie. He made me feel like crap. Even if I could persuade myself I misunderstood, I can't get past that look. He's never looked at me like that before and I–'

'Which is exactly my point,' Annie interrupted. 'Art is not a demonstrative guy. But he looks at you like you matter. I've also never seen him smile as much as he has in the two weeks before you split up. And he's certainly not smiling now, in fact he's been supremely cranky, even for him. Just ask Toto.'

'Well, he's not getting spectacular nooky any more, is he,' Ellie said, not wanting to think about Toto either. 'Men are simple creatures, sex keeps them happy. I found that out the hard way with Dan.'

'Forget about Dan, he's a skank,' Annie said. 'Art's not. And I wouldn't normally disagree with you re: the path to enlightenment for men being paved with spectacular nooky. Rob only whistles when he's up at dawn to do the milking if he got up before dawn too,' Annie said. 'If you get my drift.'

Ellie laughed, the first genuine laugh she'd had in four days, Annie's broad Yorkshire humour hard to resist.

'And Rob can get tetchy if he's not getting any, because so can I. But Art's surprisingly self-contained in that department. I think he may have trained himself to do without sex for Toto's sake.' She lifted up her hand and began counting off the points with her fingers. 'Let's look at the evidence. One. He never brings anyone back to the farm. Ever.'

'I was here already, he didn't have much of a choice there,' Ellie said.

'Two,' Annie carried on regardless. 'He dates women then discards them quickly.'

'We broke up after two weeks, so he certainly didn't break pattern there,' Ellie said.

'Yes, he did, you guys were circling each other for months. Ever since you arrived really.'

So everyone had picked up on that too. Fabulous.

'And three,' Annie added, not waiting for a reply. 'He never ever lets a woman get too close. As soon as there is even a whiff of commitment in the air, he's gone. Ask my mate, Daisy. So the fact he didn't notice you were getting too close – I think that's hugely significant.'

Who knew Annie was such a hopeless romantic? Or capable of clutching so hard at straws? Ellie would have been charmed, if only the conversation wasn't making her start to feel angry with Art now as well as hurt.

How could he have let her think she was special, knowing the whole time she wasn't? Because if what Annie was saying was true, his behaviour was beginning to look deliberate. He'd protected all the other women he slept with but not her. Had she actually meant even less to him than she thought?

Thank goodness she'd always had an exit strategy – her return to New York suddenly looked like a lifeline.

Josh and she would be able to make a clean break in three weeks' time from this misery.

She'd get over any lingering feelings for Art again like she had the last time. And when that happened she'd be able to come back and visit. But until then, it would be healthier for her to put the distance between them she needed. Three thousand miles distance to be exact.

'Annie, can we stop talking about Art now?' she said, letting the weariness show in her voice. 'We've still got ten more of these centrepieces to prepare. And I don't want to be still here at midnight.'

Before Annie could say anything, Jacob and Melody crashed into the room holding armfuls of ivy.

'Hey, you wouldn't believe how much we managed to find,' Jacob said.

'Where's Toto?' Ellie asked, pleased to be able to change the subject.

'We bumped into Art in the woods. Toto went back with him.'

Ellie's heart throbbed painfully at the mention of the man, the gaping hole still there and still making itself felt. Yup, she needed distance. Thank goodness she was going back to New York, because as long as she was still here, the hole would never heal.

Brushing his hands on his jeans, Jacob knelt beside his bride-to-be, his smile sweetly reassuring as he rested his palm on the small mound of her belly. 'Hey, good-looking, what you got cooking?'

'Maddy's got a baby cooking,' Melody said, having climbed onto her mother's lap, then promptly stuck a grubby thumb in her mouth as everyone chuckled.

Jacob ruffled Melody's hair. 'Clever girl.'

'Can I go to bed now, Mummy?' Melody yawned, round her thumb.

Tess lifted her daughter to take her home. 'I'm afraid I'm going to have to desert the field, ladies,' she said. 'Are you OK, Ellie?'

'Yes, of course, I'm happy to put in another couple of hours, if Maddy and Jacob will have me,' she said, deliberately misinterpreting the question.

Tess left, and Annie stayed and the three of them worked together, doing the last of the work to make sure Maddy's wedding would be glorious, while Jacob cooked them all dinner and kept the wine flowing. As always, Ellie found herself enjoying the camaraderie. She was really going to miss moments like these when she returned to the US. But it was better not to linger.

Nobody mentioned Art again. And Ellie was glad.

Because really, what else was there left to say?

CHAPTER TWENTY-EIGHT

Maddy and Jacob's wedding day dawned bright and clear and crisp. The slight chill in the air a signal that summer was drawing to a close.

Ellie spent the morning in the shop – the original plan had been to schedule the celebration for the evening, because they hadn't wanted to lose a day's trading and Saturday was their busiest day. But, in the end she, Dee, Tess and Annie had made an executive decision to close up at one o'clock despite Maddy's objections. They could make up the sales the next weekend with a leafleting push in Gratesbury and Salisbury. Both Maddy and Jacob had put in so much to the project and they deserved to have their special day properly marked... Plus, Ellie knew there were bound to be tons of last-minute details to see to that would require all hands on deck. The late arrival of the guys who were erecting the gazebo and a mad dash to Gratesbury to buy extra tea lights just two of the things that ended up on Ellie's troubleshooting list.

By six o'clock, with the ceremony due to start at seven, she had finally downgraded from whirling dervish to multitasking maniac.

Entering the house after decorating the gazebo with Annie and Tess, she found her mother putting muslin covers on the trays of canapés she'd prepared for the reception. With an apron slung on over a royal blue body-con dress, her salt and pepper hair arranged in an elegant chignon, Dee looked the picture of calm, competent class.

'Mum, you look gorgeous.' Ellie's stomach rumbled, she'd missed lunch in the melee – but everything was finally done. 'And so does the food.'

The gazebo was ready for the guests to arrive, the tables for the wedding feast had been arranged and decorated in the shop forecourt, the flower arrangements her mother had got up at dawn to finish looked beyond beautiful in the rustic fall colours. Rob had begun to light the jam jar lanterns they had dotted around the grounds as the sun began to sink towards the horizon and the band Rob and Mike had booked were setting up for entertainment later in the evening.

The group of students they'd hired from Salisbury's catering college to serve the meal, so that Dee could join in the festivities, milled around the kitchen stacking champagne flutes onto trays, and finishing the final prep.

The aroma of fresh herbs and roasted garlic wafting out of the kitchen and the glimpse of the wild mushroom and goat's cheese tartlets Dee had just covered made Ellie's mouth water.

'Good, that's the general idea.' Dee smiled and straightened, flicking a tendril of hair back from her face. The subtle application of make-up accentuated her mother's enviable bone structure and the cool blue of her eyes.

Ellie felt the pulse of pride in her chest. At all her mother, no, all of them, had achieved today. This would be a celebration not just of Maddy and Jacob's love for one another, but of the love they all shared for this place, this community.

The pulse of sadness wasn't far behind, at the thought of all the things she was going to miss when she went back to the US. She pushed the thought to one side – no time to mope about that now. Given the increasing awkwardness with Art now he had moved back into the house, she knew she'd made the right decision there.

'You need to get upstairs and change,' Dee admonished.

'Right, but have you seen Josh? And Toto?' She'd been keeping an eye out for them both for over an hour.

'Toto's upstairs moaning about the dress she has to wear. I haven't seen Josh,' her mother remarked.

'I thought they were together.' The two of them had headed off after breakfast to help Jacob decorate the vintage Land Rover Art had found to transport the bride and groom to their wedding night caravan. 'He needs to get showered and changed into his suit.'

'Toto might know where he is,' Dee said, before one of the catering students interrupted to ask if it was time to start frying the sweetcorn and tofu fritters.

Ellie dashed up the stairs. She did not have time to track Josh down. But, as she raced down the corridor, Art stepped out of his bedroom

She barrelled into him, his whoosh of breath matched by her squeak of dismay.

Strong arms wrapped around her, to stop her tumbling on her arse. For a split second she was inhaling his delicious scent – soap and man – overlaid with the fresh hint of sandalwood cologne, her face nestled against the fabric of a starched white shirt.

She stumbled back. Awareness shot through her like wildfire. He looked magnificent, his tall rugged physique filling out the sleek lines of the expertly tailored single-breasted suit.

'Art, sorry,' she mumbled. The flash of something hot and yearning arched between them.

'Are you OK?' He hadn't released her arm and the light touch of his fingertips made the skin pebble and pulse.

'Yes.' Although she didn't feel OK, her emotions a jumble of needs and desires and dreams she couldn't explain.

They were over – when was her body going to catch up?

His thumb stroked the inside of her elbow, setting off a riot of sensations.

'I need to find Josh, have you seen him?' she said, subtly tugging her arm out of his grasp.

'His dad turned up and took him off somewhere,' Art said, sweeping the still damp hair off his brow, the sneer in his voice unmistakeable.

'He what? When?' she said, trying to adjust her pulse from hysterical to merely frantic.

'Couple of hours ago. Toto was pretty upset about it,' he said, clearly mad with Dan.

Of course he was, this was the first day Toto and Josh had spent together since Dan's arrival. Josh had been keen to spend time with Toto this morning, and had told Ellie he didn't want to spend time with Dan, when Dan had texted. So why had he gone off with his father? And, more importantly, the wedding was starting in an hour. And Josh was a pivotal part of the ceremony.

'She's not the only one,' she said.

'Really? You didn't sanction this?' Art said, his dark brows lowering into that moody frown she'd seen far too often of late.

'Of course not, why would I?'

'Because you let that guy do whatever he wants.'

The harsh words and the accusation stunned her, almost as much as the judgemental frown.

Why was he having a go at her about Dan? When he'd made it very clear he wasn't remotely interested in her relationship with her husband? She shook off the thought. She didn't have time to worry about Art's jerky behaviour. Because she had a pageboy to locate who seemed to have gone AWOL.

'Where's Toto?' she said. Time to take the higher ground for the sake of the greater good.

'In her room,' he said, the frown still firmly in place. 'Having a strop about her dress.'

'OK, let's start there. Maybe she knows where they've gone?'

She went to dash off, but he caught her arm, the pulse of reaction another infuriating reminder of how fickle her body was where this man was concerned.

'I'll question her,' he said, his dark gaze skating over her skin. 'You go and get changed. As tempting as you look in jeans and a T-shirt, we'll have a riot on our hands from Totes if you turn up to the ceremony like that and she has to wear a dress.'

Tempting? Was he actually coming on to her? After the shitty way he'd been treating her since that night?

But before she could get her outrage past the obstruction in her throat caused by that hot assessing look, and the offhand compliment, he had stalked off down the corridor taking the last of the available oxygen with him.

*

Twenty minutes later, Ellie was showered and coiffured and dressed, wearing the bias-cut emerald green silk sheath and kitten heels she'd bought for the occasion. Art and Toto and Dee were nowhere to be found. The young wait staff had taken over in the kitchen.

She checked her phone, her panic levels rising, as she left the house, pulling on the pashmina she'd bought to go with her dress and ward off the autumn chill.

Had Josh turned up? She hadn't heard the shower going. And Dan hadn't answered his cell phone and the numerous messages and texts she'd sent.

She tapped out another one, as she picked her way across the reeds they'd laid down in the farmyard to protect people's footwear. Maddy's family and some of Jacob's friends, who were staying nearby, were already being served with champagne and canapés. The fairy lights flickered in the dusk as she rounded the side of the barn.

The scene laid out before her took her breath away for a moment.

The jump and jitter of her pulse caused by Josh's disappearance slowed to a crawl, the panic retreating to be replaced with something thick and viscous and overwhelming.

Annie and Tess stood at the entrance to the wedding gazebo, which was lit by the tiny sparkle of the lights woven into the ivy and rose garlands they'd spent most of the afternoon wrapping round the uprights. Dressed to the nines in their wedding finery – Annie's curves looking luscious in vibrant scarlet and Tess's slender figure elegant in flowing pale blue silk – they were laughing as they directed guests to the rows of folding chairs. The twins and Melody darted about between the chairs with a collection of Maddy's young cousins. Rob and Mike were nearby sharing a beer with Jacob, who looked terrified, all three of them looking ridiculously dashing in the tailored suits that matched Art's.

She scanned the growing crowd for her mum, and found her with her arm around Toto. The girl's coltish physique and sun-bronzed skin, so much like her father's, was flattered by the rose dress Maddy had picked out for her. The simple lines hinted at the beautiful woman she would become, while at the same time accentuating the tomboy beneath, there were no unnecessary frills or bows, Toto's short dark hair tied back with an Alice band.

How strange that the first time she saw Toto in a dress, her appearance would make Ellie realise how closely she resembled her father, those high slanting cheekbones and wide chocolate-coloured eyes a strong hint to her heritage.

If Toto had made a fuss about wearing the dress, she seemed resigned to it now, her blush shy and heartbreakingly sweet as Art's dark figure emerged from the crowd gathering round the bar area and leaned in to whisper something to his daughter.

Ellie tried not to look at Art, tried not to think about the great big gaping hole in her stomach, which widened a little more every time she saw him.

Toto laughed at whatever he had said to her, and Ellie felt the deep pulse of longing reverberate in her chest. But it wasn't just a longing for Art, it was much deeper and more profound than that.

It was the longing to stay.

Why was she leaving Willow Tree Farm when she had come to love it so much? She didn't want to go, and deep down she knew Josh didn't want to go either. But, until this moment, when everything she would lose by leaving, everything they would both lose by leaving, was laid out before her, she had consistently refused to ask that fundamental question of herself.

Was this the choice her mother had been talking about? Not the choice to go or stay, so much as the choice to stand up for herself and Josh's best interests.

Josh had been so happy here this summer, and so had she. And instead of being prepared to talk to Dan about the possibility of staying, and figuring out if they could make it work, she had spent all her time obsessing about Art and how miserable she felt about losing something that she had since convinced herself had never really existed.

But when had her relationship with Art become more important than what she wanted for herself? And for her son?

Clarity came like a blinding light as Art captured her gaze and, detaching himself from Dee and Toto, walked towards her.

His gaze raked over her and desire flashed across his face. A desire so dark and elemental, the deep pulsing in her chest took on a chaotic, kinetic rhythm. Living here with Art would be hard, knowing that they still wanted each other, but their relationship wasn't the whole story.

Life was full of regrets, of mistakes, of paths not taken and, as her mother said, ultimately the only way to weather them was to learn from them and forge your own damn path. From this moment forward that's what she was going to do.

'You look good,' he said, the husky voice tense but thick with desire.

For all his commitment issues, Art had made her feel so good about herself in those crazy few weeks. She could use that now.

'Thanks, so do you,' she said, letting her gaze absorb the shift of his shoulders under the suit jacket. 'Any news about Josh?'

'Toto said his dad took him to Gratesbury for a burger and promised to be back by six.'

Ellie pulled her phone out of her clutch purse to re-check the time. Six forty-five. Fear gripped her, galloping right through the renewed blast of frustration.

'They're forty-five minutes late.'

Could they have been in an accident? What if this wasn't Dan's usual selfishness, what if it was something much worse than that?

'Ellie, breathe.' Art touched her arm. 'We'll find them.'

'It's probably nothing.' She tried to reason with herself. 'Dan's always chronically late for everything. Although I don't understand why Josh went with him. I know he wanted to hang out with Toto today.'

'Toto said he didn't want to go, but Dan insisted.'

'But why?' This was just getting worse and worse.

'Ellie, is everything OK?' Dee arrived, flanked by Toto.

'Josh is missing with Dan,' Art said, still holding her arm.

'Everyone's seated, guys, is something going on?' Tess joined their huddle with Annie.

Ellie forced herself to breathe and to think. Panicking wasn't going to help.

Jacob and Rob and Mike arrived. 'Is Josh not back yet?' Jacob asked, looking as if he were about to pass out.

'No, do you think you could get in touch with Maddy's mum?' Ellie said, determined to calm the groom down first. 'Tell her to hold off arriving for a few minutes.' She needed to focus on fixing this, rather than turning it into a total catastrophe. Josh was OK. Dan was just an inconsiderate idiot who couldn't be bothered to answer his damn phone.

'Sure,' Jacob said, digging his phone out of his jacket pocket to text his fiancée's mum before Maddy arrived in her bridal gown with the place in an uproar.

'Tess, Annie, could you two tell everyone we may be slightly delayed, the bride's prerogative and all that.'

'Got it,' Tess said, as she and Annie headed off.

'Toto, how about you go into the house and find Josh's suit, he can change in the shop when he gets here.' Because he would get here soon. Very soon.

But, as Toto sped off, Art swore. 'There they are.'

The huge surge of relief at the sight of Dan and Josh appearing was quickly quashed, when Art stalked off to greet them.

She and everyone else raced after him.

Josh ran towards her.

'Mom, Mom, I'm sorry I'm late.' He sounded distraught, his lip quivering and his eyes wide with anxiety, reminding her of the boy she had brought with her to Wiltshire three months ago. 'I told Dad we had to get back, but he didn't listen. I didn't even want to get a burger. I wanted to stay with Toto.' She couldn't imagine how much courage it must have taken for Josh to finally stand up to his father. Pride for her son blossomed as Dan strolled up, behind him.

The languid stride suggested he didn't have a care in the world, as if he hadn't just deliberately given his son and everyone else a panic attack.

'Stop whining, Joshie,' he said, the feckless grin antagonising her more. 'We got here in time, just like I told you, the wedding hasn't even started yet.'

'Where have you been?' she demanded, her voice rising in pitch with her anger. 'Why did you take him off like that?'

'Because I wanted to have a burger with my son.' His gaze flicked to Art's and suddenly she knew. Dan's desire to take Josh out for lunch had nothing to do with his son and everything to do with his pissing contest with Art. He'd been staking a claim.

As if Josh's affection were a possession to be bartered, to prove that Dan was somehow the better man – and, in so doing, he'd proved exactly the opposite. 'Joshie's whining about nothing, as usual,' he said.

Anger swept through Ellie in a mighty wave, gathering in its wake all those times Dan had treated her and their son with the same careless contempt, but before she could open her mouth to tear into him, Art's big body blocked her view.

'You wanker.' The low words ground out, followed by the crunch of skin hitting bone.

Dan screamed and grasped his face, his body folding in on itself as he wheeled back and collapsed onto the grass.

'Dad!' Josh shouted.

'Art!' Dee yelled.

Toto danced from foot to foot, looking rapt.

'What the hell is wrong with you?' Dan shouted at Art, staggering to his feet and testing his jaw.

Art stepped into his personal space, the sight of his bunched fist held rigidly at his side, the knuckles bleeding, finally snapped Ellie out of her trance.

Oh crap, they are going to kill each other and ruin Maddy's dream wedding.

People were rushing across the grass to see the show. Rob and Mike grabbed hold of Art and dragged him back, to stop him landing another punch, while Dan propped his fists in front of him impersonating Gentleman Jim.

Diving into the fray, Ellie slapped a palm to Dan's chest before he could take a swing.

'Don't you dare, you've done enough damage already,' she shouted.

'Me?' he shrieked, clearly mortally offended, but he dropped his fists. 'What about Farmer Goddamn Giles?'

His lip was cut and starting to bleed, but, unlike Art's torn knuckles, the sight didn't move her in the slightest. Dan had finally met someone he couldn't charm or trick or cajole – a man who had seen through his immature posturing, just like she had. It served him right.

'I expect an apology or I'm going to goddamn sue,' Dan added, swiping at the blood with a knuckle. 'What your boyfriend just did to me is assault.'

'Is Art your boyfriend, Mom?' Josh said, his gaze darting between her and Dan.

'I can explain,' she said to Josh. 'We can talk about this later, sweetheart.' Because no way was she having this conversation with her son and Art's daughter in front of the whole congregation. She cursed Dan again. 'But first we have a wedding to do.' She tucked a finger under Josh's chin. 'You need to run into the house and get into your suit, I left it on your bed.'

Josh's face was a picture of confusion as he swivelled his head between her and Dan. 'But what about…?'

'Come on, Josh, I'll race you,' Toto said, grabbing Josh's arm.

Ellie wanted to kiss the little girl as the two of them sprinted off across the farmyard, Toto kicking off her pumps and hiking up her dress to streak ahead of Josh.

'What do you see in Farmer Giles anyway?' Dan said, disgruntled now as he continued to nurse his jaw. 'The guy's a jerk.'

Not as much of a jerk as you are, Dan.

'That's none of your business,' she said. 'It stopped being your business three months ago. And when you get that through your head we'll all be better off.' She slapped her hands on her hips, the events of the last few minutes finally giving her the courage she needed. This probably wasn't the time or the place, but she didn't want to wait.

'I don't want to come back to the US. I want to stay here in Wiltshire.'

Dee let out a little sob of breath and Dan frowned. 'What are you talking about?'

'I love it here and I believe our son does too. Our marriage is over. And I want to have the chance to build a new life here with Josh.' A new life she'd already starting building.

'But he's my kid, too? What about what I want?' Dan said, sounding petulant.

'And he'll always be your kid. And he loves you.' *Even when you behave like a dick.* 'But however much you love Josh, you have never wanted the responsibility of being a full-time dad. If you did you wouldn't have always left the important stuff to me. Like telling him about the divorce. And you would have known how important this wedding was to him. You would have got him back here on time, instead of ignoring his feelings and letting him get so anxious. You would have put his needs above your own and you never have.'

She took a deep breath, not sure how Dan would react to her next request.

'I'm asking you to do that now. Come back tomorrow and let's talk to him together and then we can see what he wants to do, because that's what really matters.'

If Josh didn't want to stay, she would respect his decision, and they would both return to the US. But after the last week of endless activities with Dan and today's argument, she had the sneaking suspicion father and son had both had more than enough quality time to last them for quite a while.

Even so, she braced herself for Dan's response.

But the fight she had been expecting didn't come. Dan gave a weary sigh and dug his fingers through his hair. He brushed the carefully styled waves, which had once captivated her, when she had been young and foolish and infatuated with him, off his brow.

That flop of hair didn't captivate her any more, but it still made him look boyish and oddly vulnerable when he said, 'Are you actually in love with that dick?'

'This isn't about him,' she said, because it absolutely wasn't, not any more. 'I want to stay here for me and Josh.'

Dan studied her for the longest time. 'Fine, talk to Joshie tomorrow and let me know what he says,' he said, the wry smile making him hiss when it split his lip. 'I think he's kind of pissed with me at the moment.'

Ellie nodded, grateful that Dan wasn't going to fight her on this. But also saddened that Dan was prepared to leave this important discussion about their son's future to her alone.

Dee stepped in and took Dan's arm. 'How about I get you washed up then you can join the wedding party?' she said.

'No thanks on the wedding, they give me the jitters.' Dan shuddered theatrically and Ellie let go of the last of her anger with him. She'd always expected too much of him, at least now his limitations as a father might work in her favour. And Josh's favour.

'I won't say no to some TLC, though,' Dan added, milking it just a little bit. 'But be gentle, that guy's got a harder right hook than Wladimir Klitschko'

Dee leant in and whispered in Ellie's ear. 'I'll hold the fort, go and find Art. He'll want to know about your decision.'

Art.

Ellie swung round to find Rob and Mike standing empty-handed.

'You're going to stay?' Mike said. 'Tess will be overjoyed.'

'Your ex isn't as much of a twat as I thought,' said Rob at the same time.

'Hopefully, yes,' she said to Mike. 'He's not my ex yet, but he soon will be.' She spotted Art through the crowd making his way towards the orchard, away from the wedding congregation that was milling around being offered canapés and champagne.

She headed after him only to get waylaid en route by Tess and Annie.

'What happened with Mr Skank?' Annie said.

Ellie turned to watch Dee leading Dan towards the farmhouse. 'He's not a skank, he's just woefully immature.' But maybe that was finally starting to change.

'Jacob said to tell you Maddy's not ready yet anyway, you've got at least another–' Tess checked her watch '–twenty minutes before the bride is going to make her grand entrance.'

'I need to speak to Art.' And, unlike last time, she wasn't going to let him stop her. One of them had to break cover, and it looked like that someone was going to be her.

Because the first thing she planned to ask him was, what the hell had he been thinking socking Dan in the jaw?

'Go easy on him,' Annie shouted after her.

Sod that, she was through being easy on him. And on herself.

No more sulking, no more heartache and no more drama. Tomorrow would be a new dawn in her life, she wasn't running away any more from difficult decisions. Or tough conversations. Or her own emotions. And, as of now, neither was he.

CHAPTER TWENTY-NINE

Ellie checked the farmhouse first, in case he'd doubled back on her, then his workshop, but there was no sign of him there either. The sun had begun to dip to the horizon, darkening the orchard and the woods with a ruddy glow.

Where on earth had he gone? And why had he hit Dan? The questions tumbled around her brain as she made her way through the woods towards the millpond. If he wasn't there, she'd just have to leave it for now, and handle him later.

But she didn't want to leave it, the urgency making her heart race as she slipped off her heels to walk through the carpet of leaves and moss on the forest floor, the chill oddly comforting.

Then she saw him, standing under the weeping willow by the water's edge, where they'd made love for the last time.

Had that really been less than a week ago? How could everything have changed so much since then? The sure solid joy in her heart that she had made the right decision to challenge Dan, to see if she and Josh could stay at the farm, was tempered by that bone-deep longing she had steadfastly refused to fully acknowledge until now.

But which had stuck around for nineteen years in some small

shadowed recess of her heart, ready to jump out and force her off course again this summer.

Her foot settled on a branch as she approached him and the crack as it broke had Art swinging round to face her. He didn't say anything as he turned away from her, then knelt on the bank to dip his bruised knuckles into the cool water.

She winced at the thought of his suit being ruined, but that wasn't why her pulse was battering her collarbone as he swept his hand through the water.

'Why did you punch Dan?'

'Because he's a wanker.' He brought his hand out of the water, flicked it, scattering drips onto the white shirt.

'That's not an answer.'

He shoved his injured hand into the pocket of his suit trousers. 'What are you doing here? Shouldn't you be tending him? He's your husband, isn't he?'

She heard it this time, beneath the bite of sarcasm, the judgemental frown, the definite whisper of jealousy.

'We're getting a divorce,' she said.

'Then why are you going back to the US with him?'

'I'm not, Josh and I...' She paused, not sure how to explain it, as nothing was settled. 'I'm hoping we'll be able to stay. If that's what Josh wants.'

'You're staying? For Josh?'

She tilted her head to one side. Was that hope she could see alongside the surprise? Or was it just a trick of the dying light?

'Yes, I'm hoping to. But not just for Josh. For my mum too, and my friends here, and the shop, obviously. And for Toto,' she added. 'I think it will be good for her to have another woman around the place.'

Instead of protesting that she'd overstepped the mark again, he stayed silent, watching her in that intense way that had always unnerved her.

'But, most of all,' she continued, 'I'm staying for myself. Because I like living here. I like being part of something that feels solid and worthwhile.' Family. She liked being part of a family, that was more than just her and Josh. 'And I know I can contribute so much to this community. I like that too.' She stopped talking.

And I like you, a lot, you big dolt.

She wanted to say it, but she couldn't get the words out. She needed something from him first. Some sign that she wasn't making a great big tit of herself again. That the reason he'd punched Dan signalled as much as she hoped it did.

He loosened his tie, and undid the top button of his shirt, his gaze dipping to the ground then away across the pond. But he didn't respond, the muscle in his jaw just below his ear lobe twitching.

'I hope that's not going to be a problem for you,' she added.

'No, but…' The low words disappeared into silence.

'But what?' She had never been good with pregnant pauses, unlike Art.

His chest expanded, making the starched cotton stretch across his pectoral muscles. The movement accentuated the broad, hard body she was going to have a devil of a time not expiring from want of in the next few weeks and months if he didn't come through now.

'But that's not all I want to know,' he finally said, once the uncomfortable silence had stretched far enough to be heard on the dark side of the Moon.

She waited. He didn't elaborate.

'You're going to have to ask me what else it is you wanted to know because—'

'What about us?' he cut in.

'What about us?' The whispered question choked out, bringing with it all the yearning needs and wants and desires that had assaulted her in the last few weeks, hell the last few months, and which he had stopped her from articulating five days ago. 'I thought you said there was no us?'

Her breath seized to a halt. The anticipation painful.

His head rose. His brows slanting down. 'I was talking crap. Of course there's an us. We were banging each other senseless for two whole weeks.'

The vice around her heart released. Enough to allow her to inflate her burning lungs.

Sex. Was he still just talking about sex?

Her lady bits chose that precise moment to start picketing her brain – having formed a committee to advocate for lots more extra-curricular banging.

But her head – and her heart – pushed back.

She couldn't start sleeping with Art again, without screwing herself. Maybe not today. Maybe not next week. But eventually she would have to demand more. And she still didn't know if Art wanted more. If he would ever want more.

She knew why it was so hard for him to ask, all the clues had always been there. He'd closed himself off years before he had ever met her. His father had abused him. His mother had deserted him. And Alicia had done the same, losing herself in drugs after giving birth to his child. Art had learned at a young age how to protect himself from hurt and he'd built that wall higher, brick by brick, over a lifetime.

But if she stayed in Wiltshire, she couldn't continue to batter her head and her heart against that wall – however vocal the lady bits committee – without knowing she had at least some chance of making a dent in it.

'We're not going to be banging each other any more,' Ellie said. 'That's not why I'm staying. And it's also way too confusing for the kids.'

'Not that confusing, once we explain everything.'

'There's nothing to explain any more.'

'Why not?'

She blinked, her rising anger going some way to puncturing the hurt still constricting her lungs. 'Because I'm staying now.'

'So?'

'So a no-strings affair was viable when I was just going to be here for the summer. But I'm not prepared to be your convenient bonk buddy for the rest of my life, Art.'

'Since when were you ever convenient?' he said.

'Is that supposed to be funny?'

'No, you're about the most inconvenient woman I've ever met, if you must know. You were at fourteen and you're even more so now.'

Bloody hell. She did not have to put up with this.

'Why?' she said, playing him at his own game. 'Why am I inconvenient, Art?' she asked. Before he could open his mouth, she jumped in to give him the answer. 'Because I have the unbelievable cheek to actually demand more from you than an orgasm? Because I have an opinion on your relationship with your daughter? On the way we run the project? Because I love how protective and caring you are with my mum? Because it rips me apart to know what happened to you as a child? Because I want to strangle your mother for being such a weak, stupid, selfish bitch? Because the more we make love the more invested I feel? Is that why I'm so inconvenient? Because I want you to feel something for me? To want me? And not just my lady bits?'

He looked stunned. As if he'd just been asked to defuse a nuclear warhead and it had exploded in his face. Exactly as he had all those summers ago.

She let the pain flood through her system. And the humiliation. Because she'd finally told him everything. Ripped it open and laid it at his feet. The way she should have done five days ago. And now he would know. How much she loved him. And he'd probably feel sorry for her. And if there was actually something worse than having to live with Art and not touch, it would be living with Art and him knowing how much it was costing her not to touch.

Still maybe this was a good thing, because if he wasn't interested, the very last thing he'd want to do now was have sex with her ever again.

*

You coward. You've got to tell her. No excuses. Not any more.

Art felt everything inside him coalesce into one raw aching nerve. The same nerve that had been exposed when he'd been seven and lying on a hospital trolley and his mother had whispered in his ear: 'Don't tell, Arty.' And he'd known she didn't care about him, or didn't care enough.

The same nerve that had been flayed when Ellie had stood in front of him all those summers ago and told him she loved him. And he'd been too terrified to believe her.

The same nerve that had been flayed when Alicia had looked right through him, her eyes glazed and unfocused and told him to stop being such a bore about their baby.

The same nerve that had been flayed again, even though he thought he'd cut it out of himself years before, five days ago, when Ellie's husband had stepped out of his fancy hire car.

But this time, instead of covering the nerve any way he could, he knew he had to go with the pain, own it, let it own him. And hope to hell Ellie didn't decide to slice right through it when he was through.

'That's not what makes you inconvenient,' he murmured.

She threw up a hand, the fingers trembling.

'Bugger off, Dalton. I'm not having this conversation any more.' The bright sparkle in her eyes threatened tears that weren't going to fall. 'I'm through. I've got a wedding to organise.' She dug into a pocket in her dress with shaking fingers and pulled out a tissue. 'Maddy's arriving in ten minutes. I'm going back to be there for people that matter to me. You can come with me or you can piss right off. I don't care any more.'

He grasped her wrist, and dragged her into his body. Enfolding her into his arms, the tension she refused to let go vibrating through her body.

God, she was so strong. So perfect. And he wanted her so much to be his. All his, that the fear she would reject him was crucifying him. But he had to get over his fear now. And put himself out there, or he had no chance of getting her. And, more importantly, he would never ever deserve her.

'You're inconvenient, because you make me feel all that stuff too,' he whispered into her hair.

Her body stopped struggling against his. At last he got up the courage to loosen his grip. She stared at him, the shock in her deep emerald eyes making his heart melt all over again.

'What?' For once she didn't seem able or willing to talk. Which meant he would have to fill the silence, put the record straight all on his own.

It was exactly what he deserved. The torture of having to try to articulate his feelings at the most important moment of his life, with words instead of moves.

Right now he'd give anything to be able to show her what he meant by bringing her to an earth-shattering orgasm. By putting his mouth on her body and making it sing. But that was the easy way. The easy way he'd taken all along. They'd done this his way. Now he had to do it her way. What a travesty, because he sucked at talking about his feelings.

'I love that you care about me, that you care about Toto.' He swallowed, now for the big one. 'But it terrifies me too. Because if I get you and then I lose you. If you decide I'm not enough...' Like every other woman he'd ever had in his life, bar Dee '...it would destroy me.'

Her hand, still trembling, reached up to cup his cheek, the tears sliding over her lids now and down her face. 'Is that your backhanded way of telling me you want more than just a sex-for-the-sake-of-it affair?'

'Only if you admit you want more than a guaranteed orgasm?' he said, hating the defensiveness, the desperation in his voice.

She chuckled. 'I'm not going to deny your orgasm guarantee is a powerful incentive to me and my lady bits. But no, Art, that's not the only thing I want from you.'

He grasped her head, let his hands sink into her hair and frame her face, let his gaze glide over her and take in all of it, the pert nose, the heart-shaped face, the tiny slant of her eyes now bright with tears, the lush lips that he could spend the rest of his life kissing while hanging on every word that came out of them.

'Good, because it's not even close to all the things I want from you,' he murmured.

How weird to think after so many years of being terrified of letting anyone know how he felt, what he might need, it had been so easy to say it to her.

His mouth sealed the deal, covering hers in a soul-searching kiss that tasted hot and cool and everything in-between.

*

Ellie felt as if she were floating above the forest floor, as they raced back through the woods to the wedding together, her hand clasped firmly in Art's.

They came out of the trees just as Maddy climbed out of the horse-drawn trap decorated with autumn greenery and two glowing carriage lanterns.

The young woman looked like a medieval queen in her vintage antique lace dress, flowers woven into her hair, sequins glittering on the neckline. Jacob stood under the gazebo, his stunned face breaking into a cheeky grin as she made her way down the aisle of folding chairs towards him on her father's arm. Josh and Toto led the way, scattering handfuls of rose petals over the carpet of reeds and most of the congregation. Melody danced with glee as Toto halted the whole procession to sprinkle petals on her hair.

The humanist minister read out the vows the young couple had written for each other in a calm steady cadence, giving Art time to duck into position, replace Rob as the stand-in best man, and hand the ring to Jacob.

Ellie joined Tess and Annie and Dee in the front row where they had saved her a seat.

'What have you two been up to?' Annie whispered, her eyebrows lifting in wicked amusement. 'You almost missed the best bit.'

Ellie chuckled, her heart as light and airy as the autumnal breeze as she watched Jacob cradle Maddy's head and proceed to kiss her senseless, declaring them husband and wife to the backtrack of whoops and cheers.

'Don't worry, I'd never let that happen,' she shouted over the noise, finding Art's dark gaze and holding it.

Excitement prickled across her skin and pummelled her ribcage in hard heavy thuds.

Especially now I know, the best bit starts now.

EPILOGUE

'Congratulations, ladies, we survived!'

Ellie popped the cork on the last bottle of elderflower champagne in the whole of Wiltshire to a round of applause from Tess, Dee and Maddy, as Annie shut the sliding glass door on the last of their Christmas Eve customers. Only ten minutes after their official closing time.

The shop looked as if a bomb had hit it, a bomb full of glitter and fairy lights and tinsel. The shelves had been ransacked, and they'd sold out of pretty much everything, including the range of hampers Dee had designed for the Christmas period, packed full of her Christmas delicacies and the array of cheeses from the dairy. The last of the Christmas trees Mike had sourced from a supplier near Gratesbury had gone a week ago – much to Art's eternal gratitude, because he'd had the onerous task of lining them up and packing them away each day.

Ellie glanced round the shop floor at the few items still remaining, and clocked some of the empty spaces. On the day after Boxing Day she planned to do a thorough inventory to make sure they were properly supplied for next year. Selling out had been wonderful for their egos, but next year she planned to be better prepared with a lot more inventory in the lines that had been particularly popular.

She pushed the thought aside. They could always do better. But they'd had a spectacular first Christmas, their customer numbers steadily swelling every single day in the two-month run-up since Halloween, and right now was pat-on-the-back time.

Ellie filled the paper cups Annie lined up on the counter. As the alcohol fizzed on her tongue and her mum and her friends toasted each other, Ellie felt the bubble of excitement in her stomach.

A whole week off. She glanced at the clock on the wall. Ten past two. Art and Toto would be back any minute from their six-hour round trip to pick up Josh at Heathrow from his flight back from New York.

He'd been away for a fortnight, hanging out with his father, and she'd missed him horribly, despite the daily Skype calls she and Toto and Art did with him. The custody arrangements were still fairly chaotic, because Dan didn't seem to understand the concept of school term dates, but she wasn't going to bitch about that now. After draining the last of her cup, she pulled her apron over her head.

'Right, we need to clear this mess up,' she said.

'Why don't you leave it to us, Ellie?' Dee touched her arm as she reached for the broom. 'You've been here since six today and Josh will be home soon.'

'I can't leave it all to you guys,' Ellie said. 'The place is a mess.'

'Course you can,' Annie said, pouring herself another cup of champagne. 'We've got it. Haven't we, girls?'

'Yes, we're good,' Tess said getting a refill from Annie. 'As long as the champagne keeps flowing and I know I never have to tie another ribbon on a bag of Dee's Christmas cookies.'

'Hallelujah,' a heavily pregnant Maddy concurred, while saluting them with her cup of fizzy apple juice.

'Until next year, that is,' Dee said, grinning when the other women all groaned.

'But what about your date with Marjorie, Mum? Don't you need to get ready?' Ellie asked.

'Don't be daft,' Dee said, looking flustered as the others all added words of encouragement.

Ellie couldn't hold back a smile as her mum blushed prettily.

Dee and Marjorie Durden, Gratesbury Secondary's head teacher, had been an item for nearly two months, but it still made Ellie's heart sing to see her mum's flushed face. The light of new possibilities had chased away so many of the shadows that had haunted her mother when Ellie had first arrived at Willow Tree that summer.

She knew Dee would always mourn Pam – the woman had been the love of Dee's life – but seeing her mother's joy in this new relationship delighted Ellie too. Her mother deserved this, because she had more courage and compassion than any other woman Ellie had ever known.

'Marjorie and me are just having a quiet night in tonight,' Dee added, her cheeks beaming.

'Not *too* quiet I hope,' Annie said, wiggling her eyebrows lasciviously as everyone laughed.

'Go on, Ellie, you've been putting in silly hours all this week, we've got this,' Tess added, once they'd all got a grip.

'Yeah, take a load off while you have the chance, before Josh gets home and you and Art have to start organising the feeding of the five thousand for tomorrow,' Maddy said, caressing her baby bump.

'Yikes, don't remind me.' Ellie smiled, already anticipating how much she was going to enjoy riding herd on Art and the two kids while they prepped the Christmas meal she and Art had invited everyone to at the farmhouse – so that Dee could have time off cooking Christmas lunch for the first time in years. And how much she was going to enjoy the celebration herself, with all her favourite people in attendance.

'OK, I'll see you all tomorrow. Thanks for being so awesome.'

Tess gave a bow, Maddy laughed, a tear slipped down Dee's cheek and Annie splashed the last of the champagne into her cup before saying, 'Oh bugger off. I refuse to start blubbing before I know for sure Rob hasn't got me the box set of *Poldark* I ordered from him for Christmas.'

*

Ellie was still smiling as she made her way across the frozen farmyard. The dusting of snow that had fallen that afternoon had started to freeze, making the trees and the hedgerows glisten, but the scent of more snow was definitely in the air. Wouldn't it be fabulous if they got another layer tonight? Josh and Toto would be ecstatic, especially when they discovered the sledges Art had made for them both under the tree.

As she rounded the farmhouse, her heart soared at the sight of Art's camper van coming down the lane. She spotted Josh waving frantically and Toto bobbing up and down next to him in the van's front seat.

My family's home.

The swell of emotion blindsided her as both kids piled out of the van.

'Mom, there's snow!' Josh said, as he barrelled into her and wrapped his arms round her waist.

'Welcome home, honey,' she said, holding him close. She placed her hands on his shoulders, which were almost level with hers now. Good Lord, how could he have grown so much, in just two weeks?

'Didn't you have snow in New York?' she asked.

'Yeah, but it's not as cool as here,' he said.

She laughed, while trying not to feel smug at Dan's expense.

The divorce had gone through two months ago with a minimal amount of fuss. And she knew her ex was trying. Josh had reported with enthusiasm all the stuff he'd done with his dad in Orchard Harbor in the past fortnight – a tour of the New York Mets Stadium, a Broadway show, a trip to the mall to buy Josh a ton of designer clothes and video games and about five trips to the local multi-plex to see all the Christmas movies. Even if the line-up of events had been the same shiny distractions Dan had always enjoyed doing with his son, Ellie could see how much Josh had revelled in all the attention.

Dan had always struggled with the responsibilities of being Everyday Dad – the man who did 'stuff' with his son, the man who could be a role model as well as a pal, who could instil discipline, who could nurture and protect and spend more than just bursts of quality time without getting bored. And that hadn't changed.

But, as Art approached them both with his hand in Toto's, she knew Josh no longer lacked that male presence in his life. Without ever being asked, Art had moved seamlessly into the role of Everyday Dad – leaving Dan free to be Vacation Dad, a role he excelled at, during the six weeks of the year they had agreed Josh would spend with him and his new girlfriend Ally in Orchard Harbor.

Somehow, so far, and against all the odds, their shared parenthood plan seemed to be working out.

Maybe there would be complications down the line. Josh wouldn't always be so sunny and adaptable – she and Art had already had a few short sharp bursts of Teen Josh, and Teen Toto, to handle in the last few months. And maybe one day Dan would want more of his time. Plus, there wasn't a lot of love lost between Dan and Art. But so far it was working. And after everything that had happened in the last six months, to her and Josh, Ellie had happily adopted a new life strategy.

Until it's actually broke, don't waste your time and energy freaking out about it.

'Me and Toto are going sledging,' Josh announced. 'Art made us sledges.'

'That was supposed to be a surprise, for tomorrow.' Ellie's gaze connected with Art's and she spotted the crinkle of amusement round his eyes.

'Not any more, I peeked,' Toto announced.

Art shrugged, as the rueful smile she had come to adore spread across his face. 'How glad am I, I spent all those nights working late in the workshop to keep it a secret for Christmas morning.'

'Toto, you fiend,' Ellie said.

'Oops,' Toto said cheekily, not chastened in the least. 'But it's silly not to use them. The snow might have melted by tomorrow and then all Dad's hard work could be wasted for another whole year.'

'Fair point, Batman,' Ellie said, and Toto grinned at her.

'So can we go sledging now?' Josh said. 'We've been talking about it for hours.'

'But it's going to be dark soon,' Ellie said, checking the skyline – her worry gene never too far from the surface, despite her new life strategy. They had an hour of daylight left at best.

'Please, Mom.' 'Please, Ellie.' Josh and Toto begged in unison.

Gathering them both in her arms, she turned to Art. 'What do you say? Should we reward Toto's espionage skills?'

The look in his eyes had something dark and intense flickering to life in her abdomen.

'Definitely,' he said.

The kids ran off, chasing each other to the workshop as Art shouted after them. 'Be back at least ten minutes before it gets too dark to see.'

As soon as the kids had disappeared around the side of the farmhouse, Art grabbed her round the waist and dragged her to him. He kissed her, thrusting his tongue into her mouth, reminding her he'd had to leave at dawn and they'd missed their usual morning canoodle.

She plunged her fingers into his hair, and devoured his mouth right back. Forced to draw back, she sucked an unsteady breath into her lungs. Heat spread up her torso at the hunger in his eyes.

Good grief, would their passion for each other never cease?

She cradled his jaw. She certainly hoped not.

'Why do I get the feeling you are not remotely upset that Toto found the sledges ahead of schedule?' she asked.

He kissed her nose. 'Because I'm not. It's all part of my evil plan.'

Grasping her hand, he led her towards the house.

'What evil plan?' she said, aiming for coy but getting breathless instead.

'Guess?' he said, slamming open the farmhouse door and kicking off his boots.

He gave her a few seconds to lose her own boots.

'I know,' she said. 'Your evil plan is to get an hour's head start on the vegetable prep for tomorrow's lunch.'

'Nope. And don't remind me of that,' he said, then bent down and hefted her onto his shoulder in a fireman's lift.

She shrieked as he spun her round, the lights from the Christmas tree a blur of motion as her heart slammed into her ribs and her head swam. 'Art, put me down.'

'Shut up.' He gave her bottom a playful swat and began to march up the stairs, bouncing her effervescent stomach on his shoulder each step of the way. 'Now guess again.'

'Your evil plan is to punish me for all the vegetable prep we're going to have to do for tomorrow's lunch by dropping me on my head,' she said, wriggling furiously, and laughing breathlessly at the same time, as excitement and anticipation shimmered through her body.

'Closer,' he said, as he dumped her on the bed in their bedroom – the bedroom that had once been hers alone during the first months of her stay at the farmhouse.

Climbing on top of her, he gripped her wrists and flung her hands above her head. Trapped under him, her heart kicked her ribs in hard heavy thuds, the fierce love she felt for him reflected in the deep chocolate brown as his gaze roamed over her face, then fixed on her lips.

'Figured it out yet?' he asked.

She nodded, the emotion too full to allow for coherent speech.

'Good.' He kissed her thoroughly, making her moan, as his

lips trailed down to her collarbone and sucked on the pounding pulse in her neck.

As he implemented his evil plan, locating each one of her erogenous zones and exploiting them mercilessly, the question that had been mocking her for days now, no weeks, lurched into the forefront of her mind. The question she had been too scared to ask. Then drifted away again, as the endorphin rush drowned out everything but the taste, the feel of Art.

*

Eventually they lay naked and sated on the sheets, her hand resting on his chest. His fingers stroked her hair as he cradled the back of her head and held her close.

She propped herself up on her elbow to look down at the harsh, handsome face she had come to adore.

'Art?'

He groaned. 'I know, we need to get up and in the shower before they get back.'

His eyelids opened and he turned to look out the window. Snow had started to fall again in big fat flakes, illuminated by the foggy light of the wintry dusk.

He closed his eyes again and tugged her closer.

'But there's no rush,' he said, snuggling her into his side. 'We both know they're not going to get back until it's pitch dark.' A lazy, satisfied smile split his face. 'Thank God our kids never do a bloody thing we tell them.'

Our kids.

The easy statement filled her heart with hope. Bright, beautiful, determined hope. Maybe it was too soon for this question. But why not put it out there and see what happened? She could wait, if that's what he wanted. But she was through being a coward about asking for her heart's desire.

'How would you feel about making this official?' she said.

'Hmm?' he murmured, still snuggling, only listening with half an ear.

'I'd like to make Toto my daughter, and you Josh's stepdad. You know, officially.'

His eyes snapped open.

Well, that had certainly gotten his attention.

'What?' he said, his voice a husky croak.

'Not straight away, obviously.' She twirled a fingernail in his chest hair, suddenly unable to look at him. 'We would have to talk to the kids first. Get their take,' she said, busy qualifying, denying.

When he didn't say anything, though, and she couldn't lift her gaze from his chest, she wished she could grab the words back.

Why the flipping heck had she said anything? She was mad. Of course this was too soon. She'd got all hyped up on her mum's new relationship and Josh's return home and Maddy's new baby and the shop's successful Christmas sales period and the all-around romance of the season – not to mention yet another spectacular orgasm – and completely lost her grip on reality.

They'd only been together five months. Art had always had trust issues. Did she really want to be testing him again after how far they'd come already? And her divorce had only been final for seven weeks. What was she thinking, talking about marriage again so soon? What was wrong with her?

He tucked a knuckle under her chin and forced her to meet his gaze.

'Are you serious?' he said. 'You want to get married?' She

couldn't tell from his voice whether he was pleased or not pleased, because all he looked was stunned.

'We don't have to do it straight away, I just thought—'

He pressed a finger to her lips, to halt the outpouring of confused qualifications.

'Yes,' he said.

'What did you say?' Had she heard that right?

'Yes, let's get married,' he said.

'Really?' she said, still not sure her ears weren't playing some sort of cruel trick on her.

'Yes, really, but I've got conditions,' he said.

'Conditions? What conditions?' That didn't sound good.

He stroked her hair back from her face, gazed at her, the smile spreading across his face making her heart leap with joy.

'We do it soon,' he said. 'I don't want a ton of fuss.'

'But I'll want to plan a proper wedding.'

'No way.'

She laughed as he rolled over, and held her captive.

'No fuss,' he added, nibbling kisses down her neck. 'I want to get this done before you change your mind.'

Arousal surged, as she met his hunger with a hunger of her own. And agreed to every one of his stupid conditions…

But later, much later, as they sat together on the couch next to the Christmas tree and listened to Toto and Josh argue over which Christmas Eve movie to watch – *Batman v Superman* or *The Avengers* – she began planning the details of her dream wedding in her head. Her great big glorious extremely fussy dream wedding next summer at Willow Tree Farm – when she would celebrate not just her love for Art, but her love for her new daughter, and his new son, and for all the rest of her new family.

Art would come around to the idea in time, she thought, as she watched him referee the argument by shoving *Arthur Christmas* into the DVD player.

Once she'd finished convincing him there was no way on earth she was ever going to change her mind.

ACKNOWLEDGEMENTS

Writing *Summer at Willow Tree Farm* involved lots of help and lots of encouragement from a variety of people. First off I need to say a special thanks to Beth McMurray at Three Trees Farm for giving me the low down on how to open and operate a farm shop (any mistakes are entirely my fault). I also want to thank my mum, Sylvia Rice, for sharing her love of the Wiltshire countryside with me, a committed city girl! Big thanks also go to my best writing mate, Abby Green, for her constant cheerleading with this book and others, my other wonderful writing mates – especially Fiona Harper, Susan Wilson and Iona Grey – and to my best friend and fellow road-trip rebel Catriona O'Kane. Thanks to all of you for helping me to get through my endless anxiety attacks while writing this book. Thanks also go to my fabulous editor Bryony Green and Anna Baggaley and the team at HQ Stories, as well as my agent Margaret Halton, for helping this story to realise its full potential. Last but by no means least, I should also say a heartfelt thanks to my wonderful husband Rob for still making me smile after twenty-plus years of marriage (not always an easy task when you're living with an author!).

ONE PLACE. MANY STORIES

Bold, innovative and
empowering publishing.

FOLLOW US ON:

@HQStories